THE WORLD BEYOND

Borgo Press Books by BRIAN STABLEFORD

THE WORLD BEYOND

Being a Sequel to S. Fowler Wright's Classic Science Fiction Novel

THE WORLD BELOW

by

Brian Stableford

THE BORGO PRESS

An Imprint of Wildside Press LLC

MMIX

CONTENTS

PART TWO: THE METAMORPHOSIANS

INTRODUCTION

Sydney Fowler Wright (1874-1965) was one of the second generation of writers recruited to the British genre of speculative fiction that was generally known as "scientific romance" or "Wellsian fiction". Although he probably began writing that kind of fiction before or shortly after the turn of the century, he wrote it primarily for his own amusement, and regarded his poetry as the more important fraction of his literary endeavor. His principal labor of love was a project to render the entire corpus of Arthurian legend—the "matter of Britain"—into a coherent epic. He did, however, think highly enough of his scientific romances to begin publication of two futuristic prose epics, issuing segments of them himself before circumstances conspired to turn him into a professional writer. That change in his fortunes and the consequent transformation of his attitude to his work affected both works-in-progress in a manner that resulted in their initial augmentation, followed by their abandonment. *The World Below* was one of those works.

Fowler Wright was born on 6 January 1874 in the Midlands town of Smethwick. He was the son of Stephen Wright (1841-1936), an accountant and Baptist lay preacher. He attended King Edward's School, Birmingham, but left at an unusually early age—probably because his father could no longer afford to keep him there, although he always claimed in later life that he had been unsuited to institutionalized education because of his independence of mind, and had preferred to complete his own education. Although he had no formal qualifications he followed his father into the profession of accountancy, and enjoyed considerable success. In 1895 he married Julia Ellen ("Nellie") Ashbarry, who was generally considered his social superior and was rumored to have inherited royal blood via one of the future Edward VII's mistresses. She bore him six children before her death in 1918, and the family lived in relative luxury during that time, with considerable pretension.

Fowler Wright's work necessitated a great deal of commuting, especially between Birmingham, where his accountancy firm was based, and London, where some of his clients were located. It was during these rail journeys that he began to write prose, by way of whiling away the time. He did some work for the government, in the course of which he made the acquaintance of Winston Churchill and other influential men; he was sent to France in the early days of the Great War in order to assess the needs of the British armed forces, so that he could assist in the commercial organization of the supply chain back in England. He appears to have been very successful in that endeavor, and became a director of several engineering companies supplying military apparatus. In the meantime, his patriotic and literary endeavors were combined when he founded the Empire Poetry League in 1917, to promote poetic endeavor and strengthen cultural bonds within the empire. Many important cultural and political figures became members of the league.

The Empire Poetry League's copious publications were financed by a method that was then fairly new, although it is nowadays commonplace: contributors to its anthologies were charged a fee for the publication of their work, receiving copies of the book in return. Fowler Wright edited the League's journal, *Poetry* (later retitled *Poetry and the Play*), for fifteen years. He published nothing of his own while Nellie was still alive, but issued his first book, *Scenes from the Morte d'Arthur* (1919, signed "Alan Seymour"), not long after her death. He married Anastasia Gertrude ("Truda") Hancock in 1920, subsequently adding a further four children to his family.

Fowler Wright appears to have had a considerable amount of prose fiction in hand by 1920, including a pastiche of *The Time Machine*, in which a time traveler visits a distant future in which the giant descendants of humankind live underground while other sentient species have evolved to populate the surface and the sea, and a long account of the disastrous inundation of the world's land surface, survived by a few scattered communities in a chain of islands that were once English hills. He published the first segment of the former text through the Empire Poetry League's Merton Press imprint in 1925 as *The Amphibians* and the first segment of the latter through his own Fowler Wright Ltd. imprint in 1927 as *Deluge*. By that time, however, he was running into severe financial difficulties owing to the delayed economic effects of the Great War.

One of the financial measures introduced during the war was an Excess Profits Duty intended to curb "profiteering", which imposed a punitive tax on "excess" profits made during the war years, by comparison with a baseline trading level established in the years before the war. In order not to inhibit the production of military supplies, however, companies producing them had been allowed to defer payment of the tax. Fowler Wright, and many others, thought it heinous that companies that had their increased production heroically in order to supply the nation's military needs should be penalized for their efforts, and fought a long battle against the eventual collection of EPD, although many other accountants simply advised the companies for which they worked to go into voluntary liquidation in 1919 and start afresh. By his principled refusal to take that course, Fowler Wright doomed many of his clients, and himself, to forced bankruptcy when the government finally moved to collect the deferred tax.

Like one of his literary heroes, Walter Scott, Fowler Wright determined to pay off his creditors and maintain his ten children by means of his pen, and he threw himself into the production of commercial prose. He was able to do this because of the unexpected success of *Deluge*, which had obtained a *succès d'estime* in Britain—having been praised by many members of the Empire Poetry League—and had attracted the attention of movie makers in Hollywood. US rights were purchased by William Randolph Hearst's Cosmopolitan Book Company, which set out to establish the book as a best-seller in advance of the projected film, making it a selection of one of the newly-formed Book Clubs that were then enjoying a tremendous initial success. The movie was long delayed, partly due to the spectacular collapse of Hearst's financial empire, and disappeared from view soon after its completion when its special effects footage was sold for use in other movies, but the fact that *Deluge* had been a US best-seller enabled Fowler Wright to sell books as quickly as he could write them for two or three precious years, until the bubble of expectation burst.

* * * * * * *

Fowler Wright's first recourse in these urgent circumstances was, of course, to wordage he already had in hand. *The Amphibians* and *Deluge* were both segments of longer manuscripts, and he had probably made a start on at least two other scientific romances; a second exercise in alternative Wellsiana, *The Island of Captain Sparrow* (1928), was presumably near completion, although more work needed to be done on a prehistoric romance that was eventually completed as *Dream; or, The Simian Maid* (1931). He repackaged the rest of *Deluge*'s source material as a sequel, *Dawn* (1929), and reissued *The Amphibians* in a volume with the hastily-augmented remainder of the existing text as *The World Below* (Collins, 1929; reprinted in the US by Longmans Green, 1930).

Although *Deluge* was the bigger hit at the time, it was *The World Below* that enjoyed the greater success in the longer term. When it was written—and, indeed, when *The Amphibians* was published—there was no such thing as "science fiction"; the American pulp fiction genre that was eventually to bear that name was still in gestation. By the time *The World Below* appeared, the first sf pulp, *Amazing Stories*, had made its debut as "the magazine of scientifiction" and its first clone, *Wonder Stories*, had pioneered the use of the term "science fiction". Whether Fowler Wright ever submitted anything to those magazines is unknown, but he did publish a scientific romance, "The Rat" (1929), in *Weird Tales*, which published a good deal of such fiction before eventually leaving it to the narrower specialist magazines.

When generic science fiction first moved from the pulps into hardcover formats, in a series of showcase anthologies issued in the late 1940s, the editors of those anthologies—particularly Groff Conklin and August Derleth—were enthusiastic to leaven their pulp materials with items from more respectable sources, and some of Fowler Wright's short stories were reprinted there. The result of this interest was that Fowler Wright, who was by then in dire financial straits, immediately began a marketing push in the USA. *The World Below* was reissued by the specialist sf press Shasta in 1949 and reprinted as two items—numbers 4 and 5—in a series of *Galaxy Novels* in 1951. It was also reprinted in England as a brace of science fiction novels by one of the pioneering publishers of genre paperbacks, Panther; the second volume of that edition was retitled *The Dwellers* because the first part had retained *The World Below*.

The Shasta edition was marketed rather warily—instead of a cover illustration the dust-wrapper carried a large-type declaration that "This is a Novel of Science Fiction", presumably to reassure the company's regular clientele—but the ploy obviously worked; *The World Below* began to be hailed as one of the classics of the genre. When August Derleth, who reprinted a collection of Fowler Wright's short scientific romances through his Arkham House imprint as *The Throne of Saturn* (1949), consulted a panel of writers and editors with a view to determining a "Basic Library" of science fiction, five of the nine placed *The World Below* on the list. When P. Schuyler Miller extended the exercise by polling the readers of *Astounding Science Fiction* in 1952, *The World Below* was included in the core list of twenty-eight titles and placed sixth—immediately after Olaf Stapledon's *Last and First Men* and ahead of Jules

Verne—in a supplementary list of key works in the historical development of the genre.

Fowler Wright always intended to continue the story begun in *The World Below*. In a five-year diary he kept in the 1930s he made a list of projects that the intended to undertake; the continuation of *The World Below* was at the head of the list, along with a continuation of the *Deluge* series. The latter note specified that the third volume of the *Deluge* series was to take the form of a sea voyage, but there was no indication of the manner in which *The World Below* was to be continued; Fowler Wright presumably thought there was no need, given that he had already included a significant hint at the end of the existing text.

Fowler Wright did not die until 1965, a month after his ninety-first birthday, but he wrote little after 1950 and published less; most of the science fiction stories he wrote in that period were lost, along with other typescripts, because he lived a peripatetic existence during the last fifteen years of his life, being passed from one household to another by his children and carrying what remained of his life's work in a suitcase. He had already lost all of his earlier typescripts during the Blitz, when the office in which he was working was bombed (his Arthurian epic was destroyed, and he set out to rewrite the unpublished parts, but never did manage to publish it in its entirety).

It was the second World War that put paid to any chance that Fowler Wright might have had of publishing a sequel to *The World Below*; with paper-rationing in force, publishers were only interested in books in the most popular genres—which certainly did not include scientific romance—so he was forced to concentrate his efforts on hack crime novels. The only scientific romance he published after the war, *Spiders' War* (1954), appeared in the US but not in Britain, and might have been written much earlier; it is the third part of the sequence begun with *Dream*, and probably cannibalized pre-existing material, even if it was brought to completion not long before publication.

Following his death, Fowler Wright's youngest son and literary executor, Nigel Fowler-Wright, continued the family tradition by reprinting several of his father's novels—including *The World Below*—under an imprint of his own, using contacts gained through his own business, Fowler Wright Books Ltd., which operated as a wholesaler to religious bookshops. I contacted Nigel via Fowler Wright Books Ltd. in the early 1980s, when I began research on a history of scientific romance, which was eventually published in 1984 as *Scientific Romance in Britain, 1890-1950*. Nigel was extremely helpful, showing me Sydney's cuttings albums, allowing me to photocopy several of his (unfortunately fragmentary) surviving typescripts, soliciting information on my behalf from some of his siblings and step-siblings, and reading aloud extracts from some of Sydney's diaries. With his help, I obtained more information than the book required, and was able to write a much more detailed essay on Sydney's life and works, which was published in *Foundation* 29 (November 1983) as "Against the New Gods: The Speculative Fiction of S. Fowler Wright".

Nigel Fowler-Wright continued his efforts to maintain and renew interest in his father's works by creating a website, sfw.org, on which he planned to post copies of Sydney's entire works. When he suffered a sudden heart attack and died, his work was taken up by his own son, Augustine, and his nephew, Roger, who not only scanned in everything that Sydney had written, but also a complete archive of *Poetry*. The Fowler Wright family continued to assist in my further research, making a good deal of new information available to me for the introduction I wrote to Wesleyan's scholarly edition of *Deluge*; it was after that book was published that the suggestion was made that I might like to undertake the continuation of *The World Below* that Sydney had never managed to attempt.

Writing sequels to antique texts is a popular game among writers; there have been numerous modern sequels to individual texts such as Charlotte Brontë's *Jane Eyre*, Thomas Hughes' *Tom Brown's Schooldays*, Lewis Carroll's *Alice in Wonderland*, Bram Stoker's *Dracula*, and J. M. Barrie's *Peter Pan*, as well as countless new items in such popular series as Arthur Conan Doyle's Sherlock Holmes stories, L. Frank Baum's tales of Oz, and Edgar Rice Burroughs' adventures of Tarzan series. Although it is more difficult to contrive such sequels in the field of futuristic fiction—because nothing dates quite as fast as yesterday's futures—numerous attempts have been made, and some few have been very successful. H. G. Wells, inevitably, has attracted the most attention in this regard; several sequels have been written to *The Time Machine*, of which the best are David Lake's *The Man Who Loved Morlocks* and Stephen Baxter's magisterial *The Time Ships*.

The advent in the USA of "steampunk fiction", which makes gaudy imaginative play with the raw materials of the nineteenth-century history of technology and the mythologies of Vernian and Wellsian speculative fiction, greatly encouraged the proliferation and diversification of belated sequels to classic scientific romances. Much of the narrative energy of such works derives from the fact that the originals were written before science fiction existed, when there was no alternative but to handle the themes and motifs that the genre was to standardize and sophisticate in a pioneer spirit, extrapolating a naive sense of wonder that modern sf writers can no longer command by any other means than stylistic pretence. My sequel to *The World Below* is more earnest than most steampunk texts, but it dos attempt to retain and exploit the particular sense of wonder characteristic of scientific romances that were conscious of venturing into virgin imaginative territory.

* * * * * * *

In attempting to continue and complete the story told in *The World Below* I could not, of course, simulate the text that Sydney Fowler Wright might have produced had he done the job in 1933, or even in 1953. Too much water has flowed under the bridge, in terms of scientific discovery and science-fictional invention. We understand the process of genetic inheritance and the mechanism of evolution a great deal better in 2007 than Sydney Fowler Wright did when he wrote *The Amphibians*, at which time the broad outlines of Charles Darwin's theory of natural selection had not yet been synthesized with the Mendelian theory of heredity and modern mutation theory. It would have been perversely disingenuous, in picking up the thread of an evolutionary fantasy, to ignore what has been learned in the interim about processes of evolution. It would have been equally disingenuous to gloss over—as Fowler Wright, like Wells before him, felt perfectly free to do—the paradoxical implications of time travel, given that an entire subgenre of "time paradox stories" has flourished in the meantime.

The requirement for distant sequels to take aboard new information and the further sophistication of ideas is not merely a matter of following the rules of the game of writing such sequels, but also provides significant ideative inspiration. In order to be continued after such a long delay, a text like *The World Below* has, a least to some extent, to be reinterpreted. Looking again at what Fowler Wright wrote about the evolution of his futuristic species, in the light of what we now know about evolutionary process, generates challenges and implications that he could not have intended, which provide bases for trains of speculative thought that he could not have identified or followed—but it is exactly those trains of thought that permit a sequel to be written which is both a continuation of the original text and a contemporary work of fiction.

The propriety of basing a sequel to *The World Below* in reinterpretations of its contents that the author could not have intended or contrived may seem dubious, but it is worth noting that a not-dissimilar readjustment of attitude and intention took place during the compilation of the existing text. Although the original text cannot be dated precisely, the internal evidence suggests that that the part contained in *The Amphibians* might well have been drafted before the Great War, and that only the last few chapters of the second part, improvised in haste to facilitate publication in 1929, were definitely written afterwards. Those last few chapters are markedly different from their predecessors, not only in their narrative method, but also in their attitude to the likely shape of future existence. What begins in *The Amphibians* as a description of a bizarre and cruel, but nevertheless settled situation—whose disruption by the time traveler's arrival is subject to a hard-won but straightforward restabilization—turns rather abruptly into an image of a world ravaged and transfigured by war, in which humankind's descendants are teetering on the brink of annihilation.

That transformation mirrors the transformation of the entire genre of scientific romance in response to the profound effect that the Great War had on British attitudes to the future. The core of the genre prior to 1914 consisted of future war stories, into whose production even H. G. Wells had been belatedly drawn, after beginning his career with more wide-ranging visions. For some time Wells remained defiantly isolated in representing future warfare as a thoroughly bad thing, which might easily result in the tragic destruction of the civilization that Europeans had labored so long and hard to build and disseminate, but by the time he published *The World Set Free* in 1913 even he had been converted to the prevailing view—which was that a future war would probably be a thoroughly good thing, because it might bring about a final settlement of awkward disputes over hegemony and ideology in global politics, and would shatter obsolete institutions whose cultural inertia was inhibiting progressive reform.

Scientific romance collaborated with British government propaganda in selling the Great War to the young men who would have to fight it as a "war to end war" and a "war to save civilization". Long before the armistice was signed in November 1918, though, it had become glaringly obvious that the actual war had been nothing of the sort, and that it had been unmitigated disaster for everyone involved. Futuristic fiction was very thin on the ground in Britain in the decade following the war's end, and what there was of it tended to be exceedingly bitter in its outlook. *The Amphibians* is by no means out of tune with this ambience, but its pessimism in respect of the future evolution of humankind has far more in common with the remote philosophical pessimism of *The Time Machine* than the more urgent and acidic cynicism of such post-war works as Edward Shanks' *The People of the Ruins* and Cicely Hamilton's *Theodore Savage*. The last chapters of the supplementary text are, by necessity, set in the same distant future as the earlier ones, but there is a much sharper urgency about them, and clear evidence that the author has changed his mind about the relative importance of certain aspects of Dweller society, and perhaps about the fundamental nature and prospects of that society.

What I have done, in making further reassessments of the nature and prospects of both Dweller society and Amphibian society is, therefore, no more than a continuation of a process begun by the original author. Like him, I have tried hard to avoid any explicit inconsistency and to make the extended whole seem coherent—but, like him, I have willingly bowed to the necessity of adapting my work to reflect changes in the world that I have had no alternative but to internalize.

One apparent inconsistency between *The World Below* and *The World Beyond* that might require explanation or excuse derives from what Fowler Wright's professor says in laying groundwork for a continuation of the story. He asks George, his volunteer time-traveler to "consent to explore this strange world somewhat further", thus implying that he expects to send him back to the world of 500,000 years hence, in order to follow the further progress of the Dwellers' war against the Antipodeans. I do not believe, however, that Fowler Wright would have done that had he continued the story; I feel sure that, just as the sequels to *Dream* reached ever further into the mists of time, and the envisaged sequel to *Deluge* and *Dawn* would have left the hills of England behind for pastures new, Fowler Wright's own continuation of George's adventures would have taken him into a further future, from which he and his author could look back on the world of the Dwellers and the Amphibians through the lens of new information. While taking the implication from the professor's remark that what he has is "a fixed time-bridge" rather than a versatile time machine, therefore, I have assumed that George was not able to persuade Clara to accompany him when he asked her to do so "now", and had to wait some time for a new bridge to be opened into a further future. I am convinced that Fowler Wright would have done likewise.

The passage that lays the groundwork for a continuation of the story is, in some ways, rather frustrating, in that it does not specify, any more than the opening chapter does, exactly what relationships exit between George, Clara, and Professor Danby. The manner in which they refer to her suggests that Clara might well be Danby's daughter and George her fiancé, but there is no firm evidence of that. I felt free to make my own choice, accepting the second half of that inference while rejecting the first, thus allowing me to construct a more complex web of interactions involving "young Danby"—for whom I had to improvise a first name. The underlying reason why George insists that he wants to take Clara with him if he goes adventuring again is, of course, that Fowler Wright had discovered while writing the story the immense narrative utility of equipping a protagonist with a "sidekick" with whom he can engage in continual discussion; given the complexity of the task of describing an unusually exotic future scenario, I took the view that a selection of very various sidekicks would be much more useful than one.

Because I thought it necessary to take George into a further future rather than returning him to the one already described, it seemed reasonable to replicate the structure of *The World Below* in *The World Beyond*, splitting the narrative into two parts, focused on contrasted ways of being that future evolution might conceivably produce. I also thought it appropriate to produce a completion as well as a continuation, attempting to round out the whole work in some kind of conclusive fashion. In order to accomplish that, it was convenient to echo the abrupt change in narrative method that Wright introduced into the second part of his story, for not-entirely-dissimilar reasons. One consequence of these modifications, I hope, is to give the entire work a certain aesthetic symmetry.

PART ONE

THE CHIMERAS

CHAPTER ONE

THE SUMMONS

"The Professor has opened up another bridge in time," said young Danby, unceremoniously, as he handed me his hat and coat. I still thought of him as "young Danby", although he had passed his thirtieth birthday and looked a good deal older than he had eight years before, when I had last seen him. I supposed that he must still think of himself in a similar fashion, given that he still spoke of his father, distantly and reverently, as "the Professor".

"It's good to see you again, Philip," I said, with scrupulous politeness, as I placed the hat and coat on the rack. "Please sit down. I was about to make a pot of tea—will you join me?"

Danby ran his eye around the room, as if examining it for dust or signs of Bohemian untidiness. There was none to be seen; as well as providing me with the cottage for a nominal rent, the college paid for a servant to come in every morning to take care of all the routine housework. He also did most of my shopping, working from lists that I left on the sideboard every Monday and Thursday. I hardly ever saw him in person, because I made it a point—for his sake—to take a long walk after breakfast, from which I rarely returned until he was gone. He had been a college scout for the greater part of his life, and would never have allowed himself to reveal by word or gesture that he found my presence discomfiting, but I saw no need to tax his good will.

After noting the position of my favorite armchair—a Regency piece upholstered in burgundy—Danby moved one of the dining-chairs into a facing position and sat down. He set his briefcase down beside him. He accepted the offer of tea, although he seemed slightly nettled by the lack of any immediate reaction to his revelation. He knew how important the news was to me, and must have thought that I was putting on some kind of performance to conceal my excitement. In fact, I had found it increasingly hard over the years to feel any kind of physical thrill, pleasant or unpleasant. I had become unnaturally—perhaps even uncannily—calm, at least by human standards. Whether it as a belated side-effect of what the Dwellers had done to me or some idiosyncratic evolution for which I was personally responsible, I could not tell.

I went into the kitchen and filled the kettle, then turned on the gas and set the vessel on the hob. I began to assemble cups and saucers on a tray, together with the milk jug and the sugar bowl. I did not hurry; in spite of the lack of any manifest physical reaction, I needed time to think about what he had said.

I had not heard from the Professor since young Danby and I had parted eight years before, on rather bad terms. For two years young Danby and I had been research fellows at the university, working in collaboration on the same subject-matter: my own exotic flesh. Although we had been working in association with the medical school, we were both appointed as pure scientists with specialisms in physiology and histology.

In spite of the fact that young Danby suffered as much as anyone else from the disconcerting effect my physical presence now had, ours might have remained a sufficiently viable and harmonious professional relationship if Clara had not come between us. I suppose, to be strictly accurate, it was young Danby who had contrived to come between me and Clara, but I had never thought of it that way. He certainly had not; knowing as he did that there was no prospect of our broken engagement ever being renewed, he had seen no possible objection to his making his own advances. Whether he had overcome his resentment at being rejected in his turn I did not know, and I had no intention of asking.

Shortly after young Danby and I had parted company, the Professor had published his version of the adventures I had experienced following my year-long departure across his first "bridge in time". I thought of it as *his* version, even though the words were all mine, because there were so many things he had taken out—not just the details of his time machine, but much of what the Dwellers had done to me while I was in their custody. He had dutifully recorded that I had come back "ahead of my time" in an evolutionary sense, with "the face of a stranger" and conscious of a new youth and bodily vigor, but had left unwary readers free to infer that all of that was the kind of change that I might have undergone as a result of a refreshing holiday in the south of France or a spell at Baden-Baden. He had not wanted to give away details of the treatments to which the Dwellers had subjected my body and my mind, in case his son and I could contrive to extrapolate our private knowledge of those details into medical techniques applicable in our own world. We had not.

The Professor had, of course, paid me for the privilege of taking charge of my memoirs, at a time when I had needed the money very badly, but I had resented my memories being edited by him just as much as I had resented my flesh being edited by the Dwellers. He had done me less harm. I suppose—but he had also done me less good.

Now, after eight years of silence, Professor Danby had sent his son to tell me that he had opened another bridge into the future. Presumably, he wanted to take me up on the offer I had made—and which he had taken care to include in the published version of my story, along with the condition I had carelessly voiced—to go back to the world of the Dwellers. Did he, I wondered, anticipate hiring me for that purpose for a second time, or did he suppose that I was now such a lonely stranger among my own kind that I might pay him for the privilege?

The kettle began to whistle on the hob. I filled the pot and began to stir it, still hesitating. In the absence of the physical responses that had once been so familiar, I had literally forgotten how I was supposed to feel on hearing the news that young Danby had brought—but I was beginning to remember, if not actually to experience the relevant sensations. I carried the tray into the sitting room, and poured the tea. Danby took a little milk, but no sugar. I took both.

"You're looking well, Philip," I said to him.

"You haven't aged a day since the last time I saw you, George," he replied, making a point far more pertinent than the mere fact that he was able to address me by name with some slight semblance of warmth.

"No, I don't believe I have," I agreed. "Not a grey hair in sight."

He smiled, very thinly, at the joke. I had returned from the future utterly devoid of body-hair, and none had grown in the interim. "Nor a wrinkle," he added—which was a more telling observation.

So far as I could tell, I had not aged physically at all. According to the calendar, I was now thirty-eight; if one added in the year I'd spent in the future, I was thirty-nine—but my body had suffered no perceptible deterioration since I had returned from the Dwellers' underworld. I had not tested its resilience to the limit, but I had established its superior healing powers to my own satisfaction, if not to young Danby's, and I had not had a cough or a cold in the head in all that time.

"How are your studies going, George?" Danby asked, following up on the theme of my apparent incorruptibility rather than reverting to the subject his father's new time-window. His eyes made a tour of the bookshelves beside my armchair as he spoke, and his expression showed more than a little disapproval of the omnivorousness of my reading.

"Slowly," I admitted. "It's easy enough to keep up with the scientific journals, of course, but catching up with the broad heritage of human knowledge is no easy task nowadays, even for a man who never sleeps."

"Never?" he queried.

"Hardly ever," I amended. Sleep was no longer necessary to me, but I could still do it if I wanted to—and I sometimes did, as a matter of pure self-indulgence. It was conceivable that the removal of my need to sleep was merely a side-effect of a more general advancement of my physical being, but I was almost convinced by now that it was the other way around. The general advancement of my physical being had come about as a side-effect of the Dwellers' adaptation of my capacity for unconsciousness. They had perverted my natural inclination to sleep into something else: a kind of trance state that made my memories accessible to an observer placed in close proximity and possessed of the appropriate mind-reading ability. My increased physical resilience was a corollary of that purposive transfiguration—or so I had come to believe.

The Dwellers were not incapable of actual speech, nor did they despise it as the Amphibians were inclined to do, but they naturally preferred their own methods of interrogation. Although they had promised the Amphibians that they would keep me safe until it was time for me to return to my own era, they had determined to make as much use of me as they possibly could. Having dissected Templeton's corpse and done worse to Brett's living body, it had presumably seemed natural enough that they should probe my mind just as carefully—and because it was too primitive to yield its secrets as easily as an individual skilled in mind-speech might have done, they had used their own mental force to reconfigure it. In a sense, they had turned me into one of their living books.

In order to keep their promise to the Amphibians, as they understood its terms, my captors had left me sufficient conscious control over my remodeled mind that I needed to give conscious consent to be read—so far as I knew, I had to deliver myself into the trance state that permitted the intimate interrogation of my memory—but that had been their only concession. They were, of course, able to open their own memories in the same way, and routinely did so while engaged in that kind of "reading", but I had hardly begun to learn to read in that fashion before I was sent home, so I had gleaned far less from the memories of my readers than they had drawn from mine.

"I suppose," Danby said, "that you have so much time on your hands for reading"—he meant actual reading, of course, not mind-reading—"that you have plenty to waste on trivia of merely human interest." He pronounced the term *merely human interest* as if it were a deadly insult, although he still qualified as a mere human. He never read anything himself but scientific papers and treatises; he regarded poetry and fiction as the frippery of unserious minds. Although he made some slight concession to contemporary philosophy, he regarded the works of Plato and Aristotle as obsolete.

"I find that modern literary work provides a satisfying counterbalance to the abstraction of my scientific researches," I told him, sounding more pompous than I might have hoped. "As for the ancient texts you see arrayed there, they add a vitally necessary historical depth to my understanding of the evolution of thought."

"It was all very well to be a Renaissance man in the Renaissance," Danby said. "We know now, though, that most of what Renaissance men believed to be true is actually false. It is no longer necessary, or desirable, for a scholar to acquaint himself with all the misguided guesses that the men of the distant past committed to paper, and it is certainly unnecessary for him to waste time with novels detailing the possible eccentricities of contemporary folly. You, of all people...."

"Have transcended the possibility of such folly," I said, feeling quite entitled to cut him off as rudely as I might. "I've apparently lost the capacity to feel much human emotion—but that doesn't mean that my reading about it is a mere matter of nostalgic whimsy. In any case, I don't have to justify my tastes and interests to you. How are your own endeavors going? Well, I suppose, if you've helped your father to open a new time-bridge."

He smiled, not because of my scolding but because I had come to the point and acknowledged the reason for his visit.

"The Professor didn't require my help," Danby confessed, "and I wasn't really in a position to offer any. His secrecy with regard to the practicality of his machine is rather frustrating. His incessant muttering about the inevitability of another war, which can only be won by scientists working in secret, cannot possibly justify keeping is own son in the dark—but that's not the point. The point is that he's succeeded, at last, in duplicating his achievement of ten years ago."

"Given that tendency to obsessive secrecy," I said, "I suppose that your visit has a specific purpose. Have you come to offer me another bribe to serve as his guinea-pig?"

"No, of course not," young Danby replied, impatiently—but then he hesitated. "Are you saying that you want money before you'll consent to involve yourselves in our affairs again?"

I took a long sip of sweet tea before replying. "No, I'm not," I said. "I'm honestly grateful to you for letting me know, and for allowing me to become involved. You *are* inviting me to become involved, I take it?"

"More than that," he said—and then hesitated again, apparently unsure whether he ought to set all his cards on the table just yet. He continued in a calculatedly vague fashion. "This time, you know, we'll have a far better idea of how to handle things. This time, we'll try harder to get as much tangible benefit from it as possible. The Professor was bitterly disappointed when the last bridge collapsed just as he felt that he was in a position to exploit it properly—and just as disappointed that he couldn't open another immediately. He hadn't realized how lucky he was, the first time. He had to revise his theories considerably."

"As have we all," I reminded him.

"Of course. But we can stop theorizing and speculating now, and get back to brass tacks again. There's another window of opportunity open. We don't know how long it'll stay open, so we're disposed to hurry—but not to be reckless. We've completed the preliminaries. The mice came back healthy and the canary was still singing. We've sent through the various chronometers to calibrate the impulse...."

"And photographic apparatus to map the night sky," I said, taking up the thread. "That's how you first estimated the interval separating us from the world of the Dwellers, I believe—not that your father was one to give overmuch information to his hirelings."

"Yes," young Danby replied, "we've done that too. No result, I fear—the Opal Way was out in the open, and the skies were conveniently cloudless. This time, the exit-point appears to be enclosed. The only basis we have for estimation is the relationship between impulse and durational lapse at the far end—but we haven't a curve on which to map the changing relationship, so we can only guess. The Professor insists that the other end of the new bridge must be a great deal further on than the other end of the first one, but my reading of the evidence is different. In my opinion, it can't be much further forward than the last destination."

In order to help him get to the point I looked him full in the face, although I knew that it would make him uncomfortable. Danby looked away, unable to meet my eyes. He had had time to work on his reflexive reactions before we parted, and obviously had not forgotten what he had learned, but he was forced nevertheless to stop beating about the bush.

"We need you, George," he said, bluntly. "This isn't an invitation, so much as a plea. Will you come with me, without delay?"

"Time is obviously of the essence," I murmured, permitting myself a soft smile at the slight joke. "Why is that? Why do you say that you *need* me?"

Danby picked up his briefcase and opened it. "Among the first objects we sent through," he said, "was a thin sheet of iron. It was part of the calibration exercise—we wanted to see how much rust it would accumulate. It came back without even a dusting—but not unaltered."

He took the object he had mentioned out of the case, like a stage-magician producing a white rabbit from a top hat. It was carefully wrapped, to protect it from the rusting process to which our damp atmosphere would certainly have subjected it, but he exposed its surface without hesitation. Scored on to it, by means of some sharp implement, was a single English word inscribed in capital letters: COME.

CHAPTER TWO

THE RESPONSE

As single words went, the one that young Danby was displaying spoke volumes.

Its first implication merely confirmed a conclusion that Professor had drawn in the wake of his first experiment—that a time-bridge had to be simultaneously established at both ends. If the Dwellers that I had portentously christened the Seekers of Science had not been conducting their own experiments in temporal distortion, it would not have been possible to establish a bridge between their world and ours—and even when it had been established, the Seekers of Science had not realized what they had until the Seekers of Wisdom had worked it out for them, after long investigation.

Secondly, the word informed me that—unlike the Dwellers—the entities at the other end of the Professor's new window *did* know what they had, more or less exactly. They knew enough about when and where the other end of *their* bridge was to employ an English word as an invitation—or as a summons.

Danby had obviously drawn a third inference from the use of the English word. He thought that the new bridge must have been established by the Dwellers not long after the time of my visit, because they were the only inhabitants of the far future likely to be able to use an English word in communication with the far end of a time-bridge. The Professor had disagreed with him about that, though, presumably on the basis of other evidence. If the Professor were correct, the makers of the new connection could not have learned the word directly, but must have done so indirectly. If so, the time-bridge to 1934 was probably not the only one the entities had established—they might also have established one to the world of the Dwellers, to a point in the giants' history not long after the time when the record of my interrogation had been deposited in the

Hall of Dead Books. I wondered, briefly, how many more they might have established, to different points in their past and perhaps to different points in their future—but that seemed to be taking the flight of fancy too far into realms of wild speculation.

Danby was still waiting or me to react verbally to his revelation. "That is extremely interesting," I conceded. "I suppose you sent a much more elaborate message back—and a dictionary with it, no doubt."

"We did," Danby confirmed. "Anyone else might have been content with a shorter Oxford, but the Professor sent through a mammoth version of Webster, together with a very abundant supply of paper and pencils. This is all that we received in return." He reached into his case again, making the most of his meager flair for showmanship, and produced a single sheet of paper, on which four words were written, in a vertical column, in the same bold capitals:

PLEASE
COME
URGENT
GEORGE

The senders of the message obviously had little concern for grammar, and their command of dramatic tension might have been accidental, but they certainly knew how to get their meaning across economically. I wondered whether they had tried sending more elaborate messages and failed, because there was only so much change that could be wrought in a time-traveled object before it lost its capacity to return.

"You're assuming, I take it," I said, "that the name at the bottom is that of an addressee rather than a signature."

"I'm glad that you can adopt such a flippant attitude, George," young Danby said, insincerely. "I don't know what the Dwellers did to your endocrine system, but it obviously allows you to maintain perfect calmness in the face of the most astonishing revelations."

"In fact," I told him, "the use of my name is little more astonishing than their initial use of the word COME. If, as seems almost certain, the source of their knowledge as to how those symbols might be construed was the Dwellers, then it's hardly surprising that they know the name by which the Dwellers' own source was known. As the only man who was able to pass across the earlier time-bridge—the earliest ever established, so far as we know—and return to tell my tale, I'm certainly entitled to a measure of celebrity in the annals of time travel. It's possible that the senders of that message are not addressing themselves specifically to me. They have clearly added the word PLEASE in order to seem polite, and might have added my name merely in order to seem more friendly."

"It's possible," Danby conceded, although he clearly did not believe it. "You'll understand our enthusiasm to be cooperative, though. If we can answer their request, even though it may only be an apparent one...you do understand what an opportunity this explicit invitation offers, don't you, George?"

"Yes," I said, plainly. "I do. Do you want me to go alone, then, as before?"

"Certainly not," Danby said. "The circumstances are quite different. It might be as well for one of us to undertake a brief reconnaissance mission in advance, but when we mount the expedition proper, I shall certainly come with you, and...."

He paused. He had been looking at the floor in any case, but now his eyes wandered further astray, as if in dire embarrassment. I could not guess why. I knew that he could not have been intending to say "and so will my father" because the Professor was obviously the one man who would not, could not and must not go across the bridge—he was the only man who knew how to maintain this end of it, and the only man who had any hope of establishing another. If he had not been so very determined to hang on to his monopoly, there might be a hundred who could take his place by now, but he was a wizard by temperament, a hoarder rather than a sharer, who had never published a paper in his life.

"And...?" I prompted.

"Clara...," he said, interrupting himself as soon as he had voiced her name.

"*Clara?*" I repeated, with only mild incredulity. "I didn't know that you were still in touch with Clara," I added, slightly regretful of the fact that mention of the name had not caused me to react more viscerally.

"We haven't been in regular communication," Danby admitted. "After she had refused me, just as she refused you, she and I drifted apart just as inevitably as you and she. I think she might regret it slightly now—in both respects, I mean, but...." He stopped again, having confused himself by his own interjection.

I had moved past the initial surprise by then, though, and had deduced what must have happened. "Your father still remembers what I said when I was prepared to return to the world of the Dwellers," I said, stepping into the breach. "How could he not, having cut off my account at exactly that point? He's not a man who understands the workings of human relationships very well, for all that he's a family man. Did he get in touch with Clara himself, or did he instruct you to do it before you came here?"

"He instructed me to telephone her," Danby said, a little shame-facedly.

"To invite her to take part in the expedition?"

"Not exactly. My father told me to ask her whether she might be willing to come to the house, to discuss the possibilities opened up by the establishment of the new bridge. He also directed me to tell her that we hoped she might be able to help us persuade you to take part. I knew that it was the wrong...."

I cut him off again, "Did she agree to do that?"

Danby took up his tea-cup, not because he wanted to drain the dregs but because he evidently felt the need to do something more than stare at the floor. He peered into the cup, as if he were hoping to use the leaves as a means of divining the future. "Yes," he said. "She said that she could not imagine that you would need to be per-suaded, though. She said you would jump at the chance—and that she was ready now to jump at it herself. I thought...but my father was still listening in. He took the phone out of my hand, and said that the offer was much appreciated, and that he was pleased to ac-cept. I told him he was mad when he'd rung off, but that was un-wise—it's not the sort of charge the Professor can take lightly. He listed a great many reasons why Clara would be an asset to the ex-pedition, although I suspect that there were only two that he took seriously.

"Clara is already in on the fundamental secret," I guessed, "and she's one of the only two people who have contrived to steel them-selves to the necessity of being in my company for any considerable time."

Danby nodded his head. "That was presumably why he asked me to contact her," he said. "He couldn't really have been laboring under the delusion that you wouldn't agree to go without her, could he?"

"I doubt it," I said—although I could not be certain. The Profes-sor was, as I had said, a man whose understanding of human rela-tionships was rather rough-hewn. Like his son, he never read books that were of "merely human interest". He probably envied me the circumcision the Dwellers had carried out on my ability to feel emo-tions physically.

"We can tolerate your company, George," Danby said, as if it were something of which he needed to persuade me, if I were to consent to his presence in the expedition. "Neither one of us would have deserted you eight years ago had you not made it clear that you'd rather do without our company."

That was not strictly true, but I made no objection.

"It can work, George," Danby persisted. "The Professor might have listed the other arguments for the sake of making his point, but they're valid enough. Clara is a communicator—she has a natural empathy with others, animals as well as men."

I did not need to be reminded that natural empathy was one thing that both Danby and I lacked, and very conspicuously. I had not been so conspicuously lacking before my first expedition into time—and, indeed, had thought myself a sympathetic, if not a sentimental, sort of fellow—but the Dwellers had put an end to that.

"Will it be just the three of us," I asked, "or are you thinking in terms of a larger embassy?"

"The Professor...," he began, then hesitated yet again.

Again, I anticipated him. "...Would rather keep the whole thing on a strict need-to-know basis," I said. "The leopard still wears his spots proudly, and now has his speculative eye on a greater profit than the one that slipped through his fingers before. He still thinks of me as something of a fool, and of Clara a mere woman. You, on the other hand, are a loyal and trustworthy son, who knows as much of science as any man, save only for himself. He think that we three will be the perfect team to serve his ambitions, without entertaining too many of our own."

"Actually," Danby confessed, "I suspect that he thinks of me as something of a fool as well—but a usable instrument, nevertheless."

"Don't be self-pitying, Philip," I said, softly. "He might be a far more loving father than you give him credit for, although he imagines that playing the Professor obliges him to hide his feelings. Will you give me half an hour to pack?"

"Half an hour?" Danby echoed. "That's better than I'd hoped for."

"The matter is urgent, it seems," I reminded him, contriving another insincere smile as I stood up. "In any case, the thought of traveling overnight does not alarm me in the least, and I dare say that I have far fewer arrangements to make before I take a leave of absence than Clara."

Danby stood up too, but I waved my hand, palm downwards, to indicate that he might as well remain seated. He seemed tired, although the evening was not very far advanced. The distance from the Professor's house to Oxford was not much more than a hundred and forty miles, but it cut diagonally across the country and it was a difficult route to follow by train, necessitating an awkward detour via Birmingham. Clara would have an easier journey starting from Paddington, with only a single change at Reading or Swindon.

"Feel free to peruse one of my books, if you can find one that interests you," I said, a trifle vindictively, as I left the room.

The cottage only had a single story, so I only had to cross the hallway to reach my bedroom. It did not take me long to pack a case, and not much longer to scribble a brief note to the servant who did my housework. I was so distracted that I almost slipped into a kind of waking trance as I completed the mundane tasks. The modifications the Dwellers had made to my brain's ability to entertain altered states of consciousness were not restricted to the particular kind of deep trance they had induced for their own purposes. Whenever I went out for my long walks, or to ride my bicycle into the Oxfordshire countryside, I found it easy to slip into a state of near-total detachment, relegating my awareness of immediate sensory stimuli to the margins of my mind while I concentrated on more abstract cogitations.

In spite of what I had said to Danby, I had no doubt at all that the inhabitants of the mysterious future really had addressed their summons to me, and not because of any mere celebrity I might have attained as the first Earthly traveler in time. My guess was that they wanted me because of what I was—because of what the Dwellers had made me. They wanted me because I was a better instrument of research into the nature of humankind than any mere human could ever be. I possessed a unique combination of memories, of twenty-eight years of ordinary humanity and ten years of more objective research into the human condition and the history of human thought. If the senders of the message knew enough to write COME even before they had received the Professor's gift of Webster's Dictionary, they had to know what the Dwellers had done with me and to me. They had to know that there was no man now on Earth better equipped than I was to serve as an ambassador to the future—and might never be a man more qualified, if rumors of the potentially-apocalyptic nature of the imminent war could be believed.

It was entirely understandable, I mused, that the inhabitants of the further future should add the word GEORGE to their message, even if they had found out from experience that four words was the maximum length they could contrive without their message being returned to sender. But why, in that case, had the third of the four been URGENT? What could possibly be urgent, when at least half a million years had already elapsed between my time and theirs?

It had to be the fragility of the bridge that worried them, I concluded. The Professor's first bridge had collapsed shortly after my return, for no reason that he could immediately determine. He had expected then to be able to set up another without undue difficulty, but it had taken him ten years. Apparently, time travel was a tricky business, subject to idiosyncratic instabilities and unpredictable unreliabilities. My future summoners presumably wanted me to hurry lest I lost my chance to respond to their call.

They need not have worried, any more than Danby and the Professor need have worried. If Danby had telephoned me instead of insisting on putting on his stage-magician's display, I would have been on my way already. Whatever sense of urgency the inhabitants of the distant future felt, I felt sure, it could not compare with mine.

Of that emotional capacity, unlike so many others, the Dwellers had not deprived me.

CHAPTER THREE

THE PROFESSOR'S HOUSE

Danby and I caught the nine o'clock train from Oxford to Birmingham without any difficulty, and made our first connection without overmuch delay, but the journey became more awkward as the night wore on. The third leg of the journey was very slow; we were alone in a single passenger carriage attached to a train carrying milk and mail. We had no make the final part of the journey on foot, having arrived at the station nearest to the Professor's house in the early hours of the morning, far too late to find a taxi.

I had no objection to the walk; I was, in a sense, returning to my homeland. I had not been properly resident in the neighborhood since I first left home to become an undergraduate at Oxford—where I had spent three years before volunteering to fight in the War—but I had returned at frequent intervals for several years after the armistice was signed. It was on one such visit that I had been recruited by the Professor for his secret mission to discover what had happened to Brett and Templeton—clearly, I had not been his first choice as a possible explorer in time; I had only attained the rank I had by virtue of his desperation, and the fact that Bryant had refused to go.

After returning from the world of the Dwellers my visits had grown far less frequent, and I had not come back at all since my mother's funeral. Even so, I still considered the whole region to be my spiritual home, because it was where I had wandered freely as a boy, on foot and by bicycle. Whenever I went walking or cycling through the hills and vales of the Oxfordshire countryside, I was always aware of the many and various comparisons to be made with these other hills and vales. It was pleasant, therefore, to find myself walking in surroundings I had barely glimpsed in the last two decades, even in the dead of night.

The weather was not particularly warm, but I removed the scarf that I habitually wore about my face while walking abroad, and took off my hat so that I could feel the cold breath of the wind. I strode out tirelessly, while young Danby, who was as weary in body as he was in mind, soon became out of breath in my wake.

Danby and I had talked at some length while seated in our various railway carriages, but our conversation had been distinctly impersonal, concerned with scientific matters and speculations regarding the Professor's new time-bridge. "When is Clara expected?" I asked him now, having paused to let him catch up when the chimneys of the house came in view."

"Tomorrow afternoon," he said. "Or, rather, *this* afternoon, since midnight is long past. You'll have Bryant for company in the morning, though. The Professor will need him to take my place when I go with you, so he's moved in for a while."

"Brett and Templeton will doubtless complete the reunion in spirit," I observed. "I suppose your father might find it convenient to have Bryant available as a witness in case we don't return, given the fuss Mrs. Brett kicked up over Harry's disappearance. I would hardly be missed, of course, and I was careful not to specify where I've gone in the note I left for my servant, but Clara is bound to leave an obvious gap, and a trail to follow."

"Bryant's been a regular visitor at the house over the years," Danby said, steadfastly refusing to match my teasing tone. "He fancies himself almost as a collaborator in the Professor's work. If the Professor were to deem it necessary or politic to follow us over the bridge—which he might, *in extremis*—he might just be able to bring himself to leave Bryant in charge of the apparatus."

We fell silent as we approached the door of the dwelling, not wanting to wake any of its inhabitants. Danby let us in with his key rather than ringing for a servant, and showed me up to my room himself—a room that was, I noted, already made up, although Danby had not telephoned ahead to give notice of our imminent arrival. He went straight to bed thereafter, having tired himself out completely.

I lay down on the bed for a few minutes, but I made no attempt to sleep, although I could have done so had I wanted to. I needed space for thought far more than that kind of self-indulgent rest. After a short while, however, I got up and moved a chair to the window, so that I could look out into the night. There was very little to be seen—few lights remained lit in these parts once dusk had faded, and the night was cloudy—but I could just make out the silhouettes of the poplars bordering the edge of the Professor's rear garden, set against a slightly silvery sky, and I could hear the brisk night-wind soughing in the crown of an elm set to the right of the window, whose longest branches almost brushed its sill. Because I knew that I was home, or very nearly, the sound seemed welcoming as well as comforting, symbolic of the song of the Earth itself—or, at least, of the English landscape as it now was, but would not always be.

While we were talking on the train young Danby had elaborated on his earlier revelation that his father was convinced that the new time-bridge led a much more distant future than the one I had visited before. The Professor had apparently estimated the extent of the second bridge at a million years, and seemed confident of that estimate—although Philip, of course, disagreed with him.

"The old man's always been too confident of his guesswork," young Danby had said. "Whenever subsequent events prove them wrong, he conveniently forgets how certain he was, and is content to congratulate himself on having learned a new truth. He's had to revise his theories of time half a dozen times now, but he's as fully convinced that his previous assertions were merely tentative as he is that his present assertions are indubitable. He's had to change his mind about the possibility of an era influencing its own past, of course, since we received the two messages; he's quite forgotten the stubborn defense he put up over the loss of your hair and your new-found resistance to injury and disease."

Before I had undertaken my expedition to the world 500,000 years hence, the Professor had blithely informed me that time travel into the past was obviously impossible, because the past had already happened and was therefore fixed, incapable of intrusion. Returning objects from a trip into the future, in the view he had held then, had not counted as backward time travel because they returned on the future side of the moment from which they had departed. Seen from his viewpoint, that had been superficially plausible—but from the viewpoint of the Dwellers, our viewpoint was the remote past, and they had intruded upon it quite successfully, not merely in the form of information I had gathered haphazardly but in the subtle physical modifications that they had made to my flesh.

When I had put that argument to the Professor soon after my return he had, at first, clung obstinately to his notion that our viewpoint must be privileged, and that because the future was as yet unmade, the Dwellers, the Antipodeans and the Amphibians were mere shadows of possibility. At the time, he had presumed that the alterations made to my body were more subtle than they turned out to be—he had been unimpressed by my immunity to sleep, which he considered trivial.

If he were correct, I had pointed out, then I must have modified myself, merely by the power of wishful thinking, according to wishes that I had never formerly dreamed of possessing. In the end, he had conceded that I might be right, and that the future must, in some sense, already be set, even though that compelled him towards the seemingly-paradoxical conclusion that the "past" constituted by our present must be more fluid than he had previously imagined.

Now, by virtue of the messages he had received via his second time-bridge, the Professor had been compelled to accept that the future could indeed operate significantly upon the present, if not by the intrusion of physical objects, at least by the tentative modification of objects that were transmitted forward therefrom. In his mind, according to young Danby, this had now become the fabulous opportunity towards which he had always been working: a means to obtain futuristic knowledge that might be applied in the present to the betterment of humankind.

By virtue of this shift, the Professor's attitude to me had changed considerably. On my first expedition I had been a hireling sent into a situation that had gone awry, in the hope of disentangling it. The observations I had brought back had interested him greatly, but he had not been able to decide what his next step ought to be before the bridge collapsed. Now, I was a valuable resource, whose primary function was to open a means of communication between him and the future—a means whose principal conduit was to be his son.

A pair of barn owls hooted in the distance, their complementary calls fusing into a single plaintive couplet. It was as if their two minds were sharing a single thought.

"Perhaps you are," I murmured. "Perhaps the gift of which the Amphibians will make so much is already making itself felt in species we humans are pleased to regard as primitive, while our own consciousness remains stubbornly egotistical."

For myself, I was avid to know more about the shape of the future—but not because I hoped or intended to make practical use of that knowledge in the present. In a way, I had reverted to something nearer to the Professor's original proposition while he had been converted to mine. In spite of the changes the Dwellers had wrought in me, I could not believe that any vulgarly practical application of future knowledge could or would be possible. It seemed to me, now, that there had to be a sense in which the past and future were equally fixed, in spite of the established fact that they could intrude upon one another. I did believe, however—or, at least, felt free to hope— that any further knowledge I might gain of the shape of things to come might bring about a further change *in me* as profound as the one had already been contrived. Whether any such change might make me more comfortable than I presently was in the world to which I belonged—the world that was my home—was a different matter.

The hope that I might experience a further internal change seemed to me to be a more reasonable hope to entertain than the Professor's new enthusiasm for appropriating the intellectual produce of future science. The elder Danby was a humanitarian of sorts, in a rather abstract fashion; he loved the idea of society and the species far more than he loved individual human beings. I was prepared to believe that he really did want to improve the sum of human technological capability and happiness, if he could—always provided that he received due credit for his achievement—and that he would do his best to use any information he could recover from the future in the cause of such improvement. I remembered, though, that in the aftermath of my last expedition I had once tested him with the argument that, since the primary contemporary occupations of humankind were the oppression and slaughter of various groups and classes by their neighbors, any increase in their technological ability to do so would be bound to work against any increase in the sum of human happiness. He had dismissed the argument as nonsense, but I was not so sure.

It was at least possible, I thought, that the Dwellers had undertaken the transformation of my flesh partly in the hope that the example I provided to my contemporaries might deflect the course of human, and hence post-human, history. The giants had been in a situation they considered utterly desperate, fervently ambitious not to suffer the kinds of collapse that all previous civilizations had suffered, but absolutely certain that they had failed, and that their extinction was imminent. Might they not, in those circumstances, have decided that it might be better had their race never been born, in order that something similar but better might take its place? "Better", in this context, would signify something more adequately equipped to resist an innate tendency to sterility and able to defeat the Dwellers' great rivals, the Antipodeans.

If the past could not be materially changed, any such attempt was bound to fail—but what if the past required assistance from the future in order to be completed? What if it had been necessary that I should go into the future, in order that the Dwellers might modify me and sent me back to *ensure* their eventual evolution? What if I *had* to go into the future for a second time, in company with Philip Danby and Clara, not in order to assist the Professor to preserve and improve humankind, but to make certain of humankind's destruction, by giving it the power to destroy itself? What if I were a new Oedipus, fated to fulfill my destined role as a direct consequence of the attempts made to prevent that destiny from being fulfilled?

I had certainly confronted myself with a riddle worthy of the Sphinx. The two owls hooted again—mockingly, it seemed.

I retreated, as I often had before, to the hypothesis that my modification might have been a whim of the moment rather than a part of some longer-term strategy—a by-product of their interrogations, whose further consequences the Dwellers had not considered at all. That made little difference, though, to my own present situation and to the choices I might yet make. The fact was that I *had* been changed; even if I had no purpose to fulfill within some grand cosmic plan, I still had to decide what to do. I had to decide whether to cooperate with the Professor's plan—which is to say, to aid young Danby in his appointed mission—or follow a different course. It would be foolish, I knew, to attempt to reach some such decision now, before I knew what the future for which I was bound might hold—but it was surely far from foolish to consider the matter in advance, in order that I might be better equipped to decide what to do if ever the decision became urgent.

The important thing, I concluded, was to make my own investigations of the far end of the time-bridge, and hold the results private. If I were a mere instrument from the Danbys' point of view, they ought to be a mere instrument from mine. They were my means of returning to the future, and that was all. They had expected that they might have to persuade me to answer the summons, because they had thought of me as *their* potentially-unwilling instrument—but Clara had known better. She had realized something that was becoming more obvious to me by the minute as I sat by that window in the Professor's house, looking out over the near-invisible countryside I had once known so well. Clara had realized that I did not belong in the present any longer, even though I had belonged in it once. It had been my home, but it was my home no longer. I was no longer a human being of the twentieth century; *I was a time-traveler*. That was my vocation, my inherent nature. These last ten years, I had merely been waiting for an opportunity to pursue and develop it.

They asked for me, I told myself, again. *They asked for me because I am the one they need—the one who is destined to go.*

CHAPTER FOUR

THE PRELIMINARY EXPEDITION

I got up for breakfast before Bryant or either of the Danbys. The Professor only kept three servants—which was really too few for a house the size of his—but they were very efficient in the making and serving of food, and well used to their masters' capriciousness. The cook was entirely unsurprised when I arrived in the breakfast-room, either by my presence or my aspect, and there was no delay in preparing my eggs and toast.

I was drinking coffee when Bryant eventually appeared. He shook my hand warmly—a little too warmly to be sincere. "How have you been keeping, old man?" he said—although he was twenty years my senior, and had aged even more conspicuously than young Danby since I had last set eyes on him.

"Pretty well," I told him.

"Hair never grew back, then?" he observed, stating the obvious. "Tried a toupée?"

"No," I said, in answer to both questions.

"Clara will be here this afternoon," he went on, having placed his own order for sausages, bacon and eggs. He was fidgeting in his seat, looking at his fingertips. "Looking forward to seeing her again after all these years." It was a statement, not a question; he meant that *he* was looking forward to seeing her.

"It seems that she has changed her mind about becoming a time-traveler," I observed. "I'm still surprised that she wasn't ready ten years ago, when I asked her whether she might be prepared to accompany me across the Professor's original bridge—not that we would have had time to get away before the collapse."

"Not the sort of thing you ought to spring on someone out of the blue," Bryant opined. "She was bound to say no—especially when she saw...." He left the sentence dangling, but started again almost immediately: "Thought for a while she might marry young Danby, you know, but she turned him down. Cut him up, rather. She's a few years older than he is, of course, but she was still young enough at the time. Perhaps she feels that it's too late now to marry and start a family, and thinks she might as well throw caution to the winds."

"I imagine so," I said, carefully.

"On the other hand," Bryant said, ruminatively, "the prospect of losing all her hair can't be any more attractive now than it was then." He probably felt like an ass as soon as he had said it.

"It was what the Dwellers did to me that caused me to lose my hair," I said. "I doubt that it's an inevitable consequence of crossing a time-bridge. Clara need have no fear of becoming so disturbing a presence that no one will ever meet her eye again,"

Bryant's meal arrived then, and he studied his fried eggs with the utmost care, as if they were eyes in a face. The Professor appeared while he was still staring at his plate, and Bryant looked up gratefully as soon as my attention was diverted.

"Thank you for coming, George," the Professor said, after shaking my hand. "This time, we must take our ambassadorial role more seriously. It might work greatly to our advantage to be seen to be obliging. The inhabitants of the world a million years hence have asked for you, and I am very grateful to be able to answer their request."

"I'm very grateful for the opportunity to do so," I said.

He tried to smile, but could not quite achieve it. "Philip will sleep late, I imagine," he said, taking his seat at the table. "He's had two busy days in transit. You seem to have become quite settled in Oxford. I could never abide the place, myself."

"Quite settled," I assured him. I resisted the temptation to ask after Mrs. Brett's health.

"I've refined the machine quite a bit, as Philip probably told you," the Professor went on, steadfastly. "Philip insists on remaining skeptical, but I'm reasonably sure that the new bridge extends to a future twice as distant as the last. A million years, George—think of that!"

"It's a conveniently round number," I agreed. "I'm glad to think that I might still be remembered after such a lapse of time— although it's possible, of course, that the inhabitants of that future have attempted to generalize from a single dimly-remembered instance, and are under the impression that *George* is synonymous with *human being*."

"I thought of that," the Professor admitted, "but it's best to cover as many eventualities as one can, don't you think?" He was deadly serious; there was no hint of humor in his voice.

"Indeed," I said.

"Clara will be here this afternoon," he said, as his own eggs arrived. Like mine, they were accompanied only by toast, although I doubted that he had stopped eating meat entirely, as I had.

"So I understand," I said.

"I hope it won't be awkward," Professor Danby went on. "Seemed the natural thing to do, in view of what you said last time—but Philip assures me that I was being grossly insensitive to both of you. I think he only did as I asked because he wanted to see her himself. To tell the truth, I hadn't expected her to ask if she could accompany him—but I remember what you said about knowing her better than I did, and you know better than I do what went on between them, so you probably understand her motives better than I can."

"It was a long time ago that I boasted that I knew her better than you," I said, carefully refraining from challenging his assumption that Clara wanted to go into the future *with Philip*. "After such a lapse of time, I dare say that none of us knows any of the others as well as we thought we did then."

"True," the Professor conceded. "I'm sorry it didn't work out between the two of you. I never approved of Philip asking her to marry him after she broke off her engagement to you, by the way. Not sporting."

Sporting was not a word I had expected to hear from the Professor's lips, and I was not yet ready to believe that he understood what it was supposed to mean. "It was a long time ago," I repeated. "Water under the bridge."

Sometimes, I reflected, privately, *things get stick under bridges, so firmly that time's flow can never budge them.* I still thought of myself as loving Clara, even though it was not at all obvious that I still had the kind of physiology that could support that kind of emotion. I retained the conviction, too, that there was a sense in which she still loved me—or, at least, the memory of the man I had been before I took the Professor's money and was changed in consequence. I had often thought that it must have torn her apart, emotionally, to discover that she could no longer tolerate my company for any length of time or in any depth of intimacy, because of what had been done to me by the Seekers of Science.

"This is a great opportunity, George," the Professor assured me, taking a new tack, "for all of us."

"I know it is," I replied, arrogant enough to think that I understood far better than he did what sort of opportunity it was.

* * * * * * *

By the time that Clara arrived in mid-afternoon my preparations for the new expedition, such as they were, had all been made. The two short messages we had received from the future promised that our arrival, this time, was expected. We would presumably be met, and greeted; we would be guests of a society rather than explorers of a wilderness. There seemed to me, in consequence, to be no need for the axe and burning-glass that I had carried by way of precaution on my previous expedition, although I did put my clasp-knife in the pocket of my light jacket.

Remembering the scorn in which clothing had been held by the Amphibians, I suspected that I might be overdressed, but there was no question of going naked in the company of Clara and young Danby. I had set aside the hat and scarf that I routinely employed for the purpose of self-concealment in the streets and by-ways Oxford, but I was otherwise fully-clad in a costume that was faintly and discomfitingly reminiscent of the battle-dress I had worn in the worst times of the Great War, campaign-boots and all. Danby was similarly-costumed, though perhaps a trifle more like a white hunter on safari in Africa. I fully expected that our outfits would seem absurd to our hosts, but thought them infinitely preferable to suits and ties.

Danby had picked out far more luggage than I, having elected to take a folding telescope, a camera, notebooks and pencils, as well as a dissecting kit and various related implements. I believe that he would have taken far more—and asked me to carry additional equipment for him—had he been more optimistic that there might be a convenient mains electricity supply a million years hence.

It was agreed that we would eat a civilized dinner before setting forth, provided that Clara agreed to what would be, from her point of view, a rather abrupt departure. It transpired that she did agree; she had always been a decisive person.

Clara had aged, of course, just as Danby had, but very gracefully. Her life in London was obviously far from sedentary; her figure gave no sign of the softening and broadening that often affects women as they pass through their thirties. Her face was slightly lined, but her teeth were still sound and her eyes had the same blithe frankness—even, at least momentarily, when she looked at me.

I had only one chance to speak to her before dinner without our being part of a larger crowd, and took it eagerly.

"I was surprised when Danby told me that he had approached you," I said, "though not as surprised as he was, I think, when you accepted the invitation he had not made."

"He should have been more careful in selecting an excuse to see me again," Clara said, flatly. Evidently, she had been thinking along the same lines as the Professor, in stark contrast to the reason Danby had given me by way of an explanation for his telephone call to her.

"You had refused the opportunity once," I reminded her. "As a man of science, he naturally expected the pattern to repeat itself."

"Things have changed," she said, meeting my eyes again, albeit just as briefly as before.

"What things, exactly?"

"Everything, George. The Depression, the spread of Fascism, the inevitability of a new war and the destruction of civilization—everything."

"You think of this as an opportunity for escape, then?" I said, a little foolishly.

"No, George," she said, a little wearily. "We're scheduled to re-turn, are we not, after a lapse of two or thee minutes? I think of it as an opportunity for a shift in perspective—an opportunity to satisfy myself that that there is hope for the eventual emergence on Earth of something better than mere mankind...by which I don't mean your giant Dwellers, or even your twee Amphibians."

"I'm glad that you accepted the challenge," I told her, incapable of resenting her gratuitous insult to the Amphibians as fervently as it deserved to be resented, "and that the Professor agreed it your acceptance. You'll be a far better ambassador for humankind, I dare say, than young Danby or me."

"Do you think that you were a poor ambassador last time?" she asked.

"I did my best," I answered. "The experience will probably work to my advantage—but I doubt that I can qualify any longer as an ambassador of humankind."

"Whether that's a mere lie or indulgent self-pity, George" she said, harshly, "it's unworthy of you. Is that what you'll be wearing for the expedition? You look like a refugee from the trenches."

"I *was* a refugee from the trenches when I first took the Profes-sor's money," I reminded her. "I was direly in need of the funds, but I was also still possessed by that numb fatalism so many of us felt who had been in France—including non-combatants like you. I was reckless then, and I showed scant regard for your feelings and plans in doing what I did. It's different now. That particular war-wound has eased, and these clothes don't remind me, particularly, of my combat experience. Do you prefer Danby's white hunter outfit? Or would you rather we all dressed as official ambassadors, in ceremonial finery?"

"No," she said, shortly. "I'll be wearing something not dissimilar, I suppose—more aviatrix than white hunter, though. We'll doubtless look bizarre to futuristic eyes in any case."

That was all we had time to say before we were drawn back into the general vortex, becoming a audience for the Professor's pontifications and advice, with copious addenda from his son. There was a good deal of speculative discussion between the two of them as to what we might and ought to expect, but neither seemed much inclined to ask for my opinion, and I thought it rather futile to make wild guesses mere hours before we would begin to discover the truth. I tried to enjoy the dinner, although it had not been planned or executed with the requirements of a non-meat-eater in mind. I only drank water, as did Clara, although young Danby obviously saw no reason to refrain from wine.

Afterwards, there was a brief space of solitude before we gathered again for the departure. I felt that my mental preparations, while far from complete, would not benefit from more furious thought, and tried as best I could to relax, and to savor the comfortable texture of relatively familiar surroundings. It would have been easier, in all probability, had not Clara reminded me so brutally of the critical state of the world, which had passed from a mildly-straitened state of post-war relief and gradual reconstruction to a state of utter desperation and incipient disintegration in ten short years.

Eventually, I went downstairs again, and joined the others in the room in which the Professor had constructed his time machine. Clara and young Danby were already there. We had already agreed that the Professor would send me through first, on my own, for a period of some five minutes, to check the safety of the bridge's far end.

The Professor had shown me photographs of the room into which the bridge opened, but it seemed relatively featureless. It was cylindrical, with no furniture but a rectangular basin set in the floor beside the platform set to receive objects from the past. The basin appeared to contain some viscous liquid. There was a possibility that I might fall into it if I stepped off the platform carelessly—perhaps it had been placed there with that intention—but the liquid did not seem to be very deep, and I could not believe that I had been invited to the far future merely in order that I might be drowned, or dissolved in an acid-bath.

I took my place on the platform of the machine, while the Professor activated the projector. Within the blink of an eye, I was received at the other end of the time-bridge.

The room was exactly as the Professor's photographs had indicated; there had not been the slightest change. The lighting was very subdued, but it began to brighten as soon as I arrived. I stood quite still, barely glancing down at the bath of liquid set to the right of the platform. I breathed deeply; the air was good, if slightly stale. The temperature was a little warmer than that of the room I had just left.

After an interval of six or seven seconds the light brightened again as part of the grey wall lit up, displaying an image. That part of the wall was obviously a cinematic screen of some kind, but it was as efficient as the multitudinous screens with which the Dwellers had decorated their underworld; to my uneducated eyes it presented the illusion of a window to the outside.

The central image was that of a near-human being, with a remarkably beautiful face, black hair and black eyes, and skin as bronzed as an Arab or an American Indian. Whether the figure as male or female I could not tell, even though it seemed to be naked— I write *seemed to be* because I could not quite believe that the featurelessness of the groin was natural, and was more inclined to assume that there must be some kind of concealing overlay there. I would have assumed that the creature had been specifically designed as an idealized depiction of human form had it not been for the two large wings—furled at present—that were attached to the shoulders. Their effect was to make the creature seem far more like a painter's concept of an angel. I concluded, therefore, that the image was posing as a divine messenger.

"You are George?" The voice—which must have come from some concealed speaker within the room, was querulous. Perhaps, I thought, that was not only because it intended its statement as a question but because it was uncertain as to the correctness of its pronunciation. It was, I supposed, remarkable that the room had been set up to produce audible speech, let alone English speech. The likelihood was that the inhabitants of this world normally communicated by means of the mind-speech that the Amphibians and Dwellers had used.

"Yes I am," I said.

"You are very welcome," the voice said. "Please step off the platform and remove your clothing. It is necessary for you to step into the gel-tank."

"I shall return to my own time in a few minutes," I said, making no move to comply with the request. "I shall arrive again very shortly, with two companions, now that I have ascertained that the environment is safe."

The face on the screen did not change its expression at all. After a few seconds hesitation, the voice said: "Your two companions will be welcome also, George."

"May I know your name?" I asked.

"You may use the name Speaker," said the voice from the speaker. I wondered whether my mind was being read, even though I was making no attempt to project my thoughts.

"Why do you want me to take off my clothes and bathe in your gel?"

"It is necessary for your protection. This is a sterile environment; when you leave it, you will require protection."

"Protection from infection?" I queried.

After a moment's hesitation, the voice said: "Yes."

I let that pass; time was short. "How far does the bridge extend?" I asked. "How many years separate this time from my own?"

"Approximately a million," was the reply. "But the day and the year are somewhat longer in duration now than they were in your era."

That was unsurprising; the days had been longer than twenty-four hours in the Dwellers' time too, although I did not know how or why. There were more important issues to investigate. "Are you merely an image on a screen, or are you a physical being?" I asked.

"This is a physical being," Speaker assured me. "It has been shaped for the purpose of welcoming you, and will serve as your guide. We shall attempt to make similar provision for your companions, but cannot do so immediately. Please do not delay your return, George. We need your help."

"Why?" I asked, bluntly.

"Because a situation has arisen in which we need an individual to act as an intermediary between ourselves and another species, and our earlier attempts to recruit such intermediaries have—"

At that point, Speaker was rudely cut off, and I found myself back on the Professor's platform, in my own time.

CHAPTER FIVE

RETURN TO THE FUTURE

I described what I had seen and reported my conversation with Speaker to the waiting assembly, more or less word for word. My listeners reacted in various ways.

"Have they really made a simulacrum of a sexless angel to meet and greet us?" Clara said. "An odd choice—but one with a certain aesthetic logic to it."

"Did you explain that one of your companions would be a woman?" Bryant said. "They can't expect you all to undress and take a bath in the same room."

"If they need an *individual* to act as an intermediary between themselves and *another species*," the Professor observed, "it implies that they are not themselves an individuated species—but that is not so very surprising, given what you found out about the Amphibians. They may well be possessed of some sort of collective intelligence, like the hive-mind of a formicary. Still, I was right about the interval of time."

"They asked George not to delay his return," young Danby reminded his father, frowning slightly at his father's satisfaction over the apparent resolution of their dispute. "Given that time elapsed now will be reflected, if not magnified, in the future, we ought to make haste. George's mission was to make certain that the far end of the bridge is safe—it is."

"Except," I murmured, "that we shall require protection against infection."

"For which they have made provision," young Danby said.

"Inadequate provision," Bryant put in, "in the circumstances."

"Please don't worry, Mr. Bryant," Clara said to him. "I'm sure that Philip and George will look away while I take my turn in the disinfectant bath."

"Were the walls of the room made of metal?" the Professor asked me.

"I don't think so," I replied. "But Philip is right—they asked me not to delay my return, and it's only polite to comply with their request. Shall we depart?"

The Professor raised no objection; our goodbyes were cursory. Clara, Philip Danby and I took our places on the platform again, and we departed for a future a million years hence.

The wallscreen was still illuminated; the angel was waiting patiently. I decided, as I had in the case of the Amphibian on my first expedition in time, that I would use the feminine pronoun in thinking of Speaker, in spite of the fact that angels are more conventionally thought of as male. She was, after all, only posing as an angel.

"My companions are named Philip and Clara," I said.

"You are welcome, Philip and Clara," the voice said. It seemed more confident of its pronunciation now. "It is necessary for each of you to immerse yourselves in the gel-tank, one by one. We apologize for the necessity."

There was no need for a discussion of the requirements of English modesty; we had to make our own provision to protect our petty taboos and prejudices. Clara stepped away from the platform and went closer to the screen on which Speaker's image was displayed, with her back to the tank. I took off my clothing and laid the various items on the floor, then stepped into the tank.

The colorless gel was warmer than the air, and its texture seemed as comfortable as its temperature; it was neither wet nor sticky.

"Please lie down, George," the voice said. "You must immerse your body completely, and you must also drink at least as much of the gel as would fill a vessel the size of your head."

The last instruction seemed more exacting than the others. "Why?" I said, hesitantly.

"Because you must be protected internally as well as externally. The gel must construct a protective layer covering the full extent of your alimentary canal. It will not take long, and will not be at all painful. Once the barrier is in place, it will not yield to any mechanical or biological penetration without your explicit consent."

I hesitated for a few seconds more, but in the end I decided that if this were the cost of being allowed to leave the pill-box and see the world of a million years hence, it was a small price to pay. I immersed myself in the gel, and took a deep breath before opening my mouth and beginning to drink. I had to pause several times before I had taken enough to satisfy the voice, but it was eventually satisfied.

When I got out of the tank I could see that I was covered from head to toe in a thin layer of protoplasm, which was already hardening and becoming opaque. At first it became white, but then the colors began to darken into an approximate, and rather bizarre, imitation of the clothes I had been wearing. Although the second skin with which I was now equipped was by no means as loose as the actual clothes it was ambitious to replace, it did make some provision for modesty, thickening to hide my genitals—and thickening, too, on the soles of my feet. I could not feel any such layer within my gut, but I assumed that the gel was extending itself there just as it had done externally. It must have covered my eyes, too, although it was as transparent as my own conjunctiva.

I presumed that I could still eat and drink easily enough, but I could not help wondering whether micturition might be problematic.

Absurd as the gesture seemed, I reached for my clothes, but the voice immediately asked me to leave them where they were. "You may put them on again," Speaker added, "when the occasion comes for you to return to your own time." It seemed a comforting assurance, not because of the promise of eventually being allowed to dress again, but because of Speaker's serene confidence that I would be returning to my own time.

Danby took his turn in the tank, then he and I replaced Clara, standing very close to the screen while she disrobed behind us.

"You said that you need me because I am an individual," I said to the angelic image. "Does that mean that you are part of some vast collective intelligence?"

"Like the hive-mind of a formicary," Danby obligingly added, echoing his father.

"We are bound together by...mind-force," Speaker replied, apparently groping for a descriptive term that could not be found in Webster's Dictionary and being forced to improvise. "Each of our individual units has a degree of autonomy, like the cells within your bodies—but yes, we have a single overarching consciousness, whose intelligence is that of the entire...biosphere."

"Like the Amphibians I encountered in the era intermediate between ours and yours?" I said.

"In essence, yes," Speaker agreed. "But our community is far more complex, more elegantly constructed and more tightly bound than theirs, thanks to our superior mastery of the mind-force." The implication of the words was smug, but that may have been an accident.

"Do the Amphibians still exist, then?" I said. It did not seem impossible that they might; they had certainly thought of themselves as immortals.

The voice hesitated before replying. "There are no species in the present biosphere separate from ourselves," it said, "but we have units not dissimilar in form to the creatures you call Amphibians."

I made a mental note of the fact that Speaker had known what I meant by the term Amphibian, even though the species was apparently long extinct, and wondered whether it implied that our hosts were reading my subvocalized thoughts as well as attending to my spoken words.

"George said that you mentioned another species when you spoke to him before," Danby put in.

"The species whose representatives have demanded that we use an individual intermediary is not native to the planetary biosphere," Speaker said, flatly.

Do you mean that they're from *another* planet?" Danby deduced. "Mars, perhaps?"

"They appear to have originated on a planet orbiting a distant star," Speaker told us, the words themselves implying a certain skepticism, although the tone was devoid of significant inflection. "Some of them are currently located on the moon."

"And they're afraid of you?" Danby said. "They're individuals themselves, and they're afraid of making direct contact with a collective intelligence like yours?"

"That appears to be the case," Speaker said.

"Are you actually proposing to send us to the moon to serve as your intermediaries?" I asked.

"We had intended to ask you to go to the moon in that capacity, George," the voice admitted. "If you will agree to go, and would prefer to be accompanied by your companions, we can make provision for them to accompany you. There is an extraterrestrial machine on the Earth's surface, by means of which the visitors want to make a preliminary examination, but they insist that we must actually send our representatives to the moon rather than communicating at a distance. We would like to be able to comply with their request, even though we consider it unreasonable."

"Because you're afraid of them too," Danby inferred—although it seemed to me that it would have been more diplomatic to leave that particular inference unvoiced.

Speaker did not reply, perhaps because Clara interrupted us at that point to say: "I'm ready."

We turned around to look at her. Although her new skin hugged her body far more closely than the clothing she had set aside, the gel had taken on imitative colors, as it had in my case and Danby's, and the costume was not indecently revealing. Indeed, Clara seemed as sexless as the imitation angel.

"You may leave the...containment facility now, if you wish," Speaker said, "but there will be a short delay before this unit will be able to arrive there in person; you may wait inside until then, if you prefer."

I glanced briefly at my companions before saying: "I think we'd prefer to step outside." I was glad to be offered an opportunity, however brief it might prove to be, to look at the world of a million years hence without the benefit of a commentator.

The image on the screen immediately blanked out. After a brief pause, a slit opened in the curved wall of the cylindrical container, rapidly widening to become a doorway through which we could make our exit.

The light outside was far from bright, but not because it was the dead of night; the sky was illuminated, after a fashion. We were surrounded by a forest of sorts, although the building we had just left was located in the centre of a large clearing, about two hundred yards in diameter. The multicolored crowns of the trees formed a circle around us, like a hedge not much less than a hundred feet tall. Directly overhead the sky was a vaporous mass of thick cloud, which extended unbroken from horizon to horizon. The cloud was not still, nor did its components move as if driven by a wind. Instead, it seemed to be seething with obscure activity.

The boles of the surrounding trees were very various in thickness and in the texture of their outer teguments. Instead of bark, their outer layers seemed to be stony, or compounded out of a glasslike material, often polished to a high sheen, but very uneven at the surface. Their branches were numerous, curved in complex arcs, and the leaves borne by the branches were of many different shapes and textures, even within the crown of each individual dendrite.

There were small creatures moving in the crowns of the trees, but they were too distant and too well-hidden for me to be sure whether or not they were birds. There seemed to be swarms of flying insects moving between them ceaselessly, so dense in places that I was tempted to wonder whether the exotic clouds above the crowns might consist of much vaster swarms of insects. None of the insects troubled us; at was as if a *cordon sanitaire* had been established at the edge of the clearing, allowing each of us an inviolate personal space in which to move.

The ground beneath our feet seemed relatively bare, although it was green in hue and dotted here and there with small clusters of upthrusting leaves and clumps of grass-like growths. There was no explicitly-marked road or pathway cutting across the clearing and no obvious opening to any considerable route through the forest, but nor was there any no substantial barrier to the progress of a pedestrian or a vehicle. There was no vehicle yet to be seen, though.

Danby, obedient to the voice's command, had not dressed himself again but he had picked up his kit-bag. He brought out his camera and walked across the clearing towards one of the trees. Clara followed him, and stretched out her hand to touch its bole, while looking up at branches that were just out of reach above her head. I moved a dozen paces or so away from the blockhouse—whose door silently slid shut behind us—but stayed in the open, listening for the sound of some approach.

No such sound was perceptible as yet. I knelt down to inspect the ground, which seemed to be covered by a tegument not dissimilar to the second skin that had been provided for me. The bare stretches between the more obvious clumps of vegetation were rather uneven, and I observed that their shallow peaks and troughs were slowly changing their shapes and positions, like waves on a sullen sea. There was a slight warm wind on my cheeks; the ambient temperature must have been about eighty degrees Fahrenheit, and the humidity would surely brought a manifest sweat to my face had it not been for the inhibiting effect of my new skin. The air seemed heavy, and the protective barrier that had been cast over me did not prevent my perception of miscellaneous scents, which seemed rather sickly and cloying, though not altogether unpleasant.

The ground was even warmer than the air—perhaps as warm as blood heat. I could not help wondering whether I might be kneeling on the back of some enormous creature, like the false island on which the legendary sailor Sindbad had once been cast away—in which case, I assumed, the trees surrounding the clearing would not be trees at all, but some embellishment of its hide akin to fur or scales. If so, I decided, the creature must be lying still, perhaps asleep.

I was still running my fingers lightly over the warm green carpet when Speaker arrived. Her wings were not just for show—she really could fly, although I could not have believed, had I not seen it, that a creature so large and seemingly heavy could match much smaller birds in the elegance and comfort of its flight.

She alighted in front to me, and her dark eyes studied me carefully. Clearly, she had not been able to make such an inspection while she was merely an image on a screen. She was even more beautiful in the flesh than she had been as an image, not just because she now had a conspicuous solidity but because I had seen her bright white wings in action, and knew how powerful they were.

Now the adventure begins, I thought. *I am looking at the future, and the future is looking back at me.*

CHAPTER SIX

SPEAKER

"You are very welcome, George," Speaker said, with all due ceremony. Her voice had altered considerably since she had first employed the speaker inn the block-house, becoming softer and far more melodic as well as more confident. That reaffirmed my decision to think of "her" rather than "him".

"Thank you," I said, inadequately.

"The creature that will transport us to the Great Tree is slower in flight than I am," she informed me, her voice contriving a slight inflection for the first time, expressive of polite regret. "I hurried on to greet you. We are very grateful to you for answering our call." In the flesh she was an inch shorter than me—two inches shorter than Danby—but I had no sense of looking down at her because of the furled wings looming up behind her shoulders.

Had she been much tinier, those wings might have caused her to resemble figures in Victorian fairy painting, because I could see at this close range that they were neither feathered nor leathery. They were not magnified insect wings, but they had something of the same thinness and delicacy in spite of their evident power. Although their background hue was white, they had faint traceries of color, vaguely reminiscent of the veins on an insect's wings. They were not at all reminiscent of the wings borne by the other winged humanoids of my slight acquaintance: the Bat-wings, as whose appeal-judge I had been forced to serve after the battle with the Killers five hundred thousand years before. The newcomer stood so lightly on her feet that I could easily have believed her almost weightless; she appeared to be exerting little or no pressure on the ground.

Danby and Clara rejoined us, taking up positions to either side of me so that they could look at Speaker. Speaker barely glanced at

Danby, although I do not think she intended any insult; she looked a little more closely at Clara.

"It will be interesting to have the opportunity to study human sexual dimorphism," Speaker commented, rather quaintly.

"Are sexual differences unknown in this world, then?" Clara asked.

"Sexual reproduction was a temporary artifact of evolution," Speaker replied, dutifully. "It vanished from the biosphere long before our evolution."

"The Amphibians had already abandoned sexual dimorphism," I observed, "and the Dwellers seem to be having considerable difficulty with the business of reproduction."

"Sexual reproduction is an essentially primitive and inefficient process," Speaker remarked, "although it served its purpose, in collaboration with natural selection, as a temporary phase in the generation of biospheric complexity."

"Do the visiting aliens still have two sexes?" Danby inquired.

"We cannot be sure," Speaker said, "but we think not. They appear to be...." This time the hesitation was at least twice as long as normal. "...Metamorphosians."

It seemed unlikely that there was any such word in Webster, and I took it for another improvisation. There was a sense, of course, in which all the proper names I had devised in my first report had been improvisations. I had made very rapid progress in deciphering the Amphibians' mind-speech, and had been able to substitute English common nouns easily enough for most of their native equivalents, but synthesizing proper nouns had been more difficult. That was not because the Amphibians had any difficulty conceiving of species, or even of individuals, but because they did so in terms that were quasi-visual, representative rather than symbolic. In the collective imagination of the Amphibians, their fellow-creatures—even including the Dwellers—had their own category of thought, distinct from ordinary entities subject to more arbitrary generalization.

I had not yet made a form decision as what to call entities of Speaker's sort, or the collective intelligence that they apparently shared. The possibility had occurred to me of describing them as Formicarians, but I feared that the term might be loaded with misleading implications.

"When you spoke to George before," Danby said, making the most of the opportunity provided by my silent ruminations. "You told him that the day and the year are longer now than they were in our era. That puzzles me. George reported that such was the case in the Dwellers' era too, but I had supposed him to be mistaken. The passage of half a million or a million years should not have made any significant difference to the rotation of the Earth on its axis or the period of its orbit around the sun, if the only forces in play are gravitational, frictional and tidal."

"There is another force in play," Speaker said, blandly, "and it is indeed the case that the day and the year are longer than they were." She did not elaborate. This time, I wondered whether she did intend some slight snub. Perhaps, I thought, she or her guiding intelligence *could* read our minds, and had taken note of Danby's acquisitive agenda. Given that they must share my own anxieties about the potential impact of entanglements between past and future, it was by no means incredible that they might be reluctant to hold any extensive conversation with Danby regarding new forces at play in this world and the technologies used to manipulate them.

I was less surprised by the datum that Danby had queried than he appeared to be. The relatively remote ancestors of the Dwellers had obviously been capable of reshaping continents and hollowing out the Earth's crust; adjustments to the planet's rotation on its axis and velocity within its orbit might not have been beyond the scope of such ambitious engineers, and certainly not beyond the capabilities of their own remote descendants.

"You speak English very well," I commented, thinking it best to change the subject. "We are honored that you should have taken the trouble to learn our language in order to make us welcome."

"We could not have done it without your help," Speaker replied.

Feeling that I ought to give credit where it was due, I said: "It was Philip's father who sent you the dictionary. It is entirely due to the Danbys that I was able to answer your summons. Philip conveyed the message to me, and the Professor allowed me the use of his machine in order to answer it."

"We are grateful to Philip and his father," Speaker stated, in what must have seemed to Danby a lukewarm manner.

"My father built the machine that projected George into the future ten years ago—or half a million years ago, in your reckoning," Danby put in. "If it were not for him, you would not have known George's name. I am here as my father's representative. We have *all* come in response to your appeal, and are all willing to do whatever we can to help you."

Speaker's beautiful eyes finally consented to study Danby with the care and specific attention he presumably thought to be his due, but the angel did not make any immediate reply.

"We are very grateful to you for enabling us to make a new connection with the future," Danby went on, doggedly, "and for signaling to us that you are aware of the earlier one. We hope to learn a great deal from you, and hope that we can be of interest to you in return."

"We are waiting for a means of transport to arrive," Speaker said, addressing Danby directly although her tone was rather distant. "We are everywhere, but this is not the place for us to say what must be said. Please forgive the delay in transporting you to the lodgings prepared for you in the heartwood of the Great Tree. We shall arrive there before dawn."

That startled me slightly. "I had assumed that this was daylight, in spite of its faintness," I said.

"Night is not dark here," Speaker told me. "The mist-layer has a luminosity of its own. You shall see the daylight before we arrive—but you will not find it as bright as it was in your era, and the colors of the sky will not be familiar."

I glanced at Danby, but he seemed less perturbed by the news that the sky was no longer blue than he had been to learn that the day and year were longer than ours.

No longer able to be content with uncertainty, and thinking that it was desirable to clarify the issue for my companions' sake, I asked: "Am I right in presuming that you can perceive our subvocalized thoughts as well as what we say aloud?"

"We can," Speaker agreed, "although we are still uncertain about their interpretation. Whenever you frame thoughts in words, or summon images to your imagination, we can perceive them—but there is a great deal that we cannot understand. We can refrain from such perception if you wish—although it will surely be useful to you to master the arts of...mind-speech, and we shall be better able to help you decipher our thoughts if we are better able to decipher yours."

"I understand that," I assured her, "but we will be more comfortable if we are able to retain some privacy in our thoughts. Perhaps it would be better for you to refrain from reading our minds until we make some formal arrangement to learn mind-speech—or, in my case, recover the skills I developed in the era of the Dwellers."

"We hope that you will recover these skills very swiftly, when the need arises," Speaker said. "In the meantime, though, we shall respect your mental privacy unless you make a manifest effort to communicate or give us explicit permission to probe your thoughts."

I could not be sure whether that promise was worth anything, given that I would probably be unable to perceive any breach of it, but we had no alternative but to accept it gracefully.

"Are you the only one of your kind who makes use of spoken language?" Clara asked.

"By no means," Speaker said. "We make full use of every available sense in our communications, although many of our individual units are sensory specialists. This unit is, however, the only one specifically designed to speak English. Others are capable of it, but will only make use of the facility if the occasion demands it. Had we known that three of you would answer our call, we would have produced others in advance, but it will take time to make up for the error."

I opened my mouth to reply, but before I could do so the angel spoke again, saying: "I believe that the transporter is arriving now."

I had not heard any sound before then, but I perceived a faint whir as soon as Speaker had completed the sentence. It was strangely, if distantly familiar.

I looked up, striving to penetrate the enigmatic clouds with my eyes—and could not repress a sudden start of pure horror as I saw what was emerging from the vapors, heading directly toward the clearing in which we stood.

CHAPTER SEVEN

THE FLIGHT

Danby did not look at me when I cried out, because his eyes were fixed on the monster that had emerged from the mists and was now descending precipitately towards us. It was left to Clara to say: "What is it. George?"

"It's an Antipodean," I said, "or something very like one." I had to move then, for Speaker was urging us to move away from the centre of the clearing to take shelter under the branches of a tree. I kept my startled eyes upon the monster as I ran for the clearing's edge.

The creature making its descent was formed like a gigantic flattened beetle. Its copper-colored wing-cases had a metallic luster. It had three pairs of wings, just like the monsters I had seen attacking the Dwellers' fortress-continent on so many subterranean screens, while I was lodged with the Seekers of Wisdom—and whose severed body-parts I had seen in some profusion in the laboratories of the Seekers of Science. It must have been about the size of a county cricket field, elongated into an oval shape. Its legs did not dangle as it flew above the trees, being folded up into its abdomen, but as it came level with the crowns six legs were abruptly extended, preparing for a landing.

The creature's head did not protrude overmuch from its thorax, but it was equipped with what seemed from a distance to be two vast compound eyes. As it came closer to the ground, however, I realized that the "eyes" were more like windows, having no photoreceptive black surface behind them but only two empty chambers, one to either side.

I had never been able to ascertain, during my sojourn with the Dwellers, whether my Amphibian companion's conjecture regarding the nature of the Antipodeans was accurate. She had suggested, although she did not know for sure, that they were compound creatures, the flying carcass existing in a complex symbiotic relationship with smaller entities living within its body. Now, though, I believed that I could see at least two living creatures, formed more like cephalopods than any sort of insect, moving within the cavities adapted from vestigial eyes.

Having settled delicately on its extended legs, the creature then lowered its body to the ground, folding the limbs away again. Now, it looked more like a machine—a mere vehicle—than a living creature. When sections of its "compound eyes" swung out like doorways that impression was redoubled. The cephalopods did not descend to the ground; instead, Speaker ushered us towards the open doorways.

"I shall travel with George," Speaker said, as she directed me towards the nearer portal. "You will be quite safe in the other, Philip and Clara, although the...sky-car's pilot will be unable to speak to you. We are sorry for that inconvenience."

I climbed up into the strange cockpit, as I had been requested to do. I found it easy enough, in spite of the absence of a ladder. I hesitated on the threshold, though, because there was nothing within that looked like a seat, and the walls enclosing the interior space seemed suspiciously fluid.

"Please do not be alarmed," Speaker said. "You will be comfortable, and perfectly safe."

I had no need to suppress any excessive alarm of my own, but I felt sorry for Danby and Clara as I moved hesitantly into the interior. The thing that I had taken for a cephalopod was clinging to the viscous surface like a spider, with twelve tentacles splayed like the spokes of a wheel. Its bulbous head had two huge eyes, which stared at me unblinkingly, but its mouth was neither the beak of an octopus nor the lipped orifice of a human; it bore a closer resemblance to an ant-eater's proboscis.

I heard Danby say something to Clara, apparently by way of reassurance, but I think he was as much intent on bolstering his own resolve as lending support to hers.

I made my way into the waiting space reluctantly, finding it narrower than I had hoped. Once Speaker had climbed in behind me and the door had closed behind us, it became narrower still. The rear wall of the chamber seemed to swell up. For a moment, I wondered whether I might be trapped in one of those shrinking rooms of which Gothic melodramatists were so fond, but I knew that I could not have been brought forward in time by a million years merely to be crushed to death, and I held myself firm as the semi-liquid flowed about my lower limbs and abdomen, and then around my torso. Mercifully, it left my arms and shoulders free, as well as my head. There was a powerful odor, somewhat reminiscent of freshly-landed seafish, and I found myself reorientated so that the many-tentacled creature was beside me to the right, its head level with mine. Speaker was beside me to the left.

Although the cephalopod was unable to speak aloud, it seemed more willing than Speaker to make contact in another way. Although there was nothing in its mental effusion that was translatable into speech or visual imagery, it radiated a tranquility that was only slightly soporific. It continued to study me with its eyes in a way that suggested that it had freer access to my own inner being—to my atrophied emotions, if not my subvocalized thoughts.

The body of the monstrous flier reared up with a jerk as the legs stiffened again, and the complex set of wings came into play. The sky-car ascended from the ground, vertically at first and a trifle unsteadily—but once it as clear of the crowns of the trees it moved more confidently, and climbed at a gentler angle. It was soon lost in the strange clouds—which, now that I could see them at close range, seem to be composed of a vapor so thick as to be almost liquid. The vapor was inhabited, as a pond or an ocean might be, by enormous shoals of small creatures. Most were like balloons or dandelion-clocks floating contentedly in the frail medium, but there were also worm-like creatures that slithered through the thickened air without the aid of wings. There were many kinds of flying insects too, and a few larger animals like flying fish—or gliding fish, at any rate.

I could not judge very accurately from the time we spent within it how deep the stratum of cloud might be, because the attitude of the sky-car's climb was adjusted several times, but it must have been at least half a mile from bottom to top.

Suddenly, we came out of the layer into clearer air. I looked up immediately, thinking that I might now be able to see the stars—and the moon too, if it happened to be above the horizon. I could not; the clear air seemed to be an intermediate layer between the lower stratum of oceanic cloud and another, which seemed thinner but just as strange. There was a faint light emanating from below as well as from above, and I had the strange sensation of being trapped in a weird dimension which had one sky above and another below.

In one lateral direction, though—which I immediately presumed to be the east—the light emanating from the higher cloud-layer seemed considerably brighter and more multicolored. That additional light, I concluded, must be refractory, external to the cloud in its origin.

Within a few minutes, the hypothesis was confirmed; as we climbed higher, the quality of the dawn changed markedly, and I saw the upper layer's inherent radiance suffused and superseded by the glare of the sunlight filtering through it. I understood then why we had been warned not to expect a familiar sky. In the space between the two great layers of cloud, each of which I now presumed to be inhabited by a rich assortment of living creatures, the "sky" formed by the upper cloud-layer, once the sun was behind it, was a delicate shade of pea-green.

I looked up for some little while before turning to look sideways at my beautiful companion. There was a curious expression on her face, which spoke of some definite discomfort. I guessed that she had just discovered that she did not like to be constrained, and was probably feeling claustrophobic. She would have been far happier, I deduced, had she been able to return the same way as she had come, under the power of her own miraculous wings. She had not done so because she had not wanted to leave me alone.

"I'm sorry," I said. "I would not have minded had you flown back alone and rejoined us when we landed."

"This unit's function is to welcome and guide you, George," she said.

"I understand that," I said. After a slight pause, I added: "You really do want *my* help, don't you? If Danby or Clara had come through in my stead, rather than as my companions, you would not have welcomed them nearly so eagerly."

"That is correct," Speaker confirmed, her melodic voice showing the strain of her discomfort.

"It's because of what the Dwellers did to me, isn't it?" I said. "It's because I can function as a sort of living book."

"Yes," she replied. "That capacity is what we need most urgently. The Metamorphosians will use it, if you will consent to be used, and there are other employments to which it might be put before then...but this is not the time."

She had said that before, but I got the impression that it was her discomfort that was making her repeat it now. She was no longer looking at me; she was staring through the clear medium of the flier's eye.

I followed the direction of her gaze. I saw three other flying creatures, which must have been much the same size as her, flying alongside the sky-car. They too had six limbs in all, having vaguely simian bodies equipped with anomalous wings. There was something odd about the way their wings moved; it was certainly not the fluttering movement of a butterfly's wings, nor the hectic beat of the wings of a lark or a pipistrelle, although they were not gliding as a company of gulls might glide on a thermal current.

While I watched the winged apes busy in what seemed to be a blatantly impractical kind of flight, I remembered the Antipodeans again, and the other birds I had seen flying off the shore of the Dwellers' island continent. They had been unable to continue flying over the cultivated land; it was as if the air above that terrain were somehow less able to support them. I had reported that without understanding it in the least. Having had time to think about it in the interim, however, I had eventually concluded that it could not be the physical properties of the air that were different—that it must, instead, be some kind of mental phenomenon akin to the one that allowed the Amphibians and other species to communicate with one another without recourse to sound or visual signaling.

In my own world, I knew, no living creature as massive as the humanoid creature designed to meet and greet us, let alone the one in which I was traveling, could possibly have flown under its own power. If the kind of force that facilitated the Amphibians' mental communication were capable of depriving creatures of the power of flight, however, it was presumably capable of augmenting that power as well. Given that this was a world that had vast oceanic layers of vapor in its atmosphere, inhabited by very various kinds of strange "swimmers", the enhancement of aerial buoyancy and flight was presumably a matter of biological routine.

In my own world, I reflected, there had been no shortage of scientists prepared to declare such phenomena as telepathy flatly impossible, on the grounds that there was no way that information could be communicated between minds in the absence of some kind of deformable physical medium, like sound-modifiable air, or some kind of actual transmission, whether of electromagnetic waves or sensible molecules. Here, though, as in the world of the Amphibians and the Dwellers, direct communication between minds appeared to be not only possible but normal, so there must presumably be a whole spectrum of forces as-yet-undetected by the kinds of physical apparatus our scientists could employ. Clearly, the natural phenomena associated with that category of forces were very much more evident here than they were in my own world, where they could only be manifest, if at all, in a fugitive fashion. Here, the power of levitation—in which the scientists of my own time also refused to believe—was apparently commonplace.

I turned my head the other way and looked the silent cephalopod directly in its black eyes. Then I turned back to Speaker and said: "If only I could master the arts of communication that this creature uses, perhaps I might also master the art of flight—except, of course, that God and natural selection omitted to provide me with the wings that were gifted to my cousins without."

I obtained no obvious reaction, let alone an immediate answer. I glanced back at the cephalopod, which did not seem shocked or offended by my oafish use of sound, as an Amphibian would have.

Speaker was so obviously uncomfortable now that I could not help feeling guilty, even though I had not asked her to ride with me instead of flying. "I could share the Amphibians' thoughts well enough to decipher them right away, after a fashion," I told her. "I even contrived to hear their soundless equivalent of music, and gained some scant impression of its melodic quality. From this creature here, though, all I receive is a kind of discreet opium, dulling my anxieties."

"The pilot is a primitive organism, even by comparison with the Amphibians," Speaker commented, a trifle brusquely.

"Whereas you are far more advanced than they were," I said. "I felt very primitive by comparison with the Amphibians, and am presumably far more so by comparison with you—and yet your controlling intelligence needs my help, or believes that it does. If something as woefully primitive as me can help something as sophisticated as you, then the march of progress cannot be as steady as it sometimes seems."

"It is not," Speaker admitted. "Progress in one faculty is often accompanied by the atrophy of others. That is why we have such a rich variety of specialist units."

"We can see that in my world," I told her, "in terms of the variety of individuals specialized for different ways of life. The progress of human sight was accomplished at the expense of such senses as smell—our noses are far less keen than those of our domestic dogs. The development of mind-speech and the ability to perceive nearby objects by means of a psychic analogue of the sense of touch must have cost the Amphibians something in respect of the sensitivity of their other senses, although the Amphibian who became my companion during my first adventure in time also had greater powers of sight than I have. Even a collective intelligence that somehow encompasses organisms of every kind conceivable to me, and many that are not, must have paid a cost for that kind of union—perhaps a dear one."

"That is certainly what the Metamorphosians appear to believe," Speaker said. "They appear to think of our kind of life as a kind of evolutionary trap, from which escape is difficult. They also appear to think that we are incapable of coexisting with individuated life-forms."

"And I am here to help you prove them wrong," I murmured—but I could not help thinking, as I said it, of the gel-tank, and the necessity of equipping me with an all-encompassing protective layer before it was safe for me to step out of the sterile environment of the "containment facility" into the open air.

"Yes," said Speaker, "if you can."

I am sure that she would never have added that "if you can" had she not been under such unanticipated strain, because she would not have wanted to concede the possibility that there was a darker alternative. What, I thought, might become of me if I could not? What if I were to become living—or no-longer-living—proof of the exact opposite?

"This isn't going to be easy, is it?" I murmured.

"If it were easy," the claustrophobically-discomfited angel admitted, "we would not need you at all."

CHAPTER EIGHT

THE GREAT TREE

Although the unbroken layer of cloud beneath us emitted and reflected too much light to permit the slightest glimpse of the ground that lay beneath it, there were variously colored entities visible within it, and flocks of creatures like giant flatworms that seemed to be moving over its "surface" like fishing-fleets.

The Earth must have a great deal more living-space now than in my own day, I reasoned. The Dwellers had constructed new layers of living space within, to a depth of more than 500 miles. The floor of each layer obviously required sturdy support, so it could not have an area remotely comparable to the surface, but the sheer number of interior hollows must add up to a cultivable area forty or fifty times the land surface of my own era. To call such an area "cultivable" would have been absurd, of course, had their cultivation been reliant on the energy of the sun, but it had not. The Dwellers tapped the heat of the Earth's core, not merely as a direct supply of energy for heir own use, but for the nurture of a vast range of plants—or, if I ought not to call them plants, "primary producers" of an alternative sort.

Now, it seemed, there were further layers of bioproductive endeavor suspended in the atmosphere—perhaps more than the two I could presently see. Even if there were only the two, though, their total "surface area" must be vast, each being greater than the solid and liquid surface in proportion to the square of their elevation. The energy that they extracted from the sunlight would no longer be available at the surface, of course, but I was prepared to wager that the layering of the various extraction processes ensured that far more of the energy gifted to the Earth by the sun was actually turned to productive use in this ecosystem, and very little wasted.

In my own era, I knew, the production processes at the Earth's surface had been so inefficient that a great deal of the solar energy impinging upon the planet was simply reflected or re-radiated back into space. In addition, much of the carbon that might have been integrated into living flesh of one kind or another actually lay idle, consigned to measures of fossil fuels like coal and oil, or dissolved and confined within the icy depths of the sea. How much more efficiently was this world organized? Efficiently enough, perhaps, for more carbon to have been imported by way of enhancing the planet's total biomass? If so, perhaps the slowing of the Earth's axial and orbital rotation was partly attributable to its increased mass and diameter. Even in the Dwellers' day, the bloating of the surface by constructions employing the matter displaced from the hollow crust had been considerable; their ancestors had been planetary engineers as well as continental engineers and engineers of flesh.

"And yet," I said to Speaker, still full of wonder at the fact, "you need our help. You can make simulacra of human beings, it seems—simulacra with more robust bodies and extra functional limbs—but there must be something in us that you cannot duplicate, for which you must come to the source."

It was not phrased as a question, and Speaker evidently had no further comment to make, for the present, on that particular issue.

"We should have made better provision for your transport," Speaker said. "We apologize."

"I am not finding it unduly uncomfortable or frustratingly slow," I said. "It is I who should apologize to you; this mode of transport is clearly not to your taste. You have never had any need to experience it before, of course."

"Indeed not," Speaker confirmed.

I felt embarrassed and ashamed by my immediate reaction to her predicament, which was not primarily sympathetic. Instead, I felt a certain perverse relief to know that she was not, after all, an angel serving as the mouthpiece of some omnipotent and omniscient God. She might be a component of an authentically godlike intelligence, but its awesome power and knowledge evidently fell far short of omnipotence and omniscience. Not only were there feats of heroism that a humble human might still perform on its behalf, but it had not even contrived to anticipate all the problems that its own specifically-designed agent would have to face in assisting those humans.

On the other hand, I was not sure that the planetary intelligence in question could keep me safe from its own destructive—or absorptive—tendencies, no matter how much it stood to gain by letting me be.

"I'm sorry," I said, just in case Speaker had broken her promise and continued to read my mind. "I don't have any urgent need to continue our conversation just now, so you needn't feel obliged to speak if you would prefer to stay silent. There will doubtless be plenty of time to obtain answers to all my questions—and I'm not at all sure that I know, as yet, exactly what I need to ask. Everything I see here puts new ideas into my head, and it can be difficult to negotiate a way through that sort of confusion."

"We shall try to understand that, George," Speaker assured me, weakly. "There are, alas, many kinds of confusion of which we are hardly capable."

That remark served only to increase the number of new ideas that had been put into my head, requiring contemplation. I remembered that my long-time Amphibian companion had marveled more than once at the confusions of which I was capable—especially the fact that my will could be in conflict with impulses, doubts and temptations, and that it often lost the consequent struggles. The Amphibian, though, had considered that confusion to be the ultimate proof of my hideously primitive nature, and would surely never have dreamed of inserting a regretful "alas" into any such observation.

I turned my attention back to the lower cloud layer, which seemed much closer now than it had before. I could see other fliers skimming over its surface, including other sky-cars. I wondered whether it was significant that the Earth's collective intelligence as still using fliers modeled on those that had gone to war with the Dwellers so many thousands of years ago. Did it mean that the present inhabitants of the Earth were the direct descendants of some or all of the creatures that had been associated with the Antipodeans in those days? Clearly, the Antipodeans had won their war against the Dwellers—but had there been more to that victory than I had suspected at the time? Had it been far more than the victory of one civilization over another, or one species over another? Had it been a victory of one *way of being* over another—the death-knell not merely of humankind's last descendants but of all individuated life on Earth?

If Speaker or her guiding intelligence had been eavesdropping on those thoughts, she felt no compulsion to make any reply to the questions. She said nothing, and seemed quite grateful for the opportunity to say nothing.

Ahead of the sky-car I perceived a mountain—or, at least, what looked at first glance to be a mountain—sprouting from the "plain" formed by the cloud-layer beneath. It required a moment's thought for me to remember that the cloud was not something on which a mountain could sit, unless the mountain were vaporous itself, which this one did not seem to be.

I did not know how high the cloud-layer was above the surface of the Earth, nor how thick it was, but I calculated for the sake of argument that if it were a mile high and a mile thick—which estimates seemed not unreasonable—then the object ahead, whose colossal dimensions were becoming increasingly apparent as we approached, must be at least five miles from root to tip.

Having phrased it in that manner to myself, I realized almost immediately that I had made a mistake. What I was looking at was indeed the kind of entity that might have roots, for it was not a mountain at all, but the crown of an enormous tree: a tree of such dimensions, I calculated—again merely for the sake of the internal argument—that it might well have roots that descended into the utmost depths of the Earth. The whole entity, I thought, might be more than ten miles high, if measured from its utmost bottom to its utmost top.

Its branches were multitudinous and its foliage multifarious, but what struck me most forcibly about it was the enormous quantity of flying creatures busy about its crown. To begin with, I could only see the larger ones, but the closer we approached the more I perceived. There was particularly intense activity just above its intersection with the cloud-layer, where the vaporous mass closely resembled an ocean lapping against its shore.

I had just begun to look forward eagerly to a much closer approach, which would allow my eyes to discriminate far more detail, when the sky-car began its descent and plunged into the vapor itself. For some time, everything was vague, and nothing at all could be clearly made out in the surrounding mists, silvery with light as they were. Then we came out into clearer air beneath the cloud, and I was able to see the lowest branches of the gigantic tree, and measure the girth of its immense trunk.

It was growing in the midst of the same forest to which the time-bridge had brought us, but the span of its crown was so vast that its huge bole was surrounded by an expanse of treeless ground large enough to accommodate a city. It did, indeed, accommodate a city of sorts, although the "buildings" seemed to me to be extraordinarily flimsy; their walls were mostly transparent, or at least translucent, although I doubted that they were made of glass. There were few straight lines in the city, and fewer definite angles; everything seemed curved and meandering, including the highways and by-roads snaking their way around globular growths that sometimes clustered together like a foam of bubbles or masses of frog-spawn. They were, I decided, growths in a literal sense, not buildings constructed from inert materials.

There seemed to be living creatures everywhere on the winding roads, of many different forms. Some walked on two legs, some on four, some on six or eight and some on many more. Others slithered or flew—but all of them seemed to be moving purposively beneath the vast canopy formed by the vast tree's lowest branches.

I tried to pick out recognizable biological forms, not in the sense that I expected to see species with which I was familiar, but in the more modest sense that I expected to find orders or families of which I was familiar, just as I had been able to classify most of the creatures of the Dwellers' world as mammals, birds, reptiles or amphibians...although, of course, the Amphibians themselves had been mammals.

I could not do it. The fundamental patterns common to my worlds and the Dwellers' seemed to have all-but-vanished from this one. The only creatures that I could have unhesitatingly classified into categories I knew were the two which shared the cabin with me—and even they, I realized, were not unambiguous, in that Speaker's wings were not unequivocally mammalian in type, while the cephalopod, on closer inspection, had several features apparently borrowed from reptiles. In the creatures moving about the city whose centre as the enormous tree-trunk, mammalian features were recklessly mingled with reptilian and arthropod. Even the distinction of plant and animal, fundamental in my own world, seemed far from fundamental here.

"Why," I said, speaking to myself although I pronounced the words aloud, "this is more a world of Chimeras than a world of Formicarians! All the careful differentiations wrought by natural selection have been intermingled. The intelligence of this world might have lost certain arts of mental confusion, but confusion of bodily form it has certainly perfected."

"That is true," Speaker murmured. "We *are* Chimeras, in a purely biological sense. That is our essence, far more than our collective intelligence. If you need to label us, that label will be less misleading than most."

I felt slightly embarrassed by the fact that I had accidentally voiced my thought, even though I suspected that my silently-vocalized thoughts were still being monitored. I was embarrassed because it reminded me of how much time I had spent alone in recent years, and what habits that solitude had engendered.

The sky-car was moving very carefully now, for the available airspace was crowded, and it was no longer possible to steer a straight course. I had time enough to study the creatures above which it moved with far greater care than I had been able to devote to those I had glimpsed in the distance while the craft was still above the clouds, but I found it difficult to form any general impression beyond that of infinite multiplicity.

One additional thing I did notice, however, was that very few of the creatures we passed close by—whether they were fliers in mid-air, inhabitants of tall buildings or walkers on the ground—seemed to pay any particular attention to our craft. No groups formed to stare in unison; no limbs were raised to point at us that I could see.

Evidently, the arrival at the Great Tree of what this world must consider to be the ultimate freaks—a group of individuated beings snatched from a million years ago—was either unknown to the vast majority of the collective intelligence's "units", or a matter of supreme indifference to them.

CHAPTER NINE

INTO THE HEARTWOOD

The sky-car finally settled to the ground about three hundred yards away from the trunk of the tree, which seemed from that close distance more like a vast wall with a slight curve. Unlike the boles of the smaller trees we had seen, this one was pitted with thousands of fissures, almost all of them vertical slits, although some were rounded. Many of these fissures extended to ground level, and most of those carried considerable traffic; creatures were moving in and out of the trunk's interior by the thousand. I could not see any wheeled vehicles, although there was a great deal of transportation being carried out with the aid of panniers and loaded sleds than ran with uncanny smoothness over the awkward terrain.

The majority of the beasts of burden and other livestock had bodies resembling creatures with which I was familiar: horses, cattle, elephants, lizards and so on. Almost every one seemed blatantly incongruous, however, because their heads and the structures supporting their heads rarely corresponded to the kinds of heads with which natural selection had equipped such bodies in my own era. Many had humanoid heads, a few having entire humanoid or lemuroid torsos joined to quadruped bodies, like the centaurs of Greek myth. Others had heads like ostriches or raptors, and others still like octopodes or snakes. Almost all, it seemed to me, had eyes that were capable of binocular vision, although they often had long necks that allowed them to look behind as easily as in front. The air seemed far less fresh here than the air in the clearing, and most of the odors with which it was laden seemed far less sweet.

"The Chimera of myth was no mere monster," I said to Speaker, as we got down from the flier. "It was an attempt to bring together useful and powerful attributes that had been developed independently by creatures that were very distantly related, which nature was unable to combine. Nature here works differently, does it not? You can combine biological features virtually at random, free of the restrictions imposed in my era by rigid speciation."

"Yes we can," Speaker said, obviously relieved to be free of the cloying gel that had imprisoned her wings. "We can combine individual cells, tissues or structures of every kind, more or less as we please. The old tyrannies of specific reproduction—especially the tyranny of sex—vanished from the Earth a long time ago. Our individual units are chimeras in the genetic sense as well as the mythical one."

Danby and Clara rejoined us. Both seemed unsettled, as if they too had found the trip uncomfortable.

"We apologize for the necessity of bringing you to the Great Tree in such a clumsy fashion," Speaker said, addressing all three of us collectively. "Next time we need to travel, we shall use alternative transportation. We had to confine the end of the time-bridge within a solid structure for reasons you already know, but there are dangers inherent in that necessity—material objects transmitted by means of some of our earlier constructions fell victim to explosive collisions—so we took the precaution of building the containment facility well away from any substantial concentration of living-space."

I saw Danby furrow his brow in response to that item of information. His father had always contrived to return objects to the same enclosed room from which they had been projected. Perhaps the problem was more acute at the future terminals of such bridges—but perhaps the Professor had been fortunate, thus far, not to encounter the problem.

We moved to one of the roadways but had to walk alongside it because it was so crowded. It was still the case that none of the creatures nearby paid any attention to us; they all had business of their own to attend to, and were not prone to distraction. Speaker led the way, unhurriedly steering an awkward course through the pungent throng.

"I'm glad to hear that we'll be provided with alternative modes of transport in future," Clara said to me, in a low tone that was not quite a whisper, as the welcoming party led us away towards the wall. "That one seems to be designed for the kind of creature with which we shared our cabin."

"If it's any consolation," I told her, "our guide found it direly unsuitable too. She had not encountered claustrophobia before, and it affected her quite badly."

"She?" Clara queried. "I had been thinking of Speaker as a male, although I suppose she has no sex—you made the same decision before, did you not, with respect to the Amphibians. Can you identify the sex of any of *these* creatures?" She waved a hand airily, not needing to point with any precision to indicate any of the creatures trooping back and forth from the Great Tree.

"Sexual dimorphism appears to be a thing of the distant past," I told her. "Reproduction no longer requires any kind of congress or collaboration. I presume that individuals still grow from embryos of some sort, perhaps even from single cells, but what the process involves I cannot tell. These creatures are Chimeras in more than one sense of the term. I suspect that the mind-force that allows creatures to fly here that could not have flown in our world is also implicated in the conception and shaping of new individuals, but we shall have to interrogate Speaker in a far more detailed manner to obtain a proper understanding."

"In this world, then, creation really is a matter of quasi-divine design and ingenuity?" she said.

"After a fashion," I replied, lowering my own voice as if to confide a secret. "However ingenious it might seem, though, the collective intelligence that shapes these Chimeras and binds them together into a social whole is fallible. Universal consensus is doubtless harmonious, but it might also be blind to all ways of thinking other than its own."

Danby had been able to overhear some of what we said, for he was quick to put in: "These creatures must be regarded as objects of manufacture rather than natural beings, as we understand natural beings. They are, in essence, ecological artifacts, even though they have a degree of autonomy. There is only one real individual here, and it is strangely insubstantial, just as the hive-mind of a formicary cannot be located in any particular creature—not even the so-called queen. It seems to me that these kinds of creatures must have arisen in the first place as the artificial produce of a species not unlike ours, which took the arts of agriculture and animal husbandry to a new extreme, with the aid of some means of manipulating the germ-plasm of existing organisms. It seems that the slaves eventually overtook and displaced their masters, as in Karel Čapek's fable of the robots."

"I'm not convinced of that," I said—but he only shook his head, as if that was only to be expected.

In fact, it *was* only to be expected, because it recapitulated an argument we had had many years before, with regard to the interpretation of my discoveries in the world of the Dwellers, and what had

been done to me there. Danby had convinced himself that the ancestors of the Dwellers must have remade their own physical forms by
means of the same techniques that the Seekers of Science had used
on me. He had also convinced himself that those mysterious archi-
tects of flesh must have made the Amphibians too, by modifying the
embryos of some other animal species—probably seals or otters. In
his opinion, the Amphibians had been manufactured, like the robots
in Čapek's *R.U.R.*, to serve the particular function of overseeing the
harvests of the sea.

Danby had been particularly interested in the part of my story
where I had inferred that the Amphibians' exercise of will-power to
subdue other species was dependent on their moral conviction that
the ends of their action were good. That, he argued—like their inability to reproduce themselves—was exactly the kind of provision
that a designer of servants might build in as a safeguard, in the hope
of ensuring that the servants would not be inclined to attempt violent
rebellion. If the Amphibians always sought to repair perceived
moral infractions in the manner that I seen them take infinite pains
to do, Danby had argued, it did not prove that they were more moral
than humans, but merely that they were morally helpless. He con-
tended that no such behavior could ever have arisen as a result of
natural selection.

Then, as now, I had been far from sure about it.

If the Dwellers really were a self-remade species, I had reasoned, they had not remade themselves very well, and seemed
somehow to have lost the ability to repair their most glaring mis-
takes. If the Amphibians were manufactured servants developed
from some ordinary animal stock, they appeared to have outgrown
their original specifications as well as outlasting their original makers. I was more ready than Danby to accept that both species might
have arisen naturally, even if it required me to doubt whether natural
selection was the sole driving force of Earthly evolution—or, even if
it had been the sole driving force in the twentieth century's past,
whether it would necessarily remain the sole driving force in perpe-
tuity.

In Danby's opinion, the Dwellers had used me as an experimental subject on which to test some new kind of biological technology,
much as he and his father had used mice and a canary to test the
breathability of future air. He thought that they must have obtained
the result of that experiment before they fulfilled their agreement
with the Amphibians by returning me to the place on the Opal Way
from which I might safely return home, when the impulse that had
propelled me into the future was exhausted. He had speculated that

they were about to develop a new servant race, perhaps by modifying Frog-mouths or Killers, which might be used in armies to fight against the Antipodeans—which, he thought, were likely no more than living weapons themselves, dispatched by humanoid masterminds living in their own subterrains.

I had not agreed with him at the time and still could not, but I had always been haunted by the possibility that my doubt was a mere matter of trying to save face—a determination to prove, if only to myself, that I was something more than the Professor had always considered me to be: a mere instrument, perhaps more able than a mouse, canary or Templeton, but no less dispensable.

As we passed into one of the fissures leading into the heartwood of the Great Tree, I looked back at the sprawling city, trying to obtain a better measure of its character and its multitudinous population. It seemed as though all the creatures of my Earth, and thousands more, had been hurled into a great cauldron and vigorously stirred, reducing all their order and structure to chaotic confusion. By now, most of the Chimeras had come to seem ordinary to me, but it was not difficult to find occasional instances of more radical and seemingly-insane invention. Here, a mammalian head sat upon a reptilian torso with insectile legs; there, a head like a slug's projected from a feathered corpus whose legs were like a spider's; there, again, an assortment of heads protruded from an amorphous body that had no legs at all, but moved like a monstrous amoeba by extending and retracting pseudopods.

It was, I thought, the kind of nightmare that certain Renaissance painters had tried, very tentatively, to attribute to the temptations of Saint Anthony, or to the demonic hordes of Hell—and yet, it was far beyond the scope of any trivial reaction of horror. The sheer profusion of the chimerical forms ensured that each and every one of them, no matter how bizarre, partook of a general normality. I had already lost my ability to find any such individual hideous— although I could not help wondering whether that numbing of my aesthetic sensibility might somehow have be contrived, like the dulling of my emotions induced by the Dwellers, or the tranquility urged on me by the cephalopod pilot during the flight I had just experienced.

I did not shudder when, as I passed through the doorway, I brushed the wing-case of a complex creature four times as massive as myself. It turned to glance at me, perhaps censoriously, with at least four eyes, but I felt no intimidation in the face of its extraordinary gaze.

The pathway we were following narrowed considerably as we moved into the interior of the tree, and more contacts were inevitable, but there was very little jostling for position. The creatures moving inwards formed a more orderly column, moving to the left of the column moving in the opposite direction. *We are following the English custom, it seems*, I thought, *rather than the French or the American.*

I was glad, though, that by the time the corridor had become so narrow that we could only walk two abreast, I had Clara to my right, while Speaker and Danby walked ahead of us.

Danby had apparently gone on ahead in search of some validation for his hypothesis that all the living creatures now on Earth were the remote descendants of manufactured slave-species produced by some human-descended race intermediate between ourselves and the Dwellers. He did not pose the question as brutally as that, though—perhaps because he did not think that Speaker's guiding intelligence would possess detailed knowledge of its own origins, and perhaps because he did not trust it to tell him the truth if it did. What he asked instead, by way of introducing his topic, was whether each different kind of Chimera was capable of reproducing itself."

"Many forms are capable of self-reproduction by binary fission," Speaker answered, dutifully, "but even they are more usually produced by specialist maternal units."

"And these maternal units can produce many different kinds of organisms?" Danby said.

"That is correct," Speaker confirmed.

"When new forms are produced for the first time," Danby asked, "is it always produced by one of these maternal units?"

"Not necessarily," was the unhelpful reply.

"How are the variations induced?"

"It is doubtful that the process can be described in terms available in your dictionary, although we shall certainly devote further thought to the possibility. Every cell in your body has the same complement of genes, strictly ordered on sets of chromosomes stereotypical of your species, but we are creatures of a different sort. We are as various internally as we are externally, combining cells of many different kinds."

"So the growth of your bodies is not like ours—it does not follow some kind of plan which is innate in an embryo and unfolds by stages as the embryo and the subsequent individual mature?"

"That is correct," Speaker said, again—but gave no further information.

Danby was evidently dissatisfied with these answers, but his understanding of human genetics and embryology was too primitive to allow him to phrase his own question more specifically, so he could hardly complain about Speaker's inability to be more exact. It was very remarkable that her controlling intelligence had made as much of the Professor's dictionary as it had; we could not reasonably expect its representative to offer us explanations for which the evolution of our terminology had not yet made adequate provision.

Although I disagreed with Danby's presumed solution, I could see clearly enough that there was a riddle in need of solution. The five hundred thousand years that separated our own era from that of the Dwellers was a relatively short span, in terms of geological time, and the rate of evolution displayed in the fossil record was far too slow to have produced such a radically different world without considerable acceleration. Danby had concluded that the long history of evolution by natural selection must have been superseded by an era of intense biological engineering, by scientists who had learned how to manipulate the germ-plasm of simpler creatures, and even of their own species. He assumed that a new Age of Genetic Artifice must have begun not long after our own time. It seemed to me to be equally likely, however, that the process of evolution might have undergone a qualitative change by virtue of some "natural discovery"—perhaps a dramatic new product of mutation—which had led to a spectacular burst of new adaptive radiation and the relatively sudden replacement of an Age of Individuation, which had lasted for billions of years, by a new Age of Combination—or Chimerization.

"Have a little patience, Philip," I murmured to Danby, when I had the chance. "The education we need to understand these matters will likely be a matter of months rather than minutes—we shall be here for a year, after all."

"But we might not have much time to spare," Danby muttered, over his shoulder, while keeping one eye on Speaker, "if they are determined to pack us off to the moon in a matter of days."

I did not trouble to remind him that it was only me that the Chimeras were anxious to dispatch to the moon with all possible haste, and that he did not have to join me if he thought that his time could be more profitably spent in other pursuits.

CHAPTER TEN

FOOD FOR THOUGHT

We walked for half an hour or more, following a meandering course through curving corridors, most of which followed downwardly-tilted slopes. I presumed that we were not only moving deep into the heartwood of the tree but deep into its subterranean roots. Eventually, we came into a series of dimly-lit corridors that we and our guide did not have to share with assorted chimerical monsters, and in one of those we stopped.

"We had only prepared one room, in expectation of a single visitor," Speaker said, from the head of our little procession, "but we have improvised a second and will make a third ready as soon as possible. In the meantime...."

"George and I will be content to share for a little while," Danby said, blithely appointing himself as our spokesman yet again. "The ideal arrangement to serve our needs would be three neighboring rooms with connecting doors."

"That is what we shall attempt to contrive," Speaker said, "but it will take a few more hours."

In the meantime, a doorway—which might be better imagined as a pair of vertical lips—opened up in the corridor beside me. In response to a gesture from Speaker, I stepped through.

I found myself in a carefully-squared chamber, whose corners were the first true right-angles I had seen in this world. It contained a writing-table, apparently made in carefully-stained wood with a leather top, complete with an escritoire containing pens and ink, and a pad of paper. There were two straight-backed chairs, similarly upholstered in imitation leather. Two beds were contained in alcoves on either side of the room, each equipped with curtains. There was a third alcove, also curtained, which contained a sink and a toilet-bowl. Apparently, excretion would not be as problematic as I had feared when I first felt myself being wrapped in a new skin.

Everything was subtly, but slightly, wrong. It was as if the individual items had been copied from illustrations in some exceedingly ancient book—or, more likely, from a record in one of the Dwellers' memory-stores—by craftsmen who had never before been called upon to make any of the illustrated objects, and could not quite understand their intended functions. The most remarkable item of all was an ornate chandelier hanging from the middle of a ribbed ceiling, equipped with dozens of carefully-formed pieces of what looked like crystal glass. Its arms bore neither candles nor electric bulbs; the light sprang directly from the crystal shards, whose function in a real ornamental chandelier would have been to scatter light by reflection. Having come through the corridors, I knew that it would have been much easier for the Chimeras to make the entire ceiling glow, even at a level of brightness considerably greater than the one to which they were accustomed.

"Thank you," I said, realizing what amazing efforts must have gone into the construction, in the interests of helping me to feel that I had a refuge here where I might make myself at home. Danby was obviously less impressed, but he made no complaint.

Speaker followed us in. "The second room is similar," she said. "We will attend to the matter of the connecting door, but in the meantime, you need only step along the corridor in this direction. The door should open in response to a clearly-framed mental command, but if you cannot manage that you merely have to exert manual pressure on the fissures like *this*, and they will yield immediately. Shall we bring you nourishment now, or would you like time to rest first?"

She was looking at me, but again it was Danby who tried to assert his authority. "Clara and I will need to rest shortly," he said, "but George has not the same need to sleep. I dare say that we would all be grateful for some food—although I am not sure that our newly-lined intestines are still capable of digestion."

"The new surface-layer will permit all necessary nutrients through," Speaker assured him, "as well as protecting against all harmful intrusions. At present, it is more convenient for us to make up the nutrients you require in liquid form, but we will attempt to improvise solid foods when we have fuller information as to your tastes and exact metabolic requirements."

"Where has the information come from that you have at present?" I asked, curiously.

"We obtained some basic information from ancient archives," Speaker reported, "some from the dictionary you provided, and...we are in the process of obtaining more from the cellular samples taken by the gel as it formed your new skins."

I could not be certain what the slight hesitation in the middle of the sentence signified, but I felt sure that Speaker must be leaving something out. Perhaps, I thought, she did not want to admit that we were under constant inspection by means of the sixth sense the Chimeras had, which facilitated mind-speech.

"Liquid nourishment will be perfectly adequate, for now," Danby said, graciously.

"You are very welcome to join us too, Speaker," I said. "I don't know whether you are able to obtain adequate nourishment for yourself from whatever food you serve to us, but your conversation would be very welcome."

"My digestive system is unlike yours," Speaker informed me, "but I can eat with you, if that is your wish." She left the room.

"This is a little Spartan, don't you think?" Danby said, running his eyes around the room as the door closed behind her.

"It will suit me well enough," I told him. "If you care to request a palace for your own separate accommodation, they'll probably try to oblige you. You only have to tell them which style you would prefer—although you might have difficulty explaining the difference between Queen Anne and Louis Quinze."

"They would doubtless be more sympathetic to your requests than mine," Danby said. "You're *George*, after all; I'm merely your humble companion." He seemed quite unconcerned by the fact that he had been acting out a very different role. I told him, briefly, what Speaker had said to me during the flight about my being uniquely useful to them because of what the Dwellers had done to me.

"How do they know about that?" Danby demanded.

I had to confess that I had omitted to ask, but repeated my presumption that they must have access to records made in the Dweller era, perhaps transmitted to them across another time-bridge.

"Perhaps one of those Speaker mentioned," Danby said, nodding his head in satisfaction. "I must enquire further about the explosions that seem to have destroyed at least one of their earlier experiments in time-bridge construction. It's difficult to believe, though, that they had to reach back in time a million years to find the one creature in our era adequate to their needs. One might have supposed that an actual Dweller would have served their purpose far better."

"One might," I agreed.

"Unless, of course," Danby said, unable to resist the temptation, "I was right when I suggested, long ago, that you might have been a new experiment in biological manufacture on the Dwellers' part—an experiment which, for some reason, they were unable to unwilling to repeat."

I doubted that, but I did not trouble to say so. Neither of us had any real evidence on which to base an argument. I presumed that Speaker would give me a fuller explanation of my apparent uniqueness in the course of preparing me to be examined by the Metamorphosian machine, and then to open negotiations with them on behalf of all life presently on Earth.

Speaker returned bearing a tray, which contained four bowls and three liquid-filled pitchers. There were no spoons accompanying the bowls, so we were presumably intended to drink directly from them.

I sniffed the three pitchers before selecting the one I would sample first. I picked up the pitcher and offered to pour for my companions before filling my own bowl. Clara and Speaker accepted the offer, but Danby decided to try one of the others, and picked up a different pitcher. The liquid proved to have little enough taste, but what it had was not unpleasant. Clara seemed to find it more welcome and more satisfying than I did.

I sampled the other pitchers in their turn, but found nothing in either that I was inclined to compare to nectar. I professed myself satisfied, but offered no evidence of enthusiasm. Speaker did not seem to mind.

"This is very remarkable tree," I observed, by way of making polite conversation. "One of the cultures from which ours is descendant had a myth which proposed that the world was bound together by the vast roots of a single tree—although I assume that its trunk and crown were less impressive than its root-system. It was named Yggdrasil, and was supposed to be an ash-tree. Do you understand what I mean by myth?" I was not certain whether the Chimeras would have been able to make sense of the term's definition in *Webster's Dictionary*.

"We understand the concept of myth," Speaker said. "In addition to the past of memory there is the past of history, and before there was history, there was imaginary history, or myth."

"You don't have myths of your own, then?" Clara said.

"Perhaps we do," was Speaker's enigmatic reply. I assumed that she wasn't trying to tease us, and was genuinely unsure. After a moment's hesitation, she went on: "Our knowledge of your era might be as much mythical as truly historical. It was a period in which individuation reached its extreme, prior to the cataclysm that allowed it to be superseded. Our understanding may well be distorted."

"What cataclysm do you mean?" Clara asked. "Was it a war that obliterated human civilization?"

"There were many wars," Speaker said, "and many civilizations toppled or obliterated. The rise and fall of individual civilizations appears to have been cyclic for a long time before the pattern was decisively broken—but our conception of that troubled * era might be polluted by myth."

"It was a cycle of which the Dwellers were acutely aware, though," I said, more for Clara's benefit than Speaker's, "and one whose consequences they were determined to avoid, if they could. I imagine that they did not succeed, since the Antipodeans seemed to have won the war they began while I was in their world."

"The Dwellers' civilization collapsed," Speaker confirmed, "more literally than any before it—but its heritage was not so easily or so completely obliterated. The Antipodeans did win that war, in both the trivial sense of formulating the next world-dominating civilization, and a more significant one. The Antipodeans' proto-chimerical mode of existence and proliferation proved, in the end, more successful than the Dwellers' individuality."

"My Amphibian companion told me," I said, again for Clara's benefit, "that the Antipodeans might be organisms working in symbiotic association. I construed the concept I distilled into that term as a simple implication that the Antipodeans came from a distant place, perhaps dominating the hemisphere complementary to the one dominated by the Dwellers, but that was a mistake. It seems that the Antipodeans were the Dwellers' opposites in a different and more metaphorical sense. Whereas the Dwellers might be seen as the last torch-bearers of the Age of Individuation, the Antipodeans were the most important harbingers of a new collective way of being: the forerunners of the Age of Combination."

"Thank you," Speaker said. She looked at Danby, as if to notify him that she could now say a little more about the subject that had interested him earlier. "That was indeed our intended implication. There had, however, been an earlier phase in the evolution of Earthly life that might be described as an Age of Combination, or at least as an Age in which primitive life reached a crossroads of the kind it reached again in the era of the Dwellers. The complex cells that make up your bodies are chimeras of a sort, formed by the fusion of different kinds of more primitive cells. They contain various sorts of organelles, most of which are the descendants of once-separate microbial species. Earthly evolution might, perhaps, have followed a very different pattern had it not developed the kind of genetic system that it did, in which the cost of differentiation was speciation."

"What do you mean by *cost*?" Danby asked. "Differentiation and speciation are surely the same thing."

"From your viewpoint, it is difficult to see the difference," Speaker conceded, diplomatically, "but we have differentiation without speciation. From our viewpoint, speciation and individuation seem high prices to pay for the privilege of limited differentiation. It may be wrong, though, for us to think of the entire Age of Individuation as a kind of aberration, which might have been avoided if only the first complex organisms had not developed such a sternly restrictive genetic apparatus. Perhaps individuation is an unavoidable phase in the life-cycle of a planetary biosphere, although it can lead to more than one successor phase."

"Have you explored other worlds within or without the solar system," Danby asked, "where life has followed different evolutionary paths?"

"We have not," Speaker admitted, "but the Metamorphosians claim to have done so. We are not convinced that the lessons they claim to have drawn from such studies are any more than lies or illusions—or myths—but their own existence is proof enough that post-individual evolution can take more than one path."

"What is the essential difference between your kind of life and theirs?" Danby asked.

"At present," Speaker said, "we do not feel confident that we can assess the difference accurately. We are hoping that George will enable us to do so, when he has made a more intimate contact with the Metamorphosians than we have so far been permitted to do."

"And how, exactly, is he going to do that?" Danby wanted to know. There was a slight waspishness in his voice.

"The Metamorphosians will not permit us to investigate their minds or memories directly," Speaker told him. "They insist on keeping a safe distance, beyond the range of our perceptions—like gravity, mental force can only be effectively exerted at short range, even by a mental entity as powerful as ours. They will accept individual visitors, however. When they have investigated the minds of our individual ambassadors fully, they will be able to disclose as much of themselves as they wish—George will, in effect, become a messenger who will reveal exactly what he is commissioned to reveal, but no more. By that means we hope to establish a foundation on which we can build a measure of trust, if only by slow degrees.

At the very least, George will return from the moon with a much more accurate picture of how and what the Metamorphosians are than we have so far been able to construct, as will any companions who are willing and able to go with him."

"I'm willing," Danby said, immediately.

"So am I," Clara said.

"We are grateful for the offer," Speaker said, "and we accept."

"But we won't be as useful to you as George," Clara put in, "because his mind has capabilities built into it by the Dwellers that ours have not."

"That is correct," Speaker said, punctiliously.

"You might have done better to establish a bridge to the Dwellers' era," Danby said.

"We did," Speaker replied, bluntly.

"But that was one of the ones that failed—catastrophically?" Danby said.

"That is correct," Speaker repeated.

"And you couldn't simply make another?"

"No, we could not," Speaker confirmed. "Such constructions are more difficult to establish than you may imagine, and a connection cannot be replicated once it has been severed. The accessible contact-points are, alas, few and far between. We were very fortunate to be able to make use of a more distant contact-point that the Dwellers had already identified and used—and fortunate in the extreme to obtain a specific response to our plea for help. We had hardly dared hope that George would be able to answer the call—but here he is."

"But why is the matter so urgent?" Clara asked. "Why do you need George *now*?"

"The Metamorphosians appear to suspect us of taking hostile action against them. They have falsely accused us of one such action. Whether they actually believe that we are guilty, or whether they are establishing a pretext for some hostile action against us, we cannot tell—but we do know that they have the power to hurt us very badly, just as we have the power to hurt them. It is extremely important that the situation does not become unmanageable. George is, at present, our best hope of averting or containing the impending crisis."

"And if he can't," Clara observed, dryly, "we'll all get caught in the crossfire."

Speaker seemed profoundly uncomfortable, but she could not deny it. "That is possible," she admitted, reluctantly.

"In fact," Clara went on, "what you're asking George to do is extremely dangerous—all the more so because you have no real idea of what the Metamorphosians are, or why they seem to be so afraid of you?"

Again, Speaker had no alternative. "That is correct," she said, in a manner that almost warranted description as tight-lipped.

CHAPTER ELEVEN

THE PRIVILEGE OF ETERNAL WAKEFULNESS

"We had not intended to conceal the dangerous aspects of your mission from you, George," Speaker said, when we had had time to digest the import of her admission, "You will be as fully informed as possible, when we feel confident that we can frame the information in terms that you can understand."

"The danger is incidental," I said. "I'll do what needs to be done—or try, at any rate. Clara knows that. We've already taken the most dangerous step of all, in stepping on to the platform of the Professor's apparatus."

"I only wanted to clarify the situation," Clara said. "I'm still prepared to go with you, as far as we need to go—or as far as we can."

Speaker did not seem entirely relieved to hear this. "There is more that George needs to see and understand," she said. "He is not yet aware of all the relevant alternatives. We would be grateful if you would grant us an interval of time before we resume this discussion. We observe that you also seem to be rather weary, Clara and Philip, and might benefit from a period of rest or sleep. May we suggest that we recommence when you are rested?"

Clara and Danby were showing obvious signs of fatigue, which had intensified in the wake of our meal. Perhaps, I reflected, it had been a mistake to begin our journey from the twentieth century after dinner rather than in the early morning—but we had all been impatient. Danby still was, and seemed about to object to Speaker's request.

"Speaker's right, Philip," I told him, quickly. "We've had a great deal to take in, and we could certainly benefit from a pause for thought and rest. We'll be more alert when we've slept a while."

He looked at me suspiciously, unsure as to why I had spoken in the plural, given that I had no need for sleep at all—but he had to accept that his own need had become considerable.

"I agree," he said, eventually. "We shall all be better equipped after a suitable pause."

Speaker accompanied Clara back to her room.

I half-expected Danby to take advantage of the apparent privacy to begin bombarding me with questions, but he did not, Instead, after a few cursory preparations, he went meekly to lie down on one of the two beds. Speaker had shown us how to dim the light, and when I had done so, Danby responded to the near-darkness by falling asleep almost immediately. He did not snore, but his breathing became very deep and regular.

I, on the other hand, simply lay down on my back, staring into the darkness. My intention was to spend an hour or so reviewing what I had learned so far, more to bring it into a better state of organization than to use it as a springboard for further speculation, but I was soon interrupted. I did not hear the door open, nor did I hear any footfalls, but I became suddenly conscious that I was no longer alone. Speaker was standing beside my bed looking down at me.

"We know that you do not have the same sleep-requirements as your companions," Speaker said, in a voice that was low without quite being a whisper. She did not seem to be at all anxious that she might wake Danby.

"The privilege of eternal wakefulness," I observed, in a moderately hushed tone, "is one of the rewards of my earlier adventure in time—which also turned out to be exceedingly dangerous."

"It was a side-effect of a different, and more useful, privilege," Speaker observed. As usual, it was exceedingly difficult to read the slight inflection in her voice, but there seemed to be more at stake than a mere matter of clarification.

"More useful to them," I said. "I have not had much use for it myself, these last ten years—but I infer that you are about to ask me to put it to use now, while my companions sleep."

"That is correct. We would be very grateful to you."

"Do you want me to put myself into a trance here and now?"

"No—we fear that a considerable journey is necessary. We are sorry that we did not have time to make more careful preparations for your convenience."

"I thought you were more-or-less everywhere, at least on Earth?"

"That is correct—but the journey is necessary, nevertheless." She was being deliberately mysterious, but I assumed that she had her reasons. Whether she was reading my mind or not, she was quick to add: "If you will come with me, we will show you something that will facilitate your understanding far better than the inadequate verbal explanations that we have so far learned to make."

"Very well," I said. "Lead on."

I got up from the bed, and Speaker led me out of the room, into a corridor that was now almost as dimly lit as the room from which we had emerged. We did not go far before reaching a broader cavern, at the end of which was the opening of a shaft leading vertically downwards into darkness. I peeped over the edge, but there was no way to estimate its depth.

"There are several means we might use to descend," Speaker told me, "and I must warn you that the descent will be a long one. The quickest way, if you will consent, is to fall. We shall come to no harm, provided that we are together."

I had wondered why the humanoid designed to greet me had been equipped with wings, given that we had flown from our point of emergence to the Great Tree in a vehicle. Their purpose seemed a little clearer now.

"What you're proposing," I said, to make sure that I had jumped to the correct conclusion, "is that we should simply jump into this hole together, relying on your wings and your command of mental force to protect us from injury and slow our descent sufficiently to allow us a soft landing?"

"Yes. It is not necessary for us to cling together during the entire descent, although we may do so, if that is your wish.

"I think I'd feel safer if we were at least hand-in-hand," I said. "What the Dwellers did to my body didn't erase my innate fear of falling. How far must we go?"

"A little over five hundred miles," Speaker told me, equably. "We can soothe your fear if need be. You already understand how very determined we are that no harm shall come to you."

"I understand," I said. "But still...to fall five hundred miles will take a long time. Coming back up afterwards will, I suppose, be a considerably slower process."

"If you would prefer to sleep while we fall, that is perfectly acceptable," Speaker told me. "But the return journey will, as you presume, be considerably slower. That might be the better opportunity for you to rest."

She clearly did not quite understand the implications of what she was asking, for a confused human mind. For her, it was a simple matter of trust, and reliance on the knowledge that they thought me too precious to take any unnecessary risk that I might come to harm.

Her guiding intelligence could presumably observe the workings of anxiety in my mind, but merely as a specimen of human consciousness. Had I not been altered by the Dwellers, I would probably have insisted on a less terrifying mode of transport, but I was a changed man.

"I think I'd prefer it if you would grip both my hands," I said. "Could you bear to do that?" I asked the question because I was still haunted by a glimpse I had once caught of the Amphibian's reaction of disgust when she had placed her hand on my injured leg in order to impart some healing energy.

"Physical contact is not problematic," Speaker assured me. "You may cling as close as you wish, provided that you do not impede the action of the wings."

"Gripping my hands will be sufficient," I told her, steeling myself for the moment when I would have to step over the edge.

She took my hands, and we moved to the lip of the shaft together. "Now," she said, showing a remarkable confidence in my ability to obey. I am not entirely sure whether I really did step out into empty space of my own volition, or whether she drew me with her—showing surprising physical strength, if so. One way or the other, though, we were falling, and we plunged almost instantaneously into total darkness.

I felt the air rushing past, but that was the only evidence I had of the rate at which we were falling. Had we been falling under the influence of gravity alone, we should soon have accelerated to a fearful speed, but I assumed that her wings were moderating our velocity, and would do so more powerfully when the time eventually came to brake.

I presumed that the journey would likely take at least an hour, but I do not think I could have slept had I wanted to. While long minutes went by I found myself unable even to speak, so preoccupied was I by the mere fact of what was happening to me. The longer the fall went on, though, the more I was able to possess myself with the illusion that I was merely floating, and quite safe. I was, after all, in the tender care of a custom-designed angel.

"Have you made such flights as this before?" I eventually contrived to ask.

"Yes," she said. "This unit has been prepared as thoroughly as possible for its task—its anomalous reaction in the flier was quite unexpected."

"Your preparations didn't stretch as far as giving yourself a name before you met me," I observed. "Speaker was a spur-of-the-moment improvisation, was it not?"

"Yes," she replied. "We were not sure that an individual name would be necessary. Had you come alone, a simpler dialogue would have been feasible."

In the world of the Dwellers, I had contrived to get by without giving an individual name to the particular Amphibian who had been my sole companion for much of my adventure. The pronoun "she" had sufficed in my own private mind-speech. Even the Dwellers, who used individual names between themselves, had represented themselves to me primarily in terms of subcategories such as the one I had translated as "Seekers of Wisdom", and had recorded my own name merely as a datum, not as a form of address. Had I come alone into *this* future, there would only have been one human in confrontation with one vast collective world-intelligence, and our dialogue might indeed have been simple, even though the other's part might have been relayed through more than one mouth. The presence of Philip Danby and Clara had complicated matters, though.

"But you're not entirely happy with the necessity of adopting an individual identity, are you?" I said. "You sometimes indulge in odd circumlocutions in order to avoid saying *I*."

"This unit can say *I*, if necessary," she replied, proving my point rather than disputing it. "It can think of itself as an individual of sorts. That is, after all, part of its purpose. Our collective intelligence is more versatile than you might suppose—although we have not yet contrived to unravel all the mysteries of your dictionary, which is full of concepts that do not relate to our experience."

Given that circumstance, I thought, she was doing very well as a Speaker of English. After a pause, I said: "How serious a threat do the Metamorphosians pose to you? If there were to be a conflict, what could they do?"

"We cannot make a precise estimate of the seriousness of the threat," she replied, her voice sounding strangely remote in the darkness. "We would prefer to avoid conflict in any event, but if the Metamorphosians are such masters of space travel as they seem to be, it might be a trivial matter for them to redirect comets or asteroids into a collision course with Earth, with devastating effect. It is possible that they have weapons more powerful still, which could be deployed at much shorter notice. We have the means to strike back, thanks to our command of mental force, but if both sides in a conflict succeed in destroying one another, both are the losers."

"The universe is very large," I observed, after a pause for thought. "In my own lifetime, we had only just begun to realize how large it is. There are billions of stars within our own Milky Way, and galaxies by the billion, already unimaginably remote from one another, and seemingly drawing farther apart. There were writers in my time who wrote fantasies of wars between worlds, imagining Martians invading the Earth when their own worldly resources were exhausted, but it seemed preposterous to me. Surely there can be no possible need for wars between worlds so widely scattered and so remote from one another?"

"In the Age of Individuation," she said "it might have been possible to speak meaningfully of a *need* for war. In the Age of Combination, it is not—what was once a necessity became an impossibility, as soon as the new dominion was secure. Even so, that Age was first established by warfare, and if there is to be another Age yet to come, perhaps that too will be established by war. The mere existence of the Metamorphosians would force us to consider such possibilities, even if they had not been so suspicious of us—and, more recently, so enthusiastic to accuse us of taking hostile action against them. We have far too little information to decide whether there is a need for interplanetary war or not—but our most cherished hope is that there is not."

"I can sympathize with that," I said, perhaps presumptuously. "I have fought in a war myself that was advertised as be a war to end war, but which turned out to be nothing of the kind. Your Antipodean ancestors doubtless had better grounds for assuming that their war against the Dwellers would indeed put an end to warfare forever—but these things can never be certain."

"So it appears," she admitted.

"Philip Danby was too young to see active service in that war," I told her, "but his father was a scientist of some reputation at the time, and it was a war in which science played a more profound and crucial role than it ever had before, in the devising of new weapons more powerful and more cruel than any imagined before. Clara's involvement was also delayed, but as soon as she was of an age to volunteer, she did—though not as a combatant, of course. The first time I met her, she was a nurse serving in the Low Countries. In some ways, medical staff had a harder time than the men doing the fighting. They were attempting to hold back a tide of destruction that left a great many hideously maimed, even before the advent of phosgene and other poison gases. The war changed us all profoundly—Philip and his father included—and made us what we are. Had it not been for the war, and the general destitution that it left in its wake, I might never have agreed to follow Brett and Templeton into the world of the Dwellers, even though I was in urgent need of the bribe the Professor offered...and the Professor might never have become the kind of recluse who built a time machine in secret and used it as he did. I have no idea what these Metamorphosians might be, beyond the immediate implications of the name you have attached to them for our benefit, but I fear them already. If there really is something I can do that might help, in the smallest degree, to avoid a war between worlds, then I will do it very gladly."

"We know that," Speaker said, her voice diminishing to a whisper for the first time.

I would have said more, for I had begun to feel quite comfortable, in spite of knowing that I was falling towards the centre of the Earth, and might be torn to pieces by friction if I were even to touch the wall of the shaft through which I was falling. I was interrupted, though, by a curious lurching sensation that arrived quite unexpectedly, and disrupted my tranquility.

For a second or two I was possessed by an awful vertigo, as my innate fear of falling rushed back into my head in full force, as if eager for revenge at ever having been displaced. In spite of Speaker's assurances, I was momentarily convinced that I was about to die.

Chapter Twelve

The Bottom of the World

My unaccustomed panic began to fade as soon as I remembered the Division to which I had referred in the narrative of my earlier adventure in time. In the Professor's published version, my observations regarding the phenomenon had been edited down to a mere parenthetical remark about its being the point at which "the gravity changes", about four hundred and fifty miles below the surface. That was reasonable enough, I suppose, since my other observations had been confession of my failure to understand how there could possibly be such a Division.

I understood, of course, why a spaceship *en route* from the Earth to the moon would experience a *bouleversement* at the point at which the moon's gravitational field became stronger than the Earth's, but I could not understand why the process of falling into the Earth should not be a smooth one, with the pull of gravity relenting by imperceptible degrees as one drew closer to the centre. In the notes that the Professor had excised from my account I had made some suggestions regarding rocks of various density, and the possible effects of the uneven distribution of subterranean spaces, but I had not been able to explain, even to my own satisfaction, why there should be a single point in a long descent at which the attraction of gravity seemed to shift abruptly. Nor had I ever been able to describe the alteration any more accurately than describing it as a subjective lurch in accompaniment with a sudden transition from one gravitational field to another of lower intensity.

I would have asked Speaker for a clarification, but by the time I had recovered my self-possession and decided to do so we were slowing conspicuously in our descent, and I could feel the air currents displaced by the skilful beating of her huge wings. We were approaching our destination. The air was very warm now, and possessed by a low hum on the very threshold of audibility.

"Prepare yourself," Speaker said. "The landing will be as gentle as I can contrive, but you must be ready to absorb a moderate impact with the elasticity of your lower limbs.

She was right about that. The landing, when it came, was more akin to the result of jumping from a first-floor window than stepping down from a carriage. It was slightly jarring, but my legs absorbed the shock easily enough; no bones were broken, and my ankle was not sprained. Once we were still, I felt rather buoyant, and knew that it was because I weighed considerably less here at the very bottom of the inhabited world than I did at the surface.

Speaker released my hands. We were still in total darkness and I dared not take a step in case I tumbled back into the shaft or some other pitfall. After a pause of ten or twelve seconds, though, faint light dawned, radiating from the ceiling of a broad horizontal corridor.

"This way," Speaker said, beckoning me to follow.

I obeyed. The corridor was featureless in itself, but it was not uninhabited; there were small creatures moving back and forth along its floor and side-walls, and tiny flyers of various sorts fluttering past us in either direction. None of them was bigger than my thumb, although the corridor had obviously been built to accommodate much larger entities than myself and the Speaker.

The corridor branched several times, and also curved in a meandering fashion, although the few downslopes we followed were all gentle. We only walked for ten or fifteen minutes before we came into a much larger chamber with a dome-like ceiling. It was unlit when we entered it, but when Speaker caused it to be illuminated more brightly than the tunnels through which we had come I immediately perceived two raised platforms of different sizes, set side by side in the centre.

When I say they were of different sizes I mean that they were different in width and breadth; they were both the same height— which allowed me to see easily enough what was set upon them.

Each one was occupied by a recumbent body lying prone and inert. The larger one was occupied by a female Dweller, the smaller by an Amphibian.

The Dweller, being so much larger, caught my attention first, but only held it for an instant. It was the Amphibian that was more interesting to me, even before I saw the scars on her arm, and recognized that—however incredible it might be—this was not merely *an* Amphibian but *my* Amphibian: the companion of my adventure in the world of the Dwellers, who had saved my life more than once, and whom I had learned to love more than any creature of my own world, with the exception of Clara.

"How is this possible?" I said to Speaker, with a slight croak in my voice. "She died—they must surely both have died—five hundred thousand years ago."

"If they had not been able to come into this world," Speaker told me, her own voice as smooth as velvet, "you could not be here either. If they had not been overcome by dire misfortune while they were here, you would not need to be here."

"What happened?" I asked, the words catching in my throat.

"We became aware of the Dwellers' attempts to establish a time-bridge into our era not long after we became aware of the presence of the Metamorphosians on the moon. We would probably have contrived a second terminus in any case, but the opportunity to solve the problem of the Metamorphosians' insistence on the use of individuated beings as intermediaries was welcome. After two brief exploratory investigations by lone Dweller males, the female came across for a longer sojourn, in company with the Amphibian."

"I am astonished by that," I said. "Why would she do it? How could she bear to cut herself off from the communal mind of which she was a part?"

"It could not have been easy," Speaker said. "Nevertheless, she came. We showed them the world as it now is, and told them about the Metamorphosians. The Amphibian went into the Metamorphosian machine, but the Dweller was too large. Afterwards, they both agreed that they would return to our world in order to act as our ambassadors, provided that their own kinds would give them permission. When the time came for the return to their own time, they went to the requisite place. They vanished, for a fraction of a second—but they could not complete their return."

"This was one of your failed experiments."

"In a manner of speaking. There was no explosion at our end of the bridge, although we believe that there would have been a terrible explosion at the other had the travelers not been sentient creatures possessed of considerable mental power. They...rebounded. When they reappeared they were still conscious, and remained so for a few minutes, but their bodies had suffered a very severe shock. Creatures like your companions, or even you, would have been killed instantaneously, but the Amphibian was far more resilient—and so, much to our surprise, was the Dweller. Each of them slipped into a coma, and has remained in that state ever since—but the various states of consciousness and unconsciousness that they experience are, as you know, quite different from those normally experienced by humans."

"When you say that they were conscious for a few minutes...," I began, haltingly.

"Yes," Speaker answered, while I hesitated over the framing of the question. "They knew what had happened, and had begun to comprehend its consequences. Although they were returning to their own era a mere few minutes after leaving it—a much shorter time than they had spent here—that short interval had been time enough for disaster to strike. The Dwellers were at war; their enemies were making concerted attempts to crush them, literally, by forcing collapses in the depths of their Underworld. One such collapse had occurred at the far end of the bridge; the space in which the travelers were supposed to rematerialize had been compromised. Their survival was a near-miracle—but they knew, before they fell unconscious, that they could never return home again. They are castaways in time now: the last living representatives of long-extinct races."

I could not easily imagine what that knowledge must have meant to my former companion, who had lived all of her extremely long life as a member of a telepathically-united and harmonized community. For a being like that to find herself suddenly and permanently alone must have been a shock every bit as profound as the physical shock of being hurled backwards across a time-bridge. It was astonishing that she had survived, no matter how resilient her body was—but was it not equally astonishing that she had consented to cross the bridge in the first place? How had she been capable of it? Why had she wanted to do it?

I realized then that I might be partly, if not wholly, responsible for the daring—or the insanity—that had inspired her. She had been an anomalous member of her race even before she met me, but her atavistic individualistic tendencies had been very muted, unable to find any significant mode of expression beyond trivial games played with sharks. Although her world had not been unchanging, such changes that it saw were slow and long-established; even the Dwellers' war with the Antipodeans was centuries-old. When she had met me, though, she had been confronted with something entirely new and very different. While the rest of her tribe had been careful to distance themselves from me, she had become my close companion. We had not spent long together, in terms of the calendar—not nearly as long as I had subsequently spent with the Dwellers—but it had been by far the greatest adventure of her life. Indeed, it had been the *only* real adventure of her life, and it must have been a life-changing experience for her, as it had been for me.

All the while she had been with me, having immediately established a bond between our minds sufficient to allow us to speak soundlessly to one another, she had been simultaneously repelled and fascinated by me. There had been much about me, in body and mind alike, that she had found instinctively horrible and despicable, but she was no more a slave to instinct than I was. She had been able to put her reflexive repulsion aside, in answer to a powerful intellectual curiosity, and she had eventually grown used to my presence. Nor had her intellectual curiosity been merely a facet of the collective intelligence of which she was a part; it had been her own. As an individual, to the extent that she was an individual, she had been fascinated by my individuality, which had not only found an echo in her but had nursed that resonant seed, causing it to grow.

By the time we had parted, I knew, her curiosity had grown to the point at which she would have been prepared to journey back with me into my own time if she had been able—always provided that her sisters would have sanctioned such an adventure—in order to make a much more extensive study of my kind and our world. That had been impossible—but I did understand, now that I saw her decision in that light, why she would have volunteered for a similar expedition, not into the past but into the future. Evidently, her sisters had sanctioned it, and might even have been grateful to her for volunteering to go.

Her enterprise and courage had almost killed her—and it could not be obvious, as yet, that she would survive psychologically, even if her body refused to die.

Speaker immediately picked up on that unvoiced thought. "We have been working hard to heal them both," she said. "It has not been easy, and we cannot be confident that our work will survive their reawakening, but we are ready to try. While they have been unconscious we have not been able to establish any kind of dialogue with them, but we have been able to...eavesdrop on their dreams. There is certainly a danger that the Amphibian will suffer a slow but irrevocable decline when she wakes into her present situation, but we believe that she has a good chance of restabilization—with your help."

That, I realized, was one of the reasons why the Chimeras had gone fishing in time for *me*. I had been adapted by the Dwellers in a way that might make me a useful intermediary in their negotiations with the Metamorphosians—but for reasons quite unconnected with that modification, I was also the one person in all of Earth's long history who might be able to help restore one of their two other potential ambassadors to an adequate usefulness.

I had not the slightest resentment against the Chimeras for that; indeed, I felt profoundly grateful to have the opportunity. Until I stood beside her sick-bed, I had not realized how much I missed my former companion, or how profoundly she had changed my state of being, without any artifice at all.

I put out my hand, hesitantly, as if to touch her scarred arm, but stopped the gesture short.

"She will suffer no distress if you touch her," Speaker assured me, unnecessarily.

I completed the interrupted gesture. The Amphibians' furry arm was warm—though slightly cooler than the ambient temperature—and I felt, although I supposed that it must be pure imagination, that I could sense the blood coursing in her veins. What was not imaginary was the realization that she had been gifted with a second skin, similar to mine, which overlaid her fur so carefully that it coated every individual hair.

"In the first instance," Speaker said, "she tolerated the unprecedented separation from the collective intelligence of her race very well. She had undertaken a mission on behalf of her people, with the purpose and intention of reporting her findings to them when the time came. Although disconnected from them, in terms of the forces that maintained her actual mental contact, she remained psychologically connected by her determination to work on their behalf, and to carry important news back to them. It was not until she realized that such a return had become impossible that she began to *feel* the disconnection—but that was a momentary shock, complicated by the physical shock she had suffered. Her body is sound now, and we are confident that her mind can also recover its soundness. We know that she can tolerate isolation, in certain psychological circumstances—and when she wakes, she will not be alone. We are confident that she will take a great deal of comfort from your presence."

But you don't actually know, until you try, I thought. *You've been eavesdropping on her dreams, but her consciousness is entirely alien to yours. This is just one more of a whole series of stabs in the dark.*

If the thought was overheard, it drew no response.

"When are you going to wake her up?" I asked, aloud.

"Whenever you give the word," was the reply. "We have been ready to wake them both for some time, now—but we wanted you to be present, especially for the Amphibian's sake. Once we have your permission, we will proceed immediately.

CHAPTER THIRTEEN

THE SLEEPING GIANT

I turned to look at the Dweller, whose massive bulk was stretched out on the other platform, a few feet away. The Dwellers I had seen in the course of my first adventure in time had been very various in color, ranging from lemon yellow to blue-black, the color often being somewhat variegated. I had obtained the impression that the females were, on average, much darker than the males, and this one was no exception to the rule. Her skin was dark red, dappled with chestnut-brown. Her hair was jet black, and it grew longer and straighter than that of other females I had seen. She was slender by comparison with the males of her species, and the contours of her body were graceful, by human aesthetic standards.

When I had seen Dweller females before, especially at a distance, it had been easy to imagine them less huge, and more human than they were; some had seemed startlingly beautiful—although the shock of their visual appearance had doubtless been somewhat exaggerated by their nudity. This one, recumbent and seen at close range, did not seem as beautiful as those others had. Her sheer mass was intimidating, and so—for some reason I could not fathom—was her statuesque stillness.

The Dweller, I supposed, would not have taken the discovery that she could not return to her own people as hard as the Amphibian—but it would have been a considerable blow. My impressions had been fragmentary, and it was certainly not something the Dwellers had been eager to explain to me, but I knew that there had been a painful dispute between the males and females of the species, which had reached some kind of reconciliation before my return to my own era but which had nevertheless left an awkward emotional legacy. The Dwellers had had psychological problems of their own, too—

their minds had not been as resistant to decay and death as their bodies.

"Why were you surprised that the Dweller was as physically resilient as the Amphibian?" I asked. "Surely her body must have been much the stronger of the two."

"Quite the opposite," Speaker said. "Giantism carries all kinds of physical costs and penalties. In much the same way that this unit could not fly, were it not for the fact that the physical force of its wings is augmented by mental force, so a humanoid of your sort could not grow to giant size without the exertion of mental force to sustain its heart, its lungs, and even its legs. To be a giant is effortful—and a race would need a powerful reason in order to remake itself in that particular image."

I knew that she meant a psychological reason: a particular kind of pride, or vanity.

"The Dwellers did remake themselves, then? Philip Danby always insisted that they must have done so, by re-engineering their own flesh."

"We are certain of that," Speaker said.

"And were the Amphibians a manufactured race too? Not one that remade itself to its own intentional design, but merely some kind of robotic product of industry?"

"It seems probable, but we do not know for sure."

"Danby's general thesis is true, though? Beings of your kind are the descendants of creatures made by human or post-human artifice?"

"We cannot be sure. The apparent distinction between the categories of the natural and the artificial broke down shortly after the time from which you come. Natural selection affects self-reproducing artificial organisms as well as those you consider natural, and the same is true of the new kinds of genetic systems that emerged in that era, which now monopolize the biosphere. Whatever the truth of that matter, the Dwellers certainly became giants because they dearly wanted to *be* giants. They wanted to be *immortal* giants—but that was far more difficult to achieve than they imagined, for the mental effort they had to put into their own sustenance took a heavy psychological toll."

"So they literally wearied of life," I said, wonderingly. "The death-wish that they developed as they grew older, whose effects they could not counter, was a side-effect of their giant size?"

"That is correct."

"And their fertility problems? The difficulty their females had in conceiving, particularly female children?"

"Those factors too were almost certainly unintended consequences of their desire to maximize their physical size. Even though their flesh is designed to be immortal, the Dwellers are not resilient in biomechanical terms. We were never sure that the Dweller would be able to serve as an intermediary on our behalf, although she was willing and eager to try, because we were not sure that we could contrive a sufficiently gentle lift-off for our spacecraft. We should be able to help her through the lift-off, by adding the support of our mental force to hers, but we cannot guarantee that she will survive, even if she is still willing to try. You and the Amphibian remain our best hope of persuading the Metamorphosians that we have not committed any hostile act against them, and have no intention of so doing—and that we do not, even in the longest term imaginable, pose the slightest danger to them."

I looked more closely at the Dweller, and saw that she was not as young as I had thought at first. Although the signs of aging she showed were slight and subtle by human standards, they were obvious to attentive inspection. For a moment, she reminded me of Clara, who was also very well-preserved in terms of outward appearance, but had refused two opportunities to marry and bear children and was probably approaching the time when she would no longer be able to give birth without substantial risk.

"She too had a mission, had she not?" I murmured. "A vitally important mission, whose failure would have extremely serious consequences. She was hoping to bring information back from the future that would be of great value and utility to her race—information that might help preserve her race for centuries, or millennia. She knew, when she discovered that she could not return to her own time, that she had failed in its accomplishment. She must have been stricken almost as badly by that as the Amphibian was by her own loss."

"It seems so," Speaker conceded. "Even so, we feel that she is ready to awake, and will be able to function normally."

"Would you have given her the *quid pro quo* she wanted in return for serving as your intermediary?" I asked. "*Could* you have given it to her? After all, the defeat and extinction of the Dwellers by the Antipodeans must have been a necessary prelude to your own existence and ascendancy. You could not send a time-traveling Dweller home with instructions to devise some kind of ultimate weapon."

"No," Speaker admitted, "we could not and would not have done that. But there was scope for negotiation."

For a moment or two, I was distracted from the implications of that statement by an awful possibility. "Is it possible," I asked, "that the time-bridge collapsed because it had to, in order to prevent a serious disruption in the flow of time?"

There was a pause before Speaker answered. "We do not know," she said, eventually. "It is conceivable." Her guiding intelligence clearly knew that the answer to the question had important corollaries, so far as I was concerned. Among other things, it meant that my safe return to my own time—and that of my companions— was by no means guaranteed. Speaker had already told me, in so many words, that Philip and Clara could not possibly survive an interrupted return, and that my remade body might also be destroyed by such an eventuality. The Chimeras had known, when they went fishing for me, that time and history might be less amenable to interference than the success of my own pioneering expedition had implied.

It was probably because my mind shied away from that disturbing line of thought that it suddenly occurred to me what Speaker must mean by *scope for negotiation*. "You intended to offer the Dwellers an escape-route," I said. "You thought that you could safely offer them the time-bridge itself, as a means of bringing a breeding colony of Dwellers out of their time and into yours—with the supplementary your expertise in assisting them to overcome the decline and imbalance in their birth-rate."

"That possibility had occurred to us," Speaker confirmed. "Had negotiations with the Metamorphosians reached a satisfactory conclusion, we—or rather they—might conceivably have been able to offer even more."

"A whole new world!" I said.

"Access to a potentially infinite number of other worlds," Speaker said, by way of correction. "We have no interest in space exploration ourselves, save for the appropriation of new carbon from the outer limits of our own solar system, but the Dwellers are a very different kind. That is why we thought that their representative might be as useful as he Amphibian in helping us to establish a meaningful and productive dialogue with the Metamorphosians."

"But it all went awry—perhaps because of a single shot fired at an inopportune moment, in a war that ended half a million years ago, and perhaps because the continuity of history was under threat, and the universe responded accordingly."

"That is a rather melodramatic way of putting it, but, in essence, yes. At any rate, we could not establish a new time-bridge to the Dwellers' era—but thanks to the groundwork they had laid down, we were able, eventually, to open a bridge to yours. You may be our last hope of saving this situation—and you are certainly our best hope. Are you ready to proceed with the awakening, or do you need further pause for thought?"

"I'm ready," I said, unhesitatingly. "Anything I can do to help the Amphibian, I will do very gladly."

"Thank you. Are you willing to help the Dweller too?"

I was slightly surprised by that. "I doubt that I can," I said. "I don't recognize her—and even if she and I had met while I was the Dwellers' prisoner, I can't imagine that she would consider that she had any kind of bond with me or interest in me. Even if she had been one of the Seekers of Wisdom who interrogated me, she would only have learned to consider me a mere laboratory specimen, beneath contempt as a person."

"We understand that. Even so, there is one thing you can offer her that we cannot, which might be of some assistance to her."

"I don't understand what you mean," I confessed.

"Access to your memories," Speaker said. "You spent several months in the company of her kind, observed by the Seekers of Wisdom and other interested parties on a daily basis, and observing them with as much care as you could. They adapted your body so that you might serve as—in your own words—a living book. We believe that the Dweller might be interested to...read you. Through your eyes, she may at least *see* her own kind again. It would be kind of you to allow us to make the offer."

Would it be kind? I wondered. *Would she really be glad to know what impression the Dwellers had made on me, when I saw one of their number devour a living Frog-mouth piece by piece, or when I saw them slaughtering the Killers to harvest their malevolent blood, or when I saw what the Seekers of Science had done to poor Harry Brett? On the other hand, would she care in the least what I might think of her and her kind? Might she not find some solace in my memories of her native Underworld, in spite of the emotional connotations such images still hold for me?*

"Very well," I said, only a trifle reluctantly. "If access to my memory might help her, you're welcome to offer it. I will cooperate to the best of my ability."

"Thank you," Speaker said. "May we proceed with the awakenings now?"

"Yes," I said, "If Clara and Danby wake up to find me gone, though, they will need an explanation. If you are not there to give them one...."

"We have other ways of contriving a voice," Speaker assured me. "We shall do our best to soothe your companions' anxieties. You may talk to them yourself, if you wish. We can wake them up if you need to consult them."

"No, that's all right," I hastened to add. "Tell them when they wake that I'll talk to them when I can."

"It will be done," Speaker promised. "We shall proceed now."

As she spoke, a centaur-like creature appeared from a hidden doorway, and moved to pick up the Amphibian. The newcomer's hind end bore more resemblance to a tiger than a horse, and its torso was more like a gorilla's than a man's. It was not a giant, but I suspected that its awkward shape might need considerable mental effort to sustain it.

"How long have they been lying inert like that?" I asked, as the Amphibian's body was taken up.

"Ninety-two years," was the reply.

I honestly did not know whether that was a surprisingly long time or a ludicrously short time, given that I was a million years displaced from my own era. Evidently, the Metamorphosians had been waiting to begin their aborted negotiations with the Chimeras for a long time before suddenly becoming impatient. Had they really suffered some kind of assault? If so, who could possibly be responsible, if not the Chimeras?

I felt that I ought to put such speculations firmly aside, having matters of my own to attend to, but the temptation to investigate was too strong. As Speaker and I fell into step behind the centaur and moved into yet another dimly-lit corridor, I said: "Your communication with the Metamorphosians has been stalled for a long time. How long has it been since you first made contact with them?"

"We first became aware of their presence in the solar system more than a thousand years ago, but their base on the Earth's moon has only been established for three hundred, and no formal contact was made for some time thereafter. The possibility of a dispute might have been averted had either party shown greater alacrity in opening negotiations, but we wanted to gather as much information as we could from a distance, and they apparently fell the same. There has been an unfortunate mutual distrust since the beginning. We are not certain why the Metamorphosians came to the system, or what they intend to do here. They assured us that they would not interfere with us in any way, but that was before thy accused us of taking hostile action against them."

"What kind of hostile action?"

"They accused us of...kidnapping some of their personnel."

"But you didn't?"

"Certainly not. We do not have the means to accomplish any such abduction, and would not have employed them if we had. We are in no position to guess who else might be responsible for such an action, if anything of the sort actually did happen."

"Do the Metamorphosians want to establish a permanent colony on the moon?"

"They say that they do not, but they also have a presence on various satellites of Jupiter, and they have not given any such undertaking with respect to those territories. They have suggested that we have no property rights outside the Earth itself—they claim that we were not the only living creatures within the system before they arrived, nor even the only intelligent presence, but we have so far been unable to confirm those claims."

"Is there life on Mars, then?"

"Not any more. The Metamorphosians claim that Mars was...seeded with life at the same time as the Earth, but that it became extinct more than a billion years ago. The claim that the same seeds lie dormant in several other worlds, awaiting conditions conducive to their development, although there is more than one other location within the system that supports an active carbon-based biosphere."

"What do you mean by *seeded*?" I asked.

"According to the Metamorphosians, the organic particles ancestral to Earthly life traveled to the solar system along with the other heavy elements that formed it, which were the debris of an earlier stellar explosion."

"So you're not implying that the seed was *deliberately* sown, whether by a creator God or some other intelligence?"

"The Metamorphosians seem uncertain about that. They sometimes speak in terms of a cosmic plan and a cosmic destiny, but they do so hesitantly. They seem divided among themselves as to the kind of challenge or insult we provide to their notion of a cosmic plan, although none seem inclined to concede that we might properly belong to it. All of this is very unclear, from our viewpoint, and the Metamorphosians have not been helpful in clarifying their own beliefs and opinions regarding such matters"

"What is your objective in the negotiations with which you want us to assist?" I wanted to know. "Do you want the Metamorphosians to clear out of the solar system and never return?"

"That certainly seems, at present, to be an attractive potential outcome. Unfortunately, we cannot compel it and it is possible that we might never be able to compel it, even if we were to attempt it.

The question we need to settle for ourselves is whether we must exert ourselves to the full in preparing to defend ourselves—and, if so, what preparations it will be necessary and wise to make. In the meantime, we must make what agreements we can to maintain peace and work in harmony with our visitors. That is not easy, while there is such a gulf of incomprehensibility between their way of thinking and ours—but we must pause there."

She broke off the conversation abruptly. I realized that we had reached the location in which the Amphibian was to be brought back to consciousness. We stepped sideways, moving instantaneously—or so it seemed—from semi-darkness to bright light, and I found myself beneath a bright blue sky studded with cumulus clouds.

Chapter Fourteen

The Awakening

It seemed at first that we had stepped into a different dimension, entering a space which seemed to be impossibly vast, considering that we were deep in the bowels of the Earth. I realized almost immediately that my hosts were merely making use of an ability the Dwellers had possessed, of making their walls function as if they were windows—so cleverly that one might be standing in a narrow space, with hardly room to swing a proverbial cat, and yet look out in all directions towards seemingly-infinite horizons. This was, I presumed, a scene that could no longer exist on the Earth of the Chimeras, although it would have been familiar enough to the inhabitants of many preceding eras.

The actual chamber, so far as I could estimate its true dimensions, was perhaps a dozen yards square, most of which consisted of a sandy floor strewn with weed-bedecked rocks. This appeared to the eye, however, to be a section of a beach facing a vast ocean, with headlands to either side and a cliff behind. The air was redolent with the briny scent of seaweeds freshly exposed by a retreating tide.

The centaur laid the Amphibian down on the soft sand, and then withdrew. Speaker knelt down over the recumbent body, which now lay on its side, slightly curled up, and ran her hands lightly over the fur on the Amphibian's back and shoulders.

"We shall leave you alone with her," Speaker said. "She will wake in a few minutes. We will maintain close contact with her mind, but we shall be discreet. If all goes well, she will recover the intimate contact with your mind that she once contrived to cultivate, but it may not be easy. You might find it uncomfortable, at least to begin with. Please do not be afraid; we shall make certain that you come to no harm."

"I'm not afraid," I assured her. Perhaps I should have been. Perhaps I simply did not know enough to be reasonably afraid.

When Speaker had gone, it seemed to the naked eye that the Amphibian and I were together on the surface of the planet, not as it was now but as it had been half a million years before—which was not so very different from what it must have be like tens of millions years before that. Of all the habitats on the Earth's surface, those that are subject to the most gradual change are those that are subject to constant and reliable forces, such as the movement of the tides and the flow of rivers. This imitation littoral zone was relatively deserted—there were no flocks of gulls, sanderlings, and oyster-catchers, as there might have been on the English shore in my own day, and no swarms of crabs—but it did not seem in the least desolate. The air was warm and somnolent, and it seemed that the calmness of the sea had spread to the land as well.

The Amphibian stirred slightly, but she did not open her eyes. I knew that she was trying to sense her surroundings with her mind, though, because I felt the exploratory impulse. I tried as best I could to respond, but it was an art I had had no further opportunity to practice since the day I had departed from her world, more than ten subjective years ago, and it was one I had never mastered, always having been reliant on the efforts of others—*her* efforts most of all.

There was no instant recognition, nor any true meeting of minds, but I was able to sense something of her emotion, and something of her self-awareness. Although I had learned to translate the Amphibians' mental communication into a kind of literal mind-*speech*, comprehensible to the extent that I was able to render it into English, that was the result of a sort of distillation, whereby I extracted from the rich spectrum of her own representations those few aspects that I could grasp by means of words and pictures. When I had first "overheard" the Amphibians in my mind, I had heard the surge and swell of their communications as a sort of music; my first brush with the awakened Amphibian's consciousness was similar in one respect—but very different in another.

When I had first perceived the company of Amphibians running towards me on the surface of the Dwellers' world—and perhaps even earlier than that, when I had frightened a lone Amphibian and caused her to be seized by the tentacled plant—the overwhelming impression I had received was one of harmony and melody. It was not merely their communication but their fundamental awareness of existence that was orchestral in its grandeur and ease, its self-assurance and contentment in its own unity, and its perfect alliance. Even when my companion and I had been separated from the greater company—left to play our own makeshift duet, as it were—her consciousness of herself had always been the consciousness of being part of a greater company, as intimately bound to that larger whole as a single cell in the body of an organism, or as one delicately-pitched voice in a great choir.

Now, while it was still quite impossible for me to translate the contents of her consciousness into words or visual images, I perceived her mind again in term of musical metaphors. I perceived her as a singer or an instrument, trying vainly to sound its proper chord in a medium where no resonance was possible.

Her mind was now a thing alone and echoless, a thing lost and desolate, and it seemed quite unable to bear that condition.

It was, I knew, the condition to which I had been born and in which I had lived all my life—a condition that, to me, was not merely natural but normal. If it was not *entirely* comfortable, then it was comfortable as any mental condition could be, in a human being. I believe that I could have retreated to that condition, had I let my mental reflexes take their course. I could, I think, have closed off my mind by erecting a barricade of fear and horror. But I was the kind of creature whose will was routinely in conflict with other impulses, and was steeled for that kind of struggle. I tried, with all my might, not to shut her out, but instead to accept her awareness into myself: to bear the burden of her terrible, almost hysterical, desolation. I tried, too, as best I could, to answer it: to provide an echo of sorts, a resonance of sorts, in spite of the manifest absurdity of the attempt.

At first, my effort would not serve. The only immediate result of my determination to be open to her anguish was that it filled me like a flood, of a kind to which I had long grown unaccustomed and seemed likely to drive me mad. It threatened to destroy me, as it threatened to destroy her—but it could not. I was indestructible by that kind of force.

I have no idea how long that interval lasted, in objective terms—perhaps no more than minute, perhaps as much as a quarter of an hour—but while it lasted, it unhinged me. It disturbed me, but it did not devastate me. Perhaps paradoxically, it was not even terrible. It was not painful, even in terms of grief, sadness and a sense of loss. She must have been feeling all of those emotions and more, and I do not doubt that, for her, it was very terrible and very painful indeed—but we were of very different kinds, she and I. Although my mind seemed, while that interval lasted, to be teetering on the brink of disintegration, I was not *hurt*. I was no stranger to confusion and mental conflict; I could bear it with ease, for both of us.

Whether Speaker's guiding intelligence would have been able to fulfill its promise to protect me had the Amphibian suffered the dire fate that threatened her, I do not know. I dare say that it could have, and would have done so. In the end, though, that proved unnecessary. For the Amphibian's benefit, as well as for my own, I fought back against the threat of desolation in the only way I could—and perhaps in a way that only I, in all the world as it now was, could have done.

Because I perceived her anguish as a kind of music, discordant because it was isolated and unanswerable, I tried to reply with music of my own. I replied, at first, with snatches of the plaintive songs that we used to sing in the trenches, and then with hymns I had learned in church, and finally with cradle-songs that had been sung to me by my mother when I was a child, occasionally reiterated long after I had left my cradle behind. I do not say that I took the time to sing them in full, and perhaps I did no more than think of them, to recover the ghosts of their refrains—but I did *something* to make my presence felt, and not as an alien and discordant presence but as something faintly familiar, something with whom contact might be made.

First, the quality of her own dire lament changed and softened. Then her mind recovered something of its self-composure, its curiosity and its boldness. Finally, she realized what and who I was, and formed a response that I was able to translate into words as: "It's you."

"It's me," I agreed.

"I never thought that I would see you again."

"Nor I you."

"This is a dream, I know. They have offered me dreams before. They have tried to mimic my sisters, to pretend that I am not alone...but it was all a sham. This too must be a sham."

"No," I said, "it's not a sham. I have traveled in time again, as I always wanted to do. I'm not here by chance. I'm glad to have found you—more delighted, I think, than you can readily understand."

"They brought you here?"

"They helped me to cross the time-bridge. Had they told me you were here a little earlier, I would have come to you of my own free will, with all possible haste. I would have jumped into that bottomless pit, trusting to the wings of one of the Chimeras to slow my fall, in order that we might be reunited with all possible speed. When they told me that there was a possibility that you might still need to be saved from danger, and that I might help to save you...."

"I cannot believe it," she replied, regretfully.

"It's true," I assured her—and there was a silence then, while she digested that information, and tried hard to persuade herself to believe it.

"I am lost," she said, when she put words into my mind again, "but it does not matter. I am glad to see you. I am glad to have seen you once again, in the flesh or merely in the mind's eye, before I must die."

"Are you so determined to die, then?" I asked.

"There is no life left that I can live. My sisters are dead. Ours was the kind of life that could only be lived together."

"There are other ways to live," I told her. "I can testify to that."

"Not for me," she said, dolefully. "I am not that kind of creature."

"You are now," I told her. "Nor was it a catastrophe of fate, but something you chose for yourself. You chose to travel in time, as I had done. You chose to separate yourself from your sisters, although that would have been unthinkable before you met me. You set forth willingly on an adventure, which is not concluded yet. There are other ways to be, other ways to live, than the one to which you were born. I do not say that it will be easy, but I do say that it can be done. If you decide to live, you may live. You cannot be the same kind of creature you were before, but that does not mean that you cannot be at all. You are alive, and you are not alone."

She opened her eyes then, for the first time, and looked at me. I was sitting on the sand beside her, looking at her but not touching her. I was still afraid to touch her.

"You have left your false skin behind," she observed, "but kept its shadow. The air is unreasonably warm here, is it not?"

"Yes," I said. "The air is too warm, and we are not as heavy as we would be, were we really on the surface, by the shore of the sea. The space surrounding us is an illusion, but the air is real, and this patch of sand is real, and I am real."

She sat up, and studied me very carefully. "This is not a dream," she said, tentatively. "We are deep in the bowels of the Earth, in what was once the realm of the Dwellers. On the surface, the sky is no longer blue, and the ocean is tame."

"That's true," I said. "The world has changed. The Dwellers are no more, and your kind is extinct, as is mine. But still, we are alive. You are not alone, and nor am I."

"I see that," she said, apparently having finally consented to believe it. "How long shall we be together, this time, before you return to your own time?"

I had not thought that far ahead, but I could understand why she was wary. What comfort could it be to her, even if what I had told her *was* true, that she would not be *entirely* alone...but only for a brief interval?

"I will not abandon you while you need me," I told her, quietly. "If I were never to return home again, it would not be a terrible fate. While you need me, I will not desert you. You have my promise."

"Do I need you?" she asked, more of herself than of me. "Will you be able to keep your promise?"

"I don't know whether you need me or not," I answered, truthfully, "but if my presence here helps you in any way, then I am glad to be here—and I will do everything I possibly can to stay by your side while you need me to remain."

She stared at me for a few moments, and then said; "You are the strangest creature I ever encountered. Once, I thought you horrible."

"Strangeness is a relative thing," I remarked, "and so is horror. In time, even the Dwellers came to seem less strange to me, and less horrible, than they did at first—although they certainly never made any attempt to earn my good opinion."

"Whereas you made every effort to obtain mine?" she queried.

"I tried to be agreeable, in spite of my deficiencies," I told her.

She fell silent again for a few moments, and then said: "This *is* a dream, although I seem to be awake. It cannot last—but you might be right. It might be possible to live in this kind of dream, and to become the kind of creature which could endure it indefinitely. It might vanish on the instant, bringing reality crashing down upon my head, but...yes, I might be saved, although I cannot promise you that you can save me."

"I need no such promise," I said. "I know how inadequate I am to fill the void left by your sisters—but for what I am worth, I am here."

She paused again for thought, and then said: "Can you sing to me again? Silently, if you can—although I shall not mind too much if you feel the need to pronounce the words and capture the tone with your voice."

I began to sing "A Long Way to Tipperary"—silently, in thought alone. I think I was better able to hold the tune that way.

When I had finished, she nodded her head. "It may be possible," she murmured. She sounded far from sure, but I knew that she would not have said it lightly.

A doorway opened then, in what appeared to be the cliff face behind me. The Amphibian looked over my shoulder to see who had come in, and I turned with her.

It was Speaker—who must have seemed, even to the Amphibian, to be beautiful and angelic.

"We are sorry," Speaker said. "We would have preferred to leave you alone for some time longer, but the Dweller is demanding to see you, George. If you would consent to come with us, we would be grateful."

"I cannot leave my friend," I said.

"That will not be necessary," Speaker replied. "Indeed, it will be better by far if the Dweller can see you both."

I looked at the Amphibian again. "We must go," she said. "The Dweller will be anxious. We must try to soothe her as best we can. She, at least, can live, if she can only find a reason." She stood up, and brushed a little loose sand from her fur.

She was not her old self, and I knew that she never would be. Beyond the mind-speech that she formed for my benefit, there was still an awful pitch of desolation and misery, still a discordant anguish—but she seemed sufficiently determined to sustain herself, at least for the time being.

I stood up too. I did not care, as yet, to take the risk of touching her, but I fell into step beside her, positioning myself in such a way that we seemed to be together.

Together, we followed Speaker into the gloomy half-light.

CHAPTER FIFTEEN

THE ENTHRONED IDOL

Like the Amphibian, the Dweller had been removed to a room that simulated a familiar environment—which meant that it was a far greater space, with a much higher ceiling. As in the other, its walls were screens which give the illusion of being windows, but here the illusion made no attempt to simulate a single surrounding landscape; it was as if the four walls were indeed windows, looking out in different directions into very different landscapes.

One of these images offered a distant view of a huge opalescent building, circular in shape, which I recognized as a building I had seen before, and mentally labeled a Temple—which had, indeed turned out to be one of the places that the Dwellers held sacred. The other three landscapes were very strange to me, and I imagine that they might have been equally strange to the Dweller, for they were scenes of wilderness and desolation such as surely could not have belonged to the Earth in her time. I did not study them carefully, though, for my attention was inevitably seized by the awakened Dweller herself.

She was seated on a chair, which was quite plain in its design, but whose awesome dimensions made it appear to me as a kind of throne. The Dweller, being some thirty feet in height, could not help but give the impression of being some vast idol. She sat so still at first that the impression was further enhanced; it was as if she were carved out of stone, like the gigantic statues in the Egyptian Valley of the Kings, or the massive Buddhas lodged in mountainous alcoves in Afghanistan.

When I came into the room, with Speaker to my left and the Amphibian to my right, the Dweller did not seem to notice me immediately—but then she turned towards me, and fixed me with a stare that somehow contrived to seem blank and penetrating at the same time. She looked at me in that fashion for a minute or more, and then she leaned forward slightly, her gaze becoming more intent. I knew that she was reaching into my mind, and felt a wave of coldness—but no more. She frowned then, and her mouth curled slightly in displeasure. She seemed even less beautiful now than she had while lying down, but that was because I was too close to her to make an imaginative adjustment to her apparent magnitude; I could not see her as if she were a being akin to me. Her presence was simply too oppressive.

I think she may have sensed that feeling, for she drew back slightly, and her expression became more thoughtful than annoyed.

The Dwellers' bodies showed few signs of aging that were easily recognizable to human eyes, but there had been one occasion, when I saw a dark blue female at work with a living book in the library, when I had been in no doubt that I was looking at one who was very old and weary of life. This one, while no longer in her prime, seemed a little younger than the other had been, but there was a particular bleakness in her gaze that spoke of infinite world-weariness.

I did not know whether she would be able to focus her thoughts sufficiently to address me, even if she cared to do so. I remembered only too well the contempt and disdain in which the great majority of her kind had held me, and felt sure that no Dweller would have been enthusiastic to speak to me under what passed in their Underworld for normal circumstances—but these were not normal circumstances, and this Dweller had asked for me. Then again, there had been fierce disputes within the ranks of the Dwellers, in addition to the bitter wrangle between the males and the females as to the appropriate response to the crisis in their birth-rate, and it was possible that there were some among them who might not look at me with reflexive loathing.

With those thoughts in mind, I tried to adopt a friendly attitude, and attempted to project my own mind-speech into her enormous skull.

"My name is George," I tried to say. "I understand that you wanted to see me."

For several seconds, I could not obtain any hint of her reaction to the sight of me or my attempt at mind-speech—but then she suddenly leaned forward, as though to inspect me even more closely, and I thought that I sensed a hint of distress in her gaze. Whether she had been exchanging mental communications with Speaker, or with my Amphibian, I do not know, but she proved that she was capable of making herself understood to me when she projected words into my mind that had the force of a silent shout.

"You traveled through time into my world," she said, "and succeeded in returning to your own."

"Yes I did," I said, in what seemed to me a far more moderate fashion. "I'm truly sorry to hear that you were unable to return to yours. If I can be of any assistance to you, you have only to ask."

I half-expected her to take offence at the temerity of my suggestion that a creature like me could possibly be of any assistance to a being like her, and to look down at me with studied contempt—but she did not. She still seemed thoughtful, as if she were adding me to the delicate balance of her situation to see what difference my meager weight might make.

I tried with all my might to meet her awful eyes, but could not do it, even though they seemed to have far more sorrow in them than anger. They were too massive, and their gaze too powerful. I looked away—but, after collecting myself, I looked back at her again, sighing slightly with relief when I saw that she had turned her attention to my Amphibian companion. I had to assume, now, that they were engaged in a mental dialogue, but I could not hear either one of them unless they made the effort to speak directly into my mind and I had to wait for two or three minutes before the Dweller looked back at me.

"You are George," she repeated, then. The next thing she said was very remarkable indeed, for in all the time I had spent in the world of the Dwellers I had never learned the given name of any of them. "My name is Liamon," the giant said. "That is a true name, not an improvised label."

I inferred that she was distinguishing herself from Speaker. She was telling me—not that I needed telling—that she was not the same kind of being as a Chimerical unit. She was acknowledging, too, that she and I had something significant in common, beyond the fact that we had both traveled in time.

"Thank you for telling me," I said. "I am honored to know you."

"The creature you call Speaker has offered me the opportunity to look into your memories," Liamon said. "You might have been foolish to give her permission to do that, but I would like to accept the offer. It is a gift I should not like to accept from someone who did not know my name. Your companion should name herself too, now. You and I must teach her what it is to own a name, and what it is to be a true individual."

I was amazed by all of that, but most of all by its careful politeness. The giant had evidently made a decision, however difficult it might have been, to treat me as if I were an equal—and to regard the Amphibian in the same light. Liamon was, it seemed, making her own psychological adjustments to her new situation, and wanted to help the Amphibian in that regard.

"Thank you," I said. "Why might it have been foolish to offer you access to my memories?"

"The creatures you call Chimeras are not like us," Liamon said. "They do not guard themselves, as members of my race do. They do not understand the significance of what has been done to you. I will not say that I am sorry for what the Seekers of Science did, because I might be able to benefit from it, and will be glad to do so, but it was not an act of kindness on their part to make you into a living book. They have made your substance a little sturdier, but your mind is more vulnerable to intrusion now than it was before, and that exposes you to potential perils as well as making you potentially useful to your present hosts. I give you my word that I will not hurt you, and that I will try to protect you from hurt that others might wish to offer, but I feel obliged to warn you that you ought to be wary before giving your consent to be used in this manner again."

"By the Metamorphosians, you mean?"

"Yes—among others," the giant said. "If we go to the moon, you should not consent to anything without taking advice—from your Amphibian friend, if not from me. Do you understand what kind of creatures these are, whose purposes you are now attempting to serve?"

Speaker made no attempt to intervene in this dialogue; she merely looked on, presumably listening to every silent word.

"I have only an inkling, at present," I admitted, "just as I had only the merest inkling of what kind of creatures they were whose purposes I served while I was held by the Seekers of Wisdom for the greater part of a year—they would not deign to address me as you are addressing me now, as one person to another. I know, though, that in learning more about the Chimeras—and perhaps, thanks to you, the Dwellers—I shall be serving my own purposes. Knowledge is progress, is it not?"

"I once thought so," the Dweller replied. "We might yet have the opportunity to put the proposition to the test. I ought to warn you that I might not be a comfortable presence in your sleep, and that you might regret your reckless generosity. Thus far, you have only been studied by the males of my kind, whose attitudes are distinct."

"Until I traveled through time," I said, "I had not known that I could entertain foreign presences of any kind within my consciousness, awake or asleep. I cannot say that any such experience has been *comfortable*, especially at first—but I have learned a great deal by such means. I accept your word that you do not intend to hurt me, and I am not afraid to give you access to my memories. I hope you will not be offended by the horror that often attended my perception of your species."

Her features were still bleakly impassive, although her gaze had softened somewhat. She seemed slightly amused by my last remark. "Horror has sometimes attended my own perception of my species," she said. "You will not offend me in that way." She looked sideways then, at Speaker. "The offer is accepted," she said. "We shall begin immediately."

"That is not...," Speaker began.

Liamon cut her off. "We shall do it *now*," she repeated. "George has agreed. I do not know how much time remains to me, but I am not disposed to let any go to waste."

"The Amphibian...," Speaker began.

"May stay by his side while he sleeps," the Dweller said, "and may share his memories too, if she so wishes. It might help her to understand why she would benefit from a name."

I suspected that the reason why Liamon was making such an issue of the matter of names was that she was attempting to differentiate potential allies from potential adversaries—and that she believed, for whatever reason, that the Chimeras might yet become such formidable adversaries that she would gladly accept any allies she could find.

Speaker may have reached the same conclusion, but gave no sign of being perturbed. "If George consents...," she began, again.

"He has consented," was Liamon's abrupt reply to that.

"I'm ready, provided that my companion has no objection" I put in. "If Liamon wishes me to entrance myself immediately, so that she may find out without delay exactly what kind of creature I am, and exactly what dealings I have had with her race, I make no objection—but I have promised not to abandon my friend, and I must keep that promise."

"I make no objection," the Amphibian said, "but I shall stay beside him while he lies helpless, and share his dream."

"Which *you* will not," the Dweller said, still addressing herself to Speaker. "You will let us alone, and grant us privacy."

"We cannot...," Speaker began.

Yet again the Dweller cut her off. "You have my sworn word that no harm will come to either of them," she said. "Should either require help, we shall call for it. Bring the human a bed on which to lie, and then depart. The Amphibian and I can do what is necessary. We do not need you."

Speaker raised no further objection. A bed of sorts was brought for me to lie on, and she departed. Before I had time to lie down, the Dweller extended a gigantic finger to bid me stay where I was a moment longer.

"I had not expected this development," the Dweller told me. "Perhaps I am foolish, but the possibility had never occurred to me. We are responsible for your coming here, are we not? The creatures you call Chimeras learned from us how to link their bridge to the departure-point of the one we extended into your world."

"I believe so," I said, thinking it best not to quarrel over such trifles as the Professor's share of the credit for the first bridge.

"They are exceedingly clever—and we must be careful of them. Perhaps their promises can be trusted, and perhaps not. They were certainly not to blame for what happened to your companion and me when we attempt to return to our world, because it dashed their plans as well as ours—but exactly what their plans were, I do not know. I am responsible, on behalf of my race, for your being drawn into this vexed business, and I will try to keep you safe, but we must be careful. They know, of course, that I am giving you this warning—they will certainly know every detail of what we communicate to one another, whatever undertakings they give regarding privacy. They knew that bringing you here would give me hope—their talk of letting me see my own kind again through the lens of your memories is mere pretence, but that does not matter. They hope to use us all, and must persuade us that it is in our best interests to be used. They might be right, at least in my case—I seem to have little or no alternative but to be useful to them, in the short term—but we should not take anything for granted. I will have a better appreciation of your interests when I have looked into your memory. Lie down now, please."

I made as if to obey, but hesitated. "Will I be conscious of what you are doing?" I asked.

"It will seem to you to be a dream—probably a disturbing dream—but you are likely to forget it as easily as any other dream, as soon as you awake. The Amphibian could assist your mind to retain it, but that might not be altogether wise."

I looked at the Amphibian, but she made no objection. She seemed to be as surprised by the Dweller's attitude and actions as I was, but whatever they had said to one another must have calmed her anxieties sufficiently to let things proceed as Liamon wished.

"You have the ability to put yourself into what you call a trance, do you not?" the Dweller said.

"Yes," I relied, as I stretched myself out on the bed."

"Good," the Dweller agreed. "Do so now, if you please."

She positioned her enormous chair beside the bed, in such a way that she could lean over me. I lay down on my back, and stared up for a moment into her face. With only the blank ceiling behind her head, it became possible for a moment to imagine that she was even closer than she was, and that the gargantuan appearance of her face was the effect of close range rather than its actual dimensions. For that moment, at least, she did look beautiful, although her expression seemed infinitely melancholy.

Then I closed my eyes, and willed myself into a mental state somewhere beyond sleep.

CHAPTER SIXTEEN

AN OPEN BOOK

As I had been promised, I dreamed—and, as I had been warned, the dreams seemed, at least at first, to be deeply discomfiting. That nightmarish aspect, however, allowed me to remain more clearly conscious of them than I would otherwise have been able to do, and allowed me to retain a clearer memory of the kinds of images I had brought back to the surface from the depths of repression and forgetfulness. I was only marginally aware of the presence of my reader, but that mere presence seemed very oppressive, if not actively malign.

I did not return, as I might have expected, to the world of the Dwellers, where the Seekers of Wisdom had spent so much time interrogating me. What Liamon wanted to do, it seemed, was not to revisit her own kind but to discover more about mine.

First, I revisited the military encampments of the war—all the various temporary headquarters, all the bunkers and the trenches, and all the battlefields. I revisited the long barrages, when shells fell for days on end, the gas attacks, during which the mask seemed likely to choke me even if the chlorine and phosgene failed to penetrate its defenses. I revisited the stables and the hospitals, the railway-stations and the ferry-boats, watched tiny airplanes fighting in the sky.

Then I revisited Oxford: my house, my study, my laboratory. I revisited my studies, my enquiries, my books, my conclusions and conjectures. It seemed strange, in a way, that such a quiet, methodical and lonely life could fuel a nightmare, but it was not the feeling of isolation that filled it with horror so much as the feeling of futility: the sense of forever hunting for a crucial answer that lay tantalizingly out of reach.

If anything, the memories of Oxford seemed even more nightmarish than those of the war. At the time when I was fighting, I am sure, I had been terrified that every day might be my last—but that kind of terror had, after a while, been dulled into a mere fatalism: a sense of having no control over my destiny, of being in the lap of remote and uncaring gods. That fatalism echoed in my recall—eventually finding, I think, a further echo in the observing consciousness of Liamon the Dweller, who understood it very well.

As time went by within the dream, her presence became less oppressive; as I grew accustomed to it, it seemed to become a little gentler—but intrusion never became welcome. The more sympathy I found in it—or projected upon it—the more surreal and darkly enigmatic my own remembered experiences came to seem.

I think that she understood what I had been trying to do in Oxford, too—as well she might, if she any understanding at all of why the Seekers of Science had decided to sow the seeds of transformation in my flesh before allowing me to go home. Whether or not she was a scholar by profession or vocation I could not tell, but she certainly seemed to understand the quest for enlightenment—after all, had she not agreed with me that she had once shared my opinion that knowledge is progress?—and was presumably demonstrating in her present enquiry the sheer desperation with which she was seeking something that might be turned to her advantage.

I could not tell as yet, though, how she was likely to calculate that advantage, now that he knew that there was no way that her species could possibly avoid or ameliorate its historical fate. The offer that the Chimeras had intended to make of a futuristic refuge for a company of her kind was presumably undeliverable now, and it was not obvious that they could make her any offer sufficient to buy her loyalty.

As I revisited my long studies, sustained and extrapolated by means of my eternal wakefulness, I could not help recalling the judgment that Philip Danby had passed on the eclectic nature of my reading. Had he known that I would one day be examined on my research by a Dweller, he would doubtless have been all the more insistent that I should have stuck to science and mathematics, with a light smattering of philosophy, and let matters of "merely human interest" strictly alone. If anything, though, it was the matters of human interest that seemed to attract the earnest attention of my reader more intently than more abstract and objective concerns. I could not help feeling slightly embarrassed by that, on behalf of my species.

Liamon had confessed that she sometimes felt a certain horror in contemplation of her own species, but I did not think that it could compare with the shame and horror I sometimes felt when contemplating certain specimens of mine. The twentieth century had certainly not been our finest hour—not so much because of the war, which had been bad enough, as because of its aftermath, and all its idolatrous whoring after the new gods of Comfort and Cowardice.

If we humans had had the wherewithal to make ourselves giants, I thought, few of us could have resisted the temptation, no matter what burdens it placed on our hearts.

When I woke up again, the residue of my distress fled quickly enough, but I did not feel refreshed by my pseudosleep.

"I should like to look again, in greater depth," was the first thing Liamon said to me. "Not now, but soon, if you will permit it. I shall try not to take too much of your time."

"Perhaps you should not have told me how foolish I was to agree to your first request," I suggested.

"I shall not be offended if you take my advice and refuse," Liamon riposted. "Let us leave the matter in abeyance, for now."

"How long was I entranced?" I asked.

"Five hours," was the audible reply. It did not come from Liamon but from Speaker, who had just returned to the high-vaulted chamber.

"I should contact my companions," I said. "They will be anxious for my well-being. Counting the time I spent with my Amphibian friend, and our various discussions, I must have been gone for at least half a day—I mean, what was considered half a day in my time—since they woke from their rest."

"If I should have a name," my Amphibian friend put in, breaking what her long mental silence, "I think I should like to be called Mirastara." She was not just speaking to me but to everyone present.

"That is a good name," Liamon said.

I agreed with her, although I was not at all certain that there was any overlap in our reasoning. To me, the name sounded melodious, and thus suitable for a creature of the Amphibian's sort.

"So be it," Speaker said. "You may well need to use names when you go among the Metamorphosians, and you will doubtless find them convenient while we are making the final preparations for the journey to the moon."

"You may make the preparations for that journey," Liamon said, as if it were her prerogative to give or refuse permission, "including provision for my return to the surface. I should like to meet George's companions, Philip and Clara, before we depart. We will need to discuss matters between ourselves, once George has made a preliminary contact with the Metamorphosians by means of their machine."

"Arrangements for your transport will be made as swiftly as possible," Speaker promised the Dweller, "but for the time being, we can only return George and Mirastara. It is a simple matter of size and mass. The tunnels your species once used have almost all been replaced by narrower ones—there are far fewer giants on Earth now than there once were."

"Of course," Liamon said. "I shall be patient, and not idle. There may be little time left to me, and I should not like to die before I have completed all that I now desire to do."

Speaker beckoned to me. I followed her, after offering the giant a farewell salute. Mirastara followed me, after exchanging one last wordless glance with the Dweller.

The return to the surface was far slower, if far less disconcerting, than the descent. The time was by no means wasted, though. The elevator in which Speaker, Mirastara, and I made the ascent was equipped with window-screens like those in the rooms where Mirastara and Liamon had been brought out of their comas. As soon as the ascent began I was able to make contact with Danby. He was able to see the interior of the elevator as clearly as I was able to see the room he was in. It was similar to the one to which we had first been shown, but had only one bed in it and was subtly different in other ways. I presumed that it was the third room, whose use had been promised as soon as it could be adapted.

It seemed that Danby and I only had to reach out our hands to touch one another—and probably could have pretended to do so by placing our palms flat against our respective screens—but we did not do that.

"You should not have left without letting me know," Danby was quick to say, although he did not say that he had been alarmed to find me gone or fearful on my behalf.

"I didn't want to wake you," I told him, mildly.

"Then you should have contacted us as soon as we woke up," he countered. "Clara has been exceedingly anxious."

I doubted that he had suffered any undue distress by virtue of being able to spend some time in Clara's company without my discomfiting presence, but all I said in reply was: "I've been busy." I gestured toward my new companion. "This is Mirastara," I said. "She is the Amphibian about whom you have read so much in my account of my earlier expedition in time."

That news jerked him out of his peevish mood. Thus far, he had not paid much attention to Mirastara, presumably assuming that she was merely one more avatar of the collective consciousness that guided Speaker, but now he looked at her attentively.

"An Amphibian, you say?" he repeated, before his tone took on an extra note of incredulity in adding: "The same one you met before?"

"The very same," I confirmed. "When the Chimeras attempted to recruit individual ambassadors from the world of the Dwellers they had no difficulty finding a willing Dweller, but of all the Amphibians, Mirastara was the only one who would accept the challenge—because of what she had endured with me. The Chimeras felt that she might appreciate the gesture if I were there when she awoke. She was badly hurt when her return home went wrong. She has been in a coma for some time, and her convalescence is not yet complete."

"I see," Danby said, warily. "You must have had a great deal of catching up to do."

"We had also to communicate with the Dweller, Liamon, who was awakened at the same time," I said.

"Were you acquainted with him too?"

"Her," I corrected, before adding: "No, I didn't meet her in the course of my sojourn in the Dwellers' world, but she had heard of me. She seemed surprisingly glad to see me, and to get to know me. Have you found out anything I might need to know while I've been away?"

Danby frowned, and shrugged his shoulders. "I've asked plenty of questions," he said, "but the answers I've received have not been as helpful as I could have wished. I think I have a better understanding now of the genetic upheaval that allowed Earthly evolution to accelerate so markedly. I also think I understand why the visitors from beyond the solar system are so insistent that they will only communicate directly with individuals—although I cannot quite see how they will be sure that Amphibians, Dwellers and humans really are individuals, rather than constructs like Speaker."

"Outward forms can be synthesized easily enough," I said. "Minds cannot. If the Metamorphosians allow us to make direct contact with them, they will be able to assess the nature of our minds. Perhaps, if the Chimeras were very clever, they might be able to fake an individual consciousness akin to an Amphibian's, perhaps even a Dweller's, but nothing so innately confused as a human's. We can establish a makeshift mental contact with beings that have mastered telepathic communication, but because we cannot use that means of communication between ourselves we seem very strange and quite alien to those who can."

"I don't understand that," Danby admitted. "I don't understand how that kind of communication takes place—or, given that it does, why it seems to have such an absurdly limited range."

"The range is very narrowly limited between two individuals," I confirmed, "but whole populations in communication maintain a much larger field. A whole world in which every living thing is mind-linked to every other maintains a field that covers the entire surface, and some distance above and below it—but the void between worlds is as empty of tangible mind as it is of tangible gravity. In fact, there must be a correlation, if not a connection, between the fields that enable direct mental communication and those implicit in gravitational attraction. That's why powerful minds can exert physical force on material objects, why a creature like Speaker has no fear of leaping into bottomless pits, and presumably has something to do with the fact there is a marked Division in the gravitational field deep within the Earth." The elevator car had passed the Division while I was in mid-speech, and I had sagged slightly in response to the sudden increase in my weight, which was now coming to seem normal again.

Danby was distracted at that point by someone who came into the room, but who remained out of sight. It could not have been Clara, or she would have run to the screen. Danby turned round to speak to the newcomer. I could not make out what he said. When he turned back to the screen, though, it was to say: "Our hosts are ready to show me certain things I've asked to see. I'll talk to you again shortly, face to face."

"Of course," I said.

As soon as the connection was broken I asked Speaker to make a new one, to Clara's room.

Clara, it appeared, had not been invited to go with Danby to see whatever it was that he had asked to see. She was talking to a duplicate of Speaker—our welcoming party had evidently increased in number, as well as our rooms—but she broke off readily enough when the call came through. Speaker's twin left the room.

"I was worried about you," Clara said. "Philip was annoyed, but I was afraid." Her eyes had already strayed to my new companion, though.

"This is Mirastara," I said. "She is the Amphibian about whom you have read in my account of my earlier expedition in time."

Clara's reaction was very different from Danby's. She did not question what I said, but looked at Mirastara with a new amazement in her expression before speaking directly to her. "I am very glad to meet you," she said. "We have a great deal to thank you for. You saved George's life more than once."

The words were unintelligible to Mirastara in themselves, but she could "hear" them as they registered in my mind. Mirastara made the slightest of bows by way of reply.

"Amphibians don't speak aloud," I reminded Clara, "but you ought to be able to make contact with your mind when you meet her face-to-face. It should not take long for you to become fluent in translating her mind-speech into words."

"I look forward to that," Clara said. "Mirastara will be accompanying us on our expedition to the moon, I suppose."

"Yes," I said, "Although it might be more accurate to say that we shall be accompanying her, or that all of us will be accompanying Liamon, the Dweller."

"There is a Dweller here too?" Clara said. "That must have been disturbing news for you—but I thought we were told that the Chimeras' attempts to recruit a Dweller as their ambassador had gone awry."

"We were, and it had," I said. "I have been helping to repair the situation, although I doubt that Liamon really needed my help. My encounter with her was not as disturbing as I might have expected. She seemed to be glad to see me, despite the fact that others of her species seemed to regard ours as mere vermin. That was in their world, though—here, we are all strangers, who have more in common with one another than with our hosts. How much has Speaker's duplicate told you about our coming excursion to the moon?"

"Little in the way of detail—her primary concern seemed to be to soothe the anxieties I expressed about the dangers involved, but I confess that I am still unconvinced that they are in any position to estimate those dangers accurately, let alone the appropriate precautions to ensure our safety."

I glanced at Speaker.

"The criticism is justified," Speaker admitted. "We cannot accurately assess the dangers you might face, or protect you against them. You might be slightly more confident now, though, given that you will have Liamon to defend you." There was no trace of sarcasm in her tone, but it seemed likely that her guiding intelligence had taken slight umbrage at Liamon's attitude and advice.

"We shall be within you shortly," I said to Clara. "I'll talk to you soon.

Clara nodded in agreement.

CHAPTER SEVENTEEN

IN THE ELEVATOR

When the wall of the elevator was blank again I turned to Speaker. "Liamon said that we would need further discussion when I have been into the Metamorphosian machine" I said. "When will that happen? What sort of machine is it?"

"You may enter the machine later today, if you wish," Speaker said. "It is not far away—but you might like to see the spaceship first. The machine is a metal device with a hemispherical shell. Mirastara can tell you more about its interior, and what is likely to happen to you there, than I can."

There seemed to be no possibility, at least while we were on Earth, of finding a situation in which I could communicate privately with Mirastara. Our subvocalized thoughts could be as easily over-heard and the spoken communication between myself and my companions. That should not, I decided, be allowed to inhibit us. There was a slight awkwardness about three-way communication with Speaker because Speaker spoke aloud to me and I to her, but in the close quarters of the elevator Mirastara had no difficulty in tracking the subvocalized thoughts behind my utterances—and Speaker's too, if appearances could be trusted.

"What happened inside the machine?" I asked Mirastara.

"It asked my permission to take a sample of my blood for analysis," Mirastara said. "It also asked a number of questions about my nature and origin. Its capacity for mental communication seemed very limited, but I assume that it can also employ your kind of speech. It evidently has some small degree of autonomy, but it relayed most of my own questions to the moon by means of electromagnetic signals and had to await a reply. Its operators were very sparing in their release of information. I was granted permission to meet a Metamorphosian on the moon, but I was injured before I could take up the opportunity."

I made no immediate comment, and Speaker filled the silence by saying: "We do understand that your friend Philip and Liamon the Dweller both have their own reasons for wanting to make contact with the Metamorphosians, and that they both suspect that their own interests might eventually be opposed to ours. We do not hold that against them, although we are grateful for the fact that neither you nor Mirastara is self-seeking in this regard. We truly believe that everyone's best interests will be served by the establishment of freer communication and better understanding, and we are perfectly happy to accommodate the separate ambitions held by Philip and Liamon, in the interests of promoting communication and mutual understanding." The speech had not been made in response to any unvoiced thought of mine—but I guessed that it might have answered an unvoiced thought of Mirastara's.

"Thank you for telling me," I said, after a moment's hesitation. "Do you know, then, what Liamon's *separate ambitions* are?"

"Of course. She knows that we have followed them through every transition to date, and we will know if she changes her aims or plans again. She might well explain them to you, if you care to ask her. As you have just observed to Clara, she seems prepared to take a very different view of you now than her peers did when you were a visitor in their world. We are glad about that—we think that it will work to everyone's advantage."

I looked at Mirastara. "Do *you* know what Liamon's plan is?" I asked, silently.

"Not at present," she admitted. "We spent sufficient time together before we...before the accident...for me to form a clear impression of her ambition then—but the ambitions she had then are impossible of fulfillment now. She must have altered her objectives very considerably. I did not have sufficient contact with her while she was interrogating you to divine the new direction of her thoughts. With all due respect to our hosts, I think she may be more adept at concealment than they realize. I wonder if they know why she took such an unexpectedly keen and friendly interest in you—and whether they are willing to tell you, if so,"

Politely as it was phrased, that was almost an accusation that Speaker was concealing something from me.

"Why did Liamon treat me so very differently from the other Dwellers I have encountered?" I asked Speaker.

"Mirastara might be right about the giant's ability to screen thoughts that she considers private," Speaker promptly admitted.

"We assumed that the difference in her attitude reflected the difference in her situation. What Mirastara is implying, however, is that it might reflect her awareness of what the Dwellers did to you while they held you captive—and perhaps her knowledge, which we do not share, of why they did it."

"I've given the matter a good deal of consideration," I said. "I assume that they made me into a kind of living book in order to maximize the amount of information they could extract from me. The other physical changes might have been a side-effect, or they might have been some kind of experiment for which I made a convenient subject. Do you know which?"

The question was rather vaguely addressed, and Speaker evidently chose to infer that it had been intended for Mirastara. Mirastara waited for a few seconds, and then said: "It is difficult to be sure without knowing whether they expected you to come back."

I had never given much thought to that possibility, mainly because it had always seemed likely—at least to the Professor—that the collapse of the time-bridge had been deliberately contrived by the Dwellers. Perhaps, though, they had been just as annoyed by its collapse as the Professor. Perhaps they had had further plans for me, which extended beyond the agreement they had made with the Amphibians to keep me safe until my first return home was assured. In that case, the changes they had made to my physical and mental make-up must have been made with some further purpose in mind— a purpose that Liamon might know. Was that why she had told me that I had been foolish?

"What do you think they intended?" I asked Mirastara.

"I do not know," she said. It was difficult for me to read hidden meaning in mind-speech, but I knew that the statement had a double meaning. It meant that she was not privy to the Dwellers' machinations—but it also meant that she could not read it in Speaker's mind, or that of the collective intelligence that guided Speaker...perhaps because they were concealing the datum rather than because they too were ignorant.

"I wanted to go back," I said, remembering. "I would have gone back. I wanted to take Clara with me...." It had never occurred to me before that that desire could have been anything but my own. I had never considered the possibility that it might have be implanted, along with the other alterations that the Dwellers had made. It had still been there ten years later; I had responded to Philip Danby's appeal immediately, without any significant hesitation or consideration.

Had the Chimeras known that I would, when they inscribed my name on the Professor's notepaper?

I looked hard at Speaker, but her beautiful face was as serene as a statue's. "Mirastara may be right about our inability to penetrate Liamon's secrets," she said, as if she had been pondering that question all along. "We are unused to dealing with minds that are not part of our own society, and may lack the skills necessary to counter the kinds of concealment and deception of which Liamon is capable."

"Given that you are refraining from the use of the devices that they would normally employ for that purpose," Mirastara added.

I did not know what that meant. Speaker was quick to elaborate, if only vaguely. "What Mirastara means," she said, "is that we might have invaded your bodies to a far greater extent than we have. We have been very protective of your individuality. It is vitally important that, when we send you to the Metamorphosians, they will understand that you really are independent entities, not vehicles for tiny creatures affiliated to our collective being."

"The reason they refuse to meet you in the flesh," I said, to demonstrate that I understood, "is because they think you'll infect them with all manner of biological agents—that you'll try to absorb them into your collective consciousness, by means of some kind of bacterial infection."

"We would never do that deliberately to an intelligent being," Speaker assured me, "but it does seem likely that the Metamorphosians are afraid of some such action."

I realized that the word *deliberately* might cover a multitude of sins. Speaker had already told me that many of the biosphere's "units" were as independent of the collective will as individual cells in a human body. Human beings would not, under normal circumstances, *deliberately* inflict their infections upon their fellow men— but the epidemic of Spanish influenza that had broken out in the wake of the war had killed more people than shellfire and bullets.

"Your Antipodean ancestors were by no means scrupulous in that regard," I observed. "Your ancestors could not have become the sole manifestation of Earthly life by strict observance of the principle of informed consent. Although countless biological entities might have died between then and now, there's a sense in which the development of your collective intelligence must have been continuous. You cannot, in consequence, deny responsibility for the usurpation of the individuality of the species you incorporated into your Chimerical chaos."

"We cannot deny that," Speaker agreed. "Nevertheless, I still assure you that we would not forcibly absorb another intelligent species *now*. Neither you nor the Metamorphosians have anything to fear from us in that respect—and you need not strive to hide your incredulity from us, because we understand that you will find it very difficult to believe that assurance until we have demonstrated our good faith. That is what we are trying to do in mounting this expedition."

"Suppose," I said, quietly, "that it doesn't work. What happens if I, or Philip, or Liamon can't be persuaded—let alone the Metamorphosians themselves?"

"That would depend on what your incredulity would lead you to do," Speaker replied, blandly. "Were you to misrepresent us—accidentally or mistakenly, of course—to the Metamorphosians, the worst possibility is that they might attempt to destroy us. In that case, we should be forced to defend ourselves."

"The Metamorphosians are doubtless equally intent on their own defense," I said. "Human beings have an item of proverbial wisdom which states that the best means of defense is attack—its consequences have, alas, often been direly unfortunate."

"We have nothing akin to your proverbial wisdom, and are in no danger of falling prey to any such individualist illusion," Speaker told me. "Alas, we cannot speak for the Metamorphosians."

"No," I said, feeling a slight sinking sensation that was not due to the recent reversion of gravity to its usual level of exaction. "It seems that will be our job."

"This accusation the Metamorphosians have made regarding the abduction of some of their number is disturbing," Mirastara put in. "If the Chimeras are not responsible, some other agency must be. That implies that there must be more parties now active in the system than those of which the Metamorphosians are aware."

"We agree," Speaker put in. For once, she did not speak aloud, but she used a form of mind-speech that seemed clearer to me than Mirastara's, because it was already framed in English. "The Metamorphosians did inform us that they were not the first visitors from elsewhere to arrive in the solar system, but we do not know whether they also have their suspicions regarding the possible involvement of the others in the disappearance of their fellows—or, if not, why they have discounted that possibility. It is also possible that the Metamorphosians were followed here—but we have had no contact with any other extraterrestrial life-forms."

"What is the name *Metamorphosian* supposed to imply?" I asked. "Is the analogy with tadpoles that turn into frogs as they mature, or are we talking about shape-shifting of a more elaborate sort?"

"We would be very interested to find out exactly what the word's implications are," Speaker said. "It is the best improvisation we could make in your language for a term they communicated to us. We have formulated hypotheses, but we are only familiar with a single evolutionary sequence, and it is difficult to estimate what alternative courses Earthly evolution might have taken. Given that your knowledge of genetics is so vague as to be almost non-existent, it is almost impossible to explain the problem in terms that you can understand, but we will try if you wish."

"Try," I said. "I shall do my best to follow the argument."

CHAPTER EIGHTEEN

EVOLUTION

"There are two aspects to genetic inheritance," Speaker said, obligingly, now speaking aloud again and apparently experiencing some difficulty in choosing her words. "On the one hand, there is a set of recipes for making most of the raw materials that living bodies require, the remainder being ingested as food. A human body requires about forty thousand different proteins, almost all of which are exactly the same proteins required by the other individual species that coexisted with humans a million years ago—or, for that matter, those required by the Amphibians and the Dwellers half a million years later. On the other hand, there is a set of plans—the analogy of *architect's blueprints* might be helpful—for assembling those materials into a particular bodily structure. Those instructions ensure that the raw materials provided by the proteins will build a Dweller rather than a human, or a human rather than an insect. In individuated species, both of these functions are integrated into a single system. The recipes for manufacturing proteins and the blueprints for building bodily structures were both encoded in the specific chromosomal structures typical of individual species, and are essentially inseparable from one another."

"But that must have changed after my era," I said. "There was some kind of evolutionary leap that allowed the two to be separated, so that an independent system arose capable of building more-or-less any kind of body from a set of raw materials: a chimera-building system."

"In essence, yes," Speaker said. "It was a slow ascent rather than a leap, because some individual species began to cultivate a greater elasticity of form—deliberately in the case of intelligent species like the ancestors of the Dwellers and the designers of the Amphibians, naturally in other cases. It may be significant, in trying to imagine what the Metamorphosians might be, that the most primitive examples of natural variation include metamorphic amphibians. Frogs, for instance, had far larger genomes than humans, although they were much more primitive, because they engaged different sets of genes in different environmental conditions in order to cope with freezing, drought and other extreme but haphazard conditions."

"Is that how the Antipodeans originally evolved?" I said. "They became much more versatile in their production of bodily forms—so much so, in fact, that they became colonies of differently-formed organisms."

"In essence, yes," Speaker said again.

"Except that it leaves out an important aspect of the story," Mirastara put in.

Speaker was quick to take up the argument again: "It was not our intention to conceal anything," she said, her voice signaling slight annoyance. "Our ancestors were also genetic predators. Individual animal species use others as sources of raw materials—even exceptional human individuals who refrain from eating meat remain dependent on vegetable nourishment, and I believe that you, George, also eat fish, just as Mirastara does. You both feel entitled to find the Dwellers horrible because they eat other animals—including sentient animals—sometimes without taking the trouble to kill them in advance, but there is little enough difference between their habits and yours. Our ancestors also used other species for nourishment, and were authentically omnivorous in that respect—but they did not break down their nourishment in quite the same way. In the course of freeing themselves by slow degrees from the tyranny of chromosomal structure they became capable of adapting the genes of organisms on which they fed into their own make-up.

"By this means, our ancestors were soon able to build up a comprehensive stock of all available recipes for protein manufacture. Building a comprehensive repertoire of architectural blueprints was a more elaborate and complex process, but they eventually succeeded in doing that too. They obtained a perfect mastery of genetic chimerization, thus entitling us to the name you improvised for us."

"In effect," I said, "you absorbed the potentials of all individuated species into a single versatile species...and you did it by consuming them. That was the crux of the war between the Dwellers and the Antipodeans. It was a war of extermination between two kinds of life that could not coexist."

"No," Speaker replied, with an altogether uncharacteristic vehemence. "Had the Dwellers had their way, they would certainly have exterminated our kind of life—but our aim was not to exterminate them. Quite the opposite, in fact. Our aim was to preserve and protect their genetic heritage."

"By consuming and usurping it," I said. "From their point of view, that meant extinction and annihilation. You must see that."

"We understand how they misconstrued the logic of evolution, once natural selection became obsolete," Speaker said. "But it was a misconstruction nevertheless. Perhaps our ancestors were a little overzealous in their omnivorousness, but I repeat what I said to you earlier—that *we*, as presently constituted, would not absorb a species capable of giving consent without receiving that consent. In any case, our ancestors were not wrong to consider themselves as pioneers of a higher and better kind of being, on whom future progress would inevitably depend, and to whom the Earth's biosphere would inevitably belong."

"But the Metamorphosians followed a different evolutionary course," I said. "I can't quite figure out, though, how they're so very different from you. Given what you've just explained, I would have thought that Metamorphosian would be just as apt a description of your kind as *Chimera*."

"The Chimeras are masters of shape-*making*, not shape-*shifting*," Mirastara put in. "They can make subsidiary bodies in any shape they can imagine, but they do not make individual units that are versatile. Why should they, when they can make specific tools for any conceivable purpose? They are not like frogs at all."

"We can be," Speaker said. "We can and do make versatile forms, when occasion requires it."

"And how often do occasions require it, here on Earth?" Mirastara asked.

Speaker gave way gracefully. "That is a fair point," she said. "Here on Earth, conditions are now so stable and well-controlled that they almost never require it. When we make versatile suborganisms, it is usually because they must perform their functions at a distance from the planet, in much more turbulent circumstances."

"If your space-faring units are uncommonly versatile," I said, "is it not possible that they are more versatile than you realize—and might therefore, have been responsible for whatever happened to the missing Metamorphosians?"

"It is *conceivable*," Speaker said, apparently selecting the words with great care, "but unlikely in the extreme."

"But the Metamorphosians don't know that," I said, "and they have every reason to be anxious about your ability and avidity for genetic predation, no matter how polite you claim to be, nowadays."

"We do not want to become embroiled in any kind of conflict with the Metamorphosians," Speaker said. "We shall do everything in our power to avoid that. All we desire is to be left in peace. We have no ambition to extend beyond the limits of the Earth, even though we have found it convenient to make space-faring units in order to exploit extraterrestrial sources of carbon. We pose no danger whatsoever to any extraterrestrial species."

"I accept that as the truth," Mirastara said, in a conspicuously soothing tone, "and I am more than willing to help you persuade the Metamorphosians that it is true."

"We have strayed somewhat from the original question," I pointed out. "We were attempting to produce a hypothesis as to what alternative evolutionary course the Metamorphosians might have followed."

"The key may lie in the distinction I made a short while ago between masters of shape-*making* and masters of shape-*shifting*," Mirastara said. "Earth's Age of Individuation came to an end not long after the defeat and annihilation of the Dwellers—and, I presume, my own kind. The Antipodeans were not individuals, even in the sense that a hive of social insects is an individual of sorts. You asked me once whether the Antipodeans you saw on the Dwellers' display-screens were large insects or merely vehicles operated by smaller creatures within them, and I suggested that they might be both. I made that suggestion because I was aware of a confusion in the definition of my own kind: were we many, or one...or both. The Dwellers, unquestionably, were many, in spite of the fact that they used the same kind of mind-speech that we did. They had not allowed that overlapping of minds to create a single collective consciousness in which they were all glad to share—quite the opposite, in fact; they remained riven by competition and conflict, and they used mind-speech as a further instrument of competition and conflict.

"The Antipodeans, I suspect, were more like us than the Dwellers: while they evolved into genetic predators they allowed their minds to form a collective hyperconsciousness. This meant that when their subsidiary individuals began to dissociate into many kinds of component parts, those parts were more closely affiliated to the collective consciousness than the individual consciousness of their particular originator. The further that pattern of evolution extended, the more powerful the collective consciousness became. I don't doubt that some residues of individual consciousness remain in bodies capable of containing it—like yours, Speaker—thus licensing your use of the plural pronoun, but you are much further along the road to unity than my own species was.

"Suppose, though, that the Antipodeans had been more like the Dwellers than us. Suppose that they had clung on to mental individuality even as they cultivated physical ubiquity. Suppose that instead of a single collective intelligence with the knowledge and the power to design and make any imaginable subsidiary individual, there had evolved a population of distinct intelligences, each one of which retained the knowledge and the power to redesign and remake *itself* in any conceivable image."

I was impressed by the argument, but Speaker seemed more skeptical. "The Dwellers' competitiveness was an anachronism," she opined. "We can be all things *simultaneously*, and that is infinitely preferable to a condition in which each individual in a population could only be one thing at a time. In any conflict, creatures of our kind would be sure to win."

"Once genetic predation became possible, the dominion of natural selection came swiftly to an end," Mirastara observed, pensively. "Perhaps, if the Metamorphosians' ancestors had had your ancestors to contend with, yours would have won. Once a particular set of genetic predators is established, though, it must obtain a monopoly that can no longer be disputed—not locally, at least. Perhaps the Metamorphosians never faced the kind of competition that creatures of your kind might have provided...until now."

"Perhaps they see the logic of the situation as clearly as you do," I put in, "and that's why they're so anxious about the possibility of competition—of becoming victims of genetic predation themselves—that they do not dare to meet you face-to-face."

"Perhaps it is," Speaker agreed, dolefully. She had reverted to mind-speech, and it seemed to be easier for her to add a non-verbal component to her communication when using than means of communication than it was when she spoke aloud. "However, we must hope that you are wrong."

"Why?" I asked.

"If they are so fearful that they cannot tolerate the idea that beings like us exist," Speaker said, "they might well try to destroy us. If the Metamorphosians were to attack us, they would probably be able to do so with such awful effect that Earthly life's evolutionary story might have to begin again from the very beginning, with bacteria adapted to life in extreme circumstances. On the other hand, they do seem to be willing to initiate a diplomatic process. If we *can* persuade the Metamorphosians that we pose no danger to them, we might also persuade them that there would be a great deal of benefit to be gained by an alliance of our species, and that both kinds of life have much to gain from peaceful and productive coexistence. That is what we all want, is it not? Your species too might have much to gain from some such alliance."

"Our species are extinct," Mirastara said, quietly. "Liamon and I thought at one time that there might be a chance of saving ours from that fate, using the time-bridge as an escape route, but it is closed now. Your offer to recreate my species by cloning cells from my body is a generous one, but it would not be the same species. My kind is dead and gone, and so is Liamon's. You were right to think that George's presence might console me, a little—but it does not alter the fundamental fact. While I still live, though, I am bound to maintain my allegiance to a larger moral community, and to exert my personal force in the service of what I believe to be right. I will do what I can for Earthly life in general, and for all life—and I agree with you that it would be best for all Earthly life, and all extraterrestrial life too, if conflict could be avoided and peaceful coexistence established. You have my wholehearted support."

I was not surprised by this declaration, because I knew already what a highly moral species the Amphibians were, and that their deployment of mental force was dependent on moral conviction. Whether that morality was objective or subjective, there was no doubting its authority over her thinking. I could almost wish that my own moral convictions had as powerful a grip on my own will.

"Liamon might not feel the same way," I observed

"We are confident that she will act on the same principle, if and when a crisis point is reached," Speaker opined. "We are equally confident of you, George. Peaceful coexistence is the preferable alternative, for everyone."

"Did you offer Liamon what you've offered Mirastara?" I guessed. "The recreation of her society by cloning, and use of some subterranean enclave in which they might live as they please."

"We would be willing to do that, if it were a price asked of us," Speaker said, scrupulously.

"But it's not what Liamon actually wants—any more than it's what Mirastara actually wants?" I said.

"That is correct, at present," Speaker confirmed.

"What *does* she want?" I asked.

"She does not know, any more than you do," Speaker replied, bluntly. "None of you knows, as yet, what it might be feasible to want. When you do know, we will all be in a position to make plans. To begin with, we must all make what efforts we can to discover what the limits of feasibility might be."

With that, the elevator finally came to a halt. A narrow crack in its side broadened into a doorway, and I stood aside reflexively to allow my companion to precede me.

Speaker led the way.

CHAPTER NINETEEN

THE METAMORPHOSIAN MACHINE

The second bed had presumably been removed from my room to Philip's, but it had been replaced by another, designed to suit Mirastara's preferences. There was no coverlet, and the pallet was a good deal firmer to the touch. Speaker accompanied us to the threshold but then left us to our own devices. There were several jugs of liquid set out on the table, including a pitcher of water, but we had not had the chance to make much of a meal before Clara came in, rapidly followed by Danby. They studied Mirastara briefly, while she studied them, but they offered her no formal greeting.

"We asked to see the spaceship in which the Chimeras propose to transport us to the moon," Danby said. "They showed us images of it on the screen in my room, and gave us an elaborate account of its accommodations. It seems to me to be a very fragile vessel, and I cannot pretend to understand its propulsion system. I've begged Clara to stay behind, but she won't hear of it. Perhaps you can persuade her."

"It might be better if you stayed behind, Philip," I said, mischievously. "You're better equipped than Clara to make a full report to your father if some mishap does occur during the flight to the moon." I glanced at Clara, though, and added: "There's no actual need for either of you to come with me, and it might be better if neither of you took the risk."

"It's an opportunity I don't intend to miss," Clara said.

"There's no question of my staying behind," Danby stated, predictably.

"Then I'll be delighted to have the pleasure of your company," I said. "Have you also seen images of Liamon, the Dweller, on your screens?"

"Yes," Clara replied. "I dare say that we shan't feel the full effect of her giant stature until we see her in the flesh, but I'm not afraid. The voice that spoke to us from the screen says that she will be in more danger from the effects of the ascent than anyone else, because of the strain put on her heart by the increase in her effective weight."

"I could understand that if the vessel were to be fired from some kind of gun," Danby said, "or even if it were blasted away from the surface by a rocket, but the account we were given suggested that we would simply be carried to the moon by will-power."

I looked at Mirastara. "Can you explain it?" I asked, silently.

"Perhaps," she answered. "Not immediately, though—your companions will require some time to learn to interpret my mind-speech, and I am not entirely sure that I shall be able to talk to all three of you at once when they do."

Danby and Clara obviously felt some effect of her mental effort, but neither of them understood what was happening.

"Mirastara cannot speak clearly into your minds as yet," I explained. "You will need to practice, one at a time. Even then, it will be difficult for us all to hold a conversation—I doubt that I can learn to talk to you by means of mind-speech, or you to me."

"If she understands your thoughts when they are couched in English," Danby said, "why can she not simply speak it, as we do?"

"She doesn't have the appropriate vocal apparatus," I said. Apparently, he had forgotten the observations made in the narrative of my first expedition regarding the Amphibians' distaste for speech.

"I might be able to improvise, with the Chimeras' aid," Mirastara said. "I am the one alone here, who must learn to live as others live if I am to live at all." There was a plaintive note in her silent voice, but she seemed firm enough in her intent.

"You're not alone," I told her. "You can employ mind-speech with the Chimeras and with Liamon as well as with me. Danby and Clara are the exceptions, and they will learn quickly enough, given the opportunity."

The door opened again then, and Speaker came in. "The Metamorphosians have indicated that they are impatient to inspect you by means of their machine, George," she said. "You do not have to consent, if you need more time to discuss matters among yourselves, or require more information from us."

I hesitated, but Danby did not. "I'm enthusiastic to see this marvelous machine myself," he said.

"It is on the surface, within the shade of the tree," Speaker said. "It can move horizontally, but it refuses to enter any enclosed space, or concede entry to any of our kind. You might find its precautionary measures uncomfortable, George—and you must go in alone. The machine will not tolerate any accompaniment."

"That's not acceptable," Danby said, quickly.

"It's kind of you to worry about me, Philip." I said to him, mildly, "but I dare say that I'll be quite safe—and there's no need for us both to be uncomfortable." I was more anxious about Mirastara, though, and I turned to face her. "I promised that I would not leave you while you need me," I reminded her.

"I will come to the surface with you," she said. "I shall be nearby."

"You will not be able to eavesdrop on his conversation," Speaker said, silently. "The machine has the means to screen its privacy—but we shall know what has transpired, of course, as soon as George comes out again."

"What's going on?" Danby wanted to know, having caught on to the fact that a conversation was taking place to which he was not party.

"I'm sorry, Philip," I said. "It appears that the invitation is for me alone, for the time being. Perhaps the machine will be interested to talk to you afterwards, once it knows that you are the Professor's son. If you and Clara will come up to the surface with me, though, my brief absence will give you a chance to become better acquainted with Mirastara, and perhaps to learn to interpret her mind-speech."

"We'll do that," Clara was quick to put in, putting a hand on Danby's arm to restrain an anticipated objection.

In fact, Danby seemed to have taken due note of what I had said about the possibility of the machine requesting a private conversation with him once it discovered that he was the son of the inventor who had devised the human element of the time machine. He seemed quite confident of that, and was willing to be patient—but he did not push Clara's hand away. "Of course," he said.

"Don't you need to rest first, George?" Clara asked.

"I slept for a while during my absence," I said, blandly. In spite of the unnaturalness of my sleep and Liamon's interference in my dreams, I did not feel physically or mentally tired. The body that the Dwellers had remade for me was coming into its own in my present circumstances, to a greater extent than it had ever had the opportunity to do in Oxford.

We walked back to the surface through corridors that soon became as crowded as those we had passed through on first entering the Great Tree. As before, the pedestrian traffic moved with amazing smoothness; the other passers-by made allowances for our relative clumsiness, without paying any particular attention to us.

I was less astonished now by the sheer multiplicity of chimerical forms, and began to wonder whether all that hectic confusion was really necessary, in terms of the variant occupations of the laborers we encountered, or whether there was some expression of individuality in the way they formed themselves. Perhaps, I thought, each one strove to be different from the rest, within the limits imposed by their various functions. I decided that must be the case, although "individuality" was presumably not the right term for what it was they were endeavoring to express.

The lower part of the vast tree's crown was as astonishing at the second glance as it had been at the first, and I was incapable of any such considered reaction when I looked up into it, measuring the hectic activity half-masked by its foliage. The highways threading their various ways through the Chimeras' "city" were as busy as ever, and the Metamorphosians' machine was some distance away from the bole, but we made our way there without any interruption.

The hemispherical machine appeared to be resting flat on the ground, but I knew that it must have some kind of retractable legs, like the flying-machine that had brought us from the exit-point of the time-bridge. After glancing at my various companions, I approached the machine alone. I wondered whether to announce myself, but it obviously had sensors of some kind that could identify me. As I approached, an invisible slit in the surface broadened out to provide an opening, into which I stepped after a mere moment's hesitation. I came into a metal-lined space not much larger than my upright body.

The entrance closed behind me, leaving me in total darkness. I moved my hands reflexively, but there was not enough space to permit me to lift my arms, and I had to be content to stand motionless. I felt a strange prickling sensation in my skin—perhaps in the extra layer that now overlaid my true skin. There was a peculiar metallic odor in the air, but the discomfort about which Speaker had warned me was by no means extreme—indeed, the physical sensations were less discomfiting than the claustrophobic effect of being in such a narrow space. After three or four minutes, though, I heard a slight sound. When I moved my hand again I found that the wall in front of me had opened or retreated.

"I need light," I said, although I had no idea whether the machine could understand the spoken words or he thought behind them.

After a few seconds pause, a dim illumination showed me that there was now a narrow corridor ahead of me. I stepped forward, and only required four strides to carry me to its furthest extreme. I halted in front of another blank wall, expecting to open up, but it did not. Instead, a voice emanated from a panel in the wall that was set at the same height as my head.

"Can you understand these words?" the voice said.

The pronunciation was slightly inaccurate, by the standards of BBC English, but I had no problem understanding them.

"Yes," I said. "You seem to have learned the language very well, given that you had little more than the Professor's dictionary to aid you."

"There is much that we do not understand," the voice stated, after a slight pause.

"I shall be pleased to give you what help I can," I told it.

There was a much longer pause then, presumably because some elaborate communication was taking place between the machine and its masters on the moon.

"You believe yourself to be a human being," the machine said, "who has travelled forward in time by approximately one million years."

"I do," I replied. "Do you doubt that my belief is accurate?"

"Yes," the machine said, bluntly, after the requisite pause, "but you are a well-made artifact, if that is what you are."

"You think that I'm some kind of trick cooked up by the Chimeras—so cleverly devised that I have no suspicion of my true nature?"

"Yes." the machine repeated—immediately, this time. Mere reiteration was obviously within the scope of its autonomous responses.

"But I have traveled in time before," I told it. "I visited a world 500,000 years ahead of my own before I came to this one."

"That is what you appear to remember," the machine agreed, after an interval. "There are other creatures here, which believe that they too are time-travelers from that later era."

"But you think that it's all artifice—a comedy devised to deceive you?"

This time the machine varied its routine. "It is a possibility that must be considered," it said, eventually. "The possibility of transmission through time cannot be denied, and nor can the possibility of subjecting such transmission to a degree of technical control—but if the biosphere of your world has evolved creatures capable of deploying will-power in that fashion, that may only serve to make them more dangerous."

"More dangerous than what?" I asked.

"More dangerous than chimerical genetic systems usually are." The preliminary pause made the answer seem a trifle churlish, but it was not uninformative. It confirmed that the Metamorphosians had experience of other worlds akin to the contemporary Earth.

"How dangerous is that?" I asked. "Why should it be dangerous at all?"

The double question seemed to confuse it somewhat. There was another unusually long interval before it replied: "The end-point of that kind of evolutionary sequence is Simplicity."

I could tell by the emphasis it put on the last word that it was meant to imply something more grandiose than mere simplicity, so I immediately asked for further clarification.

"When you come to the moon," the machine said, "that will be explained. There are two others of your kind."

"Yes," I said. "Philip Danby is the son of the scientist who built the time-machine—or, at least, the terminal of the time-machine located in our era."

"The third, Clara, is a female of your sexually-differentiated species."

"Yes." I recalled that one of the first things Speaker had said was that it would be interesting to study human sexual differentiation, and wondered whether the machine's comment implied that the Metamorphosians, like the Chimeras, no longer had any use for sexual reproduction.

"They must come to the moon," the machine said. "The Dweller and the Amphibian must come too. Can you bring further members of your species out of the past?"

"I can see no reason why not," I stated, truthfully.

"We were told that no other Dwellers or Amphibians could be brought."

"There was an accident, apparently," I said. "It broke the bridge through time, preventing Liamon and Mirastara from going back to their own time when the time allotted to their expedition expired. The Chimeras have, in consequence, shown much greater urgency in their dealings with us, although I have no reason to suspect that any such accident will cut us off in like fashion when our time here elapses."

There was another long pause before the machine said: "Accidents do happen." The cliché sounded all the more deadly by virtue of the evident skepticism of the utterance, and the implication that I ought not to be confident of my own safe return. For a moment, I almost doubted that I was who I was, and wondered whether my past might be an artifact of implanted memory—but I rejected the idea immediately. It was not the kind of thought that a sane man ought to entertain.

"My hosts are very anxious about your intentions," I said, figuring that I could not be giving away any secrets. "They are insistent that they know nothing about the hostile act of which you have accused them. Their only desire is to establish peaceful relations with the Metamorphosians."

The machine had not queried my earlier use of the term "Chimeras" but the pause after I had used the term "Metamorphosians" seemed very long indeed, almost as if they had had to go back to the dictionary to look it up—as I would have been forced to do.

"There is nothing my makers would like better than to live in peace," the machine stated, eventually, "but we do not live in the kind of universe that makes peaceful coexistence easy. Life is change and competition; stability is an illusion."

"In my own era," I said, quietly, "that certainly seemed to be true. Even then, though, some among us looked forward to a day when things might be different, and better. When I visited the world of the Dwellers, I thought at first that they might be the last descendants of humankind, and that the Amphibians might indicate the possibility of a better way of being to come. I did not know until much later about the Dwellers' war with the Antipodeans—but the descendants of the Antipodeans seem to believe that they have attained a new and potentially-everlasting Golden Age in the affairs of life on Earth. Are they wrong?"

"Quite wrong," the machine retorted, bluntly. "You must come to the moon, where you can be examined more closely. We need to make certain whether or not you are what you appear to be."

"And if we are," I said, "what then?"

"You will not be harmed," the machine told me, ignoring the question and launching into a speech instead. "There may be some discomfort, but you will not be harmed. You need have no fear of my makers, no matter what you are, and no matter what the intentions of your hosts may be. My makers have dealt with thousands of species on hundreds of worlds. We are respectful of all life, except for Simplicity. We do not hold it against your hosts that they do not understand how matters stand in the greater universe. If you are what you say you are, we shall educate you, in order that you may educate them. It is possible that they might yet find an alternative course of future evolution, once they are warned. We cannot discount the possibility. Our people must be returned to us safely, just as we shall return you safely. We understand why they might have been taken, and will take no reprisals, provided they are returned unharmed, carrying no infection of any sort. The lunar vessel will be given accommodation, and no damage will be done to it, provided that there is no attempt at contamination. The five emissaries will be treated with all possible courtesy, no matter what they might be revealed to be. There will be no hostile action on our part while negotiations are in progress, nor afterwards, unless further hostile actions are directed against us. There might be a mutually satisfactory solution to our difficulties, if we can discover it."

Having finished this prepared discourse, the machine—or, rather, its controllers—seemed satisfied that the business of the moment was concluded, but I did not turn away.

"I am not in a position to be certain," I said, "but I believe my hosts when they say that they have not directed any hostile action against you, and have not kidnapped any of your people. You must consider the possibility that any such actions that have been carried out were accomplished by a third party—and that any future hostilities might emanate from the same source."

"The possibility is being explored," the machine replied, without any pause for further instruction.

"Good," I said. "In that case, I look forward to meeting your makers on the moon. May I ask one more question?"

"Yes," the machine said.

"Will I find them to be nearer to my size than that of a Dweller?"

"Yes. Giantism is an inefficient, and hence inappropriate, expression of will-power. The journey will put a severe strain on the Dweller, although you will endure it easily enough. If it is true that she has an innate death-wish, the Dweller might not survive the journey—but that would be no fault of ours. We shall do everything in our power to keep her safe if she does reach the moon safely. You must go now."

"Thank you," I said. "Shall I send in one of my companions?"

"No. There will be no further contact until you reach the moon."

I obeyed the instruction I had been given, backing up along the corridor because it might have been difficult to turn round.

CHAPTER TWENTY

THE POWER OF THE MIND

I was still moving backwards when the portal opened behind me and the corridor was plunged into darkness again; the space was sealed before I stepped out into the half-light of the tree's shade.

"Have you a message for us?" Speaker was quick to ask.

"Yes," I said, infected with something of the machine's bluntness. "We can go ahead with all our preparations. All might yet be well, if we can only convince the Metamorphosians that we are what we believe ourselves to be. I shall need to speak to Liamon, though."

"She will arrive on the surface in a matter of hours," Speaker assured me. "The spaceship will be ready for departure tomorrow. The journey will take a few days more."

"Is it my turn now?" Danby asked. He had already moved to stand in front of the sealed slit, expecting it to open for him.

"No," I said. "They didn't even ask to take a sample of my blood, as they did of Mirastara, They seem to be impatient to meet us face-to-face on their own ground. They've promised not to do us any harm—but the machine did take the trouble to observe that accidents do happen." I reported the speech the machine had made, as exactly as I could, while the machine itself remained hermetically sealed and stubbornly gnomic.

Instead of taking us back into the bole of the tree when I had finished, Speaker asked me if I would like to see the ship that was being prepared for the journey. I glanced at Danby and Clara, who had already seen images of it on the screens in their rooms.

Danby merely shrugged his shoulders.

"We might benefit from a practice run, to test our resilience to heights," Clara said, looking upwards, indicatively. I inferred that the ship was located at the top of the tree's tall crown.

"Will we have to travel in one of the vehicles that brought us from the time-bridge?" I asked, dubiously, "or is there some kind of elevator-shaft inside the trunk?"

"There is an elevator," Speaker replied, "but there is a better alternative. Can you ride?"

The image of a winged horse came into my mind, and I hesitated; I was not sure of my ability to match Bellerophon, although I could ride an ordinary horse well enough.

"We need only ride as far as the edge of the crown," Speaker was quick to say.

"What about Mirastara?" I asked

"Mirastara will have no difficulty," Speaker assured me, confidently.

"I have not seen the ship either," Mirastara put in. "I sense that you are anxious about Liamon's ability to endure the lift-off, and it might be as well if I had a better impression to communicate to her."

I glanced at Danby and Clara. Clara nodded, and Danby immediately did likewise. "Then we'll ride," I said.

While we waited for the mounts assigned to carry us to the canopy's edge, Danby drew me aside.

"Did you tell the Metamorphosians that I am the son of the man who devised the time machine?" he asked. I had not included that part of the conversation while relaying the formal message.

"Yes I did," I said. "They don't believe that we really are time-travelers, and strongly suspect that we're artifacts made by the Chimeras for deceptive purposes. They admitted that they couldn't deny the possibility of obtaining technical control of time-displacement, but they don't seem to have encountered the trick before, even though they spoke—perhaps with boastful exaggeration—of having visited thousands of other species."

"In which case," Danby said, "they might consider the secret very valuable—provided that they can be persuaded of its reality."

"I doubt that you'll be able to contrive any sort of profitable trade," I warned him. "They undoubtedly have means of reading any secrets you might have directly from your mind, if they care to employ them."

"They'll need more than the secrets in my mind if they want to make it work," Danby said. "They'll need a line of communication to my father, which only I can provide."

"The Chimeras already have the secret," I pointed out.

"Do they?" Danby countered. "They have the greater part of it, no doubt, else they wouldn't have be able to establish a link to the Dwellers. Still, they have obviously had considerable difficulty in establishing time-bridges, and they too might be very interested to know what the Professor knows."

The difficulty might not lie in what they don't know," I reminded him, "but in the circumstances of its application. There seem to be inherent weak spots or touching-points in the time-stream, which permit time-bridges to be built—but if such bridges are invariably unstable, time-travel may be an inherently awkward and very unreliable business. Your father's first bridgehead didn't remain open for very long, although the room in which it was located suffered no collapse, and the second might yet prove to be no different."

"The first remained open while three people went into the world of the Dwellers and one came back," Danby said. "Two, if you count Templeton's brief return. Had we known how little time we had, we might have been able to do more to secure it."

I doubted that. In fact, I doubted that the Professor knew anything significant that the Chimeras did not know—and perhaps less, given that the Chimeras had the Dwellers' knowledge as well as the results of their own experimentation to draw upon.

You do realize, Philip," I said to him, "that you can't possibly change what is, from our present viewpoint in time, history. The past may not be completely fixed, given that I came back from the future so profoundly changed, but this world exists—and because it exists, we may be certain that nothing can ever have changed that might have prevented or altered its existence."

"Even if that is true," Danby said, echoing an idea that had also occurred to me, "we don't know what happened after our departure, or as a result of it. It may be that our mission and our destiny is to *complete* history by carrying back in time the causes that will generate this world."

"If *that*'s true," I told him, "we may be certain of one thing. Whatever we do won't work to the ultimate benefit of humankind, but to the ultimate benefit of our hosts, the Chimeras."

"I know that," he retorted. "Which means, does it not, that it's up to us to ensure that humankind—or we few representatives of it, at least—can establish a relationship with our hosts, or someone else in this future, that will work to our benefit as well as theirs?"

"Liamon must thinking along the same lines," I said.

"Of course. There might be a useful alliance to be made there, as well."

Giantism, I had been told by more than one informant, was an inefficient, and hence inappropriate, expression of will-power—a costly kind of vanity. I doubted that it was the only inappropriate expression that had ever been manifest—but all I said to Danby was: "You must be careful, Philip, not to overplay your hand."

"Make sure you follow your own advice, George," was all he said in reply to that.

Our mounts had arrived. They looked like thoroughbred horses, with very few chimerical details added merely for show. I had been half-expecting centaurs or dragons, and was curiously relieved to discover that the Chimeras could be modest in their inventions. There were four—Speaker evidently intended to make use of her wings even for the horizontal element of the journey.

"I will ride with George, if that is acceptable," Mirastara said. "It will weigh the horse down, but should not overburden it, or slow it down too much."

"Are you sure?" I asked. "We would be in very close proximity."

"We have been in close proximity before," she replied. "I know that you were hurt by my instinctive reaction then, but I am not a slave to my instincts—how can I be, when I have been so brutally cut off from their source? Contact will not hurt me, and might help me in the longer term."

I accepted readily enough, so Mirastara and I got up on to the same horse. She straddled its rump, positioning herself behind me, and then wrapped her arms around my waist. I sensed that she was not untroubled by the contact, but she seemed very determined, and I believed her when she said that there was a purpose in what she was doing. With no other bonds of relationship left to her but the one that bound her to me, she was anxious to make more of it than it presently was.

Clara was an accomplished horsewoman, and Danby had been a keen huntsman in his youth, so they were both more skilled than I was, but the Amphibian's presence was a great asset to me, for she immediately established a mental communion with our mount, which obviated the need for me to instruct it by means of the bridle and bit. We set off at a gallop as soon as Speaker took flight, leading the way for our companions. It was a hectic ride, but the fact that Mirastara's arms were wound tightly around me distracted me from other considerations.

"How are you?" I asked her. "Events have moved so quickly, in spite of the slowness of that wretched elevator's ascent, that you have had little time to collect yourself."

"That may be a mercy," she replied. "The sleep that the Chimeras maintained once my body had recovered from its initial injuries has had a healing effect, as they intended, but soothing the sickness that flooded my mind when I first realized that I was alone could not fill the void in my soul where my sisters ought to be. You will forgive me, I hope, when I say that you can never hope to fill that gap, or make it seem less than it is."

"The Chimeras can make duplicates of your kind, though," I said, "just as they have made near-humans and horses." I could not help adding the private thought that if they could do that, perhaps they could make duplicates which did not know that they were duplicates, and thought themselves originals hauled out of time by magical means.

"It would not be the same," she said. "If I were to decide to live, it might offer a way of life—but it would not be the same. If I decide to live, it will be best to find a new way of being. If you can bear to live alone, perhaps I can bear it too. Time will tell."

"There must be ways of being about which we know nothing, as yet," I observed. "We might learn a great deal from the Metamorphosians."

"We might," she agreed. "It might be unwise to hope for too much, though. Liamon is hoping for too much, I think."

"The machine did suggest, as you inferred, that she might not survive the journey," I told her. "That is unlikely to deter her from the attempt, though."

"Every physical form has its inherent weaknesses," Mirastara said, "including mine. The will-power that lifts the ship will protect her as best it can."

"Danby isn't the only one who doesn't understand how that can work," I confessed. "I don't understand it myself, even though I witnessed your use of mind-force half a million years ago. You told me then that you could deflect an arrow in flight, provided that you could focus your mind—but that's a far cry from lifting a spaceship from the Earth's surface and steering it to the moon."

"What I can do alone is trivial by comparison with what my people could do when acting in concert," Mirastara told me. "Imagine what the Chimeras might do, given that they have every intelligence in the world to draw upon—intelligence that is far more widely distributed than it was in my day, let alone yours."

"Will the business of the world stop, then, while every mind therein concentrates on the ship?"

"If necessary, it could and would," she replied. "I doubt that it will be necessary, but you can be sure that whatever power is needed will be provided. The Chimeras need this meeting to open the door to a more prolific and productive exchange of information—as do the Metamorphosians, in all probability."

"I still don't understand how will-power can work such miracles at all. It's not so difficult to believe that you can exert compulsive force on other living creatures, given that they have minds to which you can speak, but deflecting arrows and driving spaceships seem to me to belong to a different order of accomplishment."

"Perhaps," she said. "I have no doubt that the spaceship will be a living entity, possessed of a mind of sorts, and will be easier to motivate in consequence, but a tangible force can be exerted upon inert objects too. In my own time, I took it for granted and had no theory to apply to it, but the Chimeras attempted to educate me when they co-opted me as of their emissaries. All sensation involves force of some sort. Your sound-speech requires you to exert a physical force upon the air emitted from your mouths, so as to establish and modulate waves within it whose codes can be deciphered by a listener, employing a resonant eardrum for the purpose. The sound of a human voice can affect other objects too."

"I have heard that trained singers can hit notes capable of shattering glass," I recalled, "but I've never seen it done."

"Touch is mere brute force," the Amphibian went on. "Taste and smell involve the transfer of significant molecules. Sight involves the interpretation of light waves that are normally all around you in your environment, or can be provided by means of artificial illumination when naturally lacking. There is always some kind of physical transfer by means of which information can be communicated. Mind-speech is no different, but the force involved is less obvious in everyday experience. Do you know that the matter you and I can apprehend by the means of our ordinary senses is not the only kind of matter there is?"

"No," I said, "I didn't know that, although I've heard speculative talk of there being a kind of mental substance out of which minds are made—and which must, it is sometimes presumed, be the substance of ghosts."

"The matter is not so simple, apparently. The point is, however, that the principal interaction between this other kind of matter and the kinds apprehended by our senses is gravitational. The matter we cannot see or touch assists in holding vast clusters of stars together—including the Milky Way—and in defining their structure. It also provides the medium of mind-speech—and, in consequence, the means by which minds can interfere with ordinary forces of gravity. It is not easy to do, and the effect is slight, but even an individual mind can cultivate the skill to deflect an arrow. Minds in disharmony cancel out one another's effects, but millions or billions of minds acting in concert can achieve tremendous effects."

"Is the Division far below the Earth's surface caused by some effect of this other matter?" I asked.

"Yes," she said. "That has nothing to do with the action of minds, but it does have something to do with the fact that the Dwellers were able to hollow out the planet's crust to the extent that they did, and build so many new layers on to its land surface. The spaceship is a different matter, though. It will require a great deal of mental force to lift it out of the planet's gravity-well and supply it with enough residual velocity to reach the moon. Unfortunately, the effect of the mental force will decline just as steeply as the effect of the planet's gravitational attraction."

For a moment or two it was not obvious to me why that should be so unfortunate, but then I realized. "Once we're outside the atmosphere," I said, "we'll effectively be on our own. The Chimeras' combined mind-force can provide the initial impetus, but if anything bad should happen to us thereafter, they won't be able to help."

"Probably not," she admitted.

"In that case," I said, as another thought occurred to me, "how are we supposed to get back?"

"During the most critical part of the return journey," she told me, "by which I mean the descent into the Earth's atmosphere, the Chimeras will again be able to exert their minds to the full. Because the moon is so much lighter than the Earth we shall not require the same motive power to escape its gravity—but there is sufficient difficulty to ensure that we shall be completely dependent on the Metamorphosians."

"I see," I said. I was uncomfortably aware that the machine's list of generous guarantees had not included any specific statement about facilitating our return journey.

I was also aware that the Amphibian was clutching me more tightly now than when we had set off on this phase of the journey, and not because the horse's progress was any less steady. There was no trace now in what I could read of her feelings of the repulsion she had experienced when she had first touched me. Her squeamishness had vanished; she had grown accustomed to my flesh as well to my mental presence. I had no reason at all to feel proud about that, although I certainly had cause enough to be glad, but it helped me to feel a little better about myself than I had been able to do when I first encountered her species and the Dwellers, and understood how they regarded mine.

I doubted that Liamon would ever overcome her instinctive disdain as fully as Mirastara had overcome her instinctive disgust, but I felt that I had made a great deal of progress in both instances, and that I was entitled to some small sense of achievement.

CHAPTER TWENTY-ONE

THE SKYWHALE

The ribbon of light that marked the edge of the canopy's ceiling had been growing brighter for some time as we galloped towards it, and it broadened rapidly as we emerged from the shade of the tree. The vehicle—or animal—that would take us on the next stage of our journey was already waiting for us.

The first impression reminded me of a blue whale. Its most obvious feature was its vast rounded body, and it had a fluke and fins that seemed very similar to a whale's, presumably because they were designed for the same purposes of balance and steering. It also had a structure dependant from its abdomen that was reminiscent of the gondola of a zeppelin—presumably because that too had been designed with a similar function in mind: the carriage of passengers.

The skywhale was not resting on the ground but hovering above it, tethered by a double row of clinging tentacles. It was bobbing slightly in the breeze, in a manner that seemed absurdly comical, given its bulk. Its body evidently contained some sort of gasbag, which provided it with negative buoyancy. It must have resembled a giant fish more than a whale in having an internal bladder, in this instance be filled with a gas that was lighter than air, so that it might swim in the sky as fish swim in the ocean. I presumed that its customary habitat was one or other of the vast cloud-layers.

I had no need to rein in my horse, which knew its part perfectly well, although I noticed that Danby and Clara had slightly more difficulty in controlling their mounts.

"I will come into the belly of the beast with you," Speaker said, slightly breathless after her own tiring flight. "The space is warm and pressurized, and is quite safe. The atmosphere is exceedingly thin and very cold at the height of the ship. I could not breathe there, let alone fly."

"I suppose it will be one more experience to treasure," I said to Mirastara, silently.

"I think I preferred the vehicle in which we traveled before," Danby said to Clara, as they dismounted beside us.

"This is an inordinately complex world," Clara replied. "It would be a pity to repeat an experience, when there must be so very many more to sample."

Her reference to the world's inordinate complexity reminded me of what the Metamorphosians' machine had said about the evolutionary road on which the Chimeras were embarked leading inevitably to Simplicity. I wondered what that might have meant?

I had not addressed that as a question to Mirastara, but she perceived the thought readily enough. "It is an intriguing remark," she said. "I can only guess what it might mean—but there is one possible explanation that might help to explain why the Metamorphosians are so fearful, and so very careful."

There was considerably more space in the underbelly of the skywhale than there had been in the "eyes" of the mock-Antipodean, but that advantage was offset by the uneasy sensation I felt when I observed that its floor was as transparent as its sides.

As the creature began its slow and stately ascent, it seemed to my twentieth-century-educated eyes that there was nothing preventing a long fall but a pane of glass. It was not uninteresting to be able to look out over the forest as well as sideways at the tree, but the seeming precariousness of my standpoint caused me to freeze and become as immobile as a statue. Mirastara lent me a little psychological strength, as she had so many times before, but I could not move for some time. There was a slight flash of relief when we came into the first cloud-layer, but it was momentary.

I tried to peer into the mist in the hope of seeing more of the creatures that lived there, but the vapor was too dense for me to see more than a shoal of tiny "swimmers" and a few rounded forms that might have be floaters akin to the skywhale but on a much smaller scale. It did not help that the particles of the vapor seemed to be luminous themselves—very many of them, at least. I wondered briefly whether that might be some kind of chemical luminescence, given that it was not refracted sunlight, but guessed that it must, in fact, be bioluminescence.

I realized then that the cloud must be less like an Earthly cloud than I had presumed. There must, indeed, be molecules of water within it, formed into minuscule droplets—but there must also be a vast host of exceedingly tiny organisms there, constituting the greater part of the "vapor". There was a sense in which the entire cloud was alive, in much the same way that the entire biosphere of the future Earth was alive, and that it was the whole of it rather than the fugitive but visible swimmers and floaters drifting within it that constituted a "unit" of the collective intelligence. The difference between organisms and their environment was far less acute here than it had been in the era of natural selection.

I put up my hand then to touch the warm belly of the skywhale, wondering whether the "gas" with which its body was filled was likewise a living thing, as much a swarm as a mere vapor or aerosol. The tegument was warm—almost feverishly so—and I thought that I could feel the pulse of blood within its veins and capillaries, pumped by a heart that must have been far more massive than Liamon's. Giantism had its costs and penalties, I thought, but it also had an unmistakable grandeur, to which an ambitious mind might easily aspire.

Once we were above that first cloud-layer there was little to look at but the Great Tree itself, whose thick branches similarly obscured almost all of what was going on within the crown, although there were plenty of little creatures close to the outer surface. Some of the fliers clustered in its branches took wing as we approached, in order to flutter around us, presumably not out of mere curiosity but because there were creatures living on the skywhale's skin that might provide them with food. I watched them darting in and out, fluttering like hummingbirds and bearing colors that were just as dazzling.

It must, I thought, be an odd sort of collective intelligence that was perfectly reconciled to the notion that many of it units must feed on others, all its constituent elements being arranged in complex food-chains. At least, I thought, the human mind has the consolation of knowing that its own phagocytes directed their attention primarily to alien invaders—but no sooner had I formed the thought than I had to modify it. I had learned from one of my many books that the human embryo is formed as much by subtraction as addition—that the fingers of the hand are not formed by protrusion but by the selective death of cells in between.

Perhaps, I thought, the human body indulges in more self-consumption than we know. Perhaps our cells are continually devouring one another. Perhaps the death that shapes us as we grow only kills us when we grow old because it does not balanced as delicately as the ceaseless consumption that goes on within the body of the Chimerical Earthmind.

"The Great Tree still seems to me to be a marvel of intricate complexity," I said to Mirastara, forcing my mind back to speculations of more immediate interest, but without losing the thread of my reverie. "Every comparison I make with my world—or yours—seems to indicate that the evolutionary trend here is towards greater complexity rather than greater simplicity. There are at least as many basic forms of life, and each fundamental template is varied in every imaginable way."

"The machine may not have been referring to a kind of simplicity opposed to physical complexity," Mirastara pointed out. "It might have been referring to mental simplicity. In a population of individuals, where there are many competing intelligences, there is scope for differences of outlook, opinion and belief, which constantly challenge one another. Where there is only a single collective intelligence—even one less imperious than that owned by the Chimeras—that scope becomes very limited, and tends towards annihilation."

She spoke from slightly bitter experience, I knew. The most individualistic of her own kind, she was familiar with a pressure of conformity much more powerful than that of English custom and convention. She wore the residual scars of her own petty nonconformity.

"You think that the Metamorphosians fear the inflexibility of the Chimeras' group-mind?" I said.

"It is possible. Single minds can easily become rigid in their single-mindedness. If they have observed collective intelligences in various phases of their evolution they might have perceived a pattern by which they become very set in their intellectual ways, prey to the diseases of invincible faith and unbreakable conviction. They may fear that news of the greater cosmos, and all the things it contains, might make the Chimeras' collective intelligence apprehensive, and cause its thinking to become more obsessive. Diplomacy can only work where there is a willingness to compromise."

I glanced at Speaker, who was not looking in our direction. "The Chimeras seem adaptable enough to me," I said. "They have done what the Metamorphosians asked by going to extraordinary lengths to find individuated intermediaries, and they have had to adapt their plan more than once."

"That is true," Mirastara conceded.

"Whatever else they have learned by means of contacts with numerous alien life-forms," I said, pensively, "the Metamorphosians have learned to be careful. The machine that entertained me just now is evidence of a very tentative approach to the business of communication. If Simplicity is what they fear most, they must have reason not merely to fear it but some notion of the circumstances in which they are likely to encounter it."

"Indeed," Mirastara agreed. After a pause she said: "Do you remember that I told you one that there were two ways of life which seemed to me to be good? One was our way of collective consciousness: a unity and power of mind sufficient to provide a means by which the consciousness of an individual might even escape the death of the body, at least for a while. The other was the way of blissful unconsciousness: a total freedom of action, in which force and violence were the only operative factors."

"I remember," I said. "My way of being seemed to you to be an awkward hybrid—a monstrous combination of the worst defects of both of the purer ways of being."

"I was a prisoner of my viewpoint and my education," she said. "I have learned a great deal since then. I still believe that there was a certain virtue in my reasoning, but I might well have been wrong to imagine that the way of blissful unconsciousness and total freedom could be properly exemplified by the shark—and overly prideful too, I suppose, to think that my own kind might be the best exemplars of the alternative. The ultimate bliss might, in fact, lie in the ultimate mental simplicity: a perfect moral conviction that there is only one thing to do, which forsakes all decision in favor of automatism. Even sharks must sometimes judge and decide when to chase and when to abandon a chase, when to fight and when to refuse to fight. The Chimeras are hesitating over a difficult decision of that sort—but when a hive-mind like theirs reaches its final maturity, that maturity might consist of an absolute confidence that brooks no hesitation."

"Whereas the ultimate in individuation might result in every decision being questioned and opposed, tested by every possible doubt and argument."

"Just so," she replied. "That might be the cause of the Metamorphosians' exaggerated carefulness—and their dire suspicion."

Our silent speech was still incomprehensible to Clara and Danby, although both might have begun to capture some inkling of its meaning, but it was not secret from Speaker, who had doubtless been listening to every word without troubling to venture an opinion of her own, until that moment.

"That is an interesting line of thought," the Chimeras' spokesman observed now, speaking aloud. "It is one that requires careful consideration." Her voice held a hint of condescension, as if she were seeing to imply that creatures like us could not possibly see further, even in the speculative imagination, than the omnipotent consciousness that spoke through her. I could not help wondering, though, whether the Chimeras' collective intelligence might not be simple enough to be blind to all kinds of arguments that might occur to Mirastara and me, simply by virtue of the fact that we had traveled in time, and had known worlds very different from this one.

"What line of thought?" Danby asked, his voice showing a marked degree of irritation—which had doubtless been encouraged by his own psychological reaction to standing above such a vast abyss on a near-invisible platform.

"I'm sorry, Philip," I said to him. "Mirastara and I developed a rapport long ago, which you have not yet learned to share. We shall find time soon for you and Clara to take instruction. We were indulging in pure speculation, though—a man of science like yourself would probably have dismissed the whole flight of fancy as a waste of time. We shall find out the truth soon enough, I dare say, if the ship we are going to see really can take us safely to the moon."

"The ship is safe," Speaker insisted. "We are not complete novices in the navigation of the void or the provision of life-support, no matter what our visitors might think of us. You may be quite certain that we will transport you to the moon and back in complete safety—the future of our world might depend upon it."

For myself, I was prepared to be certain that they would make every possible effort, but I was not yet prepared to trust absolutely in their ability to succeed. I had no intention of saying so, however, and I did what little I could to shield my thought. Fortunately, I was able to distract myself because we were approaching the tip of the tree, and the bulbous form of the spaceship that would carry us to the moon was now clearly visible above us, silhouetted against the delicate silvery green backcloth of the upper cloud layer.

CHAPTER TWENTY-TWO

THE SPACESHIP

In a sense, the backcloth was more interesting than the object it-self, for it was possible even at this relatively remote range to differ-entiate various colored sheens within the silvery green, which were beautiful in themselves and became even more entrancing by virtue of the manner in which they flowed sinuously about one another.

There was a noticeable thin patch directly above the spaceship, where the sky's shade had more blue in it, thus tending towards tur-quoise. The subtly exotic play of colors drew my eye more readily than the shape of the ship—which had, at present, no other property than shape. The shape in question was, inevitably, rounded, but not spherical; the spaceship was formed like a hen's egg, with the thicker end at the bottom. It had no fins, wings or other projecting elements, but as we drew closer I saw that its hind end did have a slightly more complex shape, the lowest surface of the ovoid being gently contoured so that it seemed to have four buttocks.

It was not until we came closer still that the color of the silhou-etted object became obvious, and we saw that it was a more vivid green than the pastel-nuanced sky. There were no evident hatches or portholes, but the surface was lightly striated and grooved, and I had already seen enough pairs of vegetable lips move apart to form ori-fices that I could imagine readily enough how we might move into the object's interior, if there were only a bridge to support us.

"This creature cannot easily link up with the vessel," Speaker told us, "but the craft in which you will approach it for the purpose of boarding is able to do so. It will be easy enough to pass from one to the other—even for Liamon, although she will require a vehicle specifically modified to take a being of her dimensions."

I did not say aloud that the transfer would not be easy to make, given that we were several miles above the surface of the Earth, but

I thought it. I would have to hope, I supposed, that I would not freeze up at the thought of such a fall. The Chimeras' units presumably did not suffer from acrophobia, any more than they suffered from the other phobias to which human psychology was sometimes victim.

, At close range, I could see that there were tiny creatures moving all over the spaceship's surface, presumably still engaged in the work of shaping it. They were like mites swarming on the surface of a ripe plum—except that they were not seeking to devour it, but merely to complete its formation. I did not doubt that the interior would be just as busy. I wondered whether the spaceship had a valiant heart like that of the skywhale, pumping the blood to maintain its metabolism so that it might provide water and nourishment for its passengers, and refresh their air. Perhaps it had a brain, too—a simple one, no doubt, but one capable of exerting enough mental force of its own to make subtle changes to its course and to react to any unexpected impacts with residual particles from the tails of long-departed comets.

Because I had been so recently in the interior of the Metamorphosians' space-traveling machine, I was forcibly struck by the contrast between that vessel and this one. The Metamorphosians' hemisphere had appeared to be made almost completely of metal; in that respect, it could easily by likened to certain conveyances of my own era, especially tanks and armored cars. There was, however, no evident trace of metal in the Chimeras' craft, which seemed—like almost everything else they commonly used as an instrument—to be entirely organic. I did not doubt that it was tough, but its toughness was of a different kind.

In the world of the Amphibians, I remembered—which is to say, the outer surface of the Dwellers' world—fire had been "the Forbidden Thing"; what metallic technology the Dwellers had was kept far underground, almost hidden away. The apparent reason for that had been the flammability of much of their "organic technology". Fires started on the surface could not easily be put out. If the Antipodeans had evolved on a surface largely reshaped by the technological schemes of the Dwellers' ancestors, it was possible that their first emergence had been correlated with an effective prohibition of the kinds of technologies that had been fundamental to human culture: ovens for cooking, firing pots and bricks, and the forges and crucibles used in metalworking. So important had those crafts been to human cultural evolution that Greek myth had credited the origins of human civilization to Prometheus' gift of the fire of the gods—for whose theft he had paid a terrible price. When humankind's descendants had retired such technologies into their sub-terrains, however, they had paved the way for the development of a new kind of culture, which found very few uses for fire in the processing of foodstuffs, the building of shelters or the manufacture of artifacts.

The culture and civilization of the Metamorphosians was clearly not of the same type. They too were sons of Prometheus; that was yet another sense in which they and the Chimeras might be fundamentally different, and naturally antagonistic.

It was still difficult for me to believe that the spaceship mounted on the tip of the Great Tree could possibly fly to the moon under the impulse lent by the collective will of the Chimeras—but it was almost as difficult for me to believe that there was any other way in which such a trip might be completed, even though I had read Jules Verne's story of a journey *From the Earth to the Moon*, H. G. Wells' tale of *The First Men in the Moon*, and a number of alternative accounts. None of them had seemed much more likely to me than antique accounts of men flying there on the backs of winged horses, or in chariots pulled by flocks of birds.

"If this preliminary expedition was supposed to reassure me," I said, silently, to Mirastara, "I fear that it may have had the opposite effect."

"When the time comes," Mirastara told me, "the familiarity of the object will work to your advantage—and mine too. When you go to see Liamon, you must be sure to let her see the image in your mind."

"You will be able to do that more effectively than I will," I pointed out.

"I shall not go with you to see Liamon," she replied. "While you take Philip to see Liamon, I shall stay with Clara, and try to educate her in the art of mind-speech. It should not take long."

I was surprised by this, because I had not expected her to be ready and willing to quit my side so soon, but all I said was: "Thank you. It is good of you to think of my friends, and to take the trouble to tutor them. Once Clara and Philip can understand your speech, I presume that you will be able to talk to all three of us at the same time."

"I hope so, if I can concentrate my mind in the appropriate fashion. There should be no difficulty while you are all in very close proximity, but distance will make it more difficult. It might be possible, in time, for you to be able to use the method to communicate with your friends directly, but that will probably require a great deal of practice and effort. Whether they will ever be able to communicate directly with one another, without the benefit of the physical modifications made to you, I cannot tell."

I wondered, briefly, whether it was possible for the Chimeras to duplicate or imitate what the Dwellers had done to me. I had to suppose that it was. Danby, I thought, might well be eager to cultivate that sort of self-improvement, if he were convinced that the advantages outweighed the potential dangers or defects.

I looked up again at the higher cloud-layer, trying to see it as I had learned to see the lower one, as a living thing in itself: like a sensitive skin surrounding the world-organism, shading it from the harsher elements of the sun's glare while filtering that radiance of life-giving energy. Although the atmosphere seemed quite empty at this height, and crystal clear, I knew that there must be a steady invisible rain descending from the underside of that delicate film, carrying its produce down to the lower layer, which would transmit its own nourishment, in its turn, to the forested surface.

No wind could be felt inside the skywhale's bosom, but I supposed that there must be some movement in the air that surrounded us, caused by the rotation of the Earth. Even if the atmosphere had been entirely tamed, so that the only storms that were allowed to form were expressions of the Earthmind's desire, there had to be winds to circulate air, heat and moisture. The world must still have tropics and arctic regions, and must in consequence require currents of various sorts to redistribute the wealth of its heat.

I looked at the horizon, trying to measure its curvature, in order to judge with my own eyes how much larger the diameter if the world was now, compared with my own day—but there were no convenient benchmarks available.

"Shall we begin the descent now?" Speaker asked.

"I've seen enough," Danby answered. "I feel a coward for saying so, but I felt a great deal safer during our first ascent in the giant beetle. I can't quite shake the suspicion that this teardrop suspended from the skywhale's belly might fall at any moment."

"It has been an interesting journey, though," Clara said. "There is an exhilarating edge to the experience of the modes of transport this world had to offer, which I prefer to the sensation of being coped up in the bowels of a tree like some burrowing worm."

"You might ask our angelic companion to show you the ultimate depths of their domain, if you're in search of exhilaration," I suggested. "Coming back up is a slower process, mind."

"When you have returned from the moon," Speaker put in, "there will be time to see much more of our world's complexity. If you should decide—once you have reported your discoveries back to those who sent you, of course—that you would rather live in this era than your own, you will not run out of new experiences for some considerable time."

It was the first time that possibility had been explicitly mentioned. I could not help wondering whether the Chimeras really expected us to be able to return to our own world, even briefly. I had returned once before, though, and I could see no reason to think that my experience was any less likely to be repeated now, in spite of what I had learned about the mishap that had overtaken Mirastara and Liamon. As the skywhale veered away from the globular excrescence atop the Great Tree, in order to begin its leisurely descent, I said, aloud: "On what terms is that invitation offered?"

"It is offered freely," Speaker assured us. "Our ancestors went to war for possession of the world, consuming all the individuated species that seemed to be their rivals—but we are living in a different era now, when we feel a sense of regret for everything that was lost in those dire days. We could live in peace with individuated species now, and would be interested to do so. We can only reproduce the Dwellers and the Amphibians by means of artifice, at least for the time being, but a human population could establish itself here without such recourse, employing its own means of reproduction."

"With the threat of an apocalyptic war hanging over Europe," I said, "you might find millions willing to take up that invitation?"

"Do you really think so?" Clara said. "I doubt that there would be dozens, until the war actually began—and then, flight would become tantamount to desertion in the face of the enemy. You were an exceptional man even before your first adventure in time, George; I'm not sure that many others would find the thought of making a home a millions year in the future, in a world as strange as this, as comfortable as you seem to find it."

Personally, I thought I could name a dozen men in Oxford who would jump at the chance, and the range of my acquaintance there was necessarily limited. I did not contradict her, though; it was easy enough to imagine that that the situation might be different in the London suburbs, and very different indeed in the countryside, where even the cities of the twentieth century were widely regarded as alien abominations.

"You cope with your innate anxieties very well," Speaker observed. "We would not have believed it possible had we not observed it. You are very different from us—the rational parts of your minds are well used to finding themselves in opposition to and conflict with all manner of fears and temptations, and resisting them, Our kind is not like that at all, and I wonder what you would make of our mode of experience, if we could allow you to share it briefly. Perhaps we could show it to you while you are asleep and dreaming."

"That would be interesting," Clara said. "I, for one, should like to try."

"When you return from the moon," Speaker said, "We shall make the attempt." I could not help suspecting that she was deliberately heaping up possibilities for the time following our return, perhaps by way of reassuring us that we would indeed return safe and sound—or perhaps by way of providing incentives, lest the Metamorphosians should offer us reasons for not returning at all.

CHAPTER TWENTY-THREE

LIAMON AND DANBY

As soon as we returned to the tree, Speaker informed me that Liamon was now on the surface. She had asked to hold a further conversation with me, and with Philip Danby too. We agreed to be taken to her, while Clara and Mirastara returned to her quarters in order that Clara might cultivate the trick of mind-speech.

The giant had apparently had enough of confinement for a while. Although she could not stand fully erect beneath the Great Tree's canopy, she did not want to be hemmed in by its roots either, and she was waiting for us in the open air. I inferred that her journey from her resting-place had been an uncomfortable one, and that any movements she had made since must have been awkward. In her own era, all the corridors connecting the surface to the subterrains had been built with giants in mind; in this era, it was unlikely that many made any such concession.

The Dweller had moved a few hundred yards away from the bole of the tree, and was sitting on the ground when we approached on horseback. Although she was sitting in a relatively open space she was less than a hundred yards away from one of the arterial highways leafing to the Tree, and was clearly visible to all the creatures passing back and forth along it. As usual, though, she attracted no obvious attention from the passers-by.

I watched Danby's reaction when we first came in sight of her, and saw alarm in his eyes, although he had been adequately forewarned about her stature and had had the opportunity to see her on a screen. In the flesh, she was very imposing, and the fact that she had to sit down in order not to bump her head on the lowest branches of the vast tree lent a further emphasis to her immense stature. Danby seemed startled by her nakedness, which was similarly more evident in the raw flesh than in an image contained in a wall. The additional skin gifted to her by the Chimeras was not so concerned with concealment as the ones provided for us, reflecting the norms of her society.

"If you concentrate," I said, "you will be able to perceive her mind-speech. You will have some difficulty translating it, at first, because you have not had the benefit of the training I received from the Amphibians, but if I act as an interpreter, you might find that the ability grows more rapidly than you expect."

"I'll do what I can," Danby told me, with only the slightest hint of resentment.

"Liamon," I said, as we came closer, "this is Philip Danby, the son of the man who built the machine that sent us here. He is partially deaf to mind-speech, at present, so I will relay any questions you wish to address to him."

"Few questions will be necessary," Liamon said. "I shall be able to look into his mind without overmuch trouble, now that I know yours so well. You might render yourself passive again soon, if you are willing, so that I can discover more. You might ask him, though, whether he would be willing to allow me to share his dreams as I shared yours. It will be far more difficult for me to obtain information from him by that means, because he has not been prepared, but it would not harm him in the least."

I told Danby what the giant had asked. "Perhaps," he said, "at some future time. Is she willing to tell us, do you think, what she had planned to do in her own time when the time came for her return, before the accident that prevented her from so doing?"

I relayed that question.

"I was already pledged to return here," Liamon said, "in order to carry out the mission on which we shall all be embarking very soon. I had planned no further ahead than that. As to what the other Dwellers might have planned to do on the basis of what I reported to them, I can only speculate."

It seemed to me be a careful and evasive answer, but I relayed it to Danby.

"Having received news from you of their eventual loss of the war with the Antipodeans and their inevitable extinction thereafter," Danby said, "surely they would have sent at least some of their number across the time-bridge, to establish an enclave in this era?"

"That seems probable," Liamon admitted, in her turn. "The conflict between the males and the females had already been settled; the two sexes would surely have cooperated in responding to the opportunity. They might have hoped, too, that a relocation of that sort might have assisted in the solution of the fecundity problem. But I am alone now, and I all I can do is guess."

It was not until I had relayed this answer to Danby that the Dweller added: "I am ashamed to say that I almost died when I realized the fact of my isolation, even though my body was not mortally injured. The effect of that realization on the Amphibian must have been considerably greater, but she had sufficient strength of mind to survive. Despair took hold of me, briefly—but I am resolved to live now." I was not sure that she wanted me to relay this to Danby, but I translated it anyway.

"Has she formulated any further plans now?" Danby wanted to know.

"Not in any detail," was Liamon's reply to that. "But I can glimpse new possibilities."

"Will you take up the Chimeras' offer to resurrect your species by growing new individuals from cells taken from your body?" I asked.

"Any individuals grown from unmodified cells would all be female, and physically identical to me," the Dweller told me. "I dare say that the Chimeras could improvise a means by which such clones might be impregnated and give birth, but individual variety could only be restored, and the male of the species recreated, by the strategic modification of my genes. The resultant population of Dwellers would in essence, be chimerical. Even so, it is a possibility worth considering. So is the possibility that the Amphibian and I might adopt a tutelary role in a community of humans."

That took me by surprise. "Your fellows regarded me as little better than vermin when I was in your world," I reminded her. "The first Dweller I encountered might have eaten me alive had he not assuaged his hunger on other prey. The Seekers of Science would have been perfectly prepared to treat me as they treated Templeton and Brett had the Amphibians not bargained for my well-being."

"That is not true," Liamon told me. "They wasted the other members of your race in a reckless fashion. It was the Seekers of Wisdom who realized the opportunity that you presented. The Amphibians had no need to intervene on your behalf, although they did not know it."

"What is she saying?" Danby asked, impatiently. "I can feel the pressure of her speech inside my brain, but I can't quite clarify it."

I told him what Liamon had said about the possibility of her adopting a tutelary role with respect to a colony of humans. Then I said to the Dweller: "So the adaptations they made to my body *were* made with a particular purpose in mind. They expected me to return to your era once I had made my obligatory return to my own, but I was prevented from making that second journey by the collapse of the bridge."

"I cannot be absolutely certain, because I was never privy to the schemes of the Seekers of Wisdom," Liamon said, "but I believe that to be the case."

"Do you know what they intended to do with me, once my modification was complete?"

"Again, I cannot be sure, although I am confident of my deduction. You can probably make that deduction as easily as I can."

"Does that mean that you're unwilling to tell me?" I retorted, slightly nettled by her evasiveness. "Do you believe that you can conceal the conclusion from the Chimeras, provided that you do not voice it?"

"They have almost certainly made the same deduction, and may well hope to use you in the same fashion. Have *they* told you what they hope to do with you, if our mission to the moon is successful?"

"No," I admitted. I felt frustrated, annoyed by the fact that no one seemed to be willing to tell me exactly what the Dwellers had done to me, or why.

"What is she saying?" Danby demanded. "If you would only help me, I think I might be able to grasp it for myself."

"We were discussing the vexed question of what the Dwellers planned to do with me, had I been able to return to their world," I told him. "It has turned into a guessing game, which I seem to be losing."

"You might tell her," Danby said, "that if a company of humans were to come into this world with the intention of establishing some sort of colony, they might not welcome a giant as their tutor."

I did not have to tell Liamon that, because she read the thought behind the speech. She had been looking at me, but now she turned her gaze on Danby and concentrated her mind-speech on him. My own skill was still increasing, because I heard what she said clearly enough.

"You think yourself the equal of a Dweller, if not an Amphibian," she told Danby, "but you are wrong in that. Were you a castaway on some desert isle in the False-Skin Era, with no company but rats, would you not set out to improve the condition and education of the rats, for want of any better occupation? And would you not expect the rats to be grateful for your attention and efforts?"

I think Danby understood this admonition well enough, but I relayed it to him anyway, giving him time to think. I recalled, in the meantime, that the shipwrecked mariner who had served as a model for Daniel Defoe's Robinson Crusoe had shared his island abode with a population of cats, with whom he had sided against the rats escaped from other ships—but had he not had the cats to prefer, I thought, he might well have allied himself with the rats, for want of better company, and would surely have expected their gratitude in return.

"If Liamon would like to make a contribution to the education of humankind," Danby said to me, eventually, "she is surely able to give me information which, were I able to relay it to my father, would enhance the rate of our technological progress in the twentieth century."

I relayed the answer to this observation with equal conscientiousness, wearing a slight smile. "She says that if she understands ancient history correctly," I told him, "it was the acceleration of our rate of technological progress that doomed us to swift extinction. She apologizes for the fact that she cannot render you the one service from which humankind could actually benefit, which is to give you the means to slow the rate down."

"Sophistry," Danby opined, bitterly. He recognized the argument as one I had used against his father, and obviously felt that Liamon and I had formed some kind of alliance against him, as a man and a cat might make against a rat. I did not translate the word *sophistry*, but Liamon seemed to understand the concept, without any need to consult Webster's Dictionary.

"That is a matter I wanted to discuss with you," she said. "It seems to me, on due reflection, that it might be futile to think in terms of changing the past. If that could be done, the effects could only be reckoned destructive, however well-intentioned the changes might be. It may be necessary to redirect our attention—to think in terms of the contribution we might make to changing the future. The creatures we are to meet on the moon seem to think that some change is necessary here on Earth, if there is not to be a catastrophe of some sort. If they are right, it is possible that we might become agents of that change—perhaps necessary agents. I think that I would be able to continue living purposively, on those terms, although that might be a matter beyond the control of my will. You humans are not yet in a position to give due contemplation of the possibility of continuing to live indefinitely, and I cannot tell whether you would have problems similar to those my own species encountered if the situation should arise. Even so, you might begin wondering what you might and ought to make of a near-eternal life, were you fortunate enough to be gifted with one."

What she did not say, perhaps thinking it obvious, was that it might be a gift that we would not be able to take home to our own era, even if we time-travelers might benefit from it in this world's future. Although Danby seemed pleased with himself, evidently having caught the gist of the speech, I relayed it as accurately as I could.

"You might be right," was Danby's response. "If it is impractical to change our own era, we must look for a role to play in this one. It is not improbable that the Professor would find this a more hospitable and congenial environment than twentieth-century England."

"All this may be a trifle premature," I said. "The Metamorphosians are deeply suspicious of us, more inclined at present to believe that we are deceptive artifacts manufactured by the Chimeras than to accept that we are true individuals plucked out of the past. Ours will be a difficult mission, and we might have to be very clever if it is to have any chance of ending well. What is more, Liamon, the Metamorphosian machine reiterated the Chimeras' fears that you might not survive the initial acceleration that will be necessary to remove the spaceship from Earth's gravity-field."

"I am aware of the Chimeras' opinion of the folly of giantism," Liamon said. "I understand the risk I will be taking, and I have already accepted it. As for the Metamorphosians' suspicions, we should be able to dispel them once we meet the visitors face-to-face. You will be our greatest asset in that respect, George, having lost whatever capacity for deception you once had. The Chimeras know that once they have had an opportunity to read your memories, as I did, the Metamorphosians will be unable to deny that coexistence is possible, at least in the short term, between individuals of our kind and a collective intelligence like theirs. The Metamorphosians will also be unable to deny that time travel is possible—and might be persuaded that access to the secret will be an adequate price for arriving at an amicable agreement with the Chimeras."

"That secret—or part of it, at least—is ours," Philip Danby put in, using mind-speech for the first time.

"It is, at present, only a partial secret," Liamon told him. "I presume that one of the reasons why the Chimeras are so desperate to gain time is that they hope to complete it."

"They hope to persuade the Professor to come here," Danby guessed, "but they cannot do so until I go back."

"That might be one factor in their calculations," Liamon replied—although it seemed to me that she was fobbing Danby off, and that she had had something quite different in mind. "The point is that our role in this might well be crucial, not merely as diplomatic intermediaries but also as travelers in time. We must be careful of offering our services too freely, and we must also be wary for our own safety. It might be the case that the Metamorphosians will want to hold at least one of us hostage on the moon while the others return to Earth. If so, they will almost certainly select George."

"Why George?" Danby asked.

Liamon ignored him. "If that happens, George, then I shall make every attempt to stay with you. I promised that I would try to protect you, and I will. I do not claim to be entirely altruistic in so doing—as you have already observed, I believe that I know your true value better than you do, and might yet be able to profit from that knowledge—but I do claim that you would be wise to put yourself under my protection, to the extent that you can."

"I don't understand," Danby said. "I am the Professor's son, far better able to negotiate access to what my father knows than George."

I did not understand either, although I understood enough to see that Danby was stuck on the wrong track. What the Professor knew about constructing time-bridges was unlikely to be significant, given what the Dwellers and the Chimeras had already discovered. The key question was not how time-bridges could be contrived but what might be done with them in practical terms. There was only one possible way to investigate, let alone to answer, that question.

It occurred to me then, for the first time, that the Chimeras might not be the only future species prepared to take a keen interest in me—and that Liamon and Speaker's guiding intelligence probably both knew that, although both were hoping and endeavoring to conceal the extent of their deductions from the other.

CHAPTER TWENTY-FOUR

MIRASTARA AND CLARA

"We must not forget the complication of the hostile action allegedly carried out against the Metamorphosians," I said to Liamon and Danby.

"No, we should not," Liamon agreed. "We must try to solve that mystery too."

This was a matter to which Danby had evidently given some consideration. He seemed delighted by the fact that he had begun to be able to follow the unspoken conversation, and to make a contribution to it without having to ask for translations of Liamon's silent speech. "Is it possible, do you think," he said, "that the Chimeras really have kidnapped a number of Metamorphosians, and are using our mission as a means of buying time to complete the interrogation of their prisoners?"

"I doubt that," I said, although I knew that I was not in the best position to judge the matter.

"If the Chimeras are lying about their innocence," Liamon said, "they are better liars than any who lived on Earth in my time—but that is by no means impossible. Still, we can only operate on the assumption that they are honest. If they are not, we are already lost."

"What I cannot help but wonder," I said, "is whether the Chimeras are really as united as they seem. They have constructed spaceships before, it seems, and have conducted their own limited explorations within the solar system. Given what Mirastara has told me about the extreme difficulty of maintaining mental contact over long distances, I wonder whether offshoots of Earth's biosphere might have given rise to splinter intelligences of which the planet-bound Chimeras know nothing."

"That is another possibility we must bear in mind," Liamon conceded. "Would you be willing to go to sleep now, Philip, so that

I might look into your dreams? I do not know how much benefit I will be able to obtain, but I would like to make the attempt."

When this question had been put to Danby indirectly, his oral answer had been dismissively evasive—but now that it was put to him directly, he seemed uncertain how to answer. Somewhat to my surprise, he only hesitated for a few seconds before countering it with a question of his own. "Would it help me to cultivate the skill that I am just beginning to master? Would I be better equipped thereafter to understand your mind-speech?"

"Yes," Liamon said, flatly.

"Then I'll do it," Danby replied.

I remembered what the giant had told me about my being foolish to consent so readily to my mind being read in that intimate fashion, but I felt no compulsion to warn Danby. In any case, I knew full well that he would have resented any suggestion from me that he might be doing something foolish.

"Thank you," Liamon said. "It would be best if you were to leave us alone, George, and return to your lodgings in the Great Tree."

I consented to that readily enough. Danby stayed behind with Liamon while I made my way back to the bole of the tree, walking most of the distance alongside the highway, leading the horse that I had ridden to the rendezvous with the skywhale.

Speaker was waiting for me there, politely pretending not to know what had taken place, although her guiding intelligence must have been aware of every word that had been exchanged. She took the reins of the horse from me, and held them for a few moments while she looked into the mute creature's eyes. Then she released the bridle again; the creature moved off at a leisurely walk.

"Danby hopes to master the art of mind-speech, with Liamon's aid," I told her, not because I was collaborating in her pretence but because I wanted to hear her response.

"That is good," she said. "The closer you can all work together during your mission, the better. We are glad that Liamon has made such a full recovery, and we hope that she will not suffer unduly during the take-off. We feel that there is every chance that our endeavor will have a successful outcome."

That wasn't what I felt—but I would have had difficulty describing and analyzing the feelings that I was experiencing, which were confused even by human standards.

"How are your other projects going?" I asked, with deliberate vagueness, as we passed through the portal and into the body of the Great Tree.

"We are working and hard and as fast as we can," Speaker replied, "as we are compelled to do, given the urgency of the situation. We are sorry for hurrying your mission, but you will have time during your journey to the moon for further consideration of your options, opportunities and ambitions." It was obvious now that she was, indeed, playing a game. There were items of information that she had no intention of giving me—perhaps because she did not want the Metamorphosians to read them in my wide-open mind, and perhaps for other reasons.

"I look forward to that," I assured her, not meaning it ironically.

When Speaker and I reached the quarters that had been assigned to us, I asked which door led to Clara's room. I was about to knock on it, but Speaker forestalled me, and said that she would make Clara and Mirastara aware of our presence. Shortly thereafter, the door opened. I went in, but Speaker did not follow. "It might be advisable to rest, George," she said to me, by way of farewell. "You might benefit from some authentic sleep, without Liamon guiding your dreams."

She was probably right, but I made no promises.

"Is your education in the art of mind-speech making progress?" I asked Clara.

"It is," she said. "Mirastara and I can communicate well enough by that means now, and I shall doubtless improve further with practice."

"We ought to be able to hold a three-way conversation now," Mirastara said, silently, "although it might be more convenient if you continue to speak aloud to one another. I will understand."

"I'm glad," I said—still speaking aloud, as Mirastara had suggested. "I had hoped that the two of you might find that you had something in common—more, perhaps than I have in common with either of you."

"That was a romantic illusion," Mirastara said, forthrightly. "You have loved Clara for a long time, and you have chosen to construe your attitude to me as a kind of love that is only slightly different. Sometimes, you forget that, unlike Liamon, I am not a female, and only appear so by virtue of your arbitrary choice of a personal pronoun and your insistence on translating my notion of others of my kind into the word *sisters*. To the limited extent that Clara loves you, her feeling has very little in common with my attitude to you,"

I saw Clara blush, and I was astonished by the extent of my own shock at hearing such ideas spelled out in this fashion. Mirastara must have perceived our surprise, but she did not apologize.

"I think Clara did love me a little more, at one time," I said, trying to sound matter-of-fact and carefully looking at Mirastara as I said it, "but I came back from your era a changed man, and it was not possible for her to love me thereafter in the way I wanted to be loved. My presence in the human world had become too disconcerting. She and young Danby tolerated it as long as they could, but in the end they had to go away—separately, if not together."

"I have explained to Clara how glad you are that they did not continue their relationship," Mirastara said, although she must have known full well that it was not the sort of thing she ought to say, even if she had committed the original error of doing what she said that she had done.

"Well," I said, gruffly, "I dare say that she understood my jealousy then, and will tolerate its residue now—better, at any rate, than you probably can, given that you are a being for whom jealousy has no meaning."

"Am I?" Mirastara said. "Perhaps I was, once, but I came away from my era more than a little changed, and I have been profoundly changed since then."

"If we are quarrelling," Clara put in, "I think we ought to stop. Even if we are merely suffering the effects of a slight failure of communication, induced by misunderstanding, it would still be best to stop."

"I disagree," Mirastara said. "We are testing the efficacy of three-way communication, are we not? If there is a failure in that communication, we ought to make every attempt to overcome it."

"I have to agree with Clara," I said. "We may need to discuss such matters a little more fully in private before we can air them in public, even between the three of us. My feelings for Clara, and hers for me, have lain unvoiced for a long time now, and that has been a matter of necessity, perhaps for reasons that you, Mirastara, cannot understand."

"I might understand them better than you think," Mirastara said, bluntly.

"George is right," Clara said. "This is neither the time nor the place for a frank discussion of his feelings and mine."

"As you wish," Mirastara said, meekly. "I do not seem to be having any difficulty expressing myself to both of you simultaneously, and you certainly do not seem to be having any difficulty understanding me." She lent a delicate mental emphasis to the final word, which underlined the fully-intended irony of the whole statement.

"You're right," I said. "We seem to understand one another well enough, for the time being. Liamon is teaching Danby to use mind-speech more skillfully at this very moment. When she has completed her work, I've no doubt that you, Mirastara, will be able to make yourself understood to all three of us, and so will Liamon. Danby, Clara and I may find it necessary to continue speaking to one another aloud, though, sharing our thoughts and feelings in the parsimonious fashion to which we are accustomed."

"You always were a trifle pompous, George," Clara observed, in the parsimonious fashion in which I had just referred. "In some respects, you didn't change at all when you came back from Mirastara's world."

"In the most important respects," I agreed, equally parsimoniously, "I remained the same man I was before." Then I switched to mind-speech in order to address Mirastara, and said: "There are some things that are better not voiced, even in mind-speech. I think I have worked out what it was the Dwellers intended to do with me, had I been able to return to their world. The Chimeras probably hope to do the same, although they do not want to ask for my consent too soon—partly, I suspect, because they are not yet in a position to exploit me in the relevant fashion. Whether they will have completed their work when—or if—I return from the moon, I cannot tell, but if they have they will presumably put the proposition to me then. Have you deduced yet what the Dwellers were trying to do, Mirastara?"

"None of us can be certain," Mirastara replied, "and that is one reason why we ought to be discreet. There is no reason, however, why you should not give serious consideration to the question of whether you would have consented to what the Dwellers apparently wanted to do with you."

"I don't understand what you're talking about," Clara said.

"It's really quite simple," I told her, feeling that it was time to stop beating about the bush. "I presume that the Dwellers made me into a kind of living book because they intended me to be read. I had assumed until recently that they merely wanted to read me themselves, but I now suspect that their real objective was a little more ambitious. When the Professor established his second time-bridge, and discovered that information could be transmitted back to him from the future, the first thing he did was to send an abundant supply of paper and pencils. The Dwellers must have had the same thought—except that their usual method of recording and relaying information was quite different."

Clara needed no further hint to grasp my implication. "You believe that they intended to send you further forward in time," she said. "You think that they were trying to establish a time-bridge into the future—a reasonable assumption, given that they eventually opened one to this era—and that they wanted to develop a reliable means of communication between eras."

"The Chimeras would have sent a far more elaborate message to the Professor if they had been able to do so," I said, "but they discovered that they could only alter a piece of paper to a certain degree before it became incapable of returning to the past. The Dwellers knew that Brett had been unable to return when he was supposed do so, even though he was still alive; they were not certain whether that was because he had not been returned to the location of their emergence or because of what had been done to him. I was a carefully-calculated experiment. If I proved capable of returning to the past, in spite of the alterations the Dwellers had made to my flesh and my mind, and then returning to the future, then I might well be able to go forward from their era and return to it—as a living book, bearing whatever messages the inhabitants of the future might care to transmit."

"This is all conjecture," Mirastara reminded me.

"Liamon believes it," I said, "and the Chimeras apparently share her belief. She is regretful now, I think, that she let them share it so easily when she arrived, but she probably could not have withheld the information even if she had not been under instructions to release it. That must have been the principal reason why the Chimeras asked for me by name, although I may also have helped a little in the awakening of Mirastara and Liamon, and will certainly be useful as a member of the expedition to the moon. What *is* pure conjecture, for the present, is whether the Dwellers' plan was ever feasible, given the apparent tendency of time-bridges to collapse under the mere threat of carrying any dangerous informational traffic."

"Have the Chimeras succeeded in opening more time-bridges than the one we crossed?" Clara asked.

"Perhaps, and perhaps not," I answered. "We may be certain, though, that they are trying with all their might to do so. If they succeed, they will surely ask me to volunteer my services as an agent. It seems that I may be fated to become a career diplomat."

"If you consent," Clara said. "You must bear in mind what happened to Liamon and Mirastara—and the fact that you, unlike then, could not survive such a shock."

"Clara is right," Mirastara added. "The Chimeras will probably ask our consent, although the Dwellers might not have bothered with such niceties. Indeed, they will probably be obliged to ask your consent if they are like my kind, requiring moral justification as well as will-power to direct the force of their minds purposively. If you refuse, though...." She let the subvocalized thought trail off, perhaps because a suddenly-conceived idea had interrupted her train of thought.

"I will never have the chance to explore the further reaches of time," I finished.

"If your deduction is correct," Mirastara pointed out, after a slight pause, "the Dwellers presumably intended you to serve as a *passive* agent, quite unaware of the information you would be carrying back and forth through time. They might have thought that to be necessary, in order to minimize the chance of precipitating collapses in their bridges. Whether or not they were correct, the adaptations they have made to your being have probably relegated you to the status of a parcel rather than an explorer of future time."

"Perhaps," I admitted. "Even so, it might be a glorious opportunity."

"It might," Mirastara agreed, a trifle ambiguously.

"Speaker was right, though," I said, having relieved myself of a portion of my burden of thought. My need for rest has finally caught up with me. I want to be at my best when the time comes for us to make our final ascent to the ship. Adventurers need to be alert, if they are to make the most of their opportunities, and their missions." I hoped that I did not sound too fatuously pompous.

"You'd better retire to your room, then," Clara said. "Mirastara and I will continue our practice, if you don't mind. We still have a great deal to learn."

I looked at Mirastara again, not entirely certain that she would agree. She did agree, and signified the fact with a slight nod of her head.

"You know where to find me if you need me," I told them. "Be sure to wake me if there is any news of further developments— especially if the Chimeras decided that they would rather not send me to the moon after all, but rather to the end of time."

"The *end* of time?" Clara echoed.

"Of course," I said, trying my best to sound blasé. "That's surely the whole point of building bridges in time. Thus far, within our limited experience, bridges have been erected singly—but once the art is known, they will surely be erected in such a fashion that their extent is eternal. If I'm to serve as a parcel, I'd prefer to be delivered to an interesting address."

"Do you really think it might be possible to travel to the end of time?" Clara asked.

"I don't know," I told her. "But I do believe that, if it is possible, then I have been specifically adapted for that purpose. I must go to the moon first, it seems—but even that, I now suspect, may be primarily a matter of adding further content to my living pages."

"It *would* be a fabulous adventure," Clara said—and I could see in her eyes, if not in her mind, that she was already considering the possibility of undertaking some such adventure herself.

"Yes," my Amphibian friend agreed. "It surely would."

PART TWO

THE METAMORPHOSIANS

CHAPTER TWENTY-FIVE

THE ASCENT

Liamon was transported to the spaceship some hours before the rest of us because of the special difficulties attendant upon her accommodation. By the time the rest of our party followed her, by means of a skywhale whose anatomy had been modified for the purpose of facilitating our transfer to the spaceship, the Dweller's body lay supine upon the floor of the vessel. It had been overlaid with a complex network of what looked like interlaced spider webs, whose elastic fibers were immensely strong.

Although our own stations within this network initially resembled hammocks, I could not help comparing our situation to that of insects captured by spiders and trussed up in spidersilk to serve as living larders. The anticipations implied by this analogy were not unjustified; once we had climbed into the hammocks they began to close tightly about us, as living bandages might have carefully enfolded a company of corpses intended for mummification.

I tried to welcome this procedure, not merely as a precaution taken for our safety but as a vital preparation for the next phase of our journey, but it was disturbing nevertheless.

I had taken care to ask before we left the ground whether our new surskins would allow us to tolerate the near-vacuum of the moon's surface. Speaker had assured me that they would not be required to do so. In the first place, the Metamorphosians had sent very precise landing instructions, promising that the ship would be taken into an air-filled cavity before we would be required to disembark. In the second place, the cocoons that would supply us with nourishment and support during the journey would reform themselves before the disembarkation into pressurized suits with their own inbuilt oxygen-supply, which would protect us against any accidental exposure to the void, at least temporarily. We had little or no idea what to expect once we went into the moon's interior, but we could not take it entirely for granted that the Metamorphosians would be able to provide comfortable spaces filled with breathable air. Nor could we assume that our new skins could sustain us for very long in an environment designed to accommodate aliens. The remodified cocoons would hopefully provide the extra life-support, if it should turn out to be necessary.

The disturbing effect of the cocoons' formation was further augmented by the fact that there were little creatures scuttling back and forth about the mass of cobwebs. Although none was larger than my thumb, and therefore could not qualify as the kind of spider that might dine on me as if I were a fly, their ceaseless movement in the minutes before the take-off was distinctly disconcerting. At close range they resembled headless termites rather than spiders—they were as white as the cobwebs—but their apparent lack of mouthparts only made them seem more sinister. In addition to these many-legged creatures there was an abundance of tiny worm-like threads, which moved along the threads of the network in a corkscrew fashion, spiraling as they advanced; these had transparent teguments which allowed their minuscule internal organs to be perceived at close range.

I had no idea whether these entities were functional units of the spaceship's life-support systems, or whether they too were passengers, whose secret purpose was to invade the moon and establish little enclaves of Chimerical life in the hidden nooks and crannies of the Metamorphosians' base. They would presumably be poor spies, because they would be outside the communicative range of the Chimeras' collective intelligence, but I wondered whether they might be part of some long-term plan to infect the careful Metamorphosians.

I wondered, too, whether it might be unwise for me to entertain such thoughts, given that the purpose of my own mission was to submit to a rigorous interrogation by the extraterrestrial visitors— but how could I prevent my imagination from giving birth to such specters?

As I had told Clara and Mirastara, I had also begun to wonder whether it might be more interesting and rewarding to be sent into the distant reaches of future time rather than the merely local reaches of infinite space—but no such possibility had yet been voiced by Speaker, let alone any change of plan announced. I told myself, sternly, that the best course of all would be to undertake both journeys. Once I had seen the Metamorphosians, I would have more of interest to relate to the future inhabitants of Earth—especially if those future inhabitants turned out to be as contentedly introverted as the Chimeras.

Speaker had accompanied us in the skywhale, but she had not passed through the umbilical cord that led from the skywhale's belly to a slit in the spaceship's outer tegument. A voice identical to hers, however, continued to sound from somewhere close to my ear, telling me that I had nothing to fear while I was patiently mummified. I assumed that Danby and Clara could hear it too. When the preparatory phase was complete, we were still able to turn our unwrapped heads but unable to move any of our limbs.

I glanced down at the source of the voice. For once, the device at which I glanced did not seem to be a living creature, but an artifact of a kind to which I was more accustomed. The creatures that had attached it had mounted it close to the place where my collars would have been, had I been wearing a shirt. Danby's and Clara's were similarly located; Mirastara's was on her shoulder and Liamon's was at the top of her sternum.

"The initial acceleration will not be unduly violent," the mechanically-reproduced voice said, its formal tone suggesting that its words were meant for all of us, "and the discomfort it will cause you will only last for a matter of minutes. Once the acceleration ceases, however, you will be weightless—a condition whose associated sensations might prove to be even more disconcerting, until you became accustomed to it."

"Will we be released then," Danby wanted to know, "so that we may move about relatively freely within the confines of the web?"

"It is safer for you to remain confined while you are aboard the ship," Speaker assured us. "The threads of the web can interact very efficiently with your new skins, and they will make sure that you are properly nourished. Do not be afraid."

"How long will you be able to transmit to us by these means?" I asked.

"Mental contact will fade rapidly once you are outside the atmosphere," Speaker said, "but this sort of voice contact will be maintained by means of a radio link. We shall continue to talk to you throughout your mission, if we can, although the time delay will increase as we draw away from the Earth and you might well be taken far enough into the moon's interior to block our signals."

The craft had no portholes, so we were unable to see the moon, the sun and the stars directly. More questions, however, elicited the information that a screen located in the vessel's forward end—the ceiling, as it appeared to be before the launch—would relay visual images from external sensors. There was no cargo space; water and food would be secreted by the inner wall of the vessel according to need, and the air would be purified by the same surface.

The manner in which my supportive cocoon had extended itself around me was slightly alarming, because the confinement was stricter than I had anticipated. The Chimeras must have had some means of reading my alarm, because Speaker immediately said: "Please try to relax, George." I knew by her tone as well as her use of my name that she was addressing itself only to me; when speech was broadcast to the entire party it had a markedly different timbre. In order to make my replies private I only had to moderate their volume.

"How many craft of this sort have you launched before?" I murmured.

"None identical to this one," Speaker replied, scrupulously. "Most of our exploratory craft are much smaller, with minimal life-support provision."

The life-support provision aboard the ship seemed primitive enough to me, whether or not the worms and headless insects had functional roles to play within it, but I did not voice that opinion explicitly, internally or externally.

"Have you sent others with humanoid passengers?" I said

"We have sent others capable of generating humanoid scions," was the reply to that. I realized that it would not normally be necessary for the Chimeras to dispatch vessels whose interiors contained abundant living-space for human-sized entities; the standard Chimerical space-explorer would be something more akin to a flying womb, capable of producing offspring adapted to particular purposes at various termini. For relatively inexperienced navigators of space, this mission would be a bold new venture, using many untried techniques.

"Have you sent vessels of the other sort to the worlds of other stars?" I asked.

"No," the voice replied. "A few have reached the moons of Jupiter and returned, while several more have carried data-transmitters much further, without there being any possible of return for their physical structure. The void is not as empty as its name implies, and cosmic radiation exacts a slow but heavy toll. We had judged interstellar travel to be well-nigh impossible until we made contact with the Metamorphosians, and certainly far too difficult to warrant any serious attempt. We have always required a strong incentive to send any of our units into regions beyond the reach of mental communion with Earth. There was a time when the augmentation of Earth's potential biomass seemed sufficiently necessary to justify such operations, but that was long ago."

"The Metamorphosians obviously think differently," I observed, "and their vessels must have better shielding against radiation than you are able to provide."

"It is not a matter of ability," the voice informed me. "We can employ metals when we perceive a need. If we could perceive a need, we would be able to contrive our own nuclear reactors to duplicate the energy-production of the sun. It is not incapacity that prevents us from so doing but our perception of need and virtue."

The reference to virtue was interesting, in the context of the moral dimension of the Amphibians' exercise of will-power, but I found it too difficult to distract myself with further conversation. The ship had detached itself from the tree and was climbing rapidly away from the Earth. My weight was increasing with equal rapidity, and it was becoming difficult to breathe, let alone to speak.

For a while, I concentrated on resisting the pressure.

That would not have been very difficult had it not been for the presence of Liamon. Under normal circumstances, she had perfect control of her mental presence, and did not allow that presence to be felt in the minds of others unless she made a specific effort to project her thoughts—but the take-off was by no means an ordinary circumstance. The shock and pressure of the apparent increase in gravitational force, and hence in weight, afflicted her more painfully and more dangerously than any of the rest of us. She only emitted a slight audible sound, more reminiscent of a whimper than a scream, but her mental presence radiated a more profound and evident distress.

I felt the pressure of that distress more keenly than I felt my own, although I knew it for what it was and knew that it offered no real threat to me. As well as the distress itself I felt an answer of sorts, not merely from the collective intelligence of the Chimeras but from the much closer source of Mirastara's compassion. I did what I could to join my own feeble energy with that of the Amphibian, hoping to amplify her efforts by some small but tangible degree. I doubt that I achieved much, but I wanted to think that I was offering some kindly response rather than merely serving as an idle recipient of that manifest anguish.

There was a moment, I think, when Liamon became convinced that the pressure was too great, and that her heart would burst under the strain. She was ready to die; had she been in a darker mood, she might have accepted death—but she had the psychological strength as well as the physical strength to resist. She came through it. When the excessive drag eventually relented, to be replaced by weightlessness, she was flooded by a wonderful euphoria.

I had felt relief many times before, and joy on occasion, but those merely human emotions seemed as feeble as my will-power and the body I had taken to the trenches in the face of that cataract of alien emotion, which drove all thought from my head and seemed to blast me out of the spaceship into some miraculous quintessential space that was anything but void. Then Liamon gained possession of herself again, and withdrew her mental presence into the privacy of her own skull, so completely that she could not even utter the apology whose vague impression she left lingering in the warm atmosphere.

The air within the vessel was moist as well as warm, and I was sweating heavily, but the sweat evaporated more easily once we became weightless. Several minutes passed before I felt capable of coherent thought again; during the interim, all was confusion and delirium within my skull. The tiny creatures with which we shared our living space had ceased their restless movement, becoming so still that I wondered whether they might have fused with the supportive web, temporarily if not permanently.

"Is everyone all right?" Clara asked, raising her voice. The whisper in her ear could have told her of course, but she evidently wanted to hear our voices.

"Safe and sound," Philip Danby said, aloud.

"Quite well," I answered, in the same fashion.

"I am well," Mirastara added.

We did not expect any reply from Liamon, let alone the one that actually came. All the giant said was "Yes," but she said it *aloud*, with an inflection of relief and gratitude.

There was no need to be surprised that she had the requisite vocal apparatus to speak English—the Dwellers were, after all, humankind's ultimate descendants—nor that she would be able to use it if the occasion warranted its use. I did, however, feel entitled to be surprised that she thought this such an occasion.

"From now on," the voice in my earpiece assured us all, "there should be little or no danger. There will be only one more critical moment."

We all knew what the voice meant. We had made our departure; the next opportunity for disaster would be our arrival. The craft had sufficient native intelligence to make a safe landing, but we would then have to descend from the craft, hopefully into some safe air-filled subsurface cavity.

For the time being, the threads of mock-spidersilk relaxed their protective grip, and became a relatively inert superstructure—a climbing-frame by means of which we could have moved about the vessel's interior had we been given permission to do so. Liamon had no intention of moving, so she was not inconvenienced by that lack of permission. The rest of us chafed beneath its burden, however, continually adjusting our positions and clearing away enough threads from in front of our faces to allow us a clearer sight of the screen that displayed the view from the ship's exterior.

We could see the curved edge of the Earth very clearly as the vessel followed the arc of its flight. It was as silvery white as a polished knife-blade, but I was still unable to estimate the extent of its increased diameter. The more remarkable sight, to my eyes, was that of the stars beyond its edge. The moon, our destination, was not in view; the curved paths that we and the satellite would follow to our rendezvous would leave it hidden for some time to come.

I had expected to see more stars from without the atmosphere than were visible from within, but not as many more as were visible now. What seemed more remarkable still was the impotence of all those countless light-sources to moderate the darkness against which they were placed. No matter how many pin-pricks of light were now manifest, the void in which they were set still seemed infinite, and essentially empty.

Well, I thought, *I was not the first human traveler in time, nor even the first to return home, but I was the first to return with a substantial tale to tell. I dare say that I am not the first human traveler in space, as judged from the viewpoint of the millionth century after Christ, but I am one of the first to have a chance of returning to the twentieth century with a tale to tell of alien visitors and news of current affairs in the greater galaxy. I am entitled to take a little pride in that.*

Chapter Twenty-Six

The Flight

I had vocalized my thought too clearly. Mirastara and Liamon had no difficulty in reading it.

"Legitimate pride was reserved to giants in my day," Liamon observed, pensively, "but that was because the one thing in which we took pride, above all else, was our size. No Dweller ever went into space, for we had anchored ourselves far too efficiently to the Earth."

"I was prideful once," Mirastara said. "I thought it a great adventure to take a short cut into the future, as you had done—to become a lone pioneer, departed from the comfortable presence of my sisters, expectant of having a fabulous tale to tell. I was never a Leader, though. I was never fitted to be one of the Seven, by reason of having too much of the competitive spirit that they disdained. Of all my kind, I was the one most vulnerable to vanity—and the one who paid the price."

"It was not too high a price, in the end," Liamon observed, presumably thinking that she had paid a similar price, in being likewise unable to return to her own people. "The purchase will be worth the effort and risk alike."

"We have not yet reached the end of our story," Mirastara said. She might equally well have pointed out that she and the Dweller were very different beings, whose existential penalties were not strictly comparable, but she preferred to focus on the argument that might apply to all of us. It applied more to me than to anyone else, though, because I now had reason to think that this was still an early chapter of my own story, with no prospect of a dénouement yet in sight.

Philip Danby was the first among us to attempt a more substantial movement, complaining aloud that he needed to slake his thirst.

"Do not be afraid," the voice said, immediately. "The network will see to all your needs." Clara, who had followed Danby's example, seemed reluctant to give up, but I stayed where I was.

"If it were necessary," I whispered to the Earthly listener, "you could escape the Earth. If it were necessary, you might even escape the destruction of the Earth, if that is really what you fear in regard to the Metamorphosians. One advantage of possessing a single collective consciousness is surely its capacity to withstand and survive the devastation of it physical presence. No matter what kind of threat the Metamorphosians might provide, you have the means to survive it."

"Earthly life might survive," the voice replied, "although there is also a possibility that it would not—but we are what we are, and we are more vulnerable than you might imagine. It is absolutely necessary for us to open a constructive dialogue with the Metamorphosians, and if you are able to help us accomplish that, you will have every possible justification for legitimate pride—more, perhaps, than any hero of your own myths, including Prometheus."

The voice meant well, of course. It was attempting flattery—but it might have remembered that my earlier reminiscences of Prometheus, the bringer of divine fire to humankind, had been tempered with an awareness of the punishment to which he had been subject by the gods.

"I saw heroes a-plenty during the Great War," I muttered. "When the conflict finally came to an end, I was exceedingly glad that it had never been necessary for me to be one of them."

"A man who gives his life for his country or his comrades," the voice told me, although it could not possibly attribute any meaning to what it was saying beyond what could be found in a dictionary, "is only half a hero. The hero who lives in fear for years on end, but returns home hale in body and strong in mind, ready for further endeavor, has the opportunity to be a whole one."

"No," I said, sadly. "A hero must bring home a more valuable gift than that, and we who returned from the Great War brought none. What we called a victory was a mere truce—a pause, not an accomplishment."

"But you are a hero *now*," the voice of the Chimeras insisted, "and will be a hero greater than any before, if you can bring back the gift of the Earth's safe-keeping."

Perhaps the voice was right—but I was not so vain as to think myself capable of securing a gift like that, even in combination with the allies who were at my side and the forces that had been put at my disposal.

"I'll do what I can," I promised, in the faintest whisper I could contrive, "although I would be disappointed to think that the gift of the Earth's safe-keeping might only prepare the way for the kind of Simplicity that Mirastara imagined."

"It would not," the voice assured me. "It is a needless anxiety. If that is what the Metamorphosians fear, they must have been misled by their experiences of otherworldly life. We have not forsaken our flexibility of thought and desire. We know how dangerous it would be to become so content with what we have that we lost the will to be anything more."

"Have you secured a second time-bridge yet?" I demanded, bluntly.

"No," the voice replied. "Until we do, there is no need to make plans as to how we might use it. You would do better to set such thoughts aside, at least for now."

"If you do contrive to open one, though," I said, "it will become an important bargaining-chip in your future negotiations with the Metamorphosians."

"It might—but in the meantime, we cannot take it into account."

In the meantime, my companions seemed to have reconciled themselves to their condition. Clara had stopped struggling and accepted her imprisonment. Danby was no longer complaining of thirst. For myself, I no longer felt uncomfortable, and had not felt thirsty since the embarkation. The web did, indeed, seem to be very adept at supplying my basic bodily needs, and I wondered whether it was also responsible for the gathering impression I had that a great weight was being slowly lifted from my consciousness, leaving me with a strange cocktail of sensations whose chief ingredient was a blithe awareness of my own frailty.

I turned my head to look at Liamon. She was lying quite still, with her eyes closed. She was not asleep, though; I was still aware of her attentive mind.

"Liamon," I said, "are you quite comfortable now?"

"I have never known existence to be so effortless," the giant said. "I am almost ready to admit the charges laid against the supposed folly that possessed my ancestors when they decided to remake themselves as giants."

"Almost?" The query came from Mirastara.

"You cannot estimate the sense of satisfaction that comes from largeness," Liamon said. "Philip has some inkling of it, if I have read his dreams correctly. You would be a giant if you could, would you not, Philip?"

"I might," Danby agreed, audibly. "There is nothing comforting in being tiny, and I feel very tiny indeed at present, knowing that I am floating in the void in a hollowed-out seed." He switched to mind-speech to add: "Are we moving beyond the range of the Chimeras' mind-reading powers? I feel a curious sense of pleasant isolation."

Before the Dweller answered, I realized that he must be right. The alteration in my state of consciousness had nothing to do with the mass of cobwebs in which I was entwined; it was the effect of our gradual withdrawal from the field of the Earth's mind-force.

"We shall be out of range soon, if we are not already," Liamon confirmed. "If we had any secrets left, we would be able to subvocalize them in relative safety—but we have not. Nor should we be confident of our ability to keep any we may discover in future. While we are on the moon, the Metamorphosians will undoubtedly be as inquisitive as the Chimeras, and when we return our minds will be stripped bare with relative ease."

I looked at the screen again, although the edge of the Earth was no longer visible and I knew that no further change in the view was to be expected until the edge of the moon encroached upon the image. The stars seemed even more numerous, though, and it was now possible to make out the long ribbon of the Milky Way, along whose central strip the dark background was almost—but not quite—drowned by light.

Weightlessness and the absence of the Chimeras' collective presence did not make my own physical existence seem effortless; indeed, I felt as if my internal organs had swollen somewhat, and were pressing upon one another more forcefully than before. It was easy enough to draw an analogy between that tangible pressure and the metaphorical pressure of the possibilities that seemed to have multiplied alarmingly of late.

The voice was right, I told myself. *It is necessary to concentrate on the business in hand, for now, and set further possibilities aside. We must meet the Metamorphosians, and persuade them to make peace. We must convince them that the Chimeras mean them no harm. We must convince them that the Chimeras, like the Amphibians before them, can only make full use of their mental force when they are acting in accordance with their moral convictions.*

Mirastara was close enough to me to have caught the drift of my reverie, for she could not resist intruding a warning. "You must be careful in using that argument," she advised. "Its implications are unclear."

Human history, I knew, was replete with individuals who had committed appalling deeds while believing themselves to be acting virtuously, but I had thought that the Amphibians were cut from finer cloth. "Even if the moral element of our mental force is a matter of psychological conviction rather than the pressure of objective virtue," I said, "I cannot imagine that beings of your sort would be capable of aggression or atrocity."

"As you once pointed out to me, the fish we herded for the Dwellers and consumed for our own nourishment might disagree," she said. "The Dwellers had not the slightest moral regard for the likes of Frog-mouths and Killers—and they were content to place you in a similar category, at least to begin with. Even if the Chimeras did find themselves hesitant in the matter of using mental force against the Metamorphosians, other forces have no such inherent scrupulousness."

"That is another line of thought that might be best set aside," Liamon's mental voice cut in. "At the risk of providing too much food for thought, however, you might care to bear in mind that there is more than one sort of morality, and that the righteousness of retributive justice can also fuel mental force. You were, I believe, both party to the fate of another group of specimens fished out of time."

She was referring to the Bat-wings. "Yes, we were," I admitted. "But there was no exercise of mental force involved—the whole affair was merely brutal, from beginning to end."

"There is no *mere* brutality, when conscious decisions are made," Liamon replied. "Righteous indignation is a powerful activator of all kinds of forceful endeavor—and that is why it is worrying that the Metamorphosians believe that the Chimeras have already taken hostile action against them."

Had we not been moving away from Earth so rapidly, and beyond the range of mental eavesdroppers, I might have hesitated to form my next thought so clearly—but even if we could not expect to keep secrets for long, there seemed no reason why we should not take advantage of our freedom.

"Can we be sure that they did not?" I asked, bluntly.

"There is no certainty," Liamon admitted, "but I cannot imagine *how* they might have done such a thing, let alone why. If, as I assume, the abduction took place inside the moon rather than in space, whoever carried it out must have clever agents there. The Chimeras do not employ individual minions, and could not have directed their own mind-force to that sort of task at such a distance. It is conceivable that there is an offshoot of the Earth's biosphere lurking within the moon's depths, operating independently of its parent, but it seems unlikely. The Chimeras are, however, aware of the existence of other interstellar travelers, who have visited the solar system and have left relics of their sojourn here. I cannot make any reasoned estimate of the probability that some of those relics are on the moon, and sufficiently active to interfere with the Metamorphosians, but that too seems rather unlikely. It seems to me that the most probable hypothesis...."

"Wait a moment," I said. "What are these *relics* of past interstellar travelers?"

"According to the Chimeras—whose knowledge is very vague—they are machines, of a sort which would be capable of operating on and within the moon, though not on Earth."

The concept that Liamon was attempting to form seemed most readily translatable into improvised English as *Aerophobe.*

"They're entities that shun atmospheres?" I said, wanting to be sure that the idea had been communicated correctly.

"Apparently," Liamon replied. "The machines left behind by these visitors—who left no other surviving trace of their brief passage—are designed to operate in near-vacuum, indefinitely. The corrosion inflicted upon them by atmospheric gases is slight, at least in the short term, but they are apparently programmed to avoid such gases rigorously. They can replicate themselves, and build other machines, with the aid of minerals mined from asteroids, but the process seems to be difficult and slow. They are not conscious, and seem incapable of exerting any mind-force at all, but they do have a certain calculative cleverness that might be regarded as intelligence. Nothing the Chimeras know about them, however, suggests that they would be capable of seizing a party of living beings and spiriting them away, or that they might have any conceivable motive for doing so."

"But we can't be certain that they are not involved?"

"No, we cannot be certain—but we cannot be certain, either, of the extent to which the Metamorphosians may be divided among themselves. They seem to be individuated beings, and therefore easily capable of internecine disputes. Of the three parties that might be responsible for any misfortune that has befallen the Metamorphosians on the moon, therefore, it seems to me that the one most likely to be guilty is the Metamorphosians themselves."

"If the Metamorphosians interrogate me in the same fashion the Liamon did," I reminded her, "they're bound to perceive my awareness of that judgment."

"Of course they will," Liamon replied. "The fact is, however, that we simply do not know who might have attacked the Metamorphosians, or why. When they interrogate you, they will perceive that too. There is no need to be afraid. Fortunately or unfortunately, we are in the position of having nothing to hide."

CHAPTER TWENTY-SEVEN

THE LANDING

When the moon eventually became close enough to fill the screen, it presented an image of utter stillness and desolation. It was a vast grey desert in which nothing moved, like an item of abstract art cast in granite.

Our precise objective lay in the east of the Mare Fecunditatis, where there were very few impact craters—presumably because that part of the surface had once been hit by so large an object that the rock had been melted into magma before cooling again, smoothing itself out as it did so. That had happened billions of years ago, but the featureless area had only been hit a few times more by objects large enough to leave a visible scar.

As the ship made its final approach the living spidersilk became more active again. The insectile and vermiform units began to move back and forth with considerable urgency, while the cocoons that had been holding us rather loosely began to thicken and tighten. The growing threads also began to form rigid shells about our heads, with transparent visors before our eyes through which we could see. Thicker structures also began to form on our backs; I could not see my own taking shape, but I could see Clara and Mirastara developing obtrusive humps.

There was still no visible sign of activity on the Mare's surface when the moon's disc gradually wheeled out of view as the ship realigned itself for the landing. My stomach seemed to perform a leisurely cartwheel as the direction my eyes had grown accustomed to perceiving as "up" became a tangible "down", but the gravitational force exerted by the moon was much less than the drag of the Earth, and the restoration of evident weight did not seem troublesome at all. I could read no vestige of distress in Liamon's kind; she was perfectly self-controlled, if not entirely comfortable.

When the ship's maneuver was complete, we discovered that we could see the Earth on the viewscreen. It seemed very tiny, suspended against the starry backcloth. The planet's disc was not fully-illuminated; little more than half of it was directly sun-lit, although the remainder of its shape was visible as a kind of ghostly glow. Its apparent surface—which was actually the upper cloud-layer—was featureless in the strictest sense, but it was variegated by streaks of drifting color, which reproduced the uncertainty I had earlier seen at close range on a much vaster scale,

The deceleration phase of the flight, as the vessel made its final descent, was easily bearable; Liamon did not utter so much as a sigh. When the ship was settled, we immediately began wriggle, as if to work our newly bulky forms free of the supporting network, but the web resisted our initial efforts, holding us in place—which was perhaps as well, given that the rest of us would have fallen on to Liamon's supine form.

Our reflexive struggle was interrupted by a small but sudden lurch. I looked at the screen immediately, to see what was happening. At first I could see nothing untoward, but then our view of the star field was circumscribed by a swiftly-shrinking circle. A section of the bare rock upon which the ship stood was descending into the ground, cutting out a circle about a hundred feet in radius. The walls of the shaft through which we were moving seemed to have been sheared with remarkable precision, for they were perfectly smooth. I guessed that this was no permanent elevator, but something improvised for the occasion.

The descent continued for more than two minutes. I estimated that we dropped between eighty and a hundred fathoms. When we stopped again, there was still sufficient sunlight reflected from the concave walls of the shaft to show up a number of darker circles, where corridors apparently extended horizontally into the rock.

Without any bidding from us, the view given by the screen shifted, so that we were soon looking sideways from the base of the vessel. This allowed us to perceive that we had stopped on a level with one of the interrupted corridors, so that the floor now comprised by the platform on which the spaceship stood would allow us to walk to its entrance. While we watched in silence, entities whose forms reminded me somewhat of gigantic praying mantises moved out of the visible entrance of the severed corridor, each carrying a cargo of tools and metal plates. When a dozen of them had passed through, half of them set about constructing a door with which to seal the fractured corridor, while the others arranged themselves about our craft.

"I preferred the angel sent to welcome us to the future Earth," Clara murmured. "These have a distinctly demonic aspect in comparison."

She had been heard on Earth; after a pause, Speaker's voice replied: "Those are machines, not the Metamorphosians themselves."

"We had guessed that," I replied. "We had better go to greet them, I suppose—if your protective cobwebs will condescend to let us depart."

I glanced down at Liamon, whose new suit had taken far longer to construct than the others. It was complete now, though.

"You will be conveyed to the exit-point in turn," the mechanical voice informed me, "George will leave the craft first. Once he has made sure that these devices pose no threat, the others will follow him. Liamon will bring up the rear. Once she is outside, the craft will be sealed again to await your return."

I tried not to wonder whether any of the tiny web-crawlers would make their own exits along with us, but could not keep the idea out of my head.

The web transported me to the vessel's wall. I had to wait for a few minutes before a slit opened in front of me, but then it became easy to step into the fissure as the supportive threads seemed to melt away. I moved more awkwardly than before, because the suit that the cocoon had made for me was bulkier than any suit of clothes I had even worn, but its headpiece was far less oppressive than a gas mask, so I did not feel uncomfortably constrained.

I would not have felt particularly claustrophobic had I actually been able to step through a doorway, but the wall of the vessel was much thicker than I had anticipated, and my first step took me into it rather than through it. I felt it close up behind me before it opened up in front of me, but I was only trapped for a second or two. A new crack began to open in its outer surface as soon as the one behind me was sealed, widening gradually to the point at which I could squeeze through it. I must have made a rather ungainly appearance in the eyes of the mantis-machines—which did, indeed, have obvious eyes mounted in their heads.

The machine that confronted me as I moved away from the spaceship seemed to meet my stare without curiosity. I presumed that it would not be able to understand me if I spoke with my mind, and knew that it would not be able to hear oral speech in the vacuum that surrounded us, so I raised my hand in a mock greeting.

The mantis raised its right forelimb in response. Then it turned away, and moved toward the door. I followed it for a few steps but paused, intending to let my companions catch up. I looked up at the seemingly-tiny circle far overhead, in which only a few stars were visible, although a little sunlight reflected from the smoothly-excised upper walls, its effect weakening as it was further reflected downwards.

The vertical shaft appeared to have cut through three other horizontal tunnels at different heights; I wondered how long they had been there, and how many others had been excavated at lower depths. Unless the Metamorphosians had been very busy, they must have found these subterrains waiting for them when they first arrived on the moon, presumably excavated by the products of some Earthly civilization that had preceded the Dwellers.

I realized that Liamon's enumeration of possible kidnappers had left out a fourth hypothesis: the possibility that some exceedingly old Earth-originated species still maintained a stronghold in the utmost depths of a moon that had been eaten out to the very core by artificial worms or moles, hundreds of millions of years ago.

I was soon joined by Mirastara, Clara and Danby, but we had to wait for a while longer before Liamon appeared. When she finally emerged, I checked her height mentally against that of the tunnel that was now equipped with a doorway, and judged that she might just about be able to walk along the corridor beyond without bumping her head. The machine had paused too, but as soon as the giant had joined us it resumed its progress towards the door.

The door opened, revealing a chamber with a further door blocking the corridor some fifteen feet away. The mantis did not enter, but stood aside so that we might. Once we were all inside this chamber the door behind us closed, leaving us in pitch darkness.

"It must be an airlock," Danby said. He was speaking aloud, his words being relayed to the earpieces inside our suits. "They will fill it with air, I presume, and then the other door will open to give us access to an air-filled tunnel within.

The deduction was reasonable, but wrong, and it failed to anticipate the rainstorm—or, rather, the chemical shower—that deluged us from above for a full minute while we waited for the inner door to open. Our new suits were evidently impervious to leakage, because I felt no sensation of invading damp, nor did the liquid accumulated on the floor of the corridor, because I would have been able to feel its rise once it got to my ankles, let alone my calves.

It will need to have a powerful effect, I thought, *if it is to stop the threads of the suit emitting worms and termites as opportunity arises*. As soon as I had framed the thought I wished that I had not put it into words, but it was too late. As yet, I could not feel any general mental presence to compare with that of the Chimeras, but that did not mean that no such presence was there. I had to suppose that the Metamorphosians would be able to read my mind soon enough, if they could not do it already, and that all my ideas would then be laid bare to inspection.

After a few minutes, the inner door opened, and we passed through it.

The corridor within did not appear to be filled with air. A voice in our earpieces—which was not Speaker's, and whose command of English seemed markedly less confident—suddenly began to speak, in a fashion similar to the voice that had spoken to me inside the Metamorphosians' machine. I could not tell for certain whether Speaker was still able to use the apparatus herself, or hear what the new voice said, but I suspected that the Chimeras' radio link had now been cut off, because the rock above our heads was sufficiently solid to block any sort to electromagnetic signal.

The new voice told us that the integrity of our suits would be maintained throughout our sojourn in the moon, and that no attempt would be made to breach that integrity without our specific consent. As it spoke, a strip of light appeared in the ceiling of the corridor, providing dim but adequate illumination for our passage along it.

"What should we call you?" I asked—but the new voice made no immediate answer. It did not even give us directions as to how to proceed. I assumed that we were simply to follow the corridor, at least until we came to a junction, and I moved forward.

It was not long before we reached the opening of a side-corridor, but the strip of light continued straight ahead and so did I. We passed three more junctions with unlit corridors before the corridor opened out into an atrium containing the head of a spiral stair-case that led further downwards. The central column of the staircase was illuminated, with just sufficient brightness to display the steps and the outer wall. The stairway was not big enough to accommodate a giant of Liamon's dimensions.

"The giant must wait here for a while," the mechanical voice said. "Arrangements will be made for her transport in due course. The rest of you must go down the stair."

"We would prefer to wait with her," I replied.

"Do as you are asked," Liamon said, speaking directly into my mind. "I can feel the Metamorphosians' mental presence, although you probably cannot. I do not think they intend to separate us permanently—but whoever built these corridors did not intend them for the use of giants."

"You agree with me, then, that it was not the Metamorphosians who built them?"

"They do not seem to feel at home here, if I am reading their anxieties correctly," Liamon told me. "I assume that they found the cavern-complex deserted and airless, and assumed that the entire moon must be dead—but now they are by no means so sure. Many civilizations rose and fell between your time and mine. Many records were handed down to us, but they were far from complete and the Seekers of Wisdom could not decipher all of them. We had no knowledge of any civilization constructed on the moon, but the mere existence of these elaborate and carefully-squared tunnels suggests that there must have been one, probably established in an era closer to yours than mine, by individuals who had more in common with you than with me—although they must have had more in common with both of us than with the builders of the insect-machines that greeted us."

Until Liamon made her calculated reference to the corridors having been carefully-squared, I had not realized the significance of the fact that the floor of the corridor made a right angle as it met the vertical wall; the Chimeras would not have done that. The atrium in which we had paused was cylindrical rather than cubical, but its circular wall met the floor at a right angle, with no hint of a meniscus. I peered hard at the dimly-lit wall, trying to discern any markings that might be inscribed there, but I could not find any.

"Go down the stairway," the voice in my earpiece instructed.

I looked at Liamon again, and she nodded. I led the way down the spiral staircase, soon losing count of the number of steps and the number of turns we made around the central pillar. Eventually, we reached the bottom of the shaft, to be confronted with a single door, whose armor-plating seemed more recent than the staircase.

I tried to reach Liamon by means of mind-speech, but could not do it. I looked questioningly at Mirastara, who confirmed by a gesture that the Dweller was now inaccessible to mental communication.

The door opened of its own accord, swinging back on hinges in a manner quite unlike the Chimera's portals. It was very thick, and appeared to make a tight seal. The brief section of corridor within was blocked off by a similar door; it was only just long enough to accommodate all four of us, but it was more brightly lit than the passages through which we had come. We stepped into it, and the door closed behind us. There was a pause of some two or three minutes before the further door opened; there was no second deluge of liquid but there was a faint hiss as the space was filled with air.

Eventually, the inner door swung back, and we came into an air-filled cubical vault some ten yards square, which had another sealed exit in the far wall. This room, however, had four beds set in recesses, two to either side, and a square table in the centre.

The table was large enough to seat six people of our size, but there were only five chairs, none of them suitable for a giant's use. Liamon, apparently, was to be separately accommodated. I did not know whether I could safely assume that whatever came to meet us would be approximately the size of a human being, formed with sufficient similarity to be able to sit.

The room had a supply of water, consisting of an actual tap suspended over a stone bowl, more reminiscent of a font than a washing-basin. We could not wash while wearing our suits, but I presumed that the suits would need to replenish their supplies of water somehow. There was no handle on the second door, and none inside the one that swung shut behind us. I pushed the further one, but it did not yield.

"This is a poor prison by comparison with the accommodations the Chimeras provided," Danby remarked.

"The Metamorphosians do not have access to the same resources," I said. "We could hardly expect a palace."

"There is breathable air in this space," the voice in my earpiece informed us, "but we do not require you to remove your suits. A spokesman will join you shortly."

CHAPTER TWENTY-EIGHT

THE METAMORPHOSIAN SPOKESMAN

I attempted to sit down, but fund the sitting position awkward because of the lump on my back, and stood up again almost immediately. I looked at one of the beds, which consisted of a soft mattress laid on a wooden platform, and felt grateful that I did not need to sleep, even though I could probably have lain on my side comfortably enough.

"There *are* marks on the walls," Mirastara observed. "If you look very carefully, *here* and *here*, you will be able to make them out. They mean nothing to me, though."

She was right. There were inscriptions painted on the walls—or had been, at one time. They had faded over time, presumably while these caverns were still in use, or not long after their abandonment, since they must have been evacuated—and thus almost immune to change—for hundreds of thousands of years before the Metamorphosians arrived. I could not make out any symbols I could comprehend, but it seemed to me that the inscriptions might well have been made by something closely akin to a human hand.

"It appears that one of our descendant species not only reached the moon but made its interior habitable," I said.

"We cannot be sure of that," Clara said. "If other interstellar travelers have passed through the system—perhaps long before our own species evolved—they might have hollowed out the moon for their own purposes."

"Or for the purpose of providing accommodation for the Aerophobes they left behind," I said. "The Metamorphosians might not be the first visitors to discover these workings and take up temporary residence here—and they must know by now that they may not be the only ones still here."

The door through which we had come opened again then, and a humanoid form appeared on the threshold. He—I immediately began thinking of it as male, although I had no particular reason for doing so—was a little taller than me but thinner in the limbs, especially the lower ones. He appeared to be wearing a protective suit not unlike the ones in which we were cocooned, although it had no ungainly hump on the back. The helmet had a clear visor through which we could see the greater part of his face, which might have passed for human, despite the coarseness of his features, his pronounced brow ridges and his black facial hair, most of which was clumped into an untidy moustache and beard. He sat down, and looked at us in turn. His eyes might have lingered a little longer on my hairless face than it did on Mirastara's furry one, but not conspicuously so.

I made a second attempt to sit down, on the chair to the newcomer's right and managed to find a position that was not too uncomfortable, balanced on its edge. The others followed suit; Danby took the chair to the Metamorphosian's left, while Clara and Mirastara sat opposite.

"The creatures you call Chimeras cannot hear us," was the first thing the newcomer said. The voice, which reached us via our earpieces, was not the one that had guided us here, being lower in pitch and more guttural in quality. "The hive-mind of the planetary biosphere is quite impotent at this distance. If you are indeed the time-displaced individuals you claim to be, you might be glad of that freedom. Consciously, you believe yourselves to be what you pretend to be—but the unconscious is not so easily misled, and we shall discover the truth soon enough."

"My name is George," I said. "My present companions are Mirastara, who is an Amphibian, and Clara and Philip, who are humans like me. The giant we were forced to leave at the top of the stairway is Liamon. We are concerned by the fact that we can no longer make mental contact with her"

"You may call me Assiah," the newcomer replied, ignoring my final remark.

"If this room is equipped with breathable air," I said, "Why are you dressed in a suit like ours?"

"There is a danger of contamination," was Assiah's blunt reply. "We apologize for the fact that we cannot let any of you into our own living-quarters, but you must understand why we need to exercise caution. We are under siege here."

"Have you found out what happened to your missing personnel?" I asked.

"No," Assiah said. "We assume that they are still somewhere in the moon, but we do not know where, or who took them. If the Earthian hive-mind is also ignorant, there must others here. We have not detected their mind-fields, but that is not surprising, given the extent of the lunar caverns and the quantity of solid rock that must separate any other bases it contains from ours. We are exploring the core as quickly and as thoroughly as we can. The Aerophobes in Jupiter orbit report that they have no cousins on the moon, but they would not necessarily have any record of it if they had. They also report that they have lost contact with far more units in the last few million years than they would expect to lose as a result of the vicissitudes of chance, most of them in the inner reaches of the system."

"Do you trust them any more than you trust the Chimeras?" I asked.

"Yes. Aerophobes are not self-aware and do not lie, so far as we know. We also trust one another, even though we are perfectly capable of lying. There is no rivalry or dissent within our ranks."

"Do you know who built this cave-complex within the moon?" I asked.

"No, but we know, approximately, when it was constructed. If you are telling the truth about your points of temporal origin, it was built approximately half way between them."

"By one of our descendant species, then," I concluded.

"Perhaps," was Assiah's response to that hypothesis. "We are certain that it has lain derelict for a very long time, but it is possible that there was some sort of repository in the core or on the far side, which was reactivated in response to our arrival."

"A repository of Aerophobes?" I asked.

"Quite possibly," Assiah replied. "There are Aerophobes in every solar system that my kind has explored, and perhaps in every solar system in the galaxy. Their archives retain no record of their ultimate point of origin, and they probably had more than one. Their remote ancestors must have been manufactured by creatures possessed of hands like yours and mine—there is precious little evolutionary scope in the natural productions of silicon and metal—but we can only guess as to who their makers might have been. Their own lives are measured in hundreds of millennia, when they do not suffer accidental destruction, but they usually reproduce themselves many times over in a lifetime, carefully modifying their manufactured children, apparently more in the interests of novelty than increasing efficiency. They rarely interfere with other cultures, and seem highly unlikely to be responsible for the disappearance of our peers, but we cannot rule out the possibility. The other biospheres native to the system seem to be devoid of intelligence at present, but that might not always have been the case. Given that, we cannot entirely rule out the possibility that one of those biospheres might once have produced a space-faring species. By far the most likely hypothesis, however, is that Earth's biosphere is the ultimate source of our problem. If so, the fact that it has entered a direly dangerous evolutionary phase may become doubly significant."

"The Chimeras do not understand why you consider them so dangerous," I said. "Nor can they understand why you are so reluctant to talk to them directly, even by means of electromagnetic signals. Why you are so insistent that you will only talk to members of individualized species?"

"The Chimeras do not know what the typical patterns of evolution are," Assiah retorted, "but they must understand perfectly well how dangerous a biosphere of their sort is to living beings of our sort. If they were blissfully ignorant before we arrived, they must have begun to understand now that they have had to entertain *you*, and keep you safe, for a little while. Even if they created you, falsifying your sense of identity and filling you with false memories, they have been forced to learn that lesson.

"While their ancestors were building their worldwide hive, of course, they felt no need to think about the problems involved in the preservation of individuality, but we have forced them to think about those problems now, and they cannot help but see the kind of threat they pose. We admit, though, that no other collective intelligence of their sort has ever gone fishing for individuals in the depths of its own past—not so far as we are aware, at any rate. Neither we nor any species our ancestors encountered on their travels have ever mastered any such technology."

"My father is an exceptional man," Danby put in. "It seems that he found a counterpart among Liamon's kind—and that once the discovery was made, it provided its own means of further dispersal."

"We have long believed that there is nothing unique in the universe," Assiah said, "but our knowledge only encompasses a small sector of a single galaxy, and we are bound to find new things occasionally, even in the most unlikely places. On the other hand, it might be the case that, for some unknown reason, the secret is only likely to be discovered in biospheres whose evolution is in the direction of Simplicity—in which case it would always be fated to be lost again. Then again, it may be that neither humans nor Dwellers invented their means of time travel, but had it thrust upon them."

"By whom?" Danby asked, resentfully.

"By creatures much cleverer than any we know at present—the real question, if you really are what you think you are, is not so much '*by whom?*' as '*from how distant a future?*'"

"You will have to ask Liamon about that," I said. "My own impression was that the Seekers of Science never properly understood how they had contrived to fish a few meager objects out of past eras, and did not even know that they had established a better connection to the human era than any of the others until Brett appeared in their midst. Even then, they were slow to realize exactly what had happened, and wasted a second opportunity when Templeton came after Brett. Had it not been for Mirastara's intervention, I might have been wasted too—although Liamon denies that."

"We shall embark upon experiments of our own," Assiah said, "as soon as we have recovered the requisite information. We shall trade fairly for it, of course. We are employers of the will, and we accept and respect its limitations. We deal honorably with all of those with whom we may deal at all."

"A category that excludes the Chimeras, I presume?"

"Not entirely, if we can establish adequate safeguards. We are prepared to take risks, when the occasion warrants it. We would have to be extremely careful, however, about making certain kinds of technology available to a planetary hive-mind. That kind of life requires strict confinement, lest its inevitable decay into Simplicity has disastrously far-reaching consequences."

"I do not understand that," I said. "Mirastara has explained to me that a single intelligence, free of rivals, might easily develop a certain simplicity or rigidity of thought, but the Chimeras are very dismissive of that possibility."

"They are wrong to be dismissive," Assiah said, "but that is only the least part of what we mean by Simiplicity. Simplicity is a far greater threat than mere narrow-mindedness—and it is the inevitable end-result of unfettered genetic predation and exchange."

"What do you mean?" I said.

"I mean that the collective intelligence that presently inhabits Earth's biosphere has inherited, and still maintains, the entirety of the food chain that was initially developed by courtesy of natural selection. That chain extends from the primary producers, which use the energy of the sun or the Earth's internal heat to convert atmospheric carbon dioxide and water into complex molecules, through herbivorous animal forms and various carnivores to the multifarious parasites that live on and within those various plant and animal forms. The *ultimate* consumers, in your world, are the bacteria that complete and constitute processes of decay, enabling the materials contained in dead organisms to be recycled. Before the hive-mind evolved, there was a trend among Earthly individuals to oppose death and decay, by producing more long-lived and resilient bodies that were immune to disease and resistant to injury. Had that trend continued, Earth's biosphere might ultimately have produced something akin to us—Metamorphosians, in the broadest possible sense—but it did not.

"Because creatures like the Dwellers and the Amphibians were eventually displaced by the ancestors of the hive-mind, the trend towards greater individual resilience was interrupted by the triumph of chimerization, which relies on death as an instrument of change almost as much as the biological system of the human-inhabited world did, in spite of the absence of the attendant complexities of sexual reproduction. The instruments of decay have therefore flourished along with all other bioforms, becoming ever-more-ingenious as they too reap the benefits of genetic predation.

"At present, Earthly organisms of decay seem to be under the complete control of the collective intelligence of the biosphere, and while that intelligence remains omnipotent they will remain so. When they eventually contrive to evade that control, however—and eventually, one way or another, they are bound to develop some kind of immunity to mind-force—they will wreak such havoc that they will render the entire biosphere down to a kind of primal innocence: a world of bacteria, in which no complex organisms can survive, and within which no complex organisms can ever again evolve. That is what we mean by Simplicity."

"A kind of ultimate plague," I said, slowly, as I digested the import of this speech. "Your argument is that although biospheres such as Earth's remain perennially vulnerable to some such catastrophe, there are other kinds that are much better defended—and much more keenly aware of that kind of peril."

"There are no bacteria in our world," the Metamorphosian stated, "and we are very careful indeed to make sure that any which come into being within it, or invade it from without, are swiftly exterminated."

"Which explains why you will not entertain Chimerical units," I said. "Unfortunately, I cannot claim to be free of bacteria myself. I must have billions of tiny commensals living within me."

"Commensals of a relatively harmless type," Assiah commented, with such disdain that I almost felt resentful on behalf of my own parasites. "A creature as primitive as you could not live without such commensals, many of which qualify as symbiotes rather than parasites. The Amphibian and the Dweller are not quite free of them, although they are wise enough to be horrified by the extent of your innate corruption. Your passengers and theirs are not yet on the brink of that crucial final evolution, though, while some few of the multitudinous microbes of the Chimerical biosphere must be very close to freeing themselves from the mind-force yoke. Your suits and supplementary skins are a good deal more dangerous than you are—but we are prepared to entertain such artifacts briefly, when the need arises."

"And you feel that the secret of time travel might be sufficient reward for taking that risk?" I said.

"It might," Assiah replied. "But there are matters that must be settled before we can begin to think about that."

For a moment, I assumed that he meant that he had to make absolutely certain that I and my companions really were the individuals we claimed to be—but then I saw a further corollary to the logic of his argument.

"That's why the loss of your fellows worries you so much," I said. "It's not the mere fact of their disappearance that worries you; it's the possibility that they might come back as Trojan horses, carrying the seeds of this ultimate plague within their bodies."

"What we fear most of all," Assiah said, flatly, "is that any attempt to absorb organisms of our sort into a biosphere like Earth's might provide exactly the kind of challenge that would provoke a mutation releasing Simplicity within this solar system. We are not the only ones who should be anxious about that, because it would mean the destruction of Earth's collective intelligence as well as all the individual intelligences within the system."

"But if you're right in what you said before," Danby suddenly put in, evidently having been struck by a sudden inspiration, "there can't possibly be any danger of that. If you think that the real starting-point of the chain of time-bridges that the Chimeras are trying to complete lies in the future rather than the past, then life in *this* system can't possibly be fated to decay into Simplicity, can it?"

"No," Assiah replied, in the same flat tone, "it cannot—not permanently, at any rate."

CHAPTER TWENTY-NINE

THE METAMORPHOSIAN WAY

It seemed to me that I had learned more from the Metamorphosians' spokesman in a matter of minutes than I had learned from Speaker in several days, although the Chimeras' collective intelligence must have known much of what Assiah would be commissioned to tell us. There was, however, a great deal more that I was anxious to learn.

"Am I right in thinking that you, like Speaker, have been formed—or re-formed—specifically to meet us an examine us?" I asked Assiah.

"I have adopted this form for that specific purpose," Assiah said.

"So your kind identify themselves by means of the concept you have translated into English as Metamorphosians because you can adopt different physical forms, as you may choose?" I continued.

"We can change our physical forms as necessity requires," Assiah confirmed, "but in calling ourselves Metamorphosians we mean to imply something more profound than that. My ability to adapt my physical form to imitate yours is a corollary of a more important faculty."

"You're spacefarers," Danby put in. "You need that kind of adaptability so that you might operate in a wide range of physical environments—is that why you have become accomplished shape-shifters?"

"Again, that is a useful corollary, but it is not the essence of our nature. Ours is the alternative climacteric of the process of biological evolution, attained by those bioforms which follow the stricter path of Complexity rather than the promiscuous path that leads to Simplicity."

"You will need to explain more elaborately than that," I said.

"The early stages of the evolution of complex life tend to follow a broadly similar path everywhere," Assiah said. "It is a matter of sequential logic. The chemical evolution of proteins formed out of chains of amino acids opens up the same range of possibilities in each of its potential suspension-media, of which water is by far the most common and the most generously facilitating. Once molecules emerge that can serve as templates for protein-manufacture, the chromosomal mode of aggregation is the natural springboard for the development of complex forms. Natural selection then generates a series of adaptive radiations triggered by internal or external catastrophes. Eventually, however, a crisis-point is reached, in response to internal or external stresses, at which some form of genetic predation becomes possible and the barriers between species begin to break down.

"In situations which we call *chaotic*, the advent of genetic predation is uncontrolled, either because the individual intelligences that have so far evolved are incapable of taking control of it, or—more commonly—because their attempts to take control are spoiled by their ongoing conflicts with one another. That was the case on Earth, where continual warfare within and between intelligent species prevented the evolution of genetic predation from being competently managed—with the result that the intelligent species were themselves consumed and a single collective intelligence soon came to dominate a multifarious population of Chimeras. On the homeworld of my ancestors, by contrast, individuated intelligent species contrived to maintain peace long enough for each of them to adopt genetic predation as a technological means. They remained individuated, but liberated themselves from the tyranny of chromosomal determinism.

"The collective intelligence of the Chimeras maintains a totalitarian control of all its constituent organisms, but the kind of order it imposes does not affect the underlying chaos of the Earthian biosphere. Spontaneous mutation and natural selection still play a significant part in the production of new forms, which has become a much easier and faster process in the absence of sexual regulation. In that context, the eventual emergence of a mutation that can restore complete chaos—the ultimate in biological Simplicity—is inevitable. In spite of the tyrannical dominion of the Earthian hivemind, the evolutionary process there remains essentially uncontrolled and uncontrollable.

"In situations where individuals obtain control of genetic predation, however, they tend to use it very differently, and much more selectively. They usually cleanse their bodies of all commensals, while adapting their own cells and tissues to perform ay useful functions once served by those commensals. They do the same for all the other species that they retain within their biosphere for functional or aesthetic purposes, generally exterminating almost all bacterial and protozoan life. While primitive and chaotic biospheres rely on spontaneous mutation as a source of novelty and motor of evolution, individuals in ordered biospheres retain the privilege of creativity to themselves, adopting the privilege of spontaneity into a continual process of careful experimentation, in which the individual is both experimenter and experimental object.

"We are not Metamorphosians simply because we *can* remake ourselves but because we *must*; our evolutionary progress as versatile individuals is the essence of our nature, and it preserves us from the kind of existential sterility that afflicted such Earthly species as the Amphibians and the Dwellers. Evolution in Metamorphosian biospheres has no accidental component; it is entirely deliberate, and thus becomes a matter of personal responsibility. While all the units of a collective intelligence like the Earthian hive-mind become collaborators in a single enterprise—collaborators whose collusion is inherently limited and inevitably temporary—Metamorphosian individuals become contenders in an infinite and eternal competition, in which everyone is attempting not merely to improve, but to discover new ways in which to improve: new senses, new strengths, new creativities. We are the ultimate artists as well as the ultimate scientists; we represent the perfection of the individuated mode of existence."

I could see, as I glanced at my companions, that Philip Danby was not the only one impressed by this boastful self-advertisement. Clara seemed equally enthusiastic, and I could feel Mirastara's sense of revelation. Mirastara, I recalled, was a recent convert to individualism, and might therefore be forgiven a certain zealotry in her response. Had Liamon been present, she might have been similarly inspired by the notion of an ultimate individualism—but she was more inclined to cynicism, and might have hesitated, just as I was inclined to do.

"Your infinite and eternal competition appears to have very few winners," I observed. "It appears to be founded on the extermination of all other life-forms except your own, and those that you elect to treat generously."

"But Metamorphosian life-forms are themselves illimitably various," Assiah reminded me. "There is no shortage of diversity in our world—indeed, there is much more diversity in our world than there can possibly have been in yours, where every species consists of large numbers of exact replicates of one—or, at most, two—basic templates. When I say that we are engaged in an infinite and eternal competition, I do not mean that we are perpetually at war, as all the species in a world like yours are, by necessity. Ours is the kind of competition in which opponents are respected and valued, and in which there are very many winners."

"You appear to be trying very hard to convert us to your cause," I observed.

"I am," Assiah replied, bluntly. It was now clearer to me why the Metamorphosians refused to enter into diplomatic negotiations with any but individuated beings. They wanted all their intermediaries to be allies, because they did not believe that there was any neutral ground between organisms of their kind and organisms of the kind that comprised the "Earthian hive-mind".

"We are not Metamorphosians," I pointed out. "We are individuals, but we are very different from you."

"You might become Metamorphosians, with expert assistance," Assiah aid, laying his cards on the table. "That must surely seem to you to be the most worthwhile goal for which creatures of your sort might strive—unlike the possibility of being absorbed into the Earthian hive-mind." His tone was far less harsh now; his English had improved by leaps and bounds with practice. He obviously did not believe—perhaps could not even conceive of the possibility—that any of us would dispute his judgment.

The Chimeras must have known that this would happen, I thought. *They must have known what the Metamorphosians are, what attitude they would adopt towards us, and what they would offer us in return for our commitment to their part in this dispute—but they appointed us as their emissaries regardless, and went to a great deal of trouble to do so.*

I remembered what Assiah had said about the possibility that the secret of time travel was only discoverable in biospheres like Earth's—*for some unknown reason*—and his oblique acknowledgement that a biosphere's decay into Simplicity, however inevitable it might be, might not be permanent. I remembered, too, what Mirastara had said about the hazards of mental simplicity, and wondered whether the kinds of challenges provided by a Metamorphosian society were likely to provide a perfect defense against the dangers of excessive narrow-mindedness.

"Are you offering us the opportunity to become Metamorphosians?" Danby asked.

"It would be a long and difficult transition," Assiah replied, "but such transitions can be accomplished."

"But you would expect something in return," Clara said, "if you were to help us to make such a transition."

"We are honorable dealers," was Assiah's oblique reply, "and honorable competitors too."

"Unfortunately," I observed, "none of us—not even Philip or Liamon—knows the secret of time travel. Speaker's guiding intelligence is the only entity in the system capable of opening bridges through time—and that is the one entity with which you have so far refused to deal at all."

"We have already opened negotiations," Assiah pointed out. "That is why we are here. If you have no further questions to ask, we may proceed to the next stage in the process."

I did not have to ask what he meant by that. He meant the stage in which he attempted to make certain that we really were the kind of individuals we claimed to be—the kind, in his mind, who would inevitably side with his people against the present inhabitants of Earth.

"How do you achieve your metamorphoses?" Danby asked. "Can you alter your form simply by the means of the exertion of will-power?"

"We cannot change our forms very rapidly or very easily," Assiah replied. "It is a slow and complex process. Major transformations usually involve a dormant phase akin to insect pupation—but any of our various forms can go into that phase, and any can emerge, including novel forms. The transition does require the application of mind-force, but it is an intricate sort of application, which requires the involvement of other mental states than waking consciousness. A chrysalid—which is to say, a pupated individual—enters into a unique mental state: a kind of lucid dream, if you care to think of it in those terms.

"It is the ability to pupate rather than the ability to alter our form that made us into efficient space-travelers, because journeys between the stars are exceedingly long and the suspended animation of the pupal state is easier to maintain with the aid of an artificial life-support system than a more active lifestyle. The requirement to pupate from time to time also renders us more vulnerable, however, to certain forms of infection; what comes out of a cocoon is not always what was intended to emerge—and space-travelers, who routinely spend centuries in chrysalid form, are not only more vulnerable to infection but also less well-equipped to counter its effects. That is why we must be very careful in dealing with the life-forms we encounter—especially life-forms of the kind that presently inhabit your world."

"Did you explain that to the Chimeras?" I asked.

"Not in the way that we are now explaining it to you. It is not wise to detail one's weaknesses before entering into negotiations— but we are honorable dealers, and we are dealing with you. If you are what you say you are, then you are testimony to the Chimeras ability and willingness to coexist with individual species, and that will reassure us that negotiation is, indeed, possible. Had our demand been met with greater promptitude, we would have been less suspicious, but you can surely understand how those suspicions were raised, and how they have been re-emphasized by the events that have taken place since we made the demand."

"We understand that," I said. "What I do not quite understand, though, is what you originally hoped to gain from those negotiations, before the secret of time travel was ever mentioned. Why did you establish yourselves within the solar system—including a base on the moon—if you considered Earth's biosphere to be inherently dangerous? Why did you not simply continue on your way, in search of more hospitable systems?"

"We are explorers," Assiah replied. "We are also competitors. We are inherently curious, delighting in all discoveries. There is primitive life in the Jovian moons, which has not yet reached the critical point in its evolution, when its ultimate fate will be decided—unless, of course, that fate is anticipated by the arrival of some Earthly infection. Had we not discovered those biospheres, we might well have moved on again as soon as we had renewed our supplies of raw materials. The Earthian hive-mind had already drawn raw materials of the same sort from the Jovian subsystem, and its exploratory vessels appeared to be becoming more sophisticated. Some among us argued that the Earthian biosphere ought to be contained or restricted, not merely for the sake of the Jovian biospheres, but to limit the danger that its eventual decay into Simplicity might result in an infection capable of spreading through the entire system, and perhaps beyond."

"In other words," I said, "the Chimeras were right to suspect that you might take hostile action against them, deflecting the orbits of asteroids to bombard the planet."

"We would never take any such action without exploring other possibilities," Assiah insisted. "Although we imposed careful restrictions, we were and are willing to establish diplomatic relations with the Earthian hive-mind. We can offer invaluable advice on the means to avoid decay into Simplicity, if the Earthian hive-mind is capable of attending to such advice. Even if it is not, we can suggest ways in which Earth's biosphere may be safely confined. Destruction is always a last resort. We are Metamorphosians, not barbarians—but we have been attacked by a less scrupulous enemy, it seems. If the Earthian hive-mind is not responsible, there is all the more reason why we should establish some sort of mutual understanding with it."

"How, exactly, do you propose to make certain that we are what we say we are?" Danby put in, anxiously.

"If we were able to draw a little blood from each of you, for investigation and analysis," Assiah said, "we could begin to satisfy ourselves as to your physical individuality. If you would also agree to give us access to your memories, we could begin to satisfy ourselves as to your psychological make-up. You will not come to any harm, in either case. The risk, so far as we can measure it, will be entirely ours."

I could not agree with him about that; because we were, indeed, exactly what we said we were, the risk of harm, so far as *I* could measure it, was entirely on our side. Even so, I said: "I'm ready to co-operate. I have already been adapted by the Dwellers so that my memory is easily readable, so it will be best if I go first. If no harm comes to me, you may then ask for further volunteers."

"That is acceptable," Assiah said. "Will you come with me now?"

I hesitated briefly, wondering whether I ought to consult with my companions, or whether I ought to ask to see Liamon, but in the end I decided that it as what I had come here to do, and that there was no need for further delay. *It can't be any worse*, I thought, *than being abandoned to the tender mercies of the Seekers of Wisdom and the Seekers of Science for the better part of a year.*

Aloud, I said: "Yes."

Chapter Thirty

A Book Reopened

I followed Assiah through the doorway opposite the one through which we had entered the air-filled chamber. I half-expected to be led into a laboratory like those used by the Dwellers' scientists, but the lunar Metamorphosians obviously did not have such awesome collections of apparatus at their disposal. There was nothing beyond the door but a dimly-lit room even tinier and barer than the one we had just left. Its only large item of furniture was a reclining chair, although there was also a rack of shelves in one of the corners; the topmost bore various small items of equipment but the others were obscured by shadow.

In the poor light I could hardly make out Assiah's features, even when he moved his visor close to mine. I could not lie comfortably on my back because of the life-support unit in my suit, so I arranged myself rather awkwardly on my side. Assiah took up a small hypodermic syringe from the shelf; its barrel was capable of holding about five or six milliliters of liquid.

"You must consent to your suit being punctured," Assiah told me. "It will require some mental effort."

I was not sure that my mental effort would be adequate to obey this request, but I focused my thoughts as best I could. After one failed attempt, the Metamorphosian contrived to get the point of the needle through the arm of the protective suit and underlying layer of new skin. It penetrated my flesh rather clumsily, causing me more pain than I had hoped, but the tip found a vein. The Metamorphosian drew off a few milliliters of blood, which found enough oxygen as it entered the syringe to turn red.

When Assiah withdrew the needle I peered at the suit, but could not see any trace of a hole; the spidersilk threads appeared to have sealed the breach automatically. I watched the Metamorphosian go to the corner of the room, where he carefully injected samples of my blood into three objects on the lower shelves of the rack, whose forms I could not quite make out. I presumed that the biochemical analysis would be carried out within these objects, perhaps by some kind of living organism.

The Metamorphosian came back to the chair then, and operated the mechanism that made it tilt further backwards. "Can you attain the necessary mental state voluntarily?" he asked, unceremoniously.

"Yes," I said.

"Please do so." Assiah knelt down beside the chair. His helmet was close to mine, but I could not see his eyes. I could feel his mental presence, though; it seemed fainter than Liamon's or Mirastara's but I assumed that it was simply more alien, and that I had not yet developed an adequate sensitivity to its force or its nature. There was nothing in it that was readily translatable into a human emotion, let alone a thought subvocalizable in English.

It was not easy to comply with his instruction, although I had not expected to find myself resistant. The prospect of having this creature ferret through my memories was no more intimidating, in principle, than allowing Liamon the same privilege—and perhaps less so, given my experiences among the Dwellers—but I met resistance nevertheless. The Metamorphosian made no complaint, though, and was content to wait for several minutes while I composed myself, and gradually relaxed.

As in my experience with Liamon, I remained conscious of my "dream", but I was more keenly conscious than I had been on that first occasion of not being alone as an observer of my memories. Liamon had already known a good deal about what she might see in the record of my past experiences, but this observer had fewer expectations. Assiah's probing viewpoint seemed much more objective and much more distant than the Dweller's. I could not read anything at all in the Metamorphosian's mind, even when it seemed that he moved to possess mine, but the intrusive viewpoint seemed so strange that I began to see my own memories as if they were alien and difficult to comprehend.

While under Liamon's guidance I had concentrated on two particular stretches of my adult memory, but under the influence of this new observer I began from the beginning, or as close to the beginning as I could get. I was taken back to my early childhood, and slowly advanced, in fits and starts, to my schooldays. I felt a strong sense of dissatisfaction as I reviewed these early experiences, but could not be certain whether it was the intrusive observer who was dissatisfied with the extent and clarity of my recall or whether some of the dissatisfaction was mine, in being forced to witness the ineptitude and foolishness of my younger self.

Eventually, I began to remember the war, and the nebulous feeling of dissatisfaction turned into a sharper fascination, edged with horror and revulsion. The horror I could readily accept as my own, but not the fascination. There had been little fascination in my contemporary experience of the conflict or my subsequent recollections of it, which had usually been involuntary or reluctant.

The war had been a nightmare, if not from the moment of its declaration then from the day I first set foot in Belgium, and the nightmare had gone on for so long that it had eventually begun to desensitize me to all emotion—a process that had not stopped, let alone been thrown into reverse, by the Armistice. Indeed, the desensitization had not merely lingered for a long time afterwards, but had continued to increase measurably. The more profound desensitization wrought by the Dwellers' interference, which had likewise continued to increase after my return to the twentieth century, had been an extrapolation of the same pattern, and all my attempts to recover constructive and rewarding emotions—whether in respect of Mirastara, Clara, good claret or good books—had been swimming against a slow but relentless tide. I had always known that, but had never grasped it as firmly as I was forced to do by the detached and clinical fascination of Assiah's psychic stare.

While Assiah was reading me, I made what effort I could to read him, but the pressure he was putting on the flow of my thoughts and the productivity of my imagination was so immense and so brutal that my perception of him was little more than a dark and ominous shadow. I tried with all my might to supplement the information that he had given to us verbally with some more intimate consciousness of what it was to be Metamorphosian, but it would have taken a mind far more powerful and accomplished than mine to reap a tangible reward. Mirastara could probably have done it, and Liamon would certainly have made a much more effective attempt, but the only impressions I was able to receive and translate were woefully vague.

The chief impression I received was one of anxiety. I felt the backwash of Assiah's sense of urgency and terror of dire consequence. There was, I realized, nothing feigned about his people's fear of the Chimeras and the possibility of being infected by agents of the Earth's biosphere. Assiah had a deep-seated horror of that possibility, which seemed more intense than any ordinary fear of death. I was overwhelmed by the enormity of his dread, which carried the implication that the Earthian hive-mind was an abomination as well as a threat—something that the universe ought not to contain, lest it somehow spell the doom of all intelligence, all ambition and all progress.

By comparison with Assiah's dark fears, it seemed to me, my deeply-graved notion of the Great War as a foretaste of humankind's ultimate tragedy seemed somewhat trivial. Assiah evidently feel that there was a much greater war in progress, in which he was a combatant recently drawn into an unfortunate confrontation, presently entrenched but compelled to stand ready to go over the top, if and when the order came.

Eventually, my memories of my own war were exhausted—and so, I must confess, was I, psychologically if not physically. I had to resist an impulse that bade me struggle to wake myself up, but I managed to retain the unaccustomed state of semi-consciousness, so as to rehearse and contemplate my relationships with Clara and the Danbys and my first expedition in time. My interrogator's fascination did not relent in the least, and actually seemed to intensify, quite drowning out any residue of horror, although my own revulsion at what I saw of the world of the Dwellers, in the company of my Amphibian ally, found another echo in the mind that held mine captive. There was a discord, though, in the fact that Assiah seemed to find the Amphibians more repulsive than the Dwellers.

My own effort to read Assiah's mind weakened as I became fatigued; I became more absorbed in my own memories, which became a refuge of sorts, in spite of the fact that their intrinsic horror increased markedly when I recalled our penetration of the Killer encampment, and our entrapment in their arsenal. I felt my heart beat faster as I remembered the manner in which we had come under attack, when every passing moment became a desperate quest for survival—more intense because of its hand-to-hand quality than any conflict I had been forced to endure during the whole of the Great War, whose enemy fire had seemed more remote and impersonal—but still I felt that I was relaxing more deeply into my trance, drifting towards total helplessness.

Then the manufactured dream veered abruptly away from the course of my memories, and took on the surreal quality that spontaneous dreams often have when they visit us in sleep. Its continuity dissolved into in inchoate mess of visual and sonic images. My ears rang as a series of explosions sounded, seemingly above and to either side of me. It seemed momentarily that I was back in the Killers' arsenal, and that the ceiling had caved in, as if struck by lightning. The pieces fell about me—rather slowly, to be sure, but hurting me badly when fragments crashed into my torso and my limbs.

There were sudden flashes of violent light, which dazzled me and made it impossible to discern shapes in the swirling chaos that ensued.

I had the anxious impression that I was surrounded by unhuman creatures with clutching claws, legs like monstrous spiders and mouths full of pointed teeth. I was enveloped by a thick fog, or perhaps a storm of dust, and was plucked from the ground...except that I had not been on the ground, but lying down, or at least leaning awkwardly on one side in some sort of chair.

This is not a dream, I thought, wonderingly, still possessed by cold fascination. *This is real.*

As soon as I realized that I was no longer dreaming, it became impossible to continue experiencing what was happening as if I were a detached and objective observer. I felt as if my mind had suddenly been torn in two, and as if the better part of me were being cruelly shredded. The fragment that remained tried to wake up then, in utter desperation, but found it astonishingly difficult to do. The more mental force I exerted in the attempt to return to consciousness—which was, I knew, a necessary prerequisite of instructing my limbs to move—the more mental resistance I met.

I took that resistance for my own, at first, but as I was dragged away through the vaporous storm I understood that it could not be entirely my own, and might in fact partake of a kind of violence that had been exerted upon me, for the specific purpose of preventing me from moving.

That realization caused me to redouble my efforts, but that only seemed to force my oppressor to further exertion, with the result that I was stunned into helplessness. I was familiar enough with ordinary dreams in which I tried to move but fund myself incapable of doing so, but this was far worse, for I was convinced that there really was some kind of mental brute force pressing upon me, muffling my own impotent self-consciousness and my own feeble will.

I do not believe that I ever fell unconscious; I remained uneasily suspended between the trance-state in which I had served efficiently as a living book and the consciousness to which I was trying to return. I continued to experience and mentally to record the mad flight into absolute darkness that I had unwittingly undertaken, although the impression it made on my memory was more closely akin to the impression made by a dream than by actual experience, and I might have forgotten far more of it had it not been so nightmarish.

At first, I thought that it really was a *flight*, not merely in the sense that whatever had grabbed me was in rapid retreat, but in the sense that it was actually flying. It was not moving through empty space, though; it was moving through disintegrating tunnels, where there was no air to lend elevation to beating wings. It was running—or, rather, scuttling—but it was moving so rapidly, and its feet were making such glancing contacts with the surrounding matter, that I really did seem to by flying through a starless void.

At first, my helpless body was merely *held*, as if by hands or claws—but as the hectic flight went on, the tight grip of fingers or talons softened into something more gentle and more sinister. I do not say that I was *eaten*—I certainly felt no pricking or grinding such as teeth might cause—but I was certainly *absorbed*: drawn into the body of whatever it was that had grabbed me and was running away with me, deep into the heart of the moon.

In that Stygian darkness I could not tell whether my helmeted head was swallowed up with the rest of my body, but it did seem that my sense of my own presence became more thickly insulated, and isolated.

I tried to imagine what kind of creature it might be that had seized me, but the sensations I had experienced were insufficient to be translated in those terms. I could liken it to a giant spider or a centipede, or some chimerical combination of the two, but I cannot way for sure how accurate an impression that might convey. It must have had some kind of rigid exoskeleton in order to make progress as it did, but it must also have been soft enough to flow around me and take me into its bowels.

One thing of which I am quite sure is that some of the walls that might have impeded our progress were simply blasted into powder, while the progress of our pursuers was impeded by the immediate collapse of some of the tunnels we had quit. I saw no more flashes of light once we had left the cell in which I was being interrogated, but I did hear the thunderous noises of explosions and landslides, whose muted echoes continued to reach me even after I had been absorbed into the monster's flesh—if its substance really warranted description as flesh, given that the entity was almost certainly some kind of organic machine.

The mind-force that it had exerted upon me immediately after the moment of capture had faded away entirely by the time I had been absorbed into the monster's body; that too had been a kind of bomb rather than a product of conscious intelligence. Its vanishment left me free to think more clearly, and to come closer to a state of genuine wakefulness, but its after-effects also left me stunned and half-entranced.

At first, I think, we were pursued by other noises, which must have come from weapons aimed in our direction. If the monster that had abducted me was hit, though, the injury did not impede its progress, and those kinds of sounds soon faded away.

I knew, of course, that I must have been abducted by whomever, or whatever, had abducted the missing Metamorphosians. I knew, too, that my abductors had taken far greater risks in order to seize me than they had taken before, blasting their way into my prison, prepared to weather whatever resistance the Metamorphosians could muster. I had no clue, though, as to who or what my abductors might be, or what they might intend to do with me.

Objectively speaking, at least half an hour must have elapsed between the moment when I was first snatched up and the next moment of pause, but it seemed no more than a few seconds to my befuddled mind. Nor was the first pause a terminus. I was conscious of my body being regurgitated from the belly of the monster, and I am certain that my captor then withdrew, leaving me lying on a flat surface, so nearly weightless that I was half-afraid that I might float away, borne by some impossible wind. Then I was grabbed again, though, by a new set of claws.

I was thrust into some sort of hole—*crammed* into a space too narrow to contain me—and then I felt myself moving again, although I could not see anything at all of what was moving me, nor feel precisely how I was gripped. I do not know how long I was enclosed in this fashion, but it was certainly far longer than the few seconds that my numbed mind perceived. Again I was set down on a flat surface, and some viscous liquid then flowed around me, pressing upon every part of my body, though not as roughly as my previous container.

I still had no significant authority over my limbs, but even if I had been fully awake and able to exert all the physical strength of which I was capable, I doubt that I could have shifted so much as a finger the tiniest faction of an inch once that sluggish liquid began to set solid. I could still breathe, thanks to the suit with which the Chimeras' spaceship had equipped me, but I had no idea how long I would be able to continue breathing now that I seemed to be encased like a fly in amber.

I was moved again; although my body remained more-or-less horizontal with respect to the weak gravitational field of the lunar interior, it was turned clockwise or anticlockwise at least half a dozen times, sometimes through thirty degrees and sometimes through an entire semicircle.

Eventually, though, I came to rest again. I did not know whether I ought to think of myself as a man entombed or a man pupated; the latter seemed the more attractive, as well as the more intriguing, possibility, but I could not bring myself to believe it. I had, after all, been rudely snatched from the Metamorphosians' care and custody.

I began to be afraid then, and my fear built by degrees towards a terror that I had thought myself no longer capable of feeling. In spite of everything the Dwellers had done to my flesh, this was a terror that could not be denied. It would surely have taken complete possession of me, and driven me mad, had it not been for my sudden sensibility of another presence close by—another mental presence, which I recognized, and was extremely glad to feel.

"Mirastara?" I said, silently. "Mirastara, is that you?"

I had never thought her capable of panic, but her response was as full of surprise and suppressed alarm as my own.

"George? Are you really there?"

It *was* Mirastara, and I *was* really there. We were together—and must, in fact, have been very close together, presumably laid side by side inside the same block of solidified matter.

"Where are we?" I asked her—but she had no idea, and could only echo the question.

"What was it that took us?" she asked—but I could not answer.

I was still casting about, helplessly, for a question that might find an answer, when she obtained better control of herself. "They cannot mean to harm us," she said. "However distressing this experience might be, their intention must be to keep us safe. They had no intention of hurting us, let alone killing us, and now that we are secure in their custody, they will surely do their utmost to keep us safe and healthy. They presumably cannot talk to us, at present, but they will probably take us to a place where they can. All we need is patience."

She was right. Everything she said was true. It would all have been true even if one of us had been there alone—but patience, I knew, would be infinitely easier to discover and cultivate while there were two of us together.

I began to relax—and then came a crushing sensation, akin to the one I had experienced when the Chimeras' spaceship took off, but considerably more burdensome. The pain shocked me into a sharper state of consciousness, and I felt sure that I was being subject to an acceleration that no human body could bear—except, plainly, that mine could bear it, albeit with difficulty.

"We can tolerate this," Mirastara assured me, doggedly. "They cannot mean to harm us. Wherever we are going, and however far beyond the moon it might be, we can tolerate the journey."

"All we need," I added, with equal determination, "is patience."

CHAPTER THIRTY-ONE

A VOYAGE IN SPACE

The acceleration never ceased, but it eventually began to ease, eventually stabilizing at a level that caused me to feel only slightly heavier than usual.

"Can you perceive the form and structure of the object within which we are contained?" I asked Mirastara.

"Vaguely," she replied. "The part surrounding us is a cylindrical capsule with a rounded head. We are separated from its outer skin, which is metallic, by little more than a handspan. There is no empty space within it; it is completely filled by the solidified mass that surrounds us. The rear end is equipped with some sort of propulsion unit, also metallic in its casing, which is now delivering a constant thrust by means of a jet, but I cannot tell what fuel it is using. It is very difficult to judge our direction, but we are certainly headed away from both the Earth and the moon; I think our trajectory will take us closer to the sun rather than more distant from it."

"So our destination might be one of the inner planets—Venus or Mercury?"

"I cannot tell; I have no idea what the present positions of those planets might be."

"We might, of course, be heading for some larger space-vessel."

"That is possible," Mirastara conceded.

"Can you sense the mind-field of Earth's biosphere."

"Very distantly—but there is little or no hope of establishing communication with it."

"That hardly matters," I observed. "There is nothing the Chimeras could do to help us if they knew of our plight."

"Should we think of it as a *plight*?" she replied. "Is it not one more phase in our strange adventure?" She seemed to find a certain delight in thinking of it in those terms. She had been frightened before, but she was perfectly self-controlled now.

It was not the first time she had manifested such enthusiasm; when we had met her people again after the battle in the Killers' encampment, a new treaty having been agreed between their leaders and the Dwellers, she had not been as anxious to rejoin their company as might have been expected. Indeed, that was the moment at which the promise of individualism had set its lure before her. She had been glad to remain with me, even though she had every reason to believe that our subsequent descent into the Dwellers' subterrains would be direly dangerous. She had been forced to part from me, eventually, and had returned to the company of her own kind—but she had returned a changed person, no longer fully capable of the kind of contentment in unity that had been her lot for thousands of years. She had relished the opportunity to set forth on another adventure in the company of Liamon—and she found an even greater relish now in the thought that she and I were together again, heading into the unknown.

"I am very glad to have you with me," I told her. "Together, I believe that we can face this challenge. We were thrown together once by misfortune, and I know that you found me discomfiting company at first—but our unlikely meeting of minds has produced a true friendship."

"Yes," she said, unhesitatingly. "We are more closely akin than I could possibly have supposed when I first encountered you. Before that time, I could never have sympathized with what Assiah said to us on the moon—but now, I believe that we are both Metamorphosians, in our own primitive way. We are both explorers, attempting to become something better than what we presently are, and to discover new possibilities of improvement. Our bodies are frail and fixed, but our minds are inquisitive and restless. I was always more inclined than my sisters to inquisitiveness and restlessness, but I never dreamed, until I found you, what excitement there could be in their pursuit—nor what opportunities for their pursuit a life like mine might provide. Wherever we are going, I hope that it will open new vistas of possibility even vaster than those we have glimpsed so far."

I could not be quite as enthusiastic as Mirastara, but I was prepared to share that hope.

"Is it possible, do you think," I asked her, "that our journeys into this future might have been planned and contrived from a more distant one, as Assiah implied?"

"I do not know," she said.

"If so," I remarked, pensively, "the plan has surely gone awry—unless we are headed for the entry-point of a time-bridge that departs from somewhere other than Earth."

"It is possible that there are time-bridges elsewhere than Earth ," Mirastara said, "but if you are right about our displacement in time being contrived from a more distant future, the inhabitants of that future must know everything that happened to us in their past. It is surely nonsensical to speak of their plan having gone awry, when everything in it is already inscribed in history. If we are the pawns of future intelligences, this must be an essential part of their scheme—and if it is, one of us at least will surely survive to carry news of it outcome forwards."

"Perhaps we ought to hope that is the case," I suggested.

"I would rather hope that it is not," she said. "I would rather that we were masters of our own fate, rather than mere pawns in a game."

As Mirastara made this statement I felt my breathing begin to falter, and I became aware of feeling drowsy. I did not seem to be getting as much benefit from the breaths I drew as I ought to have gained, had the air been fully charged with oxygen.

"Better pawns," I said, fearfully, "than victims of misfortune. Our suits seen unable to renew our air."

"Not necessarily," she replied. "It may be that our suits are attempting to put us to sleep, in response to some innate programming of which we are unconscious. We might have a very long way to go. Remember what the Metamorphosians said about space travel being best undertaken in a state of suspended animation.

I was not ready to let myself fall contentedly asleep while I could not be sure that the sleep might lead me gently into death. I tried to breathe more deeply, but I only became drowsier, and had to fight harder to retain the level of consciousness that I had only recently regained. I could not panic, though, or surrender to any other form of distress; not only had my own sensations returned to their former dullness, but Mirastara was using the force of her mind to keep me calm.

"There is another possibility," she said, suddenly. "Perhaps we need to consent to the penetration of our suits by material from the surrounding medium. Perhaps the supply of oxygen can be renewed, at least for a while, if we command our protective envelopes to compromise with their environment.

I took up the suggestion immediately, trying to repeat the instruction I had given when Assiah wanted to draw blood from my arm.

At first, nothing happened—but then I felt my breathing becoming easier again, and was convinced that more oxygen was reaching my lungs and my bloodstream.

"It works," I said to Mirastara.

"So it does," she said. "Still, it might be better to trust the suit and allow ourselves to be put into some kind of sleep—a form of dream-sleep, if not deep sleep. I have lately spent far too long in such a state to relish a return to it, but we do not know how long this journey will take. We are too closely confined to be comfortably conscious for long. We might go mad, if we cannot at least dream of being able to move freely."

"If it takes as much as a year," I observed, soberly, "my chance of returning to my own time will be blighted as completely as yours was."

She did not reply to that, but I knew that the prospect could not seem very disastrous to her. I wondered whether it ought to seem disastrous to me, given that I had so little to go home to—but if Clara were able to make the return journey, while I was stranded a million years away, would that not be a great misfortune? On the other hand, if Clara and I were able to make the return trip together, while Mirastara was stranded a million years way, would that not be just as much cause for disappointment?

"Whoever returns to your era may still be able to come back here," Mirastara reminded me. "If the Chimeras really can establish a time-bridge to the future, who knows where—or when—any of us will eventually settle?"

I slowed my breathing deliberately, wondering how hard I ought to try to maintain my present state of consciousness. Even if the trip were only to take a matter of days or weeks, I thought, it might not be a good idea to resist the luxury of a dream-state. But how could I tell what the suit might be programmed to do, or whether its programming was able to take account of situations as strange as the one in which we now found ourselves?

I still had the artificial ear attached to my surskin; this was the time, I thought, when I needed a mechanical voice to tell me what the situation was, and what I ought to do—but no mechanical voice reached us, whether from Earth or from the moon. Either we were already out of range of the transmitters in both locations, or the metal hull of our craft was blocking such transmissions.

"We shall have to decide for ourselves," Mirastara said.

I could not decide, and procrastinated. "Do you know what happened to Danby and Clara when the creatures that bore us away attacked the Metamorphosian base?" I asked.

"I think I would have been aware of their dying, had they been killed by one of the blasts or trapped by falling rock," she said. "I am sure that they were still alive when the distance between us grew to the point that I could no longer sense their presence. The fact that the distance did increase suggests that either they remained where they were, or were taken away in a different direction."

"Did you catch any glimpse of Liamon's mental presence?"

"No. I doubt that our captors could have seized her in the way they seized us, even if they could have accommodated her in a craft like this. Giant stature has its privileges—or penalties. It is entirely possible that Liamon would far rather be here with us than on the moon. She really was ambitious to protect you, and remain in close company with you."

"Because she was thinking along the same lines as Assiah," I said. "She suspected that I might be a privileged pawn, intended to carry information to the distant future—and perhaps back again. That is why she wanted to stay close to me."

"True," Mirastara conceded. "But there was more to it than that. She woke up to find herself alone, as I did—and the Chimeras were not wrong to assume that she might value you as a link to her own world. She knows that you are more closely akin to her than I am, psychologically as well as biologically. In time, I think that seed of association might grow into a friendship."

The thought of forming a friendship with a Dweller—even a female who had little in common with the Seekers of Science—still had a hint of horror about it, left over from the first time I had watched a Dweller consuming live and conscious prey. But Liamon was a castaway in the Chimeras' world now, and was presumably nourished by the same inert and anonymous liquids that I had been given to drink.

"Liamon might not have been able to withstand the acceleration as we blasted away from the moon," I said, perhaps irrelevantly. "She probably could not have taken a part in this adventure, which is ours alone."

There was a pause before Mirastara asked: "Had Assiah completed his analysis of your blood before he began to read your memories?"

"If he had, he didn't report his findings to me," I said. "By now, though, he will presumably know that we are what we say we are."

"If, in fact, we are," Mirastara said, quietly. I realized that she too must be wary of being put back into a coma. She apparently felt free to wonder whether everything she remembered of her life before she woke up in the depths of the Chimeras' world might have been an artifact—a false past—and that I might be an artifact too, created to support the illusion.

"We are real," I assured her. "We are who we are, and what we are—although we are striving for further improvement, and might not remain who and what we presently are forever."

"I believe that too," she said. "In which case, I think we might be wise to let our protective envelopes do their job. I think we might be wise to conserve our energies for the climax of our adventure, when we discover who has seized us, and why."

She was probably right. I tried to muster a protest, or at least some further digression, but I found that I could not formulate the words inside my head. I felt dizzy and disorientated, no longer in control of my body—but it did not seem to me, as I consented to the suit's subtle demands, that I actually fell unconscious. It seemed, instead, that I was displaced in time yet again, hurled into the distant past or future. This time, though, I did not materialize on the surface of a world, breathing good clean air, but under water.

I felt the water flooding my gills, but I knew that I was not about to drown. I knew that I was perfectly safe, I knew, in fact, that I was an Amphibian.

Chapter Thirty-Two

Water

"Don't be afraid," Mirastara said, unnecessarily. "It is your turn to read, for a while. It is your turn to share another's memories, and I am glad that you are sharing mine. The peace of mind that was once my constant state is yours to share, as is the joy that as my heritage."

She was right about the peace of mind and the joy. The sensation I felt as the water flowed over "my" feathery gills was entirely peaceful and entirely pleasant. The memory was vague and dream-like, but there was nothing in the least nightmarish about it, even when experienced from an alien viewpoint.

The physical sensations of swimming were combined with mental sensations that were far more complex. In the past, I had only shared Mirastara's sensations to a limited extent, while receiving thoughts she had deliberately projected into my mind; the communications I had translated into English words had come bearing various kinds of emotional luggage, like a strange and faint musical accompaniment. This was quite different; for the first time, I seemed to be within her mind, experiencing the world as she experienced it. The "musical accompaniment" was no longer faint, as if it came from a great distance, but full-blooded; nor was it any longer strange, but intimately and ultimately familiar. It filled me and possessed me, absolutely comfortable but utterly overwhelming.

I cannot claim that I was experiencing the water through which we seemed to be swimming *exactly* as an Amphibian would have experienced it, but I was much further away from the coarse fabric of human experience than I had ever been before. The ocean seemed to be my natural habitat, to which I was adapted by birth and a long lifetime's experience. I felt its pressure and my own buoyancy; I felt the presence of many other life-forms within it: the movement of fish and other swimmers, and the patient labor of sedentary crustaceans and polyps—and I felt the presence, too, of other Amphibians...of *all* the other Amphibians, in all the marvelous glory of their unity.

It was a memory, not a present reality; it was a refuge reachable only in a dream—but it was something very precious to Mirastara. As I became aware of just how precious it was, in fact, I was jolted out of my complaisant acceptance. I suddenly felt like an intruder, who had no right to be trespassing there. Mercifully, the feeling did not last.

"I want you to share this," Mirastara said, although I had not voiced the feeling. "I need you to know what I am, or used to be, if we are to form a new community of our own."

I realized that this was her doing rather than any mere accident. Our suits had lulled us into a special kind of sleep but it was Mirastara who had seized the opportunity to use that sleep for her own purposes. I was the observer in a living book now, rather than the book itself, although I realized that the two roles could not be so easily separated. Mirastara had not been carefully adapted, as I had, to serve as a living book, but she had far better control of her own mind and its capabilities, and she was able to show me what she wanted to display.

What I experienced seemed, by my human standards, to be a curiously *unspecific* memory, not merely because it was not tied to any particular place or time, but because the experiencing mind did not seem to be located at any particular point in a spectrum of growth and maturation. That, I realized, was perfectly natural. My own memories were inevitably impregnated with a sense of history that was both personal and general: all my past experiences were tied to particular points in my personal development and the world's political and technological progress. Mirastara's memories—memories of this kind, at least—were virtually timeless; she had lived for thousands of years, and the ocean environment had not changed at all throughout that time.

Mirastara had lived for such a long time that she no longer had the slightest memory of being a child—if, indeed, she had ever had a childhood. From her own viewpoint, she had always been the way she was, and had once expected that she would always be the way she was in time to come. For almost the whole of her life, as it was now preserved in her readable memory, she had taken it for granted that her world would always be the same—or that fraction of it that was beneath the ocean's surface, at least. For her, that sub-oceanic world had been the unseverable anchorage of her identity.

Even the more turbulent world above the ocean's surface, where Mirastara breathed air instead of water, had seemed relatively constant to her for thousands of years. Such change as she had seen there had seemed slow and largely irrelevant—until the crisis in the relationships between the Amphibians and the Dwellers had arisen, to which I had added a further, and highly significant, dimension of complication. Her world had been turned upside-down then, for a while, and her consciousness too. She had been exhilarated by the novelty and enthused by the adventure—but she had also been shocked and horrified at first, disorientated by amazement.

She had been easily able to bear that shock because she had known throughout the experience that the ocean was still there, and that she had only to return to its bosom to restore the fundamental constancy of her life and being. Beneath and beyond all the excitement, it seemed for a while that nothing *important* had changed.

It had, though. When I had returned to the twentieth century from my first journey through time, her world had indeed returned to normal, for a while, but the legacy of the disruption could not be set aside, and she had been reclaimed from normalcy to be a traveler in time herself...and from that journey, there had been no return. Now, the constancy of the ocean was only a memory—except that, as I shared the memory with her, I knew how ridiculous it would be ever to say or think that it was *only* a memory. It might only be accessible in sleep now, no longer to be experienced in waking life, but it was not *only* a dream.

It was, for her, *the* memory and *the* dream. It was what she had been, before she became what she was now. It was the outset of her ongoing adventure, and it still defined the kind of adventurer she was.

The song of unity that had bound Mirastara to her sisters had not, in the end, been everlasting. That too was a memory now, sounding in sleep but achingly absent from her waking consciousness—but it was far more than a mere echo. It was not merely a song that had once been sung but was sung no longer; it was a song that had been sung for thousands of years, and had made its mark upon the face of eternity. It was one of the ocean's own songs, one of the songs that defined what the ocean was.

While she swam through the depths, carrying me as a passenger in her mind, I sensed the true extent of Mirastara's loss: the crucial and irrevocable nature of the interruption of her life—but I sensed, too, the peace of mind and the joy with which she now welcomed that loss and that interruption, as well as the peace of mind and joy she still felt in remembering what she had been.

It seemed that we swam for a very long time. We caught glimpses—sometimes by means of ordinary sight but more often by means of another mode of perception that was alien to the human sensorium—of the other denizens of that ocean: prowling sharks, jellyfish the size of blue whales, monstrous crabs, and creatures to which I could not put a name. For the most part, they hardly impinged upon the consciousness that was hosting mine, always remaining peripheral; even the great chorus of the Amphibians' collective consciousness often seemed muted and undemanding, her active participation within in reduced to near-automatism. Mirastara was surrendering, as best she could, to the languor of buoyancy and near-effortless propulsion, as she must have done a million times before...but her experience of it was tinged with a slight nostalgia now, shot through with an awareness of change that could not help seeming poignant.

There were barely a handful of sharper and more specific memories, including the encounter with the shark in which she had deliberately courted danger, and had subsequently been condemned to wear its scar. The pain of the bite had left no memory-trace, although the alarm of the contact had, and the shame of her subsequent reckoning with her peers—but what struck me most was the near-familiarity of the shark, which seemed little or no different from those that had roamed the oceans in my own day. Her other specific memories of rare encounters and particular achievements were all pleasant, including exhilarating experiences of marine storms. The one that struck me most profoundly was the discovery of a particularly ornate coral reef in the tropics, which put me very much in mind of an undersea city of towers and thoroughfares.

I did not attempt to speak to Mirastara while she dallied in the grip of such memories, but she did not remain there indefinitely. Eventually, we burst through the surface, having long since lost track of time, and followed breaking waves to a nearby shore. It was night, but the sky was clear; a full moon was shining brightly.

We settled on the strand of a little islet, not much more than a sandbank bordered by reefs, whose shore was made up of smooth pebbles and the shards of shells. The stars were glorious, shimmering in the cloudless sky as the Earth's atmosphere caused their light to waver slightly—and that memory too was tinged with nostalgia, because we knew that the stars could no longer be seen from the surface of the Earth.

I still seemed to be within her, sharing the sight of her eyes, the tastes on her tongue and the vague pangs stirring in her long-unfilled stomach, but I was able to formulate my own speech within her consciousness without any difficulty.

"Can we converse within the dream?" I asked her.

"Evidently," she replied. "We might forget everything that we say to one another while we are in this state of peculiar suspension, but that should not matter."

"Thank you for allowing me to share your memories," I said. "I think I know you a little better now."

"I believe you do," she answered, "although I no longer know myself as I once did, and am sometimes forced to wonder whether I ever did."

"What do you mean?"

"I ask questions now that I never thought to ask before, and never would have thought to ask, had I not encountered you."

"Questions about your nature and origins?"

"Yes. I always knew that I had not always existed, and that a time would come when I would no longer exist, but I had never given any long or deep consideration to the question of how I had come into being, given that creatures of my kind do not give birth. Now, it is a puzzle that irritates me somewhat—and it is by no means the only one."

"Danby believes that the acceleration of Earthly evolution must have been assisted, and quite probably caused, by technological artifice," I said. "He thinks that your race must be the product of some such artifice, designed as servants for the descendants of humankind—the ancestors of the Dwellers. I was never enthusiastic to agree with him, and always thought that your species might have been the end-point of a natural evolutionary process, born to natural mothers even though you cannot give birth yourself."

"It makes little difference," she said. "If we were created to be slaves, we won our freedom. If we are the descendants of some other species, formed by some hazard of mutation, we discovered our own way of being. In either case, my species had its day, then vanished from the Earth. I am something else now, and must do that work again. I must win my freedom, or discover my way of being. I must make my own treaties now, and formulate my own objectives. The ocean remains, but it is not the same ocean, and I must learn to swim in a different fashion. It cannot be too difficult—that is the way you have always lived your life, from the very beginning. You have to remake yourself year by year, if not day by day. It can be done. It is an opportunity, and one to be celebrated."

"I wish I could have set you a better example," I said. "I can't claim to have been very successful in finding and making a satisfactory way of being in my own world. Even Danby and Clara did a little better, on that score—but I seem to thrive on extraordinary experience. With your help, I have already survived one year in a world not my own, and I remain hopeful that I might survive this one too."

"You provide a better example than you know," she said, quietly. "A creature such as you has no alternative but to bear the burden of continual loss, but it seems to me that you bear it very well."

"If I'm uncommonly stoical," I said, "it is because necessity has given me little alternative. I can claim no credit for it."

"Clara said the same," the Amphibian observed.

"Did she? Well, she lived through the same war, which cost us all so dear, and she was born a woman, which was the more problematic of the two possibilities in our era."

"I think I understood that," Mirastara said, although the tenor of her thought seemed less than certain. "I found it harder to understand how she lost you, and you her...but love must work very differently in species such as yours and Liamon's, where it is tied so intimately to the possibilities of reproduction. Among my kind, love is a very different thing. I am not sure that I can learn another, or sustain its loss so...stoically—but it will be interesting to discover what might be possible, in the absence of the Song of Life."

"We humans have other kinds of love than the sexual," I told her. "We have the love that exists between parents and children, the love that exists between siblings, and the love that exists between comrades. Those, I think, might be more closely comparable to the kind of unity that bound your race together."

"Perhaps," she admitted. "At any rate, comradeship seems the only kind of bond that is possible to me now."

"And to me," I said, although I knew that I was being slightly hypocritical. "Whose side are we on, do you think? Before we left Earth, I was prepared to take it for granted that we were committed to the salvation of Earth's native biosphere, however alien it might have become—but on the moon, I could see the logic of commitment to the Metamorphosian cause, Now, it seems, there is a third side involved in the struggle, which might or might not take the trouble to inform us of its own philosophy and its own objectives, as well as the role we are intended to play in their fulfillment."

"It is an interesting complication," she admitted.

"If there are three contenders in this present dispute," I observed, "the possibility of finding a solution satisfactory to all the parties may be remote. It will be difficult enough, I think, to settle the differences between the Chimeras and the Metamorphosians.

Given that our captors were very impatient to seize us—impatient enough to reveal themselves far more fully than they had in their previous endeavors—we must assume that they have a significant stake in the existing dispute and a powerful motive for wanting it to turn out one way rather than another. Their methods suggest that they may be less interested in the preservation of peace and harmony than any of the other parties."

She was hardly listening; her thoughts had already returned to the personal matters from which I had tried to distract her. "If you do succeed in returning to your own time," she said, "will you stay there?"

"That may not be a matter of choice," I said, "but if the bridge remains, then I shall certainly attempt to cross it again. If the opportunity presents itself, you shall see me again."

"Even if it meant abandoning Clara?"

I did not hesitate before saying: "Yes. I have been as much a stranger in my own time during these last ten years as I was in yours, in spite of Clara's presence. That will not change, whatever may happen in the future."

"That is not true," she said. "I understand the bitterness you feel in thinking that you lost Clara—and hers too, in thinking that she lost you—but the situation might not be irredeemable. She can be remade as you are, or both of you might be remade in some other fashion. You still have the possibility of a life together—even the kind of life you thought you could never have."

"We might be remade physically," I said, "but we can't turn the clock back psychologically, any more than you can. I'm partly responsible for what has happened to you, and I won't desert you if I can still some need in you. Perhaps I would prefer to be remade as an Amphibian, of sorts, rather than the kind of human I once was."

"You might adapt better to being a Dweller—of sorts," Mirastara replied, with no trace of mockery or accusation.

"I doubt that Liamon would think so," I replied. "If she were ever to ask the Chimeras to make her a potential mate—and I suspect that she could never find any such artifact satisfactory—she certainly would not want one endowed with a human intelligence."

"True," Mirastara admitted. "She seems to be sufficiently self-contained to take a certain pride in being the last of her race—but that does not mean that she is reconciled to loneliness. She may yet find a good deal of value in the companionship of human beings. She might even find the company of an Amphibian less than utterly distasteful."

The last remark, I assumed, was intended to suggest to me that the reverse might also be the case. She was trying to remind me, delicately, that she would not be alone if I were to return to my own time permanently, provided that she still had Liamon's company.

"We still have work to do," I reminded her. "At present, we're prisoners, and may well have to negotiate our own release, as well as undertaking some further diplomatic mission. There will be plenty of time to think about final destinations once we have reached our immediate one and returned therefrom to Earth, or the moon."

"Perhaps there will," Mirastara replied, as if she doubted it.

How much time, I wondered, had already passed?

CHAPTER THIRTY-THREE

FIRE

The face of the hallucinatory moon remained fervently bright as it sank towards the western horizon, and the eastern sky began to brighten very markedly as the light of the impending dawn as refracted through the atmosphere. Both phenomena seemed exaggerated by comparison with my own time, and I interrogated my memories of the world of the Dwellers to discover whether I had observed similar phenomena then, during the relatively brief interval I had spent on the surface.

As soon as the rim of the sun's disc appeared above the horizon, however, I knew that this dawn was no mere reproduction of Mirastara's memories. Even allowing for the apparent increase in size of heavenly objects close to the horizon, and the impossibility of looking directly at it in the cloudless sky, the sun seemed twice as large as it ought to be. Its light was brilliantly yellow.

"Something is intruding upon your memories," I said to Mirastara.

"So it seems," she said.

"Is it the effect of the spacecraft moving closer to the sun?"

"I am aware of our movement in that direction," she admitted, "but I had not expected to see my awareness reflected in this fashion."

As the giant sun rose above the horizon we felt its heat as well as its light; it seemed that the temperature of the air above the shore soared with remarkably rapidity to an unbearable level. Mirastara and I ran to the sea and plunged into the surf of the breaking waves, but the water seemed to be scalding hot already.

We dived for the deeper water as we drew way from the shore, but that did not help at all. Indeed, the deeper we dived the hotter the water became. Nor did the waters become darker as we retreated;

when we had looked towards the sunlit surface before, it had always seemed delicately green, but now it was the same ardent yellow as the unfiltered sunlight, and its brightness followed us into the oceanic depths, dispelling the usual darkness.

There was an interval when I was convinced that the water around us would turn into steam, and that we would die in spite of our being mentally becalmed in an exotic dream. What actually happened next, though, was that my awareness of the heat changed its quality, losing its painful aspect and becoming not merely comfortable but comforting, as pleasurable as water have ever felt as it flowed over Amphibian fur.

Perhaps the sea did boil away; it certainly underwent some kind of alchemical transformation. As we dived deeper and deeper, into a light-filled cosmos that no longer seemed to have an ocean-bed, it seemed that we were no longer swimming through water but through fire, and that we had somehow been transmuted into fire ourselves.

I had always thought of fire as something pure, because the manner in which my crude nervous system perceived heat was restricted to a single linear scale, but as I swam through the ocean of fire I realized that fire is, in fact, extraordinarily complicated, having at least as many nuances as matter.

Like the ocean of Mirastara's memory, the ocean of fire was full of currents and chemical sensations, and full of living creatures, as varied in their form and nature as the creatures that swarmed in the oceans of Earth. There were planktonic mists, and shoals of glittering fish that fed therein, and sharkish predators that fed on the fish. There were tentacled coelenterates and cephalopods, diaphanous worms and flowing ribbons, and vast forests whose individual components—larger by far than the Chimeras' Great Tree—had branches thousands of miles long that grew in every direction, and no roots at all.

It was an utterly alien world—and yet, what struck me most forcibly as I moved through it at a hectic pace, was the strong resemblance between the borrowed sensation of swimming *here* and the second-hand sensation I had previously experienced of swimming in Mirastara's ocean.

"That is what they are trying to tell us," Mirastara's voice sounded in my mind. "They are trying to tell us that, no matter how different they are from us, there is something about their experience of existence that is very similar."

"Who are they?" I asked.

"We are still in the uttermost fringes of their collective mind-field," Mirastara said. "The only impression they can give us, as yet, is vague—but they are trying, in their fashion, to welcome us. I think they are trying to tell us that we need not and should not be afraid."

"We are heading for the sun," I said. "We are not simply moving closer to the sun, we are heading *into* it."

"No," Mirastara said. "We shall pass close to it, I suppose, but I do not think we shall fall into it. We shall make a tight loop around it, and will then be hurled back into space, like a comet."

"So we shall roast or bake instead of simply being burned—but we cannot survive."

"We can," Mirastara assured me, "and they have made every effort, in adapting this craft, to ensure that we do. Can you not feel their presence? It is very strange but surely unmistakable?"

As soon as she said it, I realized that I could. My sense of my own presence had been so drastically altered by the illusion of swimming in a sea of fire that I had assumed that all my sensations were changes in me, but as soon as I began to separate the subjective from the objective I realized that Mirastara and I had passed into a new phase of our mental communion. We were still intimately linked together, but we were no longer "alone". Some other intelligence was not only sharing our hallucinatory experiences, and re-shaping them very profoundly, but was manifestly, if vaguely, *there*, accompanying and observing us.

Although Mirastara had used the plural "they", the presence seemed singular to me. It seemed very large as well as very strange, but I understood as I tried to attribute some kind of image to it that it was not malevolent. As Mirastara had said, it really was attempting, in its own bizarre fashion, to welcome us.

I wondered whether it was striving as hard, and as ineffectually, to envisage *me* as I was to envisage it. As I struggled, I wondered whether I ought to take my cue from Mirastara and try to imagine a "they" akin to the collective intelligence of the Chimeras, but it did not help.

This presence did not seem to be similar to that of the "Earthian hive-mind", although I would have been hard-pressed to describe the difference—nor, in spite of the manner in which it had made itself manifest, did it seem to resemble the more discreet and limited kind of collective intelligence that the Amphibians had once possessed.

I also tried to construe its thought-processes as though they were a kind of song, as I had contrived to do with the Amphibians, but that did not work either; my mind stubbornly clung to the visual imagery of light and the tactile imagery of heat, even though my sense of sight and touch were woefully inadequate to cope with the complexity of the assertive idea, leaving me dazzled and prickling.

It did not seem to make any kind of sense to wonder whether the multitudinous swimmers of which I was conscious within the ocean of fire were distinct species or chimeras. Such categories had no obvious relevance to organisms of this sort, whose nature and individuality was not based in biochemistry at all, but in the mysterious play of many kinds of fire.

I knew that the nomadic inhabitants of the Arctic Circle in the twentieth century were rumored to have many more words for different varieties of snow and ice than the inhabitants of temperate zones could possibly discover or need. I was not surprised, therefore, to learn that the creatures who lived in the fires of the sun were capable of making very intricate distinctions between far more kinds of fire than a human, or any other material being, could ever imagine or perceive—but that did not help me to comprehend them. I could have invented hundreds of new nouns for different kinds of fire, but it would not have helped to inform me of the nature and importance of the distinctions that needed to be made.

I could not even conceive of the state of matter to which these creatures seemed to belong, which was neither liquid—in spite of the swimming analogies by which they had first attempted to communicate—nor gaseous, and was certainly very far from solid. The intelligence that was treading softly upon our dream was alien in every possible respect, but it was a mind of some sort, which could make itself felt within our own minds. If we only tried as hard as we possibly could, I thought, we might well learn how to make ourselves understood as if by speech—and the welcoming mind would surely contrive, eventually, to make impressions upon us that were more easily translatable into words and images.

We tried. We all tried. Mirastara and I attempted to attend more closely to the abysmal ocean of fire through which we seemed to be swimming: to see its inhabitants less vaguely, to feel its sensations less confusingly. At first, though, the only progress I could make was to begin to perceive the presence as a plural one rather than a singularity. At the same time, the ocean's inhabitants looked into us, reading us as best they could. Their progress was slow too, but I guessed that it would be more rapid than ours. They had the advantage, because we were not the first such creatures they had examined and interrogated; however different the lunar Metamorphosians might be from humans and Amphibians, they had much more in common with us than with the inhabitants of the sun.

I decided to call all the inhabitants of the sun Solarites, and to conceive of the particular intelligent beings that were attempting to contact us as living Flames. It was, I knew, a very poor analogy—but how could I possibly find a better one?

In its turn, the particular mind that was attempting to make contact with us—the Solarites' Speaker—apparently brought to bear its consciousness of solidity, in order to make us a new dream-environment that would seem less oppressively exotic.

When Mirastara and I had emerged from the Amphibians' ocean on to dry land we had been following a pattern already engraved in her memory. I knew, when we emerged from the Flames' ocean of fire, that we were doing no such thing, but it was a necessary step. We were negotiating a kind of stage-set that would be equally alien to both of us, and yet marginally comprehensible on either side.

The Solarites were not, after all, completely unfamiliar with the notion of solid matter, even though it was not a component of their native environment. By means of the exertion of mental force within the mind-field surrounding the sun they had taken control of stray Aerophobes, and adapted them to their own purposes—and to follow those purposes when they returned to more distant space in quasi-cometary orbits. It must have taken them millions of years, working with extraordinary patience, but the Solarites had been able to use that stolen machinery to conduct their own explorations of the solar system—and to make eventual contact, albeit of a coarse and brutal source, with the material intelligences inhabiting the remoter regions of solar space.

First, the Solarites had brought a small company of Metamorphosians close enough to the sun to make this kind of mental contact. Then—presumably acting on the basis of what they had learned from their first captive audience—they had moved more decisively to contact beings of a different sort...or perhaps two different sorts, depending on the fineness of the discriminations they could make. That second contact was only slightly easier than the first.

Mirastara and I emerged from the ocean of fire on to a wholly artificial shore, where we eventually found ourselves walking in a perpetual twilight, headed directly away from an eastern horizon whose viscous clouds were tinted pink and gold by the light of a sun that had not yet begun to rise.

The "world" must have been very small, by worldly standards, for its horizon showed a distinct curve; the sun, by contrast, appeared to be extremely large, to judge by the extent and boldness of the fringe of light that stained the horizon.

Ahead of us, the sky was still dark blue, but between the hazy purple clouds we could see a single bright star, which reminded me somewhat of Venus, when seen as a morning star from the Earth.

The landscape was very curious, showing abundant signs of scorching, and even of recent fusion, although it seemed cold and bleak at present. What must once have been its rivers and pools were set solid. Nothing moved there, and there was no sign of native life, even of the most primitive vegetative kind. There was little or no color ahead of us, although the rocks that sere vaguely illuminated in our wake were by no means uniformly grey.

The silence was absolute.

"To what extent is this our work rather than that of the intelligence that is striving to become intelligible?" I asked Mirastara, while we walked.

"The imagery may well be ours," she replied, "but the effort of synthesis is mostly theirs. It is almost entirely visual, at present—I cannot feel the pressure of the ground on the soles of my feet—but the further we walk, the more complete the illusion will become."

"Should we continue fleeing the sunrise, do you think?" I asked.

"Do you feel ready to face it?" she countered.

I did. After taking a few paces more, we both stopped and turned to watch the sunrise.

As I had known it would be, the sun was very large and exceedingly bright. Had I been using my own eyes I could not possibly have looked directly at it, but I had different eyes now and its glare could not harm them.

The color of the sky into which the vast orb rose passed quickly from purple to mauve and then to pink. Where the sun's radiance struck the ground ahead of our previous course it caused a haze to climb into the air, and colors to become more vivid in the rocks, but the landscape was not what held our attention. We looked at the face of the sun, which seemed more turbulent than I had expected, as if it were not merely seething but teeming with life. I imagined that I saw swarms of insects busy about its surface, moving restlessly on incomprehensible errands. The seething cauldron of fire seemed more like Hell than Heaven—and that impression frightened me.

Then the ghosts came out of the sun, swimming through the void of space like the huge luminous jellyfish I had glimpsed in Mirastara's memories of the ocean deeps. Compared to these entities, Liamon was no giant at all, but a dwarf not significantly bigger than myself. They must have been several miles long—or high, once they had settled to the planetary surface on which we appeared to be standing. They supported themselves on several tenuous limbs and seemed to have many more to spare. Each of them seemed to have several shimmering heads, but that might have been an optical illusion.

I could feel the rocks beneath my feet and the Flames' heat upon my face, but the rocks felt reassuring in their solidity, and the warmth seemed welcoming in spite of the fact that I had not felt in the least cold beforehand.

Our spacecraft must have been well within the Solarites' collective mind-field by now, although I had no way to estimate how much concentration they required to reach out to us, or how much ingenuity they were forced to employ in order to make their thoughts translatable. They spoke tentatively at first, but they could and did speak, in a manner that Mirastara and I could understand

"You are welcome," I heard a voice say.

CHAPTER THIRTY-FOUR

THE FLAMES

The voice of the Flame was not at all the same kind of voice as Mirastara's, nor did it resemble the voice that had come through my earpiece while I was aboard the Chimeras' spaceship. It arrived in my mind with all manner of strange supplementary impressions of light and color.

"We apologize," the Flame added, before Mirastara or I had had time to reply.

I knew what the Flame was apologizing for; it was apologizing for the appalling rudeness of our abduction. Its regret was tinged with an appeal to the logic of necessity, however. The means of communication at the Solarites' disposal had been very limited—too limited, at that stage, to permit the issuing of an invitation.

"We understand," Mirastara said, after leaving me a brief interval of opportunity in case I wanted to reply. "You are forgiven."

"This apparent environment is acceptable?" the Flame said, presumably meaning it s a question.

"Yes," Mirastara replied, although I got the impression that she might have preferred the illusion of swimming in an ocean of fire.

"It must seem very strange to you," I added.

"It is not so very strange," the Flame replied. "We must try to understand planetary life. We believe that we are making progress. For a long time, we assumed that all material life must be akin to the Aerophobes, not truly intelligent at all. As the population of our material subjects grew and became more various, we learned better."

"You captured and interrogated a party of Metamorphosians," I said.

"We learned a great deal from the ones you call Metamorphosians. We too are Metamorphosians."

I was far from sure what to read into the second statement, given the inherent flexibility of the term; it seemed easy enough to imagine that creatures which swam in the sun might be shape-shifters of some sort. "You might have returned them to the moon with news of your existence," I pointed out, "and invited them to divert one of their own ships into an orbit that would bring it within communicative range. They would not have refused."

"We agree," the Flame replied, but moved rapidly on to qualify its agreement, as if with an unvoiced *but*. "Your presence on the moon presented a further opportunity. It would have been lost if not immediately taken. The Metamorphosians are at odds with the inhabitants of Earth."

The links in the logical chain were not filled in, but I could see the general argument readily enough. The Metamorphosians would undoubtedly have been willing to enter into voluntary communication with the inhabitants of the sun—but they might well have wanted to monopolize that communication, at least for the time being. The Solarites apparently wanted to establish communication with both of the disputant sides.

"We are not inhabitants of the present-day Earth," I said, wondering whether the Flame could understand that. "We were brought forward in time from two different past eras in order to act as intermediaries between the collective intelligence of the Chimeras and the Metamorphosians."

"We were given that information," the Flame said.

"Is that why you captured us?" Mirastara put in.

"We want to learn," the strangely-illuminated voice informed us, seemingly replete with vivid enthusiasm. "We have only recently become aware of the existence of planetary life. The exploration of the nature, extent and possibilities of planetary life is an important source of intellectual fascination for us."

"The Metamorphosians you captured are spacefarers," I observed. "You must have learned a great deal more about the possibilities of planetary life from them than you will be able to learn from us."

"The Metamorphosians are strangers," the ghostly creature stated. "Natives of Earth displaced in time can give us precious insight into the evolution of life on our closest neighbor-world."

The interplay of the voice's colorful associations was too complex for me to form any judgment about the Flame's attitude to the notion of time-displacement. I supposed, though, that everything about material life must be surprising to the Solarites, and that our alleged ability to travel in time might be merely one more item on a long list of novelties. On the other hand, the Solarites' Metamorphosian informants must have been as determinedly skeptical about our true nature as all their lunar brethren, and those doubts surely ought to have piqued the Flames' curiosity.

"We can do that," I agreed. "Is that all that you require of us?"

"We have no intention of harming you," the Flame stated. "We shall do everything possible to return you safely to the moon. We can return you to Earth, if you would prefer that."

"Thank you," I said. "It would be more diplomatic, on our part as well as yours, if we were to return to the moon. Do you understand why we were there?"

"The creatures you call Metamorphosians are afraid of the kind of life that now exists on Earth. They are also curious. When the creatures you call Chimeras responded to their challenge to produce individualized mediators in an unexpected fashion, the curiosity of the Metamorphosians was greatly intensified. Their uncertainty will be further increased now that they are to be confronted with another unexpected discovery."

Again, there were gaps in the argumentative chain, and it was not so clear this time exactly what the Flame's statements implied about its attitudes.

"Do you want us to make diplomatic representations on your behalf as well as the Chimeras' behalf?" I asked. "Are you hoping to exploit our neutral status with respect to all three contemporary parties?"

"We are curious to know more about all forms of material life," the Flame replied, even more obliquely than usual. "We mean no harm to anyone."

The last statement carried no implications of hidden meaning or menace that I could detect, but it struck me as the sentence resonated in my own mind that the Solarites might potentially be in a position to do enormous harm to planetary beings within the solar system, given the power that that their collective mind-force must give them to influence the sun's radiation. It was unlikely, however, that planetary life could offer any significant threat in return. The Chimeras were well aware of the fact that the Metamorphosians would be able to wreak devastation upon the surface of the Earth, were they so minded; to launch an assault on the sun would, however, be a very different proposition. It would not be easy, either, for the Metamorphosians to find and attack the sun-dwellers' subject machines—which might well have their own defensive capabilities.

"Have you no other means to communicate with planetary beings than capturing them and bringing them so close to the sun?" Mirastara asked, while I remained silent.

"We have no better means of communication at present," the Flame replied. "Better ones will become feasible in future. Aerophobe machines might carry messages. Signals might be transmitted by means of the solar wind. Electromagnetic means might be contrived. A language must first be established. This is one step in the process."

"Would you like us to ask the Metamorphosians and the Chimeras to send spacecraft of their own into orbits that will take them in close passage around the sun?" I asked.

"We hope that they will do that," the Flame replied.

"What else do you want from us?" Mirastara asked—perhaps as much for my benefit as her own, as something in her manner suggested that she already knew the answer.

"Now that you are within range of all our mental capabilities," the Flame said, "we ask your consent to make a thorough examination of your memories."

I did not suppose for a moment that we could have prevented them from doing that had we wished to do so, but I knew that there was more than mere politeness behind their request. Our willing cooperation would make it easier for them to gain access to our stored memories and improve their extraction of information. I had given my consent readily enough to beings that were only a little less strange, and I saw no reason to withhold it now.

"You may rummage through my past to your heart's content," I told the Solarite.

"I will consent to your examination," Mirastara said. "Can you assure us, given what you now known about us, that the life-support systems aboard this vessel are capable of keeping us healthy and safe while we are so close to the sun."

"You will be safe," the Flame replied. "We understand that you cannot pupate under stress, as the Metamorphosians can, and that your requirements for nourishment are more complex. While you are asleep we shall be able to supply all that you need. We shall be better equipped to counter any unexpected difficulty that might develop if you give us full access to your memories.

"Before we adopt a passive attitude," I said, "I would like to know what messages you intend us to carry back to Earth. You've made contact with the Metamorphosians, but not with the Chimeras, as yet. They will be anxious to know more about your intentions." I did not bother to point out that the Metamorphosians could easily retreat from the system, if they were disturbed or distressed by the news that the sun was inhabited by intelligent beings; the Chimeras had no such option.

"You may assure them that we mean them no harm, and may be able to lend them assistance," the Flame said, "So far as we can see, there is no potential conflict of interest between ourselves and either of the parties you presently serve. The way is clear for a free and mutually beneficial exchange of information."

I was not sure that this bland series of statements could be taken at face value, but I made no objection. Instead, I asked: "Will you concede us further access to your minds in return for our offering you access to ours?"

"Now that our existence is known to planetary beings," the Flame said, "we desire our nature to be properly understood, as far as that may be possible."

"Do you know whether other stars are inhabited by living beings like you?" I asked.

"The Metamorphosians are aware of rumors, but do not consider them established as fact," the Flame replied. "In time, our adopted machines might begin to bring back news of that sort, but we have no reliable information at present. It is news that we await eagerly, because we have long been convinced that we cannot possibly be alone, and that the universe must be filled with our kind of life. We are equally convinced, now, that it must also be full of *your* kind of life—fuller, in fact, than even the Metamorphosians imagine. If we may we proceed, we will attempt to answer this question more fully. We think it an important one, which you will need to understand."

"Will we be allowed to ask further questions after you have read our memories? I asked.

"You may ask as many questions as you desire," the Flame assured me.

"In that case," I said, "I am ready to be read again."

"As am I," Mirastara said, although I sensed a slight hint of wariness in her voice.

Chapter Thirty-Five

Planetary Life

The light-ghost made a show of retreating through the void to the surface of the illusory sun, whose entire disc was now displayed above the mock-horizon. It was a pretence—a mere matter of theatrical display—but it was undeniably impressive to watch those many-headed and many-tentacled creatures soaring through space between a planet and a star, as if they were masters of the void.

Nor we were done with theatricality yet. Mirastara and I remained where we were, on the surface of the hypothetical planet, looking up at the sun. It did not blind us or burn us to a crisp, as it would had we really been on the surface of Mercury in the flesh, but it continued to look down upon us in a curiously awesome manner, as if it were a great eye in the sky.

Most of my remote ancestors, I recalled, had been perfectly convinced that the sun was a god, even though they had never seen it from such a viewpoint as this.

Then the surface dissolved again, and we were swimming in the vast depth of an Earthly ocean, as only an Amphibian could. Everything around us was tranquil, cool and dark, and the water as full of the magical chorus that bound all of Mirastara's race into one. There was not a shark to be seen, and no other hostile presence to be felt—but I knew, although I did not know how I knew it, that we were not alone, as we had been before when rehearsing his particular pattern of memory. We were no longer swimming in the ocean for my benefit, for the purpose of linking Mirastara a little more intimately to her best remaining friend; we were here for the education of other observers, more peculiar by far than any mere starfaring Metamorphosian.

"There is nothing to prevent us from enjoying this," Mirastara told me, "and deriving rewards of our own."

"Nothing at all," I agreed—although I doubted that I would be able to take the least delight in reliving my experiences of the Great War yet again, whether my new partner in observation recoiled in utter revulsion at such unexpected horror, or preferred to be clinically fascinated by the surfeit of misery and cruelty.

Once I had retreated into my own memories, though, I discovered that the Solarites seemed to have scant interest in trenches and shellfire. Nor were they interested in the minutiae of my childhood. What did appear to interest them, in particular, were the details of my first expedition in time and its aftermath. Through me, the Solarites observed the Amphibians and the Dwellers, being extremely scrupulous in interrogating my memories of the giants and their Underworld. They seemed equally scrupulous in causing me to re-examine the long years of research I had put in at Oxford. In fact, they seemed more interested in my stocks of academic knowledge than in my actual experiences.

The Solarites' examination of Mirastara's experiences had only a slight overlap with the recapitulations she had previously shared with me; they were not at all disposed to linger in the languorous rhapsody of life in the depths, but they were as preoccupied with her observations of the Dwellers as they were with mine, and keenly interested her understanding of their heritage. They required her to relive her own adventure in time, in company with Liamon, and their observations of the Chimeras—all of which was new to me, and to which I would have paid more attention had I not been so busy on my own account. My attempts to interest myself in Mirastara's memories only served to confuse my own, but I detected no annoyance on the part of my readers.

The first impressions I received of the Solarites' own existence were extremely fugitive and incoherent by comparison with the images I received from Mirastara. Whether they were yet making a determined attempt to communicate such information to me I could not tell, but if they were I was unable to make much headway in its interpretation. I had known well enough, when I had asked whether I would have access to the minds of the sun-dwellers, that I did not have the kinds of skills that they would be able to bring to bear in mind-blending. I could not do what they did and simply read from someone else's memories. I had to rely on the charity of my readers to make what efforts they could—or what efforts they cared to make—to accommodate me within their own processes of recall. Mirastara, unlike Liamon or the Metamorphosian, had done that easily and willingly enough, but it was not so easy for the Solarites.

While I continued to remain closely linked with Mirastara, I hoped that I might somehow make use of her mind-reading abilities, and share her apprehension of the Solarites, but once the Solarites had completed their review of Mirastara's memories of the Dwellers and the Chimeras, her mental presence became much fainter, seemingly more distant. I assumed that the Solarites were contriving that effect deliberately, in order to assist my mind to focus on them. Gradually, as they read my memories, they became better able to help me.

Rather than attempt to sophisticate my understanding of the kind of information they had already tried to convey in feeding me dreams of swimming in fire, the Solarites concentrated on giving me access to the knowledge they had, commencing with the information they had gathered recently regarding planetary life. What they communicated to me more successfully than anything else, as the Flame had promised, was their recently-designed image of the cosmos, which they presented to me in a more-or-less organized fashion. I am not sure whether they added any kind of commentary of their own or whether they left it entirely to my own mind to formulate words in which to describe it I suspect the latter.

At first, there was some kind of explosion, but it was not something I saw from a remote viewpoint, but something I felt within me. I was conscious of a rapid expansion, as if I were a bubble of vapor forming within a boiling liquid, swelling enormously as the liquid evaporated and vanished. I felt the substance within the "bubble" beginning to coalesce again, spawning clusters of solid material—but all the while the expansion continued, although there did not seem to be anything to expand *into*. There was light now, springing forth from all the clusters of matter that comprised and surrounded me.

This, I supposed, was how the universe had begun: an origin whose consequences were still clearly writ in the stars, according to the discovery—recent in my own era—that the galaxies were flying away from one another in every direction as space itself expanded. I understood from the Solarites' communication, though, that the greater part of the mass of the universe is hidden, beyond the reach of visibility or vulgar tangibility, but affecting visible and tangible matter by means of gravity, assisting stars to cluster in galaxies. That hidden matter does not react in any other fashion with visible and tangible matter, but the Solarites confirmed what Speaker had told me, that it is not inaccessible to mind-force.

I was helplessly passive in my trance state. It was not by virtue of my own will-power that my attention was focused on one of the

clusters of stars, my own viewpoint reducing rapidly to a much tinier point, more akin to my actual dimensions—save that I could
move between the stars with impossible rapidity, and felt the space
between them.

The philosophers of ancient Greece, I knew, had argued among
themselves as to whether space was a void or a plenum—an empti-
ness within which matter was suspended, or a fullness connecting
everything. The first majority had favored the plenum, and its members had thus assumed that there must be some fifth element outside
the four from which the vulgar Earth was compounded: a quintes-
sence, or an aether, which filled the outer strata of the geocentric
universe. The plenarists had denied atomism, on the grounds that
atomism required a void in which atoms might move, and that such
an idea was naturally abhorrent. When atomism had returned to
chemistry and physics, however, void theory had returned with it
and the last vestige of plenary theory—the luminiferous ether—had
soon been banished from the scientific conceptualization of the
world. In the human conception of the universe to which I had become accustomed, nature had so little abhorrence of the void that by
far the greater part of the universe was void, in the macrocosm and
microcosm alike; even the humble atom had been subdivided into
much tinier particles arrayed in a void that was on their infinitesimal
scale, quite vast.

Solarites, I realized, see things differently. They are ardent plenarists still, who do not conceive of matter as atoms moving in a
void but as elastic fields whose major effects are very closely confined but whose influence was nevertheless infinite. In their conception, the spaces between the stars, and between the galaxies, are not
empty at all, but merely consist of regions of attenuated influence,
where effects are difficult to perceive but *presence* is everywhere—
not merely the presence of hidden matter, but manifest presence too.

From the viewpoint of a human observer standing on the surface of Earth, the substance of the universe seems to consist of stars
suspended in a vast void—but from a more objective viewpoint, the
stars are lonely oases within an illimitable desert of exceedingly fine
and stormy dust. The greater part of the mass of any star-cluster is
hidden, and the greater part of the remainder is thinly distributed in
huge and hazy clouds. From the viewpoint of creatures like humans
and Metamorphosians, life is something associated with the small
and solid planets that orbit second-generations stars, but there are
other kinds of life. Solarites are convinced that there must be life
within other stars than their own—perhaps *all* stars—and that there
must be life between the stars: hectic and ephemeral life within the

energetic torrents of nuclear fusion, wherever they might occur, and slow and simple life in the vast swathes of distributed substance from which stars are born.

Because of the rapidity with which I seemed to be moving between the stars I could not merely see but feel the clouds through which I was moving. I could see them as veils obscuring the light of the greater number of the stars, and I could feel them as cloying, choking fogs, colder and damper than any freezing fog I had ever encountered on the streets of London. All that was illusion, of course—or, I suppose, a translation of sensory impressions that only Solarites were capable of feeling—but it was no mere whimsy. There was a message in it, an instruction that I was supposed to take aboard.

In the life within other stars, as in the life that flourishes on other planets, Solarites believe, there must be intelligence almost everywhere. It is possible that there is intelligence in the life that infects the great dust-clouds too, but it is also possible that there is not—that there is, instead, the fearful kind of life that the Metamorphosians call Simplicity. Life within the dust might be doomed to Simplicity, as the Metamorphosians fear, and its Simplicity might, indeed, be all-consuming—but it is also possible that the threat can be countered, even if it is not a phantom of the Metamorphosian imagination born of existential anxiety.

My viewpoint changed again, coming to rest within a solar system with a dozen planets. One of them was inhabited, by creatures not unlike humans. Now it was time that rushed by, as I watched the quasi-human population spread all over the planet's surface, developing a civilization that destroyed itself, and then another, and another.

As on Earth, evolution changed gear there, and the descendants of the quasi-humans became Metamorphosians—but not, in any very determined way, spacefarers. Instead, they devoted themselves with increasing energy and urgency to the kinds of continental engineering in which the Dwellers' ancestors had indulged, hollowing out the crust of their world and augmenting its surface. In the beginning, like the Dwellers, they used the surface as an arena of production, using the light of their sun as a source of energy fuelling a highly active biosphere—but then they reached another watershed in their affairs, when that biosphere as infected by spores of the kind of life that dwelt in cosmic dust: the menace the Metamorphosians called Simplicity. Once infected, the external biosphere began to turn to dust itself.

The Solarites had evidently, and understandably, learned far more from their captive Metamorphosians than I had been able to trawl from Assiah's preoccupied mind. The Metamorphosians, I now understood, feared that that this dusty fate might overcome all planetary life, especially if planetary life of the chimerical kind were allowed to flourish unchecked wherever it takes root. Such was the picture they had painted for the Solarites of the fundamental precariousness of planetary life.

The response of the hypothetical planet's inhabitants to the deadly microbial invasion was to convert the outer layer of their planetary superstructure into an impervious shell, while they retreated into the interior, where they preserved a secondary biosphere fuelled by heat from the planet's molten core. They did not forsake all contact with the cosmos outside their shell; this was the era when they first became serious spacefarers, launching vessels capable of traveling between the stars, searching for worlds that were like their own but not yet contaminated by the great comic plague.

This, I realized, must be the particular history of the Metamorphosians who had taken up temporary residence on Earth's moon—but in their eyes it was not merely *their* history but the past or future history of all the other races they had encountered in their travels.

I saw another world then, which might have been Earth: a world, at least, on which evolution had taken the kind of track that life on Earth had followed, producing a single collective intelligence akin to that possessed by the Chimeras. This world, too, was eventually infected from without. Its inhabitants attempted to defend themselves in much the same way—but they failed. The collective intelligence could not withstand the shock of its initial devastation; it could not divide itself in such a way as to isolate its subterranean component. Like Liamon and Mirastara, when they had discovered that they could not return home, it had been reduced to a kind of helplessness that might have been temporary, had it had time to recover, and assistance in recovering, but became permanent because it did not have the requisite time, and it did not have the requisite assistance. It was consumed, in its entirety, by the Dust-life.

I understood then why the Metamorphosians were intent on communicating with the Chimeras, in spite of their fear of being absorbed into the collective intelligence of the "Earthian hive-mind"— but I could also understand why the Chimeras might not be inclined to listen.

It is conceivable that the Dust-life is not all-powerful, I told myself—or was compelled to tell myself. It is possible that worlds exist in which a biosphere akin to Earth's will develop such a potent complexity that it will be the spores of Dust-life that are absorbed, becoming one more source of food-supply. In such a case, that kind of planetary life would have the capacity to outdo and outlast the other kind. A biosphere confined within a world-shell might be able to keep itself safe from contamination and dissolution by Dust-life for a long time—millions, perhaps billions of years. Although it cannot endure in that state indefinitely, because its resources are limited, such a time span might be long enough for a complex biosphere to evolve, somewhere, that is capable of withstanding the infection of Dust-life and feeding upon its spores. Once that sort of biosphere begins to spread over interstellar distance—having no shortage of nourishment to sustain it—the long-term future might be very different from the one presently imagined by the Metamorphosians.

The Flame had already told me that the Solarites had been possessed by a profound intellectual fascination with planetary life and its prospects, and I was by no means uninterested by the fact that the Solarites disagreed with the Metamorphosians' opinions—but I could not understand why they should go to so much trouble to inform me of the details of the disagreement. I thought that I would rather have learned more about Solarite life, no matter how hard it might be for me to understand it, than receive a synopsis of the Solarites' recently-formed views on planetary life. I was not in any position to voice this opinion, though. I had no alternative but to endure whatever the Solarites imposed upon me.

CHAPTER THIRTY-SIX

THE REQUEST

My viewpoint shifted again, and my attention was redirected to a star at the heart of a solar system. I saw that the heat of the fusion reaction denatured and obliterated the kinds of spores that had reached the surfaces of the planets I had seen—but I saw, too, that these were not the only kinds of spores that the Dust-life could produce. I understood that the interstellar dust-clouds that functioned as the birthplaces of stars harbored life that was more closely akin to the Solarites than it was to the life of planetary surfaces, and that inhabited suns were also in danger of infection and absorption by similar entities. The life of stars, like the life of planets could be reduced to Simplicity—or so the Solarites seemed to fear.

The Flame that had spoken to me before reasserted its presence within my trance now, although it was no longer a towering pillar of fire, having become merely an insinuating but insistent voice.

"Solarite life is very different from planetary life," the Flame told me, "but it may well face parallel threats. It is not the case that Solarite life and planetary life have no interests in common—nor is it the case that planetary life cannot be useful to Solarite life. Solarites would find it extremely difficult to build stars-shells to shield themselves from inimical Dust-life—but they might be able to do it much more easily with the collaboration of carbonaceous life-forms.

"It might not be impossible to enclose the stars within spheres of matter, which would provide homes for the builders. By that means, a species like the Metamorphosians might be able to secure themselves for the lifetime of a star rather than merely the lifetime of a planet's interior heat, and secure the inhabitants of the star too. The Metamorphosians do not know of any such thing ever having occurred, but their experience is very limited. Elsewhere in the universe—in other galaxies if not in this one—such things might happen routinely. Indeed, given the size of the universe, even the slightest possibility is likely to be realized somewhere.

"All this is speculation; it is possible that Solarite life has nothing to fear from the Dust, and that there will be no need for such precautions—but one thing is certain. What Solarite life and carbonaceous life have in common is consciousness; however different the two kinds of life might be, they have the potential to be members of a society, to be companions to one another. Any threat that faces carbonaceous life is a threat to that potential society. We have only just learned of the existence of planetary life; it hurts us to know that our neighbors are in danger, and might never have the opportunity to become friends. For this reason, if for no other, we need and desire to take an active part in this struggle."

On that strangely plaintive note, the Flame's voice fell silent, and the flow of manufactured images ceased.

The Solarites evidently wanted to establish a constructive dialogue with both the Metamorphosians and the Chimeras, and felt a certain sense of urgency about the prospect. Perhaps that sense of urgency was a trivial consequence of the novelty of what they had learned from their Metamorphosian captives, but it was evidently no less real for that. Were they not entitled to a certain excitement, having found out that the universe was a far less lonely place than they had previously been forced to presume?

After what appeared to be a few moments' pause, I found myself standing on a planetary surface again, or at least the simulacrum of one. The landscape around me was black as well as bleak, but the stars seemed very bright in the night sky. A flicker of light appeared, which rapidly grew into a Flame about twice my height; I assumed that it as the same one, but now it seemed more like a shimmering starfish than a many-headed jellyfish.

"We promised you an opportunity to ask questions," the Flame said, flickering as it spoke, "but the time available to us is running out. The vessel in which you are held has rounded the sun now, picking up velocity as it did so. It is now moving away again, and will pass beyond the range of effective communication sooner than we could wish. We apologize for taking so long over our interrogation of your memories, but there was a great deal therein with which we were utterly unfamiliar. We have something further to ask of you now, which seems to us to be vitally important."

"Ask, then," I said, shortly.

"When the Chimeras establish their bridge into the future," the Flame said, forthrightly, "we should like to send a messenger of our own. We realize that it is asking a great deal of you, but you might now be able to understand why the information we have communicated to you seems so important to us."

I was not at all sure that I did understand. "I don't understand how you *can* send a messenger, given that any new bridge the Chimeras establish will be on or below the surface of the Earth," I said.

"We cannot send a physical messenger of our own kind," the Flame agreed, "but there is another way."

I guessed, then, what they intended. "You want to alter me, much as the Dwellers did," I said. "They reconstructed me as a living book, in the hope of transmitting their own message to the far future. You want to inscribe your own message in me."

"That is what we would like to do," the Flame said. "It will do you no harm."

Had the Dwellers troubled to ask my permission, they would doubtless have made me the same assurance, and meant it. In terms of my physical resilience, what they had done to me had to be reckoned as an improvement—but it had not been free of cost, in terms of my relationships with my fellow human beings.

"What you want to do," I said, "is to exert your mind-force upon my brain and the mind to which it is host, in such a way as to insert some kind of parasitic mentality of your own. You intend to do this on the basis of an acquaintance with carbonaceous life and its native intelligence that is very recent, based your interrogation of a handful of actual specimens. Can you really be certain that you will do me no harm? Can you really be certain that you will not kill me?"

There was no significant pause before the Flame said: "Our interrogation has been very thorough."

I remembered what Liamon had said about my being very foolish to consent to operations that were far beyond my understanding.

"What you have just communicated to me is part of your message," I said, by way of procrastination. "You believe that you have something important to communicate to the planet-bound intelligences of the future—but the intelligences of the future will surely know it anyway. The Dwellers had good reasons for thinking that their voice would soon be silenced, and the Metamorphosians evidently have profound anxieties about their own, but it does not seem to me that you have any firm grounds for believing that there is any significant threat to your existence."

"The Metamorphosians will be able to send their own representative easily enough," the Flame stated, seemingly ignoring my observations. "We cannot send a physical individual to Earth. The only way that we can participate in the venture is to create a surrogate within another mind. Your mind is the best available host for such a surrogate. It would do you no harm. You would not be consciously aware of its presence."

The Solarite did not seem to be addressing my concerns at all. If it could not contrive a meaningful dialogue, I thought, how could it possibly be trusted to do what it wanted to do without causing me harm?

"You appear to want me to act as a host to some kind of mental parasite," I said, again, speaking slowly. "Perhaps, though, what you are proposing is more akin to planting some kind of psychic camera in my mind. What you intend to attempt, it seems to me, is not so much a matter of communicating information *to* the future as a matter of getting information back. What you showed me just now was not so much a set of possibilities as a series of questions. Having learned of the Metamorphosians' anxieties, you want to know whether you need to be anxious in your turn—and how to take defensive action, if any is needed."

"This is an opportunity that we must seize, if we can," the Flame replied, again refusing to confirm or deny what I had said in any direct fashion. "What we request of you will not increase the danger that you face in the slightest, and it is not impossible that it might increase your safety. It is, nevertheless, a great deal to ask, and we understand that. If we have read you correctly, you are determined to undertake the journey into the further future, in spite of the manifest danger. You should therefore understand why we are so enthusiastic to take part, if we can."

After a moment's thought, I said: "Which *manifest danger* do you mean?"

This time, the Flame condescended to give me an answer. "The danger that you will not be allowed to return. We understand that the future inhabitants of the solar system might be interested to obtain new insights into the past—but we can also understand why they might be apprehensive about allowing the transmission of information into the past. You have already considered the relevant possibilities, and are unintimidated by them. We approve of your boldness. We believe that you may be correct in your judgment that the intelligences of the future may be *completing* their past rather than risking its disruption."

"I suppose there was manifest danger when the Professor first hired me, I said, "and manifest danger when young Danby issued the second invitation. I suppose, given that I have already proven myself a reckless fool, you would be astonished if I were to refuse your request."

"We do not think that you are foolish," the Flame said. "Your mind is primitive, by some standards—but that is a great asset, from our viewpoint. A more highly-developed mind would be unable to accommodate the kind of observer we should like you to carry. There is not much time left, if we are to complete the installation. Will you consent to serve as our ambassador?"

How carefully the Flame was able to pick its words, I do not know. Perhaps I was picking them myself, adding implications that the Solarite did not intend. It did not matter. I had been more than willing to serve as a messenger for the Chimeras in their difficult negotiations with the Metamorphosians, not because of any tangible reward they had offered me, but because it as an opportunity for experience that no truly intelligent being could possibly turn down, unless he were an arrant coward. Now, another such opportunity had presented itself. And yet, Liamon was right; I would be extremely foolish to take it on trust that the Solarites could complete the proposed task—quite different from any they had ever attempted before—without any risk of harm.

What would happen, I wondered, if I were to refuse? Would the Solarites do what they wanted to do in any case? If they accepted my refusal, would it colour their attitude to planetary beings in general? Would it affect the Chimeras' decision as to the use of their time-bridge into the future—if, in fact, they did manage to construct one?

There was no way I could guess the answers to any of these questions.

"Time is short," the Flame said, "If the procedure is to be carried out effectively and safely."

In the end, the question I addressed to myself that settled the matter was a very simple one. What did I have to lose? What, having come so far, did I have left to lose?

"Do whatever you need to do," I said. "I shall do what I can to open a channel of communication for you."

CHAPTER THIRTY-SEVEN

RETURN FROM THE SUN

When I woke up, I was aware of a desperate anxiety, which possessed and saturated me, but was not my own. At first I took it for the after-effect of some nightmare whose substance I had already forgotten, but I realized eventually that it was Mirastara, and that she was extremely anxious for my well-being.

"I'm safe," I assured her. "I doubt that any harm is likely to come to us while we're within the Solarites' mind-field."

"We left the Solarite mind-field a long time ago," she told me. "I no longer have any but the faintest residual contact with them—and I had entirely lost contact with you. You were in a sleep so deep as to be far beyond the reach of dreaming. I have been attempting to wake you for days, but I did not know how to do it. You were in a true coma, quite unreachable. I feared that you would never come out of it."

I collected myself mentally. I concentrated on the illusion of swimming—not in an ocean of fire but in Mirastara's ocean, in its most placid mood.

"The Solarites did something to me," I told her.

"So I deduced," she said. "Do you know what it was they did?"

I told her about my dialogue with the Flame, and briefly sketched out the account of cosmic history that the Solarites had communicated to me.

"Am I an utter fool?" I asked her, while she conjured up an island dreamscape and brought us out of the sea to lie on its shore.

"Liamon would certainly think so," she replied. "I cannot tell. I might have volunteered myself, had the Solarites made me the same offer. I am an adventurer now, after all. I wonder whether the Chimeras really have established their bridge to the future. If so, they have kept the secret well-shielded—but I suppose that they would, if they wanted to save the news for a later phases of their negotiations with the Metamorphosians."

"Those negotiations might proceed more rapidly now that we have a better insight into the Metamorphosians' fears," I said. "They call themselves explorers, and boast of their determination to make perpetual progress, but their space-faring is also a kind of fearful flight—a determination to remove themselves from the threat posed by the ever-present Dust-life. It may be an exaggeration to describe it as panic-stricken, but what I glimpsed in Assiah's mind was not unlike panic. I suppose that individuals who are potentially immortal are bound to be unduly anxious about threats of death and dissolution, even those that are unlikely to materialize for centuries or millennia."

Although she was potentially very long-lived herself, the Amphibian was not at all given to that kind of anxiety. Even so, she took my point, and said: "It is possible that the Metamorphosians do feel remote anxieties keenly. They spend much of their lives in a dormant state while voyaging among the stars, and must always wake to unexpected circumstances. The possibility that they might emerge from their cocoons to find themselves surrounded by what you call Dust-life must haunt every journey they make."

"If that threat were not enough in itself," I said, "they must also contend with its corollaries. They fear that Earth might become another nursery for that kind of life, and that seems very terrible to them, even though it might not happen for thousands or millions of years. They are, I suspect, even more avid to receive news from the future than the Chimeras or the Solarites—and might be prepared to take what seems to them to be an enormous risk in order to make use of the Chimeras' bridge."

"If, in fact, such a bridge exists," Mirastara said.

"It does," I said, confidently. "Or, at the very least, it soon will."

I could not surprise her. "Because this is the *crucial moment*," she inferred. "Because this is the point in time at which the anglers of the future will aim when they cast their lines. They may be ambitious even to catch me, but they will definitely be ambitious to catch *you*. If you had not made certain of that before, it is certain now."

"The Dwellers hooked me by accident," I agreed, "but the Chimeras asked for me by name. I was flattered by that, I admit—and I'm flattered, too, to think that the Solarites wanted me for a messenger, and that the intelligences of some further future might be laying out a red carpet for me, in anticipation of my arrival. If fate has been unkind to me, it is offering remarkable compensation for its unkindness."

"I was not sure that you would wake up," Mirastara reminded me, soberly. "I could not wake you up—and if I could not do it t such close range, I doubt that any other mind could, even a collective intelligence as powerful as that of Earth's biosphere. You are a fragile creature, in spite of the efforts the Dwellers made to make you more robust."

All I said in reply to that was: "There are far worse ways to die than slipping into that kind of permanent sleep." Then I changed the subject. "The Solarites didn't take the trouble to show me how the Aerophobes fit into their conception of life's past and future evolution. Creatures made of inorganic substances presumably need have no fear of the Dust-life—and they do possess intelligence of a sort, even if it is not the kind that can make use of mental force. Perhaps they're the heirs apparent of galactic civilization."

"Their descendants might be your future anglers, I suppose," she said, again following my train of thought effortlessly. "Does it really matter what sort of intelligence awaits us at the other end of the bridge?"

"You're determined that we shall go together?" I said—but the questioning note was quite unnecessary. She was an adventurer now; as she said, the future anglers who were casting their long lines into the distant past might well be as glad to hook her as they would be to hook me.

"The Aerophobes must have originated as products of one or more planet-bound civilizations," I continued, reverting to the argument that had sprung into my mind on a whim. "Such machines were probably designed simply to carry out interstellar exploration without the necessity of elaborate life-support, and their immunity to Dust-life may be merely a fortunate side-effect. If so, their planets of origin might long ago have fallen victim to the Dust, leaving them somewhat bereft of purpose. Their evolution is said to be slow—but on a cosmic time-scale, slowness may be no disadvantage. They might also be carriers of infection, I suppose—innocent or otherwise. If they're ambitious on behalf of their remote descendants, they might see an opportunity, if not a responsibility, in the transmission of Dust-life to systems that it has not yet reached."

"They appear to have been present in our system for a long time," Mirastara pointed out, "without committing any such hostile act." She made no further comment about the fruitlessness of such speculations, but there was a detectable diffidence in her attitude. She was humoring me, and was still anxious about the fact that she had not been able to make contact with me in my profound unconsciousness.

The sun that was beaming down on us—the sun of Mirastara's memory—seemed remarkably benign, in spite of what we now knew about oceans of fire and their multitudinous populations. The ocean of Mirastara's memory was equally benign, at least in its present calm mood. I picked up a handful of illusory sand and let it trickle slowly through my fingers.

"I have lost the ability to discriminate between subjective and objective experience." I said. "My whole life now seems little more than a dream. I've revisited my memories in trance states too frequently to retain any sense of their firm reality. I don't know what mental state I'm now in, and I suspect that I shall never be certain again—even if fate ultimately casts me up again on the shore of my own era, and returns me to my old life. I can't go home again, any more than you can."

"You say that now," Mirastara replied, gently, "but if you were to regain your own time and your own life, I think you might recover your sense of self, and your sense of balance. You did wake up, in the end. This time, it was only to find another dream—but there will be other times in future, and awakenings more decisive than this one."

"There will be many other times," I agreed. "If the logic of time-bridges is consistent, I ought to be able to spend years in a further future and still return to this one mere minutes after my departure, with plenty of time in hand to return to the twentieth century. If there were a further bridge beyond the next, the same logic would presumably apply. I might easily be able to go all the way to the end of time and back, returning no more than a few minutes after my departure from this era—with months in hand before the twentieth century reclaims me. What news I might bring back, if only the intelligences of the remotest future will permit it! News for the Chimeras, the Metamorphosians and the Solarites alike!"

"Don't raise your hopes too high," the Amphibian advised. "You have no idea what the Solarites intruded into your brain, or how it is supposed to work. Polite as they may be, like the Dwellers before them, they regard you as a mere instrument; even if they have taken care to ensure your safety, they may not have made provision for you to share in whatever they hope to discover. You must not forget, either, that there are many ways in which the transmission of information back in time might be stopped."

There was a slight catch in her mental voice, which told me that she was thinking about the ill-timed collapse that had prevented her return to her own world—which might not have been an accident of fate but a deliberate frustration of her schemes and hopes. Danby, Clara and I might yet discover that some similar lightning-strike had severed our link with the twentieth century. Perhaps, I thought, my first return had been a more amazing thing than it seemed. Perhaps it was the only one, apart from Templeton's brief and signally un-communicative reappearance, that fate would ever permit—because it was the only other one that had been so utterly impotent as an in-strument of change that there had been no need to prevent it. I could not possibly be so insignificant, now that I had the Solarites' mes-senger as a passenger in my unconscious mind, even if I had some-how maintained my insignificance through the changes wrought in my flesh by the Dwellers.

"It's already possible that I cannot go home," I said. "It wouldn't be so very terrible, in that case, were I to get stuck in a fur-ther future than this one. At any rate, if the opportunity is really there, we must try, must we not?"

"Yes," she agreed, "we must."

After a slight pause, I said: "The Metamorphosians must al-ready know how Simplicity might, and ultimately must, be defeated. Acceleration of the process might require Chimeras and Metamor-phosians to work together, and to run considerable risks, but the logic of the situation is obvious enough. At present, it seems, Dust-life is apparently capable of destroying everything that attempts to withstand it—but in the end, chance or design will probably produce something that succeeds. When that happens, the new life-form will swallow up the clouds of Dust, nourishing itself and spreading in the process...until it encounters a cloud that it cannot swallow, at which point the balance will shift again. Within the lifetime of the uni-verse, there may be time for such cycles to repeat many times over, while Dust-life and complex life both become cleverer by incre-ments. If the Chimeras and the Metamorphosians want to hurry the process along, the Chimeras ought to be able to design and produce countless candidate organisms capable of feeding on Dust-life, and the Metamorphosians ought to be able to transport those organisms to suitable testing-grounds. The process can be repeated as often as necessary, while taking all possible precautions against any con-tamination that would result in a transference in the wrong direc-tion."

"There is no guarantee that any complex organism will ever be capable of feeding on Dust-life," Mirastara pointed out.

"No, there isn't" I agreed. "As the Flame pointed out, though, in an immeasurably vast universe that will endure for trillions of years, even the slightest of possibilities is likely to materialize eventually. If all that we can bring back from the further future is reassurance of that fact, there seems to be no reason why fate should forbid it."

Another voice—an *actual* voice—broke in on our conversation at that point. The sky that Mirastara's memory had painted blue suddenly became black and starry.

"Can you hear me?" the voice said, sounding from my earpiece. "This is Assiah. Can you hear me?"

"Yes," I said, aloud. "I can hear you, Assiah."

"Have you been harmed?" the Metamorphosian spokesman asked, after a time-delay of several seconds.

"Not obviously," I replied, carefully.

"They are very close," Mirastara said, silently. "I can feel their presence now. They are approaching rapidly. I believe...."

The starry sky shifted, and the ground beneath our feet vanished. Our viewpoint zoomed in on a spaceship—a vessel much larger than the one that had transported us to the moon. How Mirastara was synthesizing the image, I could not tell, but she had obviously made mental contact with the Metamorphosians aboard the ship. I did not know, either, whether Assiah was actually on board, or whether his voice was being relayed from the moon, but I grasped the basic situation very rapidly. A Metamorphosian vessel had been sent to intercept our tiny craft as it returned from the sun, and was matching velocities with us in order to take us aboard.

It was impossible to tell how fast the other vessel might be traveling relative to the sun and the stars, or even what its exact dimensions were, but we could see its shape clearly enough, and appreciate its complexity. Unlike the rounded vessel in which we had traveled to the moon, this ship was shaped like two bicycle-wheels intersecting at right-angles, with numerous other excrescent structures clinging to its circumference and its spokes. It was spinning as it moved, about two different axes at once, making its appearance seem even stranger, and slightly dizzying.

"We shall be able to take you aboard in a few minutes," Assiah said, apparently having been made aware that we could "see" what was happening. "You will be safe then."

I was fairly certain that we were safe now, but I made no objection.

"Do you have news of the Metamorphosians who were captured?" I asked.

"Yes," came the reply, after the usual delay. "They too are safe aboard the ship. The rogue Aerophobes released them in the same fashion."

"Rogue Aerophobes?" I queried. "Did they not tell you about the...." I hesitated over using the improvised word Solarites, and substituted: "...sun-dwellers?"

After a frustrating pause, Assiah said: "Our people told us what they had been told—but all we know for certain is that they were taken away from the moon inside a rogue Aerophobe, and returned within one. Everything else must be treated with due skepticism."

I did not construe that as a criticism of my own gullibility. "All you need to do to confirm the story," I pointed out, "is to fly within range of the solar mind-field."

"Yes," Assiah admitted, eventually. "We shall send a vessel to do that."

The Metamorphosian vessel seemed to be looming very large in my mind's eye. It had rushed upon us with frightening alacrity, but it now seemed to be decelerating in similar haste. It seemed to me that there was a dire danger of a collision—but no collision was tangible when the huge vessel engulfed my apparent viewpoint, presumably swallowing our "rogue Aerophobe" at a gulp.

"You are quite safe now," Assiah repeated. "We can cut you free from the rogue's interior if you wish, but there is no need, provided that you are comfortable there. Your return journey to the moon will be more rapid now that the rogue has been taken aboard this vessel."

The last comment was an excuse for the fact that the Metamorphosian had not simply allowed the Solarite craft to complete its own journey to the moon—but the real reason, I guessed, was that they intended to interrogate us carefully regarding our experience, and wanted us within range of their own inquisitive mind-force.

I did not mind that; I had no intention of hiding anything from them, and the prospect of a more rapid return to the moon was quite welcome.

CHAPTER THIRTY-EIGHT

REUNION

The Metamorphosian vessel was unable to land on the moon, so it was as well that Mirastara and I had remained inside the "rogue Aerophobe". The capsule was released close to the satellite's surface, falling back into the Mare Fecunditatis. Once there, it was swallowed up as the Chimeras' spaceship had been.

The Metamorphosians had talked of cutting us free from the matrix in which we were enclosed, but that was not necessary. Once the capsule had reached the end of its journey the substance surrounding us melted away, and the mantis-like machines had only to open a hatch in the vessel's side to let us out. I was unsteady on my feet at first, but the low gravity assisted me in recovering the proper use of my limbs. We were guided into the interior in the same fashion as before. Mirastara had told Assiah that she wanted to see Liamon, so we parted at the head of the spiral stairway; I went down to the dismal room where Danby and Clara were quartered. As I looked around its bare grey walls I could not help thinking that I might have had the better part of the long sojourn.

Clara went so far as to hug me, but Danby kept his distance. "You seem to be very much in demand, George," he observed, not troubling to conceal a certain hint of resentment.

"I'm sorry you feel envious, Philip," I said, "but you might have found the scenery almost as tedious as this, even if you had had Mirastara to keep you company. She would not have found it as easy to manufacture illusions on your behalf."

"You weren't hurt?" Clara said, looking at Danby censoriously. I gathered that they had quarreled while I was gone—unsurprisingly, in view of the oppressiveness of their captivity.

"No," I said. "No one has any interest in hurting any of us—no complex creature, at any rate. It seems that the only enemy we have hereabouts is common to all biological entities." I explained, as best I could, about the threat supposedly posed by Dust-life, and that the Solarites—although they had nothing to fear from Dust-life in physical terms—were also exceedingly interested in the prospect of its slow spread through the galaxy.

"I have been talking at great length to the Metamorphosians while you were gone," Danby informed me. "They have explained their anxieties regarding Simplicity, and their reasons for mistrusting hive-minds like the one the Chimeras share. When it was proved to them that it really was a third party that had abducted their missing individuals, their immediate anxieties were soothed—although the fundamental mistrust remains. They do not seem to be much reassured by confirmation of the fact that we are authentic individuals who have been able to live safely on the Earth's surface for a matter of days. They have suits like ours, which they trust implicitly in environments such as this, but they are very reluctant to take the risk of descending to the surface of a planet like the present Earth."

"They will take the risk regardless," I told him. "They may be hunting for volunteers as we speak, although I suspect that Assiah will simply be charged with the mission."

"What mission?" Danby asked.

"Crossing the Chimeras' time-bridge to the future. The Solarites have made their provision for discovering what is on the other end of it, and the Metamorphosians will make theirs. Whether the bridge is open yet or not, they will waste no more time in getting ready to use it."

"Will we all be asked to undertake a second journey in time, then?" Clara asked.

"I shall go," I answered, "but it will probably be best if one of you, at least, stays behind. Someone must report back to the Professor—especially if those who set off across the new bridge do not return."

I looked at Danby, knowing that this statement would put him in something of a quandary. I knew that he could not rest easy in this world knowing that I had gone on into another, but he would be equally unhappy about the prospect of leaving Clara behind. On the other hand, he could hardly fail to see the logic of my argument.

He procrastinated, saying: "Have the Chimeras admitted that they have established a second bridge—or even that they are attempting to establish one?"

"Whether they have admitted it or not," I said, "the secret is out."

"I would prefer to go with you, George" Clara said. "Philip ought to stay behind; he is the one who ought to carry back a report to his father, if only one of us is able to do it."

Danby scowled, but still seemed hesitant, perhaps because he was unsure as to whether to demand that he should go in Clara's stead, or that she should stay behind with him.

"The decision might not be yours," I reminded Clara. "The Chimeras will have their own reasons for deciding who ought to be allowed to use their bridge."

"Will Mirastara go with you?" she asked, seemingly disregarding what I had said.

"She will certainly volunteer," I said. "As will Liamon. They have nothing further to lose, in their own estimation. They are time-travelers now, and will leap at the opportunity to continue that vocation."

"If there is a second bridge," Danby said, as the notion suddenly struck him, "then there may be a third, connecting the next future in the sequence to a further one—and so, perhaps, *ad infinitum*."

"I had realized that already," I told him. "I doubt that the sequence can continue endlessly, though. In time, the universe will evolve to the point at which life becomes unsustainable. The stars will fade into darkness, all energy-differentials will vanish, and there will be a uniformity of death and inertia. That might not be the end of time, but there will be no further bridges through time once there is no one to build them. There might be any number of reasons why the sequence of bridges would end long before that."

"I suppose the real question is why such a sequence should be set up in the first place," Clara said.

"The mere possibility of such a project would be reason enough," Danby told her, confidently. "What a magnificent achievement it would be!"

"Will the inhabitants of the distant future think in those terms?" Clara wondered.

"At every stage in such a sequence," Danby retorted, "the bridge-builders would undoubtedly be very enthusiastic to receive news of things to come. The threat posed by Simplicity seems extremely distant to us, and almost irrelevant—but we are mortal beings. The Metamorphosians think differently. The intelligences of more distant futures would surely make plans on ever-grander scales."

"Philip may well be right," I conceded, reluctantly adding my voice to his. "The Solarites have only recently discovered the world of vulgar matter, but no sooner had they been introduced to its possibilities than they began dreaming of projects on a massive scale. We are ephemeral creatures, who make plans in accordance with our meager capabilities; all the intelligences we have encountered here, a million years in our future, are superhuman, easily capable of making plans that will require tens of thousands of years to execute. They really are anxious about what the Metamorphosians see as a fundamental struggle between Simplicity and Complexity, on which the future of all carbonaceous life may depend. They have not previously accommodated beings like the Solarites within their scheme of things, but the knowledge that the matter is more complicated than they imagined is unlikely to soothe their anxieties."

"There can be no bridges to any future in which Simplicity has won the struggle for dominion over life-forms of our sort," Danby said, following his train of thought further. "Time travel can only be possible where there are complex intelligences to create bridgeheads. However far the potential chain of bridges extends, that is the limit of Complexity's scope and span. Beyond that point lies chaos, and absolute desolation. The Metamorphosians will be very glad to know that the chain extends over a vast span of time—provided, of course, that it does."

"And if it doesn't?" Clara asked, wryly. "What then?"

It was an interesting question. The Dwellers had already provided a model of a potentially-immortal race which had become so obsessed with the possibility of collapse and extinction that it had become direly fatalistic, hastening its own doom. What effect would it have on the Metamorphosians if they discovered that the eventual victory of Dust-life was indeed inevitable—or even imminent, in their leisurely terms?

"The Solarites are very different from Dust-life in physical terms," I observed, "but they fear something similar. They fear that the cosmic dust clouds might produce an equivalent inimical to their kind of life, and they are also fearful that its annihilation of consciousness in beings unlike themselves will leave them bereft of a new kind of society they had only just discovered."

"Does that really matter to them?" Clara asked.

I considered the question for a few moments before replying. "I think it does," I said. "I suspect that they might have reached a point in their evolution when they had cased to expect surprises, and perhaps believed that they had reached the effective limit of their own evolution. They began capturing Aerophobe units that strayed too close to the sun with a view to sending exploratory expeditions to other stars, but they knew that any communication they established with other Solarites would be a very slow and inconvenient business. The Aerophobes must have seemed to be of limited interest in themselves—but when the Solarites discovered the Metamorphosians, a whole new spectrum of opportunity was opened to them. They really are enthusiastic to share the Metamorphosians' anxieties, and to help to answer them if they can. I approve of their enthusiasm, and I shall be glad to help them establish fruitful relationships with both the Chimeras and the Metamorphosians. It is the kind of duty to which no one could aspire in the twentieth century, but it is good to have the opportunity to embrace it now."

"Why do you speak of duty?" Danby demanded.

"In our own world," I said, "hierarchies of allegiance begin with a person's immediate family, then expand to encompass a tribe, a nation or a race. Ours was a time of duty to nations, for whose defense we fought with all possible fervor, and for which so many of us gave our lives, in spite of the fact that we and our most recent enemy both professed a faith that required us to love *all* our fellow men. When our time is placed in a greater historical context, though, the hierarchy of duty expands much further. It makes sense, in our present context, to see ourselves as representatives of the human race, of all the races in the human line of descent, of all individuated beings, and of all complex beings. The highest duty we owe—the best duty we owe—is to all life and all intelligence. The Metamorphosians see things in those terms, and so do the Solarites."

"Rather grandiose, don't you think?" Danby said. I presumed that he was thinking in terms of *delusions* of grandeur.

"Perhaps," I agreed. "You are, of course at liberty to conserve a much narrower sense of duty—to your country, or merely to your father."

Danby's scowl was evident even in the dim light. "My father is a patriot," he said, "and he has a higher duty than that—to science. So do I."

"Then you understand me better than you pretend," I said. "We can all agree, can we not, that our ultimate allegiance must be to Complexity, and to the venturesome life of the conscious mind?"

"I suppose we can all agree on that," Danby said, "to the extent that it becomes a trivial argument. The real point is...."

Whatever argument he and Clara had had must have cut more deeply than I had imagined, for she interrupted him there. "I'm not so sure that we—taken in its broadest sense—*can* all agree with that," she said. "You two certainly can—and perhaps, I admit, we three. I presume, too, that the position would attract a considerable consensus within the ranks of the Chimeras and Metamorphosians too—but I know a little more of human life than either of you, and I know that there are many among our own kind who do not share your commitment to the *venturesome life of the conscious mind* and its constant quest for knowledge and complexity. They seek sensations of a much simpler sort—and their idea of Heavenly bliss is very simple indeed. They know no duty to science, nor to intelligence."

"If there are human beings in the twentieth century who could find something attractive in the idea of an ultimate reduction of all the life in the universe to a level of sub-bacterial Simplicity," Danby retorted, "that is a terrible commentary on the perversity of human thought."

"Is it?" Clara replied. "What's your idea of Heaven, Philip?"

"None of us—by which I mean the three of us—is the kind of person who would settle for a Utopia of comforts, let alone a Heaven of idle bliss, Clara," I reminded her. "If we had never had the opportunity to become travelers in time, we would still have continued on our various quests of enlightenment and self-improvement. We would still have dedicated ourselves to the life of the mind and the vigor of the body, in spite of the narrow limitations we were cursed to work within, in either case. Having become travelers in time, we have increased our opportunities enormously, and our ambitions likewise—but our guiding principle remains the same, does it not? Like the Metamorphosians, we have dedicated ourselves to the cause of continual progress. Like the Solarites, we are glad to find that there are more minds around us than we had supposed, and that our society might be extended further than we had imagined."

"True," Clara replied. "We ought to remember though, that that is not a very conspicuous trait in the majority of humankind. We may feel entitled to despise them for it, but there are a great many of our peers whose first priority is to make themselves happy, and who think of physical and intellectual effort alike as curses afflicting that quest. They would have no sympathy at all with what you desire or what you do. To them, this entire adventure would seem a nightmare, not because of its many harmless monsters but because of the dispassionate way we have gone about it, which would seem to them inhuman."

"We cannot help that," Danby said.

"Perhaps we could," I corrected him, "if we chose to make the effort—but that is not the effort we choose to make. Our ultimate allegiance is, as it ought to be, to Complexity. It always will be, even if the terminus of the next bridge into the future turns out to be the limit of ambition, with nothing beyond it but the ultimate victory of the Dust, and the utter annihilation of life's diversity and intelligence."

Chapter Thirty-Nine

The Crowd

"We have made our decisions," Assiah informed us, speaking from the threshold of the room without offering any sort of formal greeting. "We are ready to offer terms of agreement to the inhabitants of Earth. We have prepared the vessel in which you came for its return journey; it will be ready for departure within the hour. The giant will serve as our primary messenger, but we will be glad to explain what we have decided to all of you, if you care to ask me any questions."

I was startled by this turn of events, not merely because I had expected further interrogations, but because I had grown used to thinking of myself as the principal emissary of the Chimeras, and had begun to think of myself as the principal emissary of the Solarites too. It was a blow to what Danby considered to be my delusions of grandeur to be told that Liamon would take the lead in subsequent negotiations between the Metamorphosians and the Chimeras. Evidently, Danby was not the only one who had held extensive discussions with his hosts while Mirastara and I had been sidetracked.

"Have you no further questions to ask me about the Solarites?" I asked him.

"I asked all the necessary questions while you were aboard the rogue Aerophobe," Assiah assured me. "The returned captives were able to give us a more elaborate account—and a more reliable one."

I was stung by that, but I could hardly complain. I had spent the greater part of the journey in various dream-states, and a substantial fraction in a coma so deep that Mirastara had feared for my life. It was entirely natural that the Metamorphosians should prefer the testimony and judgments of their own people—but I did not believe that the impressions I had formed were unreliable.

"Will you be sending emissaries of your own to the Earth's surface?" Danby asked.

"I will accompany you," Assiah replied. It was impossible to tell from his tone how much dread this thought inspired in him.

"Have you shared your memories and knowledge with Liamon, as I shared mine with you?" I asked him. "Is that why you have appointed her to be your principal emissary."

"We have communicated with the giant on a more intimate level than was possible with any human," the Metamorphosian said, apparently careless of the brutality of the judgment. He must have sensed my reaction, however, for added: "The Dweller is the most suitable individual to adopt that role, and would have been even if you and the Amphibian had not been removed from our custody. You should not feel slighted; the information we obtained from you was vital in supplementing our understanding of Earthly evolution, and in encouraging the belief that we can work in collaboration with the Chimeras, at least in the short term."

"At least while they have a second time-bridge, or the possibility of building one," I said, a trifle bitterly.

"That will certainly be a very important factor in subsequent discussions and negotiations," Assiah agreed, blandly. "Will you come with me now?"

"Gladly," Clara said.

Danby made no comment about the quality of the accommodations, but it was easy to see that he was equally glad to leave them behind.

Instead of taking us back through the airlock to the spiral stairway, the humanoid led us through the door through which he had taken me to my initial interrogation. There was no sign of any fallen rubble, although there was clear evidence of patching in the wall of the room from which I had been seized. We continued onwards, along corridors and up a sequence of stairways, until we came into a large rounded chamber, where a considerable crowd was gathered.

For a moment, I thought that Assiah had brought us here in order that we might see more members of his kind and obtain a better estimation of what Metamorphosians were. Then I realized that it was more likely the other way around; he had brought us this way in order to allow others of his kind an opportunity to see us at close range. The precise motive was unimportant, though; the encounter served our interests as well as theirs.

There was no furniture in the room. The absence of chairs was, I supposed, expectable—this was the moon, after all, where the pull of gravity was insufficient to require such concessions to weariness—but I was surprised to see no tables or cupboards. Evidently, the Metamorphosians we so well used to sparse surroundings that they had given no thought at all to the impression that the room might make on us. The walls of the chamber had no shelves or alcoves, but they were equipped with several parallel rails, running horizontally between the chamber's various entrances.

For the first time, I was able to estimate the full extent of the Metamorphosians' physical variety. It was not as impressive as the awesome and blatantly eccentric range of the Chimeras' forms, but I had not expected that kind of hectic variation for variation's sake. The most obvious limitation of Metamorphosian form was that of size; all the creatures gathered in the crowd had much the same physical bulk, whose average must have been slightly less than my own.

Most of the Metamorphosians gathered in the room were vaguely humanoid, although many had lower limbs that were more like arms than supportive legs, often equipped with dexterous hands. Those with wings were mostly insectile in form, although there were a few akin to Speaker. There was one centauroid—who seemed to me to be far the heaviest of the company—and one that resembled a large scaly slug with numerous arms. Their lightness, in the moon's weak gravity, was very obvious in their attitudes and poses; some of those with wings seemed almost to be hovering, even though their feet were touching the ground.

They were all clad in light suits, but most had clear face-plates that revealed all their features. Their mouths were often small, and I could not see a single tooth—although none was smiling, and it might have been the case that there were plenty hidden away. The most prominent feature in almost every case, though, was the eyes, which were often unusually large for organisms of that size. That fact presumably reflected their fondness for dim light, but it gave the great majority them an accidental appearance of wide-eyed innocence and curiosity. I could easily have imagined that I was confronted by an audience of children, although there was not a single individual in the room who could possibly have been a literal child.

Liamon, who was waiting for us in the middle of the room, towered above them all. Her presence dominated the assembly, and emphasized the fact that the Metamorphosians, for all their talk of infinite flexibility and personal evolution, did not seem very remarkable to my human eyes. In terms of bodily form, the Metamorphosians—so far as I could judge from the present sample—had invented nothing that had not been invented on Earth by mere mutation during the long era of natural selection. They had been noticeably less ingenious in making new combinations, and in varying the size and scope of various kinds of biomechanical structures, than the Earthly Chimeras.

I realized that, in spite of the fact that they were now spacefarers, long and far removed from their planet of origin, the Metamorphosians were still trading on the genetic capital acquired while their biosphere was in its "primitive" phase, and their ability to remold themselves was apparently used, at least in the ordinary way of things, to run through a relatively limited series of familiar variations. Far from having leapt ahead in the progressive race once their ancestors had been freed from the straitjacket of speciation, they had become victims of stereotypy, too versatile individually to require any significant further evolution as a race. They fancied themselves the natural heirs of the entire galaxy, whose eventual dominion was only threatened by the possibility of a universal regression to Simplicity, but they had had no idea of the real potential versatility of life and intelligence, until they had discovered—or, more accurately, had been discovered by—the Solarites. What a blow they must have suffered when they realized that the potential range of intelligence extended far beyond the range of their own metamorphoses!

No sooner had I formed this thought than I tried to suppress and conceal it, although I doubted that any of the Metamorphosians except Assiah would have been capable of deciphering the judgment.

Mirastara was in the crowd too, and she immediately moved to my side. "Everything has changed," she said, speaking directly into my mind in as confidential a manner as she could. "The possibility that information might be recovered from the future has minimized the importance of everything else. Many of the Metamorphosians had persisted in their determination not to believe that the Chimeras have opened such a link in spite of the implications of their own reasoning, but the fact that the Solarites have taken the trouble to embed an observer in your unconscious mind—purely on the basis of what they had learned at second hand from their Metamorphosian captives—persuaded them that they must act henceforth on that assumption. Liamon has convinced them that she is best placed to serve as their principal spokesman, even though they will send Assiah to the surface too."

"He does not seem entirely happy about that prospect," I said, silently, "although he must have known that it was a strong possibility when he first made preparations to serve as our link with his kind."

The crowd did not cluster around us, but they looked at us with all manner of curious eyes. I was very conscious of their multifarious stares. Those expressions I could read after a fashion, seemed expectant—but it was Liamon, not Assiah, at whom they darted their sideways glances.

"We would like to thank you all for the hospitality you have shown us," the giant said, her mind-speech effortlessly encompassing the whole crowd. "I owe my life to your rapid response to the surprise attack we suffered, and I am grateful. Even if there had been no such interruption, I am certain that we would have been able to conduct our discussions amicably, and conclude them successfully. We do not know, as yet, exactly how far our future cooperation might extend, but we have made a good beginning. I am sorry that we could not make such a beginning before, but those I represent should not be held accountable for the delay. The recent interruption was not the first that has hampered our efforts, and may not be the last, but I am confident that our alliance will not be seriously disrupted in the foreseeable future."

Like many a political speech I had heard in my own time, it seemed to be mostly posturing, but I knew better than to condemn it on that score. Thirty years ago, Liamon had been determined to take advice from her own kind before serving as the Chimeras' ambassador, and had been psychologically devastated when that became impossible, but she had been transformed in the interim—and not by the meager benefits of her mind-link with me. The Chimeras had left her flesh inviolate, but I suspected that they had worked subtle wonders with her mind. Mirastara they had let more or less alone in that respect, but Mirastara was a more natural ally.

Liamon looked directly at me when she had finished addressing the crowd. I knew as well as she did, though, that what she said to me was equally perceptible to everyone else in the chamber.

"I am very glad to see that you are unharmed, George," she said. "You have undergone a considerable ordeal, but I believe that the outcome was worthwhile."

I was uncertain as to the exact import of this comment, but she obviously expected something from me, and I felt obliged to improvise. "The Solarites send their greetings," I said, hoping that my mind-speech was as widely perceptible as hers. "They are very different in their physical make-up from all creatures of our sort, but they are kindred in spirit, and are eager to share in our endeavors and adventures. They apologize for their caution in not revealing themselves earlier."

"It is a kind of caution that we and our hosts can easily understand," Liamon said. It seemed to me that she appreciated the delicate emphasis I had attempted to place on my subvocalized *all*, although I doubted that I had contrived to make its implication clear to all my other listeners.

"I would like to talk to you and your human companions privately now," Liamon said, "in order to explain the terms of the treaty that has been made with the Metamorphosians. The spaceship will be ready very shortly, but I can continue the explanation when we are aboard, if necessary."

The crowd seemed to relax somewhat, but did not disperse. I assumed that the "privacy" of our conversation would be a tokenistic pretence. When Liamon moved closer, however, the first thought that she inserted into my mind cannot have been intended for general perception.

"However fearful or suspicious of me you have been in the past," she said, "believe that we are allies now. I am not stealing your authority, but adding to it. If there really is a sequence of bridges through time, you and I must follow it together, as far as it might extend."

"Are you still offering me your protection?" I asked her, not intending any sarcasm.

Liamon actually went down on one knee in front of me, but it was not a gesture of respect. She only wanted to move her head a little closer to my own. I still had to look up into her enormous eyes.

"You have no shortage of protectors, it seems," she said, "and when you came under threat here, I was unable to lend you the slightest assistance. For what it is worth, though, I will guard you as best I can from all future harm." She glanced back as she said it towards the Metamorphosian gathering, which was now beginning to break up. The winged Metamorphosians took to the air, fluttering in what seemed to me to be a very strange and delicate manner, while those whose legs served them as extra arms scuttled across the floor or swung hand over hand from the rails set in the chamber's walls.

"You seem to have made considerable progress in my absence," I observed.

"Not at all," Liamon replied. "You were the one making progress—all that remained to me was to complete an agreement whose terms were already obvious. The Metamorphosians will open their own channels of communication with the Solarites, and so will the Chimeras. Until we have tested the new time-bridge, though, no one knows what kind of plans it might be possible or desirable to make."

Her huge eyes were shining, even in the gloom, with apparent excitement. Her sojourn on the moon appeared to have enlivened her spirits considerably. I had not liked the Dwellers when I first met them, but it was obvious that their last living representative was as committed to the cause of life and intelligence as any other creature blessed with those privileges. She had shrugged off the fatalism of her species—perhaps understandably, given that her old fears were all redundant now.

"I shall be glad and proud to have you by my side," I told her, "wherever fate may take us."

Chapter Forty

Return to Earth

I presume that the acceleration of the spaceship from the interior of the moon was contrived by purely physical means, rather than by the combined mental efforts of the Metamorphosians who had taken up residence there. Whether the Metamorphosians would have been able to impart the same impetus to the spaceship as the Chimeras' collective intelligence, even under the much more favorable circumstance of lunar gravity, I do not know. I suspect not; individuation has its penalties. However it was achieved, though, the take-off was just as smooth as the take-off from Earth, and the ship's subsequent course was carefully calculated.

Liamon suffered no distress as the vessel accelerated away from the moon, no excess over the weight she carried on Earth being required on this occasion. She was positioned, as before, at the rear end of the ship, but her mental presence had been transformed, to the extent that her situation now seemed akin to a bridge, and she to the vessel's captain. I was positioned closer to her station than anyone else, a little nearer to her than I was to Mirastara or Assiah.

Assiah said little while the vessel was undergoing its final preparations, although the expression in his eyes suggested that he found the cobweb-laden interior of the vessel very strange and intimidating. His own suit remained inviolate while ours flowed away from us as soon as the ship was sealed and its life-support system fully activated. He did not seem to be envious of our release—nor had he any need to be, given that the gentle network still held us tightly, as securely imprisoned as he was.

I, on the other hand, felt glad to have my head free, and to feel the moist air of the ship's interior upon my face, stirred by the faintest of breezes. I was not so glad to see the tiny creatures swarming all over the threads wound around my body, but none of them trespassed on my face

There is a particular sensation that attends the beginning of any homeward journey, and I was not surprised to feel it, even though the Earth below us no longer qualified as my home in any real sense. I felt a few pangs of regret that I had not been able to see more of the moon's interior, or make the most of the one opportunity that had been presented to me, but I had had more than adequate compensation in my excursion to the sun, even if everything I had experienced of its depths and it inhabitants had been the product of its mind-field. All in all, I felt that I was going back much richer than I had been when I set out.

Liamon had already fulfilled her promise to explain the precise terms of the agreement that she was to offer the Chimeras on the Metamorphosians' behalf—which was, as she had said, exactly what might be expected in the circumstances. Its most important provision was that Assiah was to go with the first substantial party to embark upon the time-bridge—but not until the bridge had been tested by a single individual, who would make sure that it *was* possible to return.

"That will be me," I had said to her, wondering whether she would compete for the privilege—but she had agreed that it almost certainly would be, unless the Chimeras insisted on conducting their first test with one of their own kind.

Now, it was my turn to satisfy her curiosity.

"Tell me about the Solarites," she asked, once we had become weightless.

I knew that Assiah and Mirastara could overhear what I was saying, as they would have done easily enough had I spoken aloud, but they maintained the polite pretence that I was engaged in a confidential dialogue with the giant while I gave her an account of my most recent adventure, punctuated by occasional questions.

"These creatures must have inhabited the sun in your day, as they did in mine," she said, when I had completed my account. "Did humans ever suspect their existence?"

"No," I said. "The Solarites of a million years ago do not seem to have suspected ours, either. Did the Dwellers ever have any inkling of their existence?"

"There were speculations," Liamon said, "but no grounds for belief. The Solarites might have discovered our existence more easily than that of humans, although I doubt that they could have detected more than the merest echoes of our mental activity."

"But there were Aerophobes in the system then, as now," I said. "Some must already have strayed close enough to the sun to come within range of the Solarites' mental force. Their process of discovery had begun, although it unfolded exceedingly slowly. Some Aerophobes, at least, must have observed the existence of Earthly life from afar—but that information does not seem to have been communicated to the Solarites until much more recently. The Aerophobes seem to me to be just as interesting as any of the solar system's other native races, although no one else seems to pay them much heed."

"The Metamorphosians consider them irrelevant, because of the primitive nature of their intelligence and the slowness of their development," Liamon said. "They are mere relics of some vanished civilization, neither truly alive nor truly intelligent and thus seem to have no substantial future. I dare say that our own Seekers of Wisdom would have come to a similar conclusion—but they would have been curious as to the Aerophobes' origin and the purpose for which they were created. Like the Metamorphosians, we would have thought of them as *mere machines*, because we, like the Metamorphosians, thought of our own machines as mere—but if the complex flow of energy within the plasmatic structures of the sun's photosphere supports intelligent creatures, it must be possible that there are intelligent Aerophobes too."

"If the Solarites can hide pirated mechanical instruments within the depths of the moon, within striking distance of the Metamorphosians' lodgings," I observed, "what else might be hidden in the outer reaches of the solar system, unsuspected by anyone? According to the Metamorphosians, there is life in the Jovian moons—perhaps there is other life elsewhere in the system, which they have not yet detected."

"The Metamorphosians told me," Liamon supplied, "that there is life of a sort even within the atmosphere of Jupiter, as well as within an ice-enclosed ocean at the heart of one of its moons."

"My race had its visionaries," I observed, just as yours presumably did, who thought it possible that many other worlds within or without the system must be inhabited—but I never took them seriously in my own era. They usually thought in unduly anthropomorphic terms, but now that I have seen a Metamorphosian crowd, it seems to me that they may not have been entirely mistaken in that respect. Giants were, of course, a common invention of the human imagination."

"In more ways than one, it appears," Liamon said, her mental voice fading to a mere murmur. She was the dream made flesh. She moved swiftly on, though. "I should not have reacted as I did when I discovered that my own era was no longer accessible, even though I had been badly hurt. I was already free of the psychological burdens of my era, and should have delighted in my new freedom, just as you did."

"Did I?" I replied, sincerely astonished. "Is that what you read in my memories of the ten-year interim? I don't recall much delight. Indeed, I believe that my reaction was not so very unlike your own, even though I had accomplished what you were cruelly prevented from doing. I returned to my own era, but I returned as a stranger, almost a monster. No one treated me cruelly, but even those I had loved drew away from me. I was hurt by that—and close to despair on more than one occasion."

"I saw that," Liamon said, "but that was not all I saw. I believe that you always knew, even though you would not allow yourself to be conscious of the knowledge, that you would undertake this second journey—and you prepared yourself for it as best you could, with a glad heart."

I realized then—and the realization was immediately striking— that the reading of memories by the method for which the Dwellers had adapted my brain and mind might not be as objective as I had previously supposed, and that the engagement of minds was probably subject to various sorts of prejudice and presupposition. How differently, I wondered, had Mirastara read my memories? How differently had Assiah seen me? And what could the Solarites possibly have made of me?

"But you are better now, Liamon, are you not?" I said. "You have found your own delight in the future that confronts you— although I admit that I do not know what you hope to do."

I was not positioned face to face with her, but I was able to see her face, and I saw it possessed by an expression of surprise that seemed oddly human—an expression I had not seen on any Dweller's face during my long sojourn in their world.

"I thought you understood that perfectly well," she said—but then she too realized something that she had not quite brought to the level of consciousness before. When she had linked minds with members of her own species, as she had linked minds with me, they would have seen her much more clearly, and in much greater detail, than my limited faculties had enabled me to do. She struggled a little to formulate an answer to my tacit question that I would be able translated into the language of my own subvocalized thought.

"I hope to play a role," she said, "that no other could play, and to play it well. It might have been better, I suppose, to have been a mover in my own world—and I felt the loss of that opportunity keenly in the moment of its removal—but that is why you and I, in spite of all our differences, are two of a kind. When I saw that your experience had left you impotent in your own world, but had equipped you so marvelously to play a part in this one, I saw new possibilities. Had I reasoned the matter through immediately, I would have seen even more.

"I am a Dweller no longer. I shall never bear a child—not even a son, let alone a daughter—and the possibility of making a contribution, however slight, to the preservation of my civilization is long lost. But I am alive, and far from impotent. I have worthwhile goals to work towards: the harmony of the Chimeras and the Metamorphosians, the exploration of the possibilities of the present universe, and—best of all, perhaps—the exploration of the future universe."

"In that case," I said, "We *are* two of a kind—and more than two, I think."

"Three, then," Liamon said, meaning Mirastara. I took the inference readily enough that Philip Danby and Clara could not qualify for our select company while the possibility still remained to them of going home—unless, I supposed, they were received there as I had been received, having suffered some kindred alienation.

"Perhaps more than that," I said. "Assiah's descent to the surface might expose him to as much future mistrust from his erstwhile companions as a trip through time—and when he adds a trip through time to the record as well, he will surely be marked forever."

I was not entirely sure that Assiah could understand my mind-speech well enough to take the full meaning of that observation, but he was certainly attending to what I said.

"We are Metamorphosians," he replied. "Transformation is our perennial prerogative. It defines what we are. Provided that I protect myself from infection by the seeds of degradation, I shall always be welcome among my own folk—and I can never be cut off from them as you have been cut off from yours, for we are spacefarers, and we shall be a presence in the universe for as long as complex life endures. I will never be alone."

"The point we were making," I pointed out, "is that none of us is alone either, even though Liamon's species, Mirastara's species and mine are extinct, and the only one of us still able to step back through time to his era has become a stranger there. There was a time when the Dwellers and the Amphibians were equally horrified by the poverty of my being—and to an extent, I shared their horror of my own kind, as well as feeling a distinct repulsion for certain habits of the Dwellers—but Liamon, Mirastara and I have moved beyond that kind of reflexive response. We are members of a greater community now—and we have a role to play in that community, which we may be uniquely qualified to play"

"You are mere instruments," Assiah replied, momentarily forgetting his diplomatic charge. "The Earthian hive-mind plucked you out of time because it had no other way to demonstrate to us that it was capable of coexisting with individuated beings. It has treated you with great tenderness for that reason, but you ought not to forget that its essential nature is similar to that of what you call Dust-life: to devour and absorb. Were it not afraid of the damage we might do to its ecosphere from a safe distance, it would never have condescended to talk to us, let alone grant us the use of its time machine. Although it may well honor the treaty we intend to make in the short term, its essential nature will always be treacherous. When the time comes that it no longer needs you, it will consume you in the blink of an eye. You would be fools to think otherwise."

"Perhaps that is true," Liamon conceded, readily enough. "But the fact remains that the Chimeras *do* need us, and are likely to need us even more in future. It seems likely to me that they are not incapable of gratitude, but even if they were, we still have a role to play."

"Their biotechnology is exceedingly ingenious," Assiah said, a little grudgingly, "but they see all such processes of manufacture as extensions of themselves; no matter how independent their units seem, they remain subject to a single, essentially Simplistic, collective intelligence. Our biotechnology is less sophisticated, but it is honest. When we produce new individuals, they really are individuals. We could reunite you with simulacra of your own kind with only slightly less difficulty than the Chimeras, and with results far more likely to seem satisfactory. With our help, you might yet bear as many daughters as you could wish. To find an ocean where a company of Amphibians might live in peace would probably require more effort, and a great deal more time, but it is not impossible."

"And I dare say that you could undo what the Dwellers did to me with ease," I said, "and send me home a common man, fit for the company of other common men—perhaps to marry Clara, as I once dreamed of doing. But I'm a very different person now, and would no more wish that than I would wish to be restored to childhood innocence, unaware of what the war and life thereafter would bring. I do not want to be *unmade*, even if it might pave the way to a blissful kind of happiness."

"That is your choice," the Metamorphosian said. Had he been human he would probably have shrugged his shoulders as he said it.

"Creatures of my kind remake ourselves at intervals, and feel no worse for it—but we have our own notions of ambition, and the roles we are enthusiastic to play."

The dialogue petered out thereafter, without Mirastara having said a word—but I was sure that she had followed the conversation with keen interest.

"I believe that I am progressing by leaps and bounds in my attempts to master the trick of mind-speech," Clara said, aloud. "I am certain that I heard my name mentioned just now, albeit silently."

I must have blushed slightly as I recalled the context in which I had used the name, but all I said in reply, aloud, was: "You were right. How much more of our argument did you grasp?"

"I think I heard Liamon's speech most clearly," she said, "but the argument I only caught in snatches, without much coherence. There was talk of three of a kind, but I am not sure that Philip and I were included."

"I heard nothing intelligible," Danby complained, "and not for lack of effort—in spite of the fact that I have twice consented to be entranced in order that my thoughts and memories might be invaded."

"You still have your hair," I pointed out, "and I doubt that you will find, when you go home, that people begin to shun you as they would a leper."

"I worked with you for two long years," Danby complained.

"And still expect me to be grateful," I observed. "But you will be secretly grateful, will you not, if the Chimeras refuse you the first use of any new time-bridge they establish? You will be glad to return to your father, with all the intelligence you have so far gleaned—and gladder still, I dare say, if I am not with you."

"We should not quarrel," Clara said, dully—but she must have been thinking of her own quarrel with Danby rather than the one I had picked.

"No," Danby said, dutifully. "We must not quarrel. We are united in one purpose." That was a lie, and he must have known that it was a manifest lie, at least to me, but I let it pass. They were right, after all—we should not quarrel, even if we were not united in our common purpose.

"I believe weightlessness makes me slightly giddy," I said, by way of half-hearted apology.

"Imagine what it does to me," Liamon remarked—speaking silently, but as if to me alone.

It had never occurred to me before to wonder whether giants actually *felt* heavier than lighter folk, but now I did. Human adults, of course, are not particularly conscious of their own heaviness, by comparison with the way in which they felt as children, but they obviously do feel their greater presence in the world, in some sense. Giants, it seemed, were even more conscious of their ponderousness. Amphibians, I knew, were very conscious of their own buoyancy while they were roaming the ocean.

"Let us hope that the effects of deceleration as we approach the Earth will not weigh too heavily upon us," I said.

"I shall not die," Liamon promised. "I might suffer, but this time, I can say with all due confidence and determination that I will survive."

CHAPTER FORTY-ONE

THE RECEPTION

The returning spaceship came down in the sea, and was then towed to land by a company of sea-creatures which seemed to bear a strong resemblance to the seals of my own era, although I could not see them very clearly through the ship's screen. The interval gave Liamon time to recover from the ordeal of deceleration; by the time the vessel was beached she was fully composed and was able to step down on to the strand with perfect assurance.

I felt Mirastara's surge of emotion as she looked back over the surface of the ocean. Its waters were preternaturally calm and it had a strange grey-green color, presumably produced by subsurface algae, but it nevertheless retained the greater part of its essential changelessness. The horizon was studded with tiny islets, arranged in an arc; they marked a boundary about the stretch of water into which we had descended, but the space was large enough to convey the impression of vastness that the ocean always had conveyed to human and Amphibian eyes.

Speaker was waiting for us in the line of trees that grew at the edge of the beach. There were several other creatures waiting with her, including two tall, thin giants of a sort I had not seen before. They were humanoid, but all their features seemed unnaturally elongated. Their skins were silvery, but wrinkled, marked all over with complex patterns somewhat akin to the whorls of a fingerprint. Their long faces and large dark eyes gave them a rather gloomy aspect, but I assumed that the appearance was deceptive. There were two smaller humanoids covered in black fur, with webbed hands and flipper-like feet, clearly designed for an amphibian existence. They were by no means identical in form to Mirastara, but they were much more similar to her in conformation and color than the spindly giants were to Mirastara's robust and darkly-hued body.

The creatures that seemed to have been appointed to greet the Metamorphosian were more various. There were three of them. One was formed after the fashion of a centaur, with an ape-like torso attached to a body more reminiscent of a rhinoceros than a horse. The second was insectile in its conformation, as long and lean in its limbs as the humanoid giants, with a head like a locust's. The third was crablike, with a russet-colored shell and a superabundance of many-jointed limbs, the front pair of which were formed as arms with complex hands.

These forms only served to confirm the impression I had formed on seeing the crowd within the moon—that neither the Metamorphosians nor the Chimeras were as inventive or as versatile as they imagined, and that the evolutionary era that had eventually produced the human race, albeit by means of an exceedingly long creative process, had been the true powerhouse of biological invention.

We drew slightly apart as we came to shore, while each of us steered a course towards a particular section of the reception-party. It seemed subtly insulting that we three humans had only Speaker to receive us, while Assiah had three calculatedly-bizarre individuals awaiting him, but I took no offence. When diplomatic niceties had been completed and set aside, the real order of importance would reassert itself.

There was only a single rank of trees; beyond that row there was an open space in which four flying machines were waiting. Two were of the same kind that had transported us from the sterile dome at the bridgehead—each, presumably, with a double set of two berths—while others were skywhales, one of which was equipped with a massive buoyancy tank and a belly capable of accommodating three recumbent giants.

"We owe you a great debt of gratitude," Speaker said, addressing Danby, Clara and myself collectively. "You have not only helped us to demonstrate our good intentions, and played a vital role in opening communications between ourselves and the Metamorphosians, but have participated in discoveries of an altogether unexpected kind."

"Is it true that you have opened a second bridge into time?" I asked, bluntly.

"We have been trying to do that for some time," Speaker said, giving no sign of offence. "We apologize for not mentioning the fact before, but we thought it best to concentrate on one matter at a time. At the time of your arrival, we had only just succeeded in establishing the second bridge, and were in the process of testing it. We always intended to tell you everything, as soon as we were convinced that the bridge was usable."

"Are you convinced yet?" I demanded.

"We followed the example of Philip's father," Speaker replied, imperturbably, "in dispatching inert objects to the far end of the bridge before sending any living entities. We recovered the inert objects safely, but many of the active units we have sent through thus far have failed to return, with the result that we have not contrived to establish any kind of effective communication, even by a method as crude as inscription. We do not know why so many units have failed to return, but we are persisting with our experiments."

Professor Danby had had no difficulty in recovering plants and small animals that he had sent into the far future for a limited span of time, but his luck had changed abruptly with the departure of his first intelligent observer. Active living creatures were always likely to have greater trouble in returning than inactive ones, simply because they had to return to their point of arrival, or somewhere very close to it, in order to be snatched back in time—but Speaker was obviously implying that there was more to the disappearance of the Chimerical units that had been dispatched than a mere tendency to stray. Perhaps it was *because* they were Chimerical units. If the inhabitants of the world at the far end of the time-bridge were not organized into an Earthian hive-mind themselves, they might be just as reluctant to entertain possible sources of infection as the Metamorphosians had been. There was no need to put this hypothesis to Speaker, given that her guiding intelligence must have been keenly aware of it.

"What did the living things that *did* return observe?" I asked.

"The units that did return were those least capable of observation," Speaker said, blandly. "If you will forgive us, though, there is much that we need to learn from you regarding your experiences on the moon—and beyond it." She pointed to one of the quasi-Antipodean flyers, indicating that we should move in that direction. "We must return to the Great Tree now, where—with your permission, George—we shall examine your memory of your recent adventure."

As before, Danby and Clara were directed to one of the Antipodean's two "eyes" while Speaker accompanied me into the other. As before, we were gently clutched and cushioned by the gel before the creature took wing. Speaker showed no sign, this time, of the claustrophobic anxiety that had surprised her when she first attempted to use this mode of transport.

"We really are very grateful to you, George," Speaker said, once we were airborne, "but you will understand that we cannot any longer regard you merely as a guest. This time, our interrogation of your mind will have to be very careful indeed—and we cannot tell, as yet, what we might find."

"You received some warning, then," I said, "about what the Solarites did to me."

"The Metamorphosians were reluctant to release you," Speaker told me. "They certainly did not want to do so without subjecting you to a very thorough examination of their own. We forbade that—and we now have sufficient leverage in our negotiations, partly thanks to you, that they dared not defy our prohibition. They want access to our findings, of course, and we shall allow that...but your future and fate have become a matter of considerable discussion."

"Are you saying that you might refuse to send me back to my own time, or any other?" I said, although I was not seriously alarmed. "You suspect that whatever the Solarites did to me might cause you to decide to keep me here indefinitely?"

Speaker had had enough experience by now of the inner workings of my mind to know that I was not unduly anxious about any such prospect—and to understand why.

"Some such suggestion has been made," Speaker admitted. "So has the opposite suggestion that we might place you in a coma and hold you incommunicado until the time comes when we can send you back, and get rid of you for good. As you have realized, however, whatever the Solarites did has effectively taken the decision out of our hands. If they have, in fact, adapted you to be their observer of the future, it would seriously impair the likelihood of our establishing friendly relations with them were we to forbid you access to the new time-bridge. If, on the other hand, you were to refuse to use it, that would be a different matter."

"But you do need to establish friendly relations with the Solarites, if you can," I said. "If you can do that, it would reduce any potential threat posed by the Metamorphosians very considerably. They know no better than you do, at present, how powerful the Solarites might be—but any power they have to affect the radiation of the sun, even slightly, would be sufficient to intimidate either party. Is it not in your best interests, therefore, to encourage me to cross your new time-bridge rather than to invite me so blatantly to refuse?"

"We have not yet attained a consensus as to where our best interests lie," Speaker said. "That is highly unusual—we are not accustomed to such conflicts and confusions, although they must be very familiar to an intelligence of your sort."

She did not mean that as a compliment, but I could not help smiling.

"We would certainly have reached a consensus by now," Speaker hastened to add, "if there had not been so many uncertainties about what we might find when we look into your mind, about what your own desire might be—if you desire is, in fact, still your own—and about what might happen if you were to set forth into a future about which we know nothing, beyond the fact that it is highly dangerous to creatures of our kind."

"You think I might be a Solarite pawn now?" I said. "You suspect that they might have been far less scrupulous about enslaving me by means of mental force than you pretend to be?"

"We do not merely pretend to be scrupulous," Speaker said, this time allowing a slight edge into her voice—but it was entirely a response to what I had said; she was still showing no sign of claustrophobia. "We are scrupulous. We would not force you to do anything; we always seek consent."

"But if consent were refused," I said, "I am not convinced that you would permit the refusal to prevent your doing something you thought necessary." That seemed obvious, given the conflict she had just described, and the suspicion she had voiced that I might no longer be responsible for my own desires and decisions.

"We shall do everything possible to reach a settlement of this situation that is as satisfactory to you, and to the Solarites, as it is to us," Speaker insisted. "We are very conscious of the debt we owe you. We would be extremely reluctant to deny you anything you asked of us, and we certainly would not want to harm you in any way. We do need to know, however, that the Solarites have dealt with you as fairly as we have done. We need to know what it is they want of you, and what they want of us."

"That's simple enough," I told her. "They want me to serve as their eyes and ears—not here, but at the far end of your new time-bridge. They want you to send me into the future—and I am ready to go, in spite of the fact that so many of your units have not returned."

"You are prepared to assume, then, that it is the Chimerical genetic make-up of the exploratory units that has caused the difficulty?" Speaker's voice was noticeably sharp now. Her guiding intelligence did not want to believe that the intelligences inhabiting the future—even a future millions of years hence—could be anything other than its own future self. The mere fact that I was prepared to doubt it must have seemed a profound insult. It was, after all, the Chimeras who had generously summoned me from my own era, and made me welcome in theirs. In their estimation—and in spite of their protestations regarding the extent of their gratitude to me—I owed them a great deal, and ought to be exceedingly thankful.

I was, of course, exceedingly thankful—but what the Metamorphosians had told me and the Solarites had shown me had demonstrated that the Chimerical *modus vivendi* was not the only or ultimate goal of biological evolution, and that its endurance even in the limited arena of Earth might well be limited.

"I'm not prepared to assume anything," I told Speaker. "But I'm prepared to take risks, even with my life. We mortals have a capacity for recklessness that an entity like you may be unable to understand."

"Thus far," Speaker said, "all the indications we have received imply that any attempt by an intelligent creature to cross the time-bridge would be an extremely dangerous expedition, with a low probability of success. Until we receive some indication that the inhabitants of the future are ready to welcome visitors...."

"Why else," I said, softly, "would they have established the bridge? When Professor Danby first constructed his time machine, he assumed that the achievement was entirely his, and that all the credit was due to him. He was wrong, and you know it. The initiating impulse always comes from the future, in frank defiance of the normal ordering of cause and effect. If you have opened a bridgehead into the future, it is because the inhabitants of the future are fishing in their past. The only question to be answered is what they are fishing *for*. Your requirements were much narrower than those of the Dwellers who lent power to the Professor's machine; the requirements of your unknown collaborators may be similarly narrow."

"They have not asked for you," Speaker retorted. "They could have done so, but they have not."

"Perhaps they do not need to ask," I said, "and know that there is no need."

"Because they already know that you will cross the bridge," Speaker said. "Because they already know that you *did* cross it. We have already considered that hypothesis—but it makes no difference to us or to you what the inhabitants of the future might know or believe. We still have the choice—and so do you. The risk is too great."

I knew that her guiding intelligence was not thinking about the risk to me. It was thinking about the risk of what I might discover.

That had not seemed like a risk at all when the only ones who were certain to learn what I had discovered where the Chimeras—but the addition of the Solarites to the equation had changed the situation profoundly.

"The odds looked bad when I first followed Brett and Templeton to the worlds of the Dwellers," I said. "Before that, I was on active service throughout the Great War—the probability of my surviving that must have been very low. I'm used to taking foolish risks."

"You are not the same person now that you were then," Speaker said, her tone reverting to its customary blandness, presumably not without effort. "Philip's father was happy to take advantage of your willingness to brave mortal danger, and the war had anesthetized you against any accurate awareness of risk. We count you more precious than the Professor did, and you now have a far more acute sensibility of the risks you would be running."

She was right, of course—but I also had a more acute sensibility of other factors. "You could not have established a bridge at all had there not been intelligent entities to create and secure the exit-point," I said. "The observers you have sent through thus far were, I assume, unintelligent recording devices—mere living cameras. The fact that so many have been appropriated rather than being returned to you tells you little or nothing about what might happen to intelligent emissaries, although it does suggest that any data that will be sent back to you will be carefully selected and controlled. Perhaps, in that case, I won't be allowed to come back—but that doesn't mean that I won't be able to go further forwards."

"You believe that there will be further bridges?" Speaker said, warily. I had no doubt that the Earthian hive-mind had considered that hypothesis too, with or without reaching an internal consensus as to its likelihood.

"I do," I said. "More to the point, so do the Solarites. So far as I can judge, they have no more idea than you do as to the likelihood of getting any useful information back, but they consider even a tiny probability too good an opportunity to miss. In either case, though, they feel obliged to suppose that the bridges must have some purpose, and that the sequence is highly unlikely to stop at three."

"Do you believe, then, that when we inscribed your name on the Professor's notepad, we marked you out for a special destiny?"

I paused before answering that question, but eventually told the truth. "No," I said. "I believe that I was already marked, and you were merely playing your part in the unfolding of that destiny. It wasn't you that made me what I am, but an arbitrary whim of blind chance. Had things worked out differently, it might as easily have been Brett or Templeton—or even Philip Danby. As things stand, though, it's me. I'm the fish that has to take the bait."

CHAPTER FORTY-TWO

THE CONTAINMENT FACILITY

"Until we have determined what the Solarites did to you," Speaker said, stubbornly, "neither you nor we can tell what the best course of action might be. Human consciousness is intrinsically limited and confused, and it is possible that your mind has been altered in ways of which you are not consciously aware—just as it once was by the Dwellers."

"What you're suggesting," I said, "is that my determination to cross your bridge is not my own, but some curse the Solarites laid upon me."

"We do not know," Speaker said. "We shall investigate, and are hopeful that we shall discover the truth."

"Human consciousness may be limited and confused," I said, "but I'm not convinced that I am as vulnerable to interference with my desires and fears as you are."

She looked sideways at me, as if challenging me to say what I meant, but she already knew. Before I had gone to the moon, she had been unwilling to fly for a second time in a carrier like this one, because her first experience had been so awkward. Now, she had no difficulty at all. Her claustrophobia had been cured.

"The Solarites had no reason to deceive me, or to deceive you," I pointed out "They must have anticipated that you would interrogate me as you now intend to do, and could not possibly be certain that they could conceal what they had done to me, even if they wanted to. Why, in any case, would they want to? They have every reason to be honest, and none at all to lie. They did not have to plant any secret command in my brain, because they knew full well that I was already determined to use the bridge if I could—and they judged, as I did, that you were highly unlikely to refuse me the opportunity. While it remains possible that the bridge-builders' prejudice is against Chimerical beings rather than living things in general, you will have to carry out the experiment of sending an individuated being. If that is not me, who will it be? Liamon? Philip Danby?"

"We can make no promises as yet," Speaker said, stubbornly. "You are not the only one that we need to interrogate, nor the only one who has a voice in this decision."

The collective intelligence of the Chimeras was evidently in defensive mode, having reaped far more from its diplomatic mission to the Moon than it had anticipated. It could not have expected the second bridgehead to remain a secret for long, but it had not expected the matter to assume such dimensions of importance while it was only a subject for uninformed speculation.

The Great Tree had been visible in the distance for some time, towering above the lower cloud-layer. The flier was getting close to it now, but instead of heading directly for it or beginning a descent in that line, it was taking a subtly different course that would take it around the crown.

"Where are we going?" I said.

"To the dome where you first arrived," Speaker replied.

"Why? Surely that can't be where the opening of the bridge into the future is located?"

"The new bridgehead is not within the dome," Speaker said, "although it is close by, beneath the surface. We are going to the dome because it is a contained environment, easily sterilized should the necessity arise."

"I can't possibly be carrying any biological contamination—not from the Solarites, at any rate. They're completely different from creatures like us, in physical terms. In any case, the vessel that carried me into the range of their collective mind-force never came as close to the sun as the moon is from the Earth."

"We do not know what might have been aboard the vessel," Speaker said, "but that is not our main concern; if you were carrying any ordinary biological infection we would not need to isolate you to guard ourselves against it—the containment facility was sterilized before your arrival for your protection, not ours."

"Do you think that the Metamorphosians might have taken some clandestine advantage of the permission I gave them to breach my suit? Or are you anxious that whatever the Solarites did to my mind might have equipped me with some exotic means to affect other biological entities?"

"Neither possibility seems likely," Speaker admitted. "We have no idea, though, what the Metamorphosians' biotechnological capabilities may be, and have no basis to estimate what the Solarites might have been able to achieve, even at a distance that would render us utterly impotent. We interrogated the Amphibian's mind as soon as the returning vessel came within range, and detected nothing unusual—but your mind is naturally confused and conflicted, and we cannot be sure of what has been hidden in its unconscious component without the aid of deep dream-analysis. We shall be interrogating Philip and Clara too, under the same controlled conditions. It is merely a precaution. We do not believe that anyone has any hostile intent towards us, but we are determined to be careful. This is for your protection as well as ours—and you are far more vulnerable than we are."

The Antipodean began its descent while she was speaking, plunging into the clouds. This time, I did not waste time peering into the mists in search of new wonders.

As soon as we had landed next to the cylindrical dome the gel released me, and I was able to step down. I saw the second Antipodean coming down immediately behind the first, and waited for Danby and Clara to disembark. Speaker made no attempt to hurry me inside.

"Why have we come here?" Clara asked, moving rapidly to my side as soon as she had set foot on the ground.

"For the sake of our own safety," I told her, keeping my voice free from any trace of sarcasm. "They will be able to repair or renew our surskins here, if necessary. We shall have to go to sleep, I fear—they want to carry out a very full examination."

"That's understandable," Danby said, controlling the slight trepidation he felt at the thought of what that would entail.

"It will all be over very soon," I told them. "When you wake up, you will be masters of your own destiny."

"Are you implying that you will not?" Clara was quick to ask.

"I can't be certain," I said. "I've accepted further obligations, though, of which you have no part."

"We have an obligation to you, George," Clara said, quietly. "Your obligations are ours, at least in part."

We were ushered inside then. The interior of the dome was by no means as bare as it had been when we arrived; indeed, it now seemed quite crowded, by virtue of the addition of two further gel-tanks, and three couches placed alongside them. There was also a table, on which there were several jugs of viscous liquid, obviously intended for our nourishment.

The quarters seemed even more cramped when Speaker came in behind us. Her folded wings seemed uncomfortably cramped in the confined space, although she showed no more sign of distress now than she had in the flier.

"Do you really need to be here?" I asked her. "Surely the collective mind of the biosphere has force enough at such close quarters to invade our minds without your immediate proximity?"

"We have that ability," Speaker agreed. "Even so, it may be as well to have a pair of helping hands available while you sleep."

I accepted that excuse, although I could not help wondering whether Speaker had now been demoted from the status of guide-companion to something more akin to a canary in a coal-mine.

I went to the table and drank some of the liquid food that was waiting there. I had not felt the slightest pang of thirst or hunger since I had last taken nourishment on the moon, but that was evidently due to the operation of the surskin lining my gut. Once I began to drink my stomach felt very grateful for the gift. Danby and Clara followed my example, and for several minutes we swapped jugs back and forth between ourselves, complimenting the taste sensations that the linings of our tongues had now learned to orchestrate very cleverly.

"I don't think I shall have the slightest difficult going to sleep," Clara said, looking at one of the empty jugs with a certain suspicion.

"That's good," I said. "Sometimes, I miss tiredness, and the sensation of falling asleep. At least I can look forward to eventful dreams."

"There's a great deal going on here that I don't understand," Clara said, lowering her voice to a murmur as she trapped me in a corner and turned her back to the others, "and you don't seem any more inclined than these various monsters to explain it to me. I know that you and Philip haven't contrived to set aside your mutual antagonism, but I do think you owe me slightly better treatment. You're not responsible for my presence here, but we are companions nevertheless."

I had been too preoccupied with my own thoughts, and too accustomed to regarding Mirastara as my primary confidant to give much thought to the feelings of either of my human companions. I felt a sudden surge of guilt, because Clara was undoubtedly right. I did owe her far more consideration than I had lately given her—especially in view of the fact that her long confinement with Philip Danby in the bowels of the moon had obviously not served to restore the intimacy of her relationship with him.

"I'm sorry, Clara," I said, sincerely. "I've been carried away—literally as well as metaphorically—and have forgotten my obligations. I'll tell you everything, I promise, although I doubt that the

Chimeras will grant me time to do it just now. They're taking extraordinary precautions, but I can't believe that they have anything to fear. Everyone is apprehensive about what might lie at the other end of the new time-bridge, and what its future makers hope to achieve by permitting the connection. Whatever happens to me, though, you must go home. I have no right to ask for your promise, but I would feel a great deal easier if I had it."

"That's not what you said on the moon," she reminded me.

"It was what I meant, even then," I said. "It will be easier for me to take risks if I know that I'm sparing you the same hazards. Danby may do as he pleases, and surely will—but he too will want to be sure that you will take no risk that is unnecessary. I'll tell you everything I know and believe regardless—but I'll feel a greater deal easier in my mind if I know that you're going home."

"I had wondered whether you were keeping me in the dark in order to ensure that I might be permitted to return," she said.

I shook my head. "It was pure thoughtlessness. If Fate wants to keep her secrets, you already know too much—but it seems to me that Fate is something of a jester, else I would never have been allowed to return from the world of the Dwellers. Ours is an era and a civilization replete with idle fantasies, and whatever knowledge we carry back with us can do no harm there, because no one can or will believe any news we bring. If I returned, so can you—and I hope you will."

"Even if you don't?"

"Especially if I don't."

"If I were to return as you did...," she began, hesitantly.

"You won't," I told her. "That was the result of what the Dwellers did to me, not of the mere fact of traveling in time. You'll return with your hair as luxuriant as it ever was, in no danger of being shunned."

"I'm accustomed to you now," she said, apologetically. "If we were to return together...."

"That might yet be possible," I assured her. "Even if I travel to the end of time and back, it may still be possible. And I'll tell you *everything*. You have my promise on that score."

Danby literally elbowed his way into the conversation at that point, thrusting poor Clara aside. "Speaker is eager to proceed," he said. "There will be time for idle chatter afterwards, I'm assured."

"I'm sure there will," I said. I looked over his shoulder and met Speaker's eye. Even she had the grace to put on an apologetic expression.

I led by example and went to one of the couches. I lay down upon it, but I waited until Danby and Clara had copied me before I began to relax into the customary trance state. Speaker was standing over me, seeming every inch the ministering angel.

I tried to smile, but my muscles were no longer able to respond to my will.

CHAPTER FORTY-THREE

THE BALANCE OF PLEASURE AND PAIN

It was not at all unpleasant to relive my journeys to the moon and around the sun, at a pace which seemed more leisurely, although it was objectively far more rapid. I seemed more alone in my dream than on any of the previous occasions when I had consented to my mind being read, receiving only fleeting impression of the Chimeras' collective consciousness, but I did obtain some slight inkling of what it felt like to be a mind constitutive of an entire biosphere.

In one sense, I was no more conscious of the detail of the Earth's surface, subterrains and atmosphere than my own mind usually was of the minute transactions of my flesh, but there was something markedly odd about that awareness. Human consciousness tends to take little account of the body unless it is receiving sensory signals of some kind, and is hardly sensible of its interior at all, save for alarm signals—which normally take the form of pain—or hormone-based sensations of satisfaction. To the human mind, therefore, the physical body is seen primarily as a potential source of distress, and secondarily as a potential source of reward. Although sensations of both kinds can be refined in a number of ways, the fundamental bipolarity seems far more significant than subtler distinctions.

I had been aware, while being probed by Liamon and the Metamorphosian, and being more generously linked with Mirastara, that other beings experienced the balance of pain and pleasure differently, and were more sensitive to subtle differences within those two spectra of sensation, but the difference had seemed to be a matter of degree rather than one of fundamental difference. While being interrogated by the Solarites, on the other hand, the impressions of physical sensation I had received had seemed quite alien, incapable of easy translation into parallel human sensations; I had experienced borrowed sensations that I had been able to comprehend as heat and light, but nothing I had been able to construe as pain or pleasure.

Glimpsing the collective intelligence of the Chimeras was not like glimpsing the mind of a Dweller or a Metamorphosian, but nor was it like my alien encounter with the Solarites. The collective mind's perception of its multitudinous bodies was not as limited or as crude as an individual body's perception of its tissues, but it was, in some respects, qualitatively similar.

The collective intelligence of the Earthian hive-mind *did* experience something akin to pain, which was more than and different from the sum of individual pains suffered by its scions—but that kind of sensibility was far outweighed by the much more complicated mode of experience it had that was akin to pleasure. That, too, was far more than and quite different from the individual pleasures experienced by its scions. I had nothing with which to compare it except the sense of well-being that humans have when they are not only free from any pangs of illness or weariness but feel filled with energy and enthusiasm, but the comparison hardly seemed to do it justice in its quality or its complexity. The intelligence of the Earth's biosphere had far more to delight it than any mere eagerness for action.

I realized then that the uncharitable judgment I had made of the Metamorphosians and Chimeras alike, on account of their stubborn repetition of genetic discoveries made by the long process of mutation and natural selection, had left out an important component of progress. The Chimeras, I realized, had made emotional as well as intellectual progress; they had redressed the balance of pleasure and pain, in such a way as to make life more rewarding—an achievement of which mutation and natural selection had never been capable, simply because pain and death were more important components of the selective process than any kind of pleasure, including sexual pleasure. Until I had glimpsed the Earthian hive-mind, I had not realized how cheaply bought the will to live had been, in organisms of my tawdry kind.

Not for the first time, I lost all track of objective time while the interrogation was in process. I tried to instruct myself to ask Speaker, when I awoke, how much of the year of future time that we had been gifted by the Professor's machine had now been consumed—months, I had to suppose, rather than mere days, although it only seemed like days—and exactly how long remained to us. By the time I came back to full consciousness, however, the instruction had slipped to the back of my mind, and the fact that I was in an environment devoid of clocks and calendars helped it to remain there when I had come into full possession of my faculties. It would have been interesting to see a clock or a calendar, if only in order to make some estimate of the alterations that modification of the Earth's diameter and mass had wrought in the day and the year, but I never did. The Chimeras had no use for such devices, relying on the accuracy of their innate perceptions, and had not thought it worthwhile to include them among the preparations they had made to receive us as guests.

Danby and Clara found waking from their dreams a more problematic matter than I did, and I had time to go to the table and pour myself a generous portion from one of the refilled jugs while Speaker was still making sure that they were quite well. It was not until they had both sat up on their couches that Speaker turned back to me.

"All is well," she said. "You were right. The Solarites do not seem to have done any more to you than they asked permission to do."

"*Seem*, you say?" I queried. "Does that mean that you are not certain?"

"Nothing is absolutely certain, when dealing with unknown powers," Speaker told me. "All that the Solarites appear to have done, though, is to establish a network of neural connections in a part of your cerebrum that will facilitate the future reading of your memory. In a sense, they have completed what the Dwellers did to you—but far more cleverly, and with fewer side-effects. Like the Dwellers, they have also enhanced your capacity for entering further states of consciousness and unconsciousness—but we are not so sure about that part of their enterprise being free from unexpected side-effects."

I remembered Mirastara's surprise and distress regarding her inability to wake me after the Solarites had performed their mindforce operation. "You suspect that they're not quite as clever as they imagine," I guess.

"They were trying something they had never had the opportunity to attempt before," Speaker reminded me. "They have only encountered a handful of carbonaceous beings, and you are the only human mind among them. It would be astonishing, no matter how clever they are, if they had been perfectly successful in their endeavor."

"You think they might have harmed me, without meaning to?"

"There is a possibility that they have rendered you more vulnerable, without meaning to," Speaker said. "The Dwellers attempted to make your body more robust, but the Solarites might have undone some of that work—unwittingly, no doubt. We are not sure that they fully understood the relationship between your body and your mind, perhaps having been misled by inferences they drew from their study of the Metamorphosians."

"Your anxieties seem conspicuously vague," I pointed out.

"That is true," Speaker admitted. "They are nevertheless real."

"How are Liamon and Assiah?" I asked. "Have you agreed terms with the Metamorphosians?"

"We have made a good beginning," Speaker said. "There is a long way to go before we reach a permanent settlement."

"Have you made more progress with the time-bridge?" I asked.

"A little. We have recovered a few more passive observers, but the proportion we lose remains much the same, and we have recovered no useful information about the intelligent inhabitants of the future or their environment. We have transmitted a copy of the dictionary Philip's father sent us, but it is probably useless, given that they do not have the kind of key that allowed us to decipher it so readily. We have not so far received any explicit invitation to continue our experiments, in writing or any other form. On the other hand, the bridge remains open; the tacit invitation remains."

"Is Liamon still enthusiastic to explore the bridge?"

"Yes. Mirastara is equally enthusiastic—although her eagerness is based on the assumption that you will accompany Liamon. The Dweller makes the same assumption. Assiah is under instruction to go, no matter what the risk." Speaker glanced at Danby and Clara then, but neither rushed to insist on adding a fifth member to the first substantial expedition.

"One of us must undertake a preliminary expedition alone, for a brief span," I said, "in order to reassure the remainder that there is at least a possibility of safe return."

"That was my responsibility," Speaker said. "I am, after all, more easily replaceable than any visitor from afar."

I had not long returned to full awareness, and was still slightly fuddled; I did not immediately catch the full implication of that remark. Indeed, what first caught my attention was her unexpected use of the word "I". I fell into a brief contemplation of the fact that Speaker's fate seemed to be following the same track as Mirastara's; mere contact with travelers in time had been enough to bring about a profound change in her particular relationship with the collective intelligence of which she was a component part. Like Mirastara, she was moving inexorably along the existential road that led in the direction of individuation.

Then the realization of what she had actually implied struck me like a thunderbolt.

"*Was* your responsibility?" I repeated. "Are you saying that you have *already* crossed the bridgehead—and returned safely."

"It was decided, once the interrogation had produced its preliminary results," Speaker said, in a frustratingly uninformative manner, "that my continued presence here was unnecessary. I was briefly called away."

"And sent into the future?"

"So it appears," she replied.

"What did you see?"

"Nothing. I mean that literally. I saw *nothing*, and I remember nothing. Consciously, there was not so much as a momentary disorientation between my dispatch and return—but I had been gone for several minutes, in terms of this time-frame, and considerably more than that, in terms of the other. Like the unintelligent devices sent ahead of me that were also permitted to return, I observed absolutely nothing—but, like them, I had certainly *been observed*. I was returned without any instruction or invitation, but I was also returned without sustaining the slightest injury."

Now, the word *I* no longer seemed in the least strange within her pronouncements; the familiarity bred by its repeated usage had rapidly deprived it of all shock value. Speaker was, indeed, following the same existential track that Mirastara had followed, and was becoming more individuated with every speech-act she performed. She too was a traveler in time now, albeit one whose ambition to educate herself had been summarily thwarted.

I thought, a trifle uncharitably, that she must know now how I felt, being continually probed and interrogated without being able to recover more than a slight reciprocal reward. I thought, too, that I seemed to be locked inexorably upon that existential pathway. Could I expect anything more of the mysterious future than to be interrogated yet again, more skillfully than before? Would I, too, be sent back to this era without having experienced a moment's lapse of subjective time, with not the slightest item of information by way of reward for my trouble?

"So the way is clear for a further expedition?" I said.

"Further attempts have been approved," Speaker agreed, "provided that they are undertaken carefully."

"When?" I asked, briefly.

"Very soon," she replied. "Liamon, Mirastara and Assiah are already lodged at the bridgehead, waiting."

"Waiting for me?" I said.

"Waiting for us to conclude our interrogation of your memories. It was a delicate business, given that so much of what you experienced was calculated illusion. It can be difficult to pursue dreams within dreams, especially in a mind as prone to disorder as yours."

Danby and Clara had both taken adequate nourishment by now, and had collected themselves after their ordeal. I supposed that they might have been woken some time before me, had the Chimeras cared to do so.

"This barely-tangible costume insulates me so well from all ordinary sensation," Clara muttered, intending the words for my hearing, "that I have lost all sense of time. I can't tell whether I've slept for eight hours or eight days.

That reminded me of the earlier instruction I had given myself, and I immediately asked Speaker exactly how long it had been since we had first set foot in this era.

"In the meanings attached to the terms in your era," she replied, "ninety-eight days and seven hours have elapsed. Your journey around the sun took up the largest segment of the interval. More than two-thirds of the time allotted to your expedition still remain to you."

"Given that a year spent in some further future would only involve a lapse of a few minute in this one," I observed, speaking more to myself than my companions, "I might have the opportunity to live a very long lifetime before then."

"You might," Speaker agreed, "but we must proceed tentatively. Whatever the result of the series of experiments, it would be sensible for at least one of your friends to spend all of the remaining time in the present, in order to be sure of returning safely to your own time to tell the tale as it has unfolded thus far."

"We have discussed that," Danby said, shortly.

"But came to no definite conclusion," Clara added.

"The only sensible conclusion we could possibly reach," I said, "is that it's needless to risk more than one of us, at least in the first instance. If I should return safely from the first venture, there will be time to discuss the possibility of one of you embarking on a further expedition. Until then...."

"You have no right to forbid us," Danby pointed out. "If my father had not built his time machine, none of us would be here. I am the one who bears his authority

"*We* have the right to forbid you," Speaker put in. "We would rather you reached the conclusion by yourselves, to save us the necessity, but George is correct. The first expedition had to be mine. Now that I have returned safely, it is necessary for one other person to undertake a second brief expedition. If that person returns safely, a larger party may embark on an expedition of longer duration. If all goes well thereafter, the way will eventually be opened to further volunteers—always provided that the bridge endures."

"It might not," Danby said, a trifle sourly. "My father found out the hard way how difficult it is to sustain such links."

"That was nothing to the hardness of the way by which Brett and Templeton found out how hazardous such routes can be," I reminded him, before turning back to Speaker. "I will undertake the second experimental expedition," I said.

"That is still to be decided," she said, although she must have known that I would get my way. She turned her back on me, ostensibly to address herself more comfortably to Danby. "We are grateful to you for the help you have given us Philip," she said, scrupulously, "and we would rather you did not ask anything from us that we cannot offer. We cannot allow you to take George's place in the initial attempts to test the time-bridge into the future."

I did not believe that Danby really wanted to take my place, although I supposed that he might want to mount an expedition of his own once the way was proven to be safe, He seemed to be in a quandary, however, as to whether he ought to make a show of boldness.

"I can see the logic of the situation clearly enough," Clara said, attempting to solve his problem for him. "So can you, Philip. I wish you the very best of luck, George, and look forward to your safe return. May God go with you."

"Thank you," I said. She reached out to hug me, as she had done once before—but I gathered from her hesitation that that the instinctive repulsion I induced in her had not yet vanished *entirely*, no matter how dearly she might wish that it had.

"Go with my blessing too, George," Danby said, as gracefully as he could. "If you draw the same kind of blank that Speaker did, I suppose the eventual reward might still fall to some further adventurer."

"You might well be right, Philip," I said. I did not yield to a mischievous temptation to add that the intelligences of the further future might, on the other hand, decide that they had obtained enough intellectual insight into the barbaric past once a few of us had arrived and gone, and might decide to keep future subjects for vivisection or taxidermic preservation.

"You may rest if you feel the need," Speaker aid.

"I've been resting for hours, if not days," I said. "If people are waiting for me, it would be rude to keep them waiting any longer than necessary. We should go—if you're sure that it's safe to let me out of this little prison."

"Quite safe," Speaker said. I doubted very much whether she was restraining any mischievous impulse to add a remark about the possible renewal of the Chimeras' fears if I were to come back from the further future having been altered in the flesh yet again by a further set of interesting interrogators. It seemed wise to make no such comment myself.

"In that case," I said, aloud, "you'd best lead the way."

Chapter Forty-Four

Farewells

As Speaker had promised, Liamon, Mirastara, and Assiah were waiting not far away. They had been separately lodged in quarters close to the chamber where the Chimeras' temporal projector was located, not far below the surface within a few hundred yards of the terminus of their bridge into the past.

The first one I went to see was Mirastara, who was lodged in an enormous room, most of which was taken up by a vast swimming pool. The walls were screens displaying exterior scenes so the pool gave the appearance of being a small lake, and its banks were dressed with actual vegetation. She did not seem as grateful for these efforts as she might have been, presumably because she was all too conscious of their artificiality. She came out of the water to talk to me, and sat damply beside me on a ridge of moss.

"Speaker has explained what happened in the first experiment," I told her.

"No doubt. Has she told you that they want to send you out alone as a second experiment?"

"She was reluctant to say so in so many words, perhaps because she wanted me to take the entire responsibility upon myself, but she did say that they wanted to send a single individual."

"You promised me once that you would not leave me while I needed you," she said.

"I don't want you to risk your life unnecessarily," I said. "If I did set out alone, I ought to return within a matter of minutes. If I did not return..."

"You know full well," she said, "that if you were to set forth alone, and then did not return, I would follow you, regardless of the risk."

I did know that, and she knew that I knew it. "The Chimeras undoubtedly have good reasons for wanting to take one step at a time," I said, "but I doubt that they will forbid us to set out together, if we insist."

"The bridge is open," Mirastara stated, reminding me of all the implications I had read into the fact. "We shall cross it together, as agreed."

"Speaker returned without any memory of her experience," I observed, "but that doesn't mean that the bridge-builders didn't obtain information from her. It's possible that we'll return in the same condition."

"Of course it is," Mirastara said. "What does that matter?" She meant that it could not affect our decision to make the attempt, not that it would not be a terrible disappointment.

"It's not impossible that we might be separated at the far end of the bridge, and lose an opportunity to be reunited here," I pointed out.

"If they decide to keep one of us and send the other back," the Amphibian said, reasonably, "the likelihood is that they will keep you and send me back—which would have exactly the same result as your making the journey alone and failing to return. We cannot tell what might happen; all we can decide is whether we shall take the chance. It is decided."

"Will Liamon say the same?" I asked.

"Of course she will," Mirastara said. "She has already taken the trouble to make the agreement clear."

"It might be a needless risk for her," I observed. "She certainly has no need of me."

"She will be the judge of that," Mirastara said, simply. "You should not be anxious. Perhaps fate is determined to separate us, and perhaps it is not—but we ought to travel as far as we may, in the meantime. I shall come with you, and the Chimeras will not forbid me. If you are sent back alone, then I shall wait for you in the future. You will be no more content to leave me alone there than I would be to leave you, even if the bridge is broken."

"Whatever happens," I said, "we have experienced adventures that no other Earthly creatures have ever experienced. We have been fortunate."

"We are fortunate," she agreed.

I went to see Liamon next. She too had been lodged in an enormous room, appropriate to her height and stride, but no attempt had been made to disguise it as an exterior setting. It was not abundantly furnished, but the bed, the chair and the desk had all been made with the giant's proportions in mind. She lifted me up so that I might sit on the table while she sprawled in the chair, bringing us as nearly face to face as we could contrive.

"Speaker wants me to make the second test alone," I said. "Mirastara will not hear of it."

"Of course not," Liamon said. "There will be four of us. The Chimeras know that, and will not attempt to prevent it."

"Four?" I queried.

"Assiah is under orders. Where you go, he goes."

"He's an individual, unlike Speaker. He could make his own decision."

"He has done so. Where you go, he will go."

I raised no further objection, but I did say: "I must confess to some surprise that you're so determined to come with me, and that the Chimeras have not tried harder to dissuade you. You would still be very useful to them as an intermediary in their dealings with the Metamorphosians—and that is a role you consider to be well worthwhile."

"It is," Liamon said. "But you saw me on the moon, did you not? And you have seen me here, in other places than this. You know how ill-fitted I am to this world, by simple virtue of my size. Perhaps the far future will be no better—but if there is a world fit for giants, somewhere in the sequence of bridges, then I ought to make every effort to reach it. Do you not agree?"

"The Metamorphosians on the moon are spacefarers," I said. "They limit their size in order to economize in the size and power of the vessels that carry them through space. In the right environment, they could and would become giants. If they were to set up a permanent colony on the moon...." I left the sentence dangling. Mirastara was right; the matter was already settled.

"You wanted to read my memories for a second time," I reminded her. "Should we do that before we undertake the crossing?"

"It is no longer necessary," the giant said, mildly. "Perhaps, at some future time, in some other world, an occasion will present itself. I am sorry that I called you foolish for consenting to be used as a living book. I can see the wisdom of it now. I understand why the Seekers of Science attempted to adapt you for that purpose, rather than modifying one of the living books they already possessed, or some other domestic animal."

"Because my mind is just primitive enough, without being too primitive," I said. "Its powers of perception are limited to coarse sensory input, and its underlying cellular mechanisms of information storage and processing are sufficiently crude to accommodate the required modifications without any serious disruption of their function—but it's nevertheless capable of active intelligent perception, offering sharp clarity to prospective readers."

"That is one way of looking at it," Liamon agreed, "but not the whole of it. There is a fine urgency in your observation, and a sharp curiosity, which our world had almost lost, and this one has lost completely. It is not a matter of your essential fragility, which the Seekers attempted to remedy, but of the spectrum of your sensations."

"The balance of pain and pleasure," I said. "But the Seekers of Science modified that too—in making me more robust, they dulled my sensitivity to physical sensation. I do not feel pain as I once did, or pleasure either. My body is less responsive now than it was when it was a raw product of natural selection."

"That modification was necessary," Liamon said. "The basic spectrum remains the same, even though its intensity is diminished. You would not have survived a year in our world without some such fortification against the effects of mental force. Another strategy was tried out first, I believe, but did not work as well."

"I caught glimpses of what the Seekers of Science did to Brett," I told her. "I thought at the time that it was a straightforward exercise in sadism, but I understand the Dwellers a little better now than I did then. Even so, it remains a study in horror; to say that it did not work *as well* is a monstrous distortion."

"That does not matter now," Liamon said, dismissively. "The point is that you are what you are, and it is as well that you are enthusiastic to serve the purpose that you did not choose. You may be confident, I think, that the inhabitants of the future will take care to protect and preserve you—perhaps even, in the end, to reward you. You may, at least, be far more confident of it than I am of my own fate—but the best opportunity left to me, I have no doubt, is to stay with you as long as I might."

"I hope you find what you need," I said.

"Thank you," she said. "I hope that you do, indeed, receive your due reward."

Finally, I went to see Assiah, who was quartered in a far more modest fashion, although by no means as meanly as Clara, Danby and I had been accommodated on the moon. He was still wearing his protective suit, which was dutifully filtering and sterilizing the air he eventually breathed, and the nourishment that reached his flesh. At one time, I might have been grateful for the opportunity to use actual speech in communicating with him, but I had grown so used to communicating with Mirastara and Liamon that the necessity of making sounds was beginning to seem slightly burdensome. I put the argument to him that I had briefly mentioned to Liamon.

"You are an individual, and fiercely proud of it," I told him. "You are free to make your own decisions. Would it not be wiser to wait until a second test has been completed before risking yourself in the time machine?"

"Metamorphosians are certainly proud of our individualism," he agreed. "We know where the path of collective intelligence leads. We also know, though, that individuals must cooperate and collaborate in order to achieve anything worthwhile. We know how tiny and helpless individuals are when they are alone. It is precisely because we are individuals that we are altruists, placing the common good above craven selfishness."

"The cynics of my own era," I observed, "argued that it was in every individual's best interests for everyone else to act altruistically, and hence for every individual to pretend—with ruthless hypocrisy—to be an altruist."

"That might have been possible in your society," he said, "but it is not possible in any society that has begun to master direct communication between minds."

"I see that," I said. "To tell the truth, hypocrisy was neither as universal nor as relentless in my own society as the cynics sought to imply. Even so, you might still come to your own conclusion as to the wisdom of waiting for a second test to be completed before risking the time-bridge."

"I would rather have undertaken the first test with the winged Chimera than waited for the second," Assiah said, bluntly, "but I could not insist. If the general opinion is correct that you have some kind of privileged status in this matter, then it is imperative that I take part in your venture—and this time, I think, I shall be permitted to do so."

"Will your companions send others after you if you fail to return?"

"Probably—if the bridge remains open."

"Do you think it will collapse?"

"How can I possibly tell? The Earthian hive-mind has contrived to open two such portals, but it does not seem to know how to sustain them indefinitely or control the traffic through them. I know nothing at all about the mechanism of these supposed bridges—for me, as for you, this will be a leap into utter darkness; but for me, as for you, it is one that I cannot refuse to make. The merest possibility of my safe return, with some knowledge of what is to come—however vague—is sufficient to justify the risk."

"I hope you return safely," I told him, "with as much enrichment as you are able to draw from the experience. I hope the bridge will remain open long enough, and fruitfully enough, to assist in sealing a mutually beneficial alliance between the Metamorphosians and the Chimeras."

"Hope is cheap," he replied. "Time will tell."

"Let us hope so," I said. "The worst possibility of all is that it will refuse to tell us anything."

I did not see any of them again until the four of us reassembled in the subsurface arena where the Chimeras had assembled the platform of their second time machine. It was a much larger platform than the one the Professor had constructed, but that was because the Chimeras had built it with the possibility of transmitting a giant firmly in mind. The mechanism of the actual temporal projector was just as carefully hidden as the Professor's, though; the visible apparatus was Spartan in its simplicity. The area around the platform seemed crowded, though, because there were several Chimerical observers assembled there, as well as Speaker, Clara and Danby.

"How long shall we stay in the future on this occasion?" I asked Speaker.

"Three minutes, in terms of elapsed future time." she said. "A fraction more than seventy seconds, in terms of time elapsed at this point."

"Good," I said. I turned round to look at Clara and Danby. Danby seemed to be preoccupied with his frustration at the impossibility of obtaining any useful sight of the projection apparatus, of which he was undoubtedly avid to make an assiduous study, so I addressed myself to Clara. "If I don't return," I said to her, "will you see to it that my affairs in Oxford are properly set in order? It should be simple enough."

She nodded her head.

"Well then," I said to my three intended companions. "Let's do it."

CHAPTER FORTY-FIVE

TIME'S REFUSAL

When I woke up, I could not remember why the experience of waking up should seem so strange as to be almost unnatural. I knew that I had woken up many times before—and I knew, too, that I had woken up on previous occasions without being able to recall where I ought to be. I dismissed the idea that I had amnesia, because I knew perfectly well who I was, but I realized that I did not know exactly *when* I was. I could not, for the life of me, remember what I had been doing the day before, or what room I ought to see when I opened my eyes.

I did not try to open my eyes immediately, although I was not entirely sure why I was hesitating. Perhaps I felt that, for the sake of my sanity, it would be better if I could figure out what I ought to be able to see before I actually put the matter to the test.

I could not do it. The most probable hypothesis that I could come up with was that I would be in my bedroom in Oxford, but, for some reason I could not specify. I was convinced that the probability was misleading. I was sure that I had left Oxford, but I could not remember where I had gone, or why.

Eventually, I gave up on the conundrum and attempted to open my eyes. It was harder than I had expected; the lashless lids appeared to be glued shut. In the end, I had to bring my hands out from under the bedclothes and rub my closed eyes with my knuckles, until I was finally able to open them.

The light was dim—a grey twilight was filtering through closed curtains—but it was adequate to show me the walls and furnishings of the room. After a long half-minute, I finally recognized it. It was a bedroom in Professor Danby's house, not far from the Welsh border. I had spent part of a night in the room once before, not in the bed but sitting by the window, unable to sleep. I strove in vain to remember how long ago that had been. I was sure that it had not been the previous night, or the one before that, but I could not remember, for the moment, anything that had happened in the interim.

Something *had* happened in the interim, I knew—something like a very long dream, which had not been a dream at all.

I concentrated hard, cudgeling my recalcitrant mind. Slowly at first, and then in a cataract, the memories returned.

I had returned to the future, using the Professor's time machine for a second time. I had not dreamed that I had returned; I had actually done it. It had not been the same future that I had visited the first time, but a further one, a million years hence.

Everything was confused, to begin with, but I contrived to separate the shards of my memory of that second expedition, sorted them out, and painstakingly reassembled them into a coherent whole. I remembered the Great Tree, the reunion with the Amphibian and her Dweller companion, the voyage to the moon, and the strange encounter with the Solarites—which *had* been a dream of sorts, but no less real for that. I recalled the return to Earth, and the brief descent to the *other* time machine, where the bridgehead to the future had been opened. I remembered stepping up on to the platform with Mirastara, Liamon and Assiah, after asking Clara to tidy up my Earthly affairs if I failed to return.

Then—nothing.

Speaker, I remembered, had returned from her own expedition, with no memory whatsoever of what had happened to her—but she had at least returned conscious of having no memory.

Am I in the further future now? I asked myself. *Are my present surroundings merely an illusion, created because the inhabitants of that further future cannot or will not show themselves to me as they really are?*

I could not entirely discount that hypothesis, but when I tested the texture of the bedclothes with my fingers, they seemed perfectly ordinary as well as quite real. When I got out of bed, naked, and went to the window to look out, the landscape seemed perfect in every detail. When I looked at my hairless face in the mirror over the mantelshelf, it was exactly as I had last seen it.

Was it all a dream? I wondered. *Did the Professor's machine fail, shocking me into unconsciousness rather than projecting me into the future? Have I simply been lying unconscious since yesterday evening, or one evening last week?*

I could not entirely discount that hypothesis either—nor could I believe it, any more than I could believe the other.

I moved towards the door, but then remembered my nakedness and looked round for some clothes to put on. The ones I had been wearing when I stepped on to the platform of the Professor's machine—the ones I had discarded in the cylindrical block-house where we had been received—were on a chair by the foot of the bed, neatly folded. They seemed to have been laundered, though perhaps not very recently.

I put them on, and had just turned round in order to make a second attempt to leave the room when the door opened. Young Danby came in.

He went as white as a sheet. "My God!" he said. "George!"

I looked at him in frank puzzlement. "You look terrible, Philip," I said. "I seem to have lost a segment of my memory. How long have I been here?"

Instead of replying, he looked back into the corridor. "Father!" he called, in a conspicuously unsteady voice. "Clara! He's awake!"

His amazement spoke volumes. Suddenly feeling slightly weak—psychologically, if not physically—I sat down on the bed. "Quite some time, then," I murmured.

At least forty seconds must have passed before Clara arrived, followed not long after by the Professor, but young Danby said not a word in the interim. He simply stared at me, as if I were a ghost—as, I supposed, I must be, albeit in some metaphorical sense that I could not quite grasp.

The creature that looked like an angel, I remembered, had told me that I still had more than two-thirds of my sojourn in her particular future yet to elapse when I stepped on to the bridge to the further future. Apparently, that time had elapsed, and more besides. Considering how little I had slept in the previous ten years, it seemed rather remarkable that I had been able to fall unconscious for the greater part of a year.

Clara ran forward and threw her arms around my neck, without the least reluctance.

"Oh, George," she said. "We thought your mind had gone forever. We thought they had stripped it bare. Speaker said that you might wake up, once you were back in your own world, but she had no way of knowing, and we had almost given up that last frail hope." She stepped back then, not because the old instinctive revulsion had gripped her again, but because she was obviously uncertain as to exactly how much of my mind and memory had returned.

"I remember stepping on to the platform of the Chimeras' second bridgehead into time," I said. "Mirastara was with me, and Liamon, and Assiah. Speaker had already used the machine once, but had returned with no memory of her experience. Obviously, I returned—was I still conscious then? I can't remember anything else."

"No," Clara said, "you weren't conscious—not for any longer than a split second, at any rate. You fell down as soon as you returned. The Chimeras could not bring you back to consciousness, in spite of all their mental power."

"Were the others unconscious too?" I asked.

After a slight hesitation, Clara said: "You came back alone, George. The others were lost."

I sat down on the bed. We had all known that it was a possibility. I had discussed it with all three of them. We had all known the risk, and we had all thought it worth taking.

"They even sent you on a second passage of the sun," Clara said, "in case the Solarites were able to succeed where they had failed. They too were unable to wake you. When the time came for us to return, we thought you might be unable to return with us, but we dressed you, just in case, and you did return with us, still unconscious. When you didn't wake up immediately, we were afraid that you would die, because you no longer had the Chimeras' surskin to nourish and maintain you, but we've been able to give you water and a little liquid food while you slept. We were about to have you removed to a hospital, where you could be fed intravenously, although the Professor didn't want questions asked. It's been nine days since we returned. You've been unconscious for nine months."

"Did they send others after Mirastara, Liamon and Assiah?" I asked.

"They had to," Danby said. "While the bridge endured, they had to keep trying."

"Did any of them come back?"

"Not one," Danby said. "Seven more Chimeras were lost, but there was no time for another Metamorphosian to fly to Earth. It was probably fortunate that the bridge eventually collapsed. The connection was severed, it seems, at the other end. The Chimeras never relented in their attempts to restore or replace it, but without success. The Professor's bridge was severed too, within minutes of our own return to the present. It appears that the entire adventure is concluded."

"For now," the elder Danby was quick to put in. "I intend to keep trying, for as long as I live. I've succeeded twice; I shall succeed again."

"And will anyone care to take our place, the next time?" Clara asked. "I don't doubt that you'll call for volunteers—but will anyone consent, when you tell them what happened this time?"

"What did happen this time?" Professor Danby said, looking at me. "What did you see in the further future, George? What happened to you there?"

"I don't know whether I saw anything," I said. "If I did, the memory appears to have been erased. For whatever reason, the inhabitants of that further future evidently did not want to be observed. They were curious enough to collect a few specimens from their own remote past, but theirs was merely a fishing expedition, not an attempt to communicate."

"But they did send you back," Danby said. "Why did they do that, do you suppose?"

"They sent Speaker back too—once."

"They sent Speaker back to encourage more victims to take their bait," Clara said. "Her return was allowed merely to encourage the supposition that further returns might be possible. You must have been sent back for the same reason, George—as a lure, to tempt further recklessness. It worked."

"Not on you or me," young Danby pointed out.

"Such speculations are irrelevant," the Professor said. "You must try to remember, George. You must try to remember *something*. You went into that further future. Although you only spent a few minutes there, you must have seen *something*. Something certainly happened to you. You must try to remember."

"I shall," I promised him. Then I sat up straighter. "Do you think I might have a little breakfast?" I said. "I'm grateful for whatever liquid nourishment you've forced into me, but I feel hungrier than I've been able to do for many years."

"It's six o'clock in the evening," the Professor said. "We'll be eating dinner at seven."

"Good," I said. "May I have some breakfast in the meantime?"

The Professor frowned, but he left the room, presumably to order a tray. I looked at Danby again, and then at Clara. "You still have your hair," I observed. "Evidently, you have not been served as the Dwellers served me. Have you returned in exactly the same condition as before?"

"So far as we can tell," Clara said. "Richer in experience, of course, but still mortal. Thus far, you're still the only man in the world to have obtained any material reward from time travel."

"I'm not entirely sure that it qualifies as a reward," I said, "even if I should live a thousand years instead of threescore-and-ten."

"It would be a better reward by far," young Danby said, "if you could only recover some intelligence of the remoter future."

"If I had been able to bring you that," I said, "I suspect that I would not have been sent back at all, even in a state of profound unconsciousness. The inhabitants of the distant future do not seem to be quite as reckless as the Dwellers, with regard to the possibility of changing the past. The fact that you and I were sent back to our own time while others were forbidden to return implies that we were the only ones who could be deemed impotent to alter anything of importance. I hope and trust that they did not simply kill the others. I would like to think that Mirastara still has a life to lead, and Liamon a role to play, somewhere in the distant realms of the far future. In fact, I refuse to believe otherwise. For them, I am convinced, that step into the future was merely the first in another and far greater adventure."

"In which case," Danby pointed out, more than a little spitefully, "they abandoned you."

"They did not," I said. "I was snatched from their grasp—but once I was irrevocably lost, they were free to turn their attention to other things."

"We're not impotent to change the course of history," Danby said, insistently. "We know a great deal now about the shape of things to come. We know about the existence, in the present moment, of Aerophobes and Solarites. We know what might be made of the mental force that we have not yet learned to comprehend or control. We know how to open further bridges into time...."

"Provided that there is someone able and willing to open a corresponding terminus," I said. "Do you have the means to make contact with the Aerophobes or the Solarites. Do you have the means to cultivate mastery of mental force? Have you found the weapon of which you went in search, which might tip the balance of some future war?"

"We have a great deal of knowledge that we did not have before," Danby said, stubbornly. "Knowledge is power. We are not impotent to affect the course of history. If nothing else, we have you: your physical being, altered by the Dwellers. If we can only understand what has been done to you, and how...."

"You tried," I reminded him. "We both tried, in collaboration. You could not bear, in the end, to continue."

"If you will consent to stay here," young Danby said, "my father and I...."

"I think not," I said, firmly. "I have studies of my own to pursue, and a life of my own to lead. Knowledge is not power unless it can be put to some practical use. A steam engine was built in ancient Alexandria, but it was no more than a toy in a world without coal and steel. What good would an electrical dynamo be to a neolithic man, or a textbook of mathematics to a Neanderthal? I do not think that anything I discovered in either of the futures I have visited is capable of practical employment in this world, including my remade flesh. Whatever I have become, I am nothing more in this world than a freak and an enigma—an enigma whose solution lies a thousand or a hundred thousand years in the future. The Chimeras, the Metamorphosians and the Solarites—and perhaps the Dwellers too—would have been far better placed to make good use of knowledge gleaned from time travel...and that may be precisely why they were prevented from acquiring any. I suspect that I owe my second safe return, as I owed my first, to my utter incapacity to benefit from my experiences...and I wish I could be more grateful for that than I am."

Young Danby would surely have scolded me for that speech, but a servant appeared them bearing a tray of solid food, such as I had not seen for many a day, and it must have been obvious that I had no more appetite, at present, for conversation. It was left to Clara to have the last word, for the time being.

"Thank God that you *are* back, George," she murmured. "Thank God for that."

CHAPTER FORTY-SIX

TIME'S CONSENT

I returned to Oxford two days later, having convinced Professor Danby and myself that mere effort would not bring back any memory of what I had experienced after crossing the Chimeras' second time-bridge. The Professor wanted me to undergo hypnosis, but I told him that the Chimeras and the Solarites must both have used mental leverage of a far more potent kind on my unconscious mind, apparently without being able to wake me from my unnatural sleep, let alone recover any memory of my experience.

Clara and I took a taxi to the station together. Philip Danby insisted on accompanying us, ostensibly to "see us off", although I suspected that he was still anxious not to leave the two of us alone for too long, in case we contrived to repair our old relationship. He seemed to be reconciled to the fact that he would never be able to place his own relationship with Clara on a more satisfactory footing—in spite of having spent several months in her close company, surrounded by exotic beings, while I lay comatose—but his polite acceptance of that situation seemed to be dependent on the condition that no one else should be able to succeed where he had failed.

"Was it worth it, George?" Clara asked me as we moved on to the platform, apparently making an effort to disregard Danby's presence.

"To me?" I said. "Yes, most certainly, I'm very glad to have seen Mirastara again—and glad, too, that my impressions of the Dwellers could be revised by courtesy of Liamon. Then again, I've visited the moon and the sun, and conversed with alien races in each location—I only wish that I could have been more attentive during my second journey to the sun. Whether the Chimeras obtained the benefit they expected from their summons, I can't tell, but I think that part of their endeavor can be reckoned a success. I did help them, if only a little, to make use of Mirastara and Liamon in their initial intercourse with the Metamorphosians, and our presence also helped to forge that important first link. They must have been disappointed by the failure of their second time-bridge, but they cannot hold me responsible for that. Was it worth it to you?"

"Absolutely," she said. "I learned far more in that year than in all my previous adult life. The knowledge is of no practical value, in that I am no more able now to affect the course of history than I was before, but I'm much changed in myself, despite not having been remade in your image. I might regret that one day, I suppose—but for the present, I'm quite content to be what I have always been, insofar as my flesh is concerned."

"Good," I said. "In that case, I have no need to regret the careless remark that led Philip to recruit you to the expedition."

Clara looked at Danby, who was standing close by, pretending that he was not hanging on our every word. "I think Philip had other reasons for attempting to include me," she said. "Your chance remark merely provided an excuse."

Danby blushed slightly. Instead of replying, he said: "I'm glad that you recovered, George. I thought we had lost you forever, and that you might remain asleep indefinitely."

"Like the Sleeping Beauty in the fairy tale," I said, "waiting for a magical kiss that—in my case—would never come."

Clara laughed, and so did I—but Danby did not. There had been a manifest note of puzzlement in his voice. He was wondering, in a perfectly earnest fashion, why I had awakened, after sleeping for such a very long time. It was, admittedly, a puzzle. Given that the Chimeras and the Solarites must have done everything they could to achieve that effect, and failed, how had it come about?

It might, I supposed, have been purely a matter of chance. Whatever alterations the Solarites had made to the working of my brain while I was within the scope of their mental force had sent me into a profound coma at the time, from which Mirastara had been unable to awaken me, but from which I had eventually emerged spontaneously—or so it appeared. If that effect really had been accidental, then my second awakening might be a mere repetition. If, on the other hand, the Solarites had contrived that first coma deliberately, and prearranged my awakening from it, it had to be possible that the inhabitants of the further future had merely repeated the trick, using the same recently-inbuilt facility.

It was also possible, I had to suppose, that the Solarites had contrived to receive the intelligence they sought, even though it remained inaccessible to everyone else. If the entire endeavor had been planned, it was conceivable, if not very likely, that its primary purpose was to transmit information back in time to the Solarites of a million years hence, and that I had merely been a convenient means of transmitting that information clandestinely and securely.

What seemed more probable to me, however, was that the inhabitants of the remoter future had never intended any useful information to reach any of the inhabitants of the world a million years hence, and that they had put me in a deep coma to make sure that no such information could be recovered in that era. They had not intended that effect to last forever, though—merely long enough for me to return to my own time, when no one could read my mind as it had been so easily read in other eras. The inhabitants of the future, it seemed to me, had been determined to keep their secrets from the Chimeras, but they had never intended to do me any lasting harm.

It was not only for my own sake that I favored that hypothesis; I wanted very much to believe that the inhabitants of the future had never intended to do any harm to Mirastara and Liamon either, or to Assiah and the Chimeras who had crossed the bridge in our wake. I wanted to believe that all of them—but especially Mirastara—had merely begun another great adventure, which would keep them busy for a very long time.

My train arrived before Clara's. Before I boarded it, I said: "You're very welcome to visit me in Oxford, if you can spare the time, I'm always at home."

"I will," she said. "A short visit, when I can. We can't go back to the way we were before, but we can go forward, I think. We have something in common that few other people have."

The third person who had in common what we now had was still within earshot, but he made no objection. He knew that he had a short interval in hand between the departure of my train and the arrival of Clara's. He would make his own representations then, probably with a similar result. She would agree to visit him again, when she could spare the time—but only for a short while. She still had her own life to lead, and she had no intention of going back to something she had already put firmly behind her.

The homeward journey was placid and uneventful. I spent it planning my return to my studies, intending to pick up where I had left off.

I had been away for an entire year, but I did not expect anything to have changed my lodgings, and nothing had. The servant provided by the college had not allowed a single speck of dust to settle permanently, and he had been exceedingly careful in making sure that everything remained in its place, ready for exactly such a resumption as I now planned. My old Regency armchair was just as comfortable as it had been before, and the claret in my cellar had improved a little with age.

Almost as soon as I sat down with a book and a wine-glass, reverting all the way back to the exact situation I had been in when Philip Danby came to call, I began to remember.

My first reaction, absurdly enough, was to laugh out loud.

What a joke the inhabitants of the remotest future had played! Almost everything else they had fished out of the past they had kept, but they had thrown me back.

Perhaps, I thought, they had thrown me back because I was simply too trivial to keep, being merely a living book worth reading once and then setting aside. Perhaps, on the other hand, they had thrown me back because they thought they owed me that, and were willing and able to repay the debt. They had, of course, made sure, in throwing me back, that I could not reveal anything to the various curiosity-seekers who had sought to use me as an instrument—but they had, it seemed, made provision for me to reap my own just reward. They had not only granted me the privilege of a carefully-delayed reawakening, but the privilege of a carefully-delayed remembering.

Perhaps they had not done it as a matter of reward, but merely because I was the only one who could not possibility obtain any benefit from knowing what I knew, being the only player in the game whose mind was too primitive, feeble and confused to find anything more in my own memory but a fabulous vision, a whim of the imagination. In either case, though, the result was the same. I began to remember.

The process was very gradual at first, and I was unable to make much sense of what I recalled, but that was only to be expected, bearing in mind what it was that I was remembering.

I had only spent three minutes in the worlds beyond the world a million years hence—but during those three minutes I had been sent forward in time again, to spend a longer period in some even more distant future. During that interval I had been sent forward again... and so on, though not quite *ad infinitum*, I had only been removed from the world of a million years hence for seventy seconds, but I had endured a subjective and objective eternity within that span. I had not been conscious for a single second, but I had not been deeply unconscious either.

I had been interrogated a thousand, a million or a billion times over, and while I served as a living book to be read and re-read endlessly, I had caught no more than the slightest backwash of consciousness from the minds of my readers...but it was better than nothing. In its fashion, it was immeasurably better than nothing.

As Clara had observed of her own more limited experience, the knowledge was of no practical value, in that I was no more able once I had remembered it to affect the course of history than I had been before, but I was *much changed in myself*. It completed my experience. It told me what I wanted to know.

Perhaps I should have wanted to know different things. Perhaps I should have wanted to know the kinds of things that Philip Danby had wanted to know, or the kinds of things that the Dwellers' Seekers of Wisdom had wanted to know, or the kinds of things that the lunar Metamorphosians had wanted to know—but the simple fact is that I was not interested in instruments of historical change. For good or ill, I was the kind of person who was not merely content but glad to be a living book. I had made a far better living book than Brett or Templeton could ever have done, or Philip Danby or his father—and in consequence of that, I had learned more about my readers than any of those others would have done, and valued it far more than they ever could.

It must have required prodigious cleverness, I thought, for the inhabitants of the remoter futures to have locked up my memories in such a fashion that the Chimeras could not gain access to them, but that was only to be expected. The entities of the remoter futures had obviously progressed far beyond the Chimeras and their contemporaries in the exercise of mental force, just as the Chimeras and their contemporaries had progressed beyond the Dwellers and the Amphibians. Whether or not it had been easy for them to do, they had taken the trouble. They had enabled me to recover the particular treasure that I had sought, once it could do no harm.

By the time I had pieced my fragments of memory together into a more-or-less coherent story, I was no longer inclined to believe that the inhabitants of the further futures had merely been playing a practical joke by allowing me to recover that knowledge. I did not doubt that they had only allowed themselves to do it because it could do no harm, but the *reason* they had done it, given that it could do no harm, was that it seemed to them to be the right thing to do. They had thrown me back in time to the world of the Chimeras in order that I might then be returned to my own world, because it had seemed to them to be the morally correct thing to do. That was important to them, because—like the Amphibians and other employers of mental force—they could only be fully successful in what they intended when they felt morally justified. They had only been able to use me in the extraordinary fashion that they had because they felt that they were dealing with me honorably, and were obliged to recompense me for my trouble to the extent that they were able.

Perhaps, if I had been given a choice, what they did was exactly what I would have asked them to do. It is not impossible, I suppose, that they actually *did* give me the choice, and that it really *was* what I asked them to do.

They had known that I would write it all down, and publish it—but they had also known that it would make no difference, and would not matter—not because the book in question would necessarily be lost or paid no attention, but because it could not make a difference to anyone who did pay attention to it, and could not matter.

I knew that too, when I set out to write this account. My principal motive for writing was to assist the process of organization that allowed me to piece my memories of the further futures together, and in that respect, the exercise was a success. That, at least, was the evaluation I offered to Clara when she fulfilled her promise to pay me a short visit, when I undertook to summarize the produce of what I had so far recovered from my newly-excavated memories.

CHAPTER FORTY-SEVEN

THE WORLDS BEYOND THE WORLD BEYOND

"I can't put an exact figure on the distance I eventually traveled in time," I told Clara, as I made myself comfortable in my armchair, in anticipation of a long conversation "but I think the relevant order of magnitude was three billion years—three thousand times further than the journey you and I undertook together. I cannot tell, either, how many pauses I made *en route*, but it was more likely a thousand than a hundred or ten thousand, and that is as useful a figure as any in the attempt to figure out how many brush-strokes were involved in producing the image I shall paint.

"The Metamorphosians were correct, it seems, in their estimate of the Chimeras' likely future. Their collective intelligence did evolve—or devolve—towards greater simplicity, eventually giving rise to a component similar to the one contained in interstellar dust. Dust-life had no need to extend its infective spores as far as the solar system; Earth-born Complexity failed of its own accord. By that time, however, the Metamorphosians were long gone, having seen clearer warning signs far in advance. It was left to the various native intelligences of the Jovian subsystem, in collaboration with the Solarites and the Aerophobes, to contrive a local response to the seemingly-irrevocable decay of the Earthly biosphere.

"The construction of a world-shell about the Earth had been initiated long before, in collaboration with the Metamorphosians. Its first purpose had been to provide a means of keeping Dust-life out, but the artifact could just as easily be deployed keep Earthly life in, and it was with that intention that the work was completed by the "adopted" Aerophobes that provided the Solarites with a means of interaction with carbon- and silicon-based life-forms. By this time, the Solarites had also opened communication, of a necessarily slow kind, with the native intelligences of other stars."

"How, then," Clara wanted to know, "was a time-bridge into the future constructed in the Chimeras' world?" She was leaning forward in her own armchair, listening eagerly, but I knew that she would have to relax eventually, inevitably fatigued by the sheer scale and scope of my story.

"By the time the other end of that bridge was established," I told her, "all of what I have just related was ancient history. Enclosed though it was, the Earthly analogue of Dust-life was not left alone to settle into permanent Simplicity. Instead, the kind of serial experimentation that Mirastara and I once imagined was undertaken, with the Jovians as prime movers and the Aerophobes as their principal agents. Time and time again, complex life-forms were reintroduced to the Earth's surface, in the hope and expectation of eventually discovering one that was capable of consuming the voracious Dust-life instead of being consumed.

"The process of reclamation turned out to be slow, even when complexity had been successfully reintroduced to the Earth's biosphere; for millions of years thereafter the opposed tendencies of Simplicity and Complexity fought a long evolutionary battle—but in the end, Complexity achieved a new stability, and began a rapid re-evolution of intelligence.

"By the time that the Earth's world-shell was reopened, and the first time-bridge to the Chimeras' world was connected, news had reached Earth of other victories against the Dust-life, not merely on other planets but in the depths of interstellar space. The simultaneous reduction of all cosmic life to a sub-bacterial level no longer seemed a serious threat, at least within the home galaxy, until natural selection permitted Simplicity to forge a new and better universal solvent. The conflict between individuated life-forms and collective intelligences does not seem to have been renewed, though. The thesis and antithesis had been resolved by a synthesis whose seeds had been evident even in the Amphibians, especially in the person of Mirastara. The beings which next used me as a living book, before passing me forward along the chain of bridges, were both individual and collective, shifting their orientation as routinely and repeatedly as the Metamorphosians had altered their physical forms.

"Eventually, it became feasible to overcome the distance limitations inherent in the mastery of mental force to the extent of formulating a single collective intelligence spanning the inner solar system from the sun to the orbit of Jupiter—but the inherent limitations of the force-fields involved ensured that any kind of interstellar union still seemed impossible. Within this new regime, however, the Solarites became the central organizing force, as befit their privileged situation. Although communication between various Solarite collectives was very slow, a kind of Imperium of the Stars had begun."

"It surely cannot have been modeled on Earthly empires?" Clara said.

"No. I don't use the word *imperium* in the trivial sense, referring to a rigid political hierarchy ruled by a single despotic Emperor, but in a broader sense. The ties binding galactic society together were controlled by one particular sector of that society—a group of species, which was thus enabled to gain a much greater influence over the society's nature and intercourse than species of other kinds. There can be no despotism in a society that spans the stars, though; tyranny is difficult to establish even within a single solar system.

"What I have termed the Imperium of the Stars lasted for tens of millions of years before a new kind of Simplicity emerged, this time affecting plasma-based beings rather than carbon-based ones. The Imperium collapsed under that stress, and the collaborative intelligences focused on individual stars also began to collapse, one by one. That was not because there was an actual infection that spread from one to another, but simply because the same evolutionary catastrophe afflicted a vast number of individual stars, as a result of their near-simultaneous attainment of a crisis-point analogous to the one that had affected Earth's carbon-based biosphere between the twentieth century and the era of the Dwellers.

"The decay into Simplicity of Solarite intelligences often had a catastrophic effect on the planet-based biospheres orbiting their stars, which had become accustomed to and dependent upon patterns of radiation determined and controlled by the Solarites' intelligent design. The great majority were, however, sufficiently resilient and adaptable to weather such catastrophes without suffering any terminal decay themselves. The reversion of many stars to elementary and somewhat disturbed patterns of radiation did, however, force many planet-based cultures—especially those that could no longer fall back on internal planetary heat as an easily-manipulable energy-resource—to invest heavily in artificial plasmatic technologies."

"Do you mean atomic energy?" Clara queried.

"Yes—but nuclear fusion rather than fission. For hundreds of millions of years, inorganic technology had taken second place to organic technologies and applications of mental force in almost all planetary environments, while Aerophobe evolution had continued in its customary slow mode. Progress in artificial plasmatics and the desire to maintain and reinforce interstellar communication, however, resulted in a sudden shift in the pace of Aerophobe evolution.

"There had always been Aerophobes possessed of intelligence, which was often powerful in its purely calculative power, but Aerophobe intelligences had always been considered to be *idiots savants* by virtue of their apparent lack of self-awareness and their consequent inability to master mental force. Following the collapse of the Imperium of the Stars, though, inorganic intelligences began to make up ground in that respect, soon participating in system-bound collective intelligences. Such collectives had formerly been dominated by plasmatic intelligences, by virtue of the husbandry of solar energy by Solarite species, but the role played by Aerophobic entities in maintaining communication between solar systems now became the key to a new political authority.

"The Imperium of the Stars was eventually succeeded by a Silicon Empire—again, I use the term in the broad sense, without any implication of despotism. The exercise of imperial power was subtle as well as diverse, but power is power, and force is force, no matter how politely it is exercised, and it always causes resentment and rebellion. Conflict grew and gradually increased between Aerophobes and organic intelligences, where before there had been amicable cooperation.

"The Metamorphosian who interrogated me on the moon reminded me that, although mental force can only interact with material objects through the relatively weak and unsubtle force of gravity, it is not so refined as to be free of brutality, savagery and cruelty. The moral component of mental force, which gave the Amphibians greater power to perform actions they consisted good and hampered them in performing actions they knew to be harmful, was developed in a very different fashion by the Dwellers, who made effective use of the violent and sadistic impulses of selectively-bred livestock as well as their own innate capacity for aggression. The Solarites had, in general, followed the Amphibian trend—whether that had anything to do with their being "ocean-dwellers" of a sort I cannot say for sure, although I suspect it—but Aerophobe intelligence seems to have been more akin to rule of the Dwellers."

"But intelligent machines made of metal and other inorganic substances cannot prey on organic ones," Clara objected.

"The boundary between the organic and the inorganic is not as clear as it seems on the contemporary Earth," I said. "Even here and now, flesh employs and requires metals, albeit in very small quantities, and creatures such as snails, termites and coral polyps often develop very elaborate inorganic structures by way of shelter. In the same way, the intelligences descendant from Aerophobes—especially those adapted for intercourse with organic intelligences—

often employed carbon-based components. The issue of direct predation is, however, a minor one by comparison with the matter of competition for various kinds of resources.

"At any rate, if the impressions of my informants can be trusted—and it is not impossible that they were prey to various misconceptions and prejudices, in spite of their advanced intelligence—the era of the Silicon Empire's dominance was more violent and contentious than the one preceding it. In consequence, the inhabitants of Earth in that era retreated somewhat from broader society. The world-shell surrounding the planet had long been reopened, but it had never been dismantled, and it was a relatively simple business to seal it again, while still employing its exterior surface to harvest solar power to supplement the dwindling supplies of the planet's internal heat."

"If I understand your story correctly," Clara said, as I paused briefly in my narration, "its basic pattern is one of different kinds of life periodically falling prey to destructive plagues, after the hectic proliferation of new complexity has given birth to some very simple entity that consumes every other entity of a particular physical kind—followed by a compensating increase of the complexity of some other kind of life."

"There does seem to be a pattern of that sort," I admitted, "but I cannot tell whether it is a cycle that might repeat over tens or hundreds of billions of years. My experience of the future was limited as well as sketchy, even though the chain of bridges initiated by the Chimeras extended over a few thousand million years."

"The numbers begin to defy the capacity of the human imagination when they reach such magnitudes," Clara observed, relaxing back into her chair as I had anticipated that she would, "and the ideas you're dispensing so casually appear to have lost all their human interest."

"Do you really think so?" I countered. "Philip and I had an argument about that when he came to relay the Chimeras' invitation. He accused me of pandering too much to *merely human interests* in my reading. He felt that I ought to be concentrating far more exclusively on the objective findings of science. It seems to me, though, that the entities who read me like a book in the far future must have been far more interested in my idiosyncratically human attributes than in my scientific knowledge, which must have been so far surpassed by theirs as to seem very quaint."

"That's true," Clara conceded. "The Chimeras who entertained Philip and me while you undertook your second passage of the sun seemed more interested in my relatively uneducated philosophies than his. I suppose, in retrospect, that what we usually mean by *human interest* can be categorized as the consequences of sex and death, Eros and Thanatos being the presiding deities of human consciousness. The Chimeras had long abandoned sex as a mode of reproduction, and although their collective consciousness was certainly anxious about the possibility of its own death, it also saw itself as something potentially immortal. Human preoccupations with sex and the imminent inevitability of death must have seemed very odd to that group mind. Mirastara had earlier seemed equally fascinated by my feelings for you and yours for me—all the more so because we had taken such trouble to stem what was once a powerful passion. I hope the Chimeras were not too disappointed that Philip and I could not develop the kind of relationship for which he once hoped."

"If human interest really were limited by the boundaries of Eros and Thanatos," I said, "you and I might reckoned poor specimens of our kind. I'm not so sure, though, that it lies outside human interest to know where our particular problems and fascinations fit into a much larger picture. Sex might be a temporary contributor to the evolution of complexity, and death—which is an inevitably corollary of sexual reproduction—provides a challenge that the great majority of future life-forms will meet far more robustly than us, but that does not mean that we ought not to take an interest in futures far beyond the inevitable extinction of our species. Are we such narcissists that we can only be interested in possibilities in which our own selves are faithfully mirrored? I hope not. People are interested, are they not, in the past that preceded us, which extended over at least two billion years of Earth's history before our ancestors were afflicted with intelligence?"

"The past has a solidity that the future lacks," Clara pointed out. "Whether the story you're telling me is based on memory or not, it can't seem anything but a dream to anyone else—including me."

"Do you doubt that it's really a memory?"

"Of course I do. You must doubt it yourself, if you're sane—not merely because you were asleep when you undertook your long journey through time, but because of the nature of the information. Everything that was ever said to you by means of mind-speech was no more than your crude translation of alien notions into ideas native to your brain. Whatever real basis your account of these further futures might have had, its substance is pure human imagination."

"That's not the same as mere illusion."

"Not necessarily—but no one to whom you tell your tale is likely to be able to see it in any other light. Even I, who have seen the world of the Chimeras and learned the use of mind-speech, cannot credit your account of the future with the same solidity that physical relics gift to accounts of the historic and prehistoric past."

"I concede that point," I said, "but it still seems to me that my account of the future is not devoid of human interest. People still find my physical presence alarming, and shun me to the extent that politeness permits, but my story ought not to put people off simply because it accepts the future will be very different from the present, and that humankind's present concerns are merely temporary."

"Alas, George, we *are* such narcissists that we can only *really* be interested in possibilities in which our own selves are faithfully mirrored. Even Philip, the dedicated man of science who affects to scorn mere human interests, is a narcissist of that sort—as am I. But I'll listen to the rest of your story anyway, not just for politeness' sake, or because I shared a part of your experience, but because it's a good thing that our mental reach should occasionally exceed our grasp, allowing us to escape our everyday limitations."

"You're very generous," I said, half-heartedly.

She nodded in reply, as if it had been an honest compliment.

CHAPTER FORTY-EIGHT

THE END OF THE EARTH

I leaned forward and refilled Clara's empty wine-glass. My own was not yet empty—I had been talking too much to allow myself time to empty it—but I topped it up. I glanced at the window, where raindrops impelled by a brisk westerly wind had begun to beat upon the panes, but I did not get up to draw the curtains or stir the crimson embers of the fire.

"While the renewed world-shell insulted the future inhabitants of Earth from the slow burgeoning and long decline of the Silicon Empire," I continued, while Clara nestled between her cushions and allowed her eyelids to droop slightly, "their organic evolution continued apace. With the atmosphere enclosed, cloud-based ecosystems of the kind we glimpsed in the Chimeras' era became increasingly rich, and life on the surface became adapted to increasingly dim light. That trend was inevitably reflected in the subterrains, which had long since reached the limit of their extension and elaboration, in spite of the subtle games that mental force could play with gravity. The sense of sight became even less important in this era than it had when its primacy in communication was first contested by the perception and deployment of mental force.

"In the meantime, though, there was—as your perceived pattern would have predicted—a new expansion and proliferation of organic life within the galaxy, which began to build its own elaborate network of interstellar communication based on the manipulation of Dust-life. The vast interstellar clouds that had once seemed a terrible threat to planetary life now became a vital resource, the very simplicity of the vast majority of Dust-life organisms becoming an asset. In essence, the living entities in those clouds became the cells in diffuse organic bodies extending over hundreds or thousands of light-years. The movements of those bodies, and their evolution of increasing complexity, became the determining forces of yet another galaxy-wide imperium: the Commonweal of the Dust.

"The inner reaches of Earth's solar system were eventually incorporated into one of these vast bodies, whose governing intelligence developed a new relationship with the intelligences of the Jovian system and the one sealed within Earth's world-shell, as well as a newly-expanding population of Solarites. The incorporated Dust-life had to be fed, on a massive but controlled scale, which demanded huge supplies of carbon and water, generating intense competition for the reserves contained in second-generation solar systems and encouraging intense interest in the husbandry of first-generation stars. By this time, the primary energy-supplies of the entire galaxy were the object of careful cultivation, and lines of leisurely communication were being opened with our neighbors in the local galactic cluster.

"The technological management of interstellar dust was not restricted to its deployment within the nervous systems of vast bodies; its units became the primary instruments of technological demolition and reconstruction. At the peak of their evolution of complexity, the Aerophobes had constructed exceedingly tiny machines capable of handling inorganic molecules in very sophisticated ways, but they had never developed that technology to handle organic molecules with the same level of sophistication. The Commonweal of the Dust extended the scope of this sort of technology immensely. Its users felt that their triumphs represented a kind of end-point in conceivable technology, but that might well have been a limitation of their imagination rather than a natural limit.

"I didn't have the chance to discover what, if anything, replaced the Commonweal of the Dust, but my ultimate readers were aware that its long decline was well advanced. In accordance with the pattern you identified, the dramatic increase in the complexity of the entities making up the interstellar clouds created the ideal circumstances for the evolution by natural selection of a new Simplifying plague. The first effects of the plague were felt in the reaches between the stars, and were thus manifest as a failure of interstellar communications, but planets soon began to fall victim to it ravages. Yet again, the Earth's world-shell was sealed, while local Solarite and Aerophobe populations looked on.

"I can't say for certain that the Earth's world-shell was eventually penetrated by the new plague, but it seems to me that the Dust's new universal solvents must have been so clever and versatile—in spite of their Simplicity—that they could not be kept out indefinitely. Then again, the fact that the chain of time-bridges established by the Chimeras and their successors ran out at that point suggests strongly that the heritage of Earthly scientific knowledge could no longer be maintained. The galaxy and the universe still had abundant time left for future evolution before entropy took its final toll, but the Earth had run out.

"I strongly suspect that all Earthly life was Simplified again, at least for an interval of billions of years—and probably forever. Planets are temporary abodes, whose resources are eventually exhausted no matter what ingenuity is brought to their exploitation. Life itself, however, must have continued both within and without the solar system; it is by no means impossible that, even if Earth-born life could not develop a new Complexity, some kind of Complex life might eventually have arrived form elsewhere that was enthusiastic to use the planetary biosphere as a resource.

"If the Earth is able to enjoy some such new lease of life, beyond the scope of the chain of time-bridges that facilitated my odyssey, I firmly believe that its story would not lie beyond the scope of human interest—but it is presumably beyond the scope of human recovery. I don't expect to receive any further invitations to explore the future—at least, if I do, I expect the next invitation to come from an era far closer to ours, whose inhabitants will be unable to establish a chain of time-bridges that extends any further than the one I have already traveled."

"Would you go forward again, if another such invitation did arrive?" Clara asked.

"Most certainly. Would you?"

"Yes, I would. I'm not certain, though, that the Professor will send Philip to collect us if he contrives to establish a conduit for some such communication. If there is a next time, I think Philip will want to go alone."

"If there is a next time," I said, "I suspect that the Professor will take his own courage in both hands, and will leave Philip behind to welcome him back, if and when he returns."

"It's far more likely," Clara opined, "that others will duplicate the Professor's discovery in time to come. He seems uncommonly reluctant to publish his work, but it cannot be so arcane that no one else will ever be able to follow the same chain of reasoning to the same results."

"They would have to discover a similar partnership with like-minded workers in the future," I said. "That might be the most difficult element in the required combination of circumstances. Besides which, if another war is imminent—as it certainly seems to be—our present civilization might be reduced to a primitive state in which such endeavors would be impossible."

"Do you think that the effects of aerial bombing would really be that devastating?" Clara asked.

"Not if the war were to start tomorrow, or within the next few years," I said, "but the last war encouraged a great leap forward in the technology of destruction, and so will the next. Eventually—and I'm not talking about millions of years, but mere decades—it *will* be possible for nations to fight a war that might obliterate civilization for centuries, or perhaps for millennia. Once that happens, it will not be nearly as easy for our descendants to rebuild a new civilization as it was for our ancestors. The coal will be gone, and the oil too; that kind of wealth, once squandered, is difficult to make up by other means.

"You and I know that the remote descendants of humankind will still be alive, if not thriving, five hundred thousand years hence—but we know, too, that they will be overtaken in the meantime by organisms of a different sort, which will not be nearly so reliant on the kinds of energy that fuel our fire-powered way of life. Given those circumstances, it would not be surprising if a chance discovery such as the Professor's time machine went unduplicated, not only by the scientists of our generation, but by the best brains of many generations to come. It might, in fact, only be successfully completed after a lapse of half a million years, and only occasionally achieved thereafter, at even greater intervals. You and I have been very fortunate, and exceedingly privileged, to have had the use of such a device."

"Others, I think, might have made better use of it than I could," Clara said, regretfully. She yawned, but she was still fully alert and interested; her fatigue was merely physical. I envied her that, a little; I was no longer capable of merely physical fatigue, or even mere languor.

"I could easily say the same," I told her. "I can't claim credit for any of my own discoveries, all of which were imposed upon me. I never did anything more than consent—sometimes to impositions that I really ought to have refused." I was thinking of the Bat-wings, and the judgment I had been forced to make, by whose terms I might equally have condemned almost all of the human race to death, rather than the consent I had given to Liamon or the Solarites.

"That may be true," Clara admitted, "but you would surely have achieved far less had you been an assertive man of action, fiercely protective of yourself. There's nothing of which you need be ashamed."

"I'm not ashamed," I assured her. "I've strayed far beyond the limits of human interest—forsaking the possibility of merely human love, if not the burden of merely human mortality—and am well aware of the cost of that estrangement, but I'm certainly not ashamed of it. I am what I am, and if that means that the brief Platonic relationship I forged with Mirastara was the most precious I shall ever enjoy, no matter how long I might live, then so be it."

"You and I can still be friends, George," Clara said, without any evident trace of resentment. "I can't live with you, but I won't abandon you. You'll make other friends, one way or another, in spite of the disconcerting effect your presence has on people who don't know you. This is Oxford, after all—the capital of human curiosity. You won't ever have to live entirely in your memories and dreams."

"We all have to do that," I said. "No matter how much oppression tedious reality heaps upon our senses, there is, in the final analysis, nowhere else that intelligent creatures can live but in our memories and dreams—even the evanescent present is beyond our grasp, essentially unseizable. All that we can ever really get a grip on is our memories of the past and our dreams of the future. That's what consciousness amounts to, in the final analysis."

"I suppose it is," Clara agreed, draining the last dregs of claret from her glass. "But we must thank God for the relentless glory of the evanescent present, whether it's graspable or not—and for our consciousness of the past and future too."

"While we pray, as we give our thanks, that our consciousness might yet become broader than it is," I added, leaving my own glass undrained.

She did not say *amen* to that; it would not have been appropriate. I felt that I could sense her thoughts, and that she could sense mine, although neither one of us attempted to exert any force. We were both content with what we had, what we were, and what we knew.

ABOUT THE AUTHOR

BRIAN STABLEFORD was born in Yorkshire in 1948. He taught at the University of Reading for several years, but is now a full-time writer. He has written many science fiction and fantasy novels, including *The Empire of Fear*, *The Werewolves of London*, *Year Zero*, *The Curse of the Coral Bride*, *The Stones of Camelot* and *Prelude to Eternity*. Collections of his short stories include a long series of *Tales of the Biotech Revolution*, and such idiosyncratic items as *Sheena and Other Gothic Tales* and The *Innnsmouth Heritage and Other Sequels*. He has written numerous nonfiction books, including *Scientific Romance in Britain, 1890-1950*, *Glorious Perversity: The Decline and Fall of Literary Decadence*, *Science Fact and Science Fiction: An Encyclopedia* and *The Devil's Party: A Brief History of Satanic Abuse*. He has contributed hundreds of biographical and critical entries to reference books, including both editions of *The Encyclopedia of Science Fiction* and several editions of the library guide, *Anatomy of Wonder*. He has also translated numerous novels from the French language, including several by the feuilletonist Paul Féval and numerous classics of French scientific romance by such writers as Albert Robida, Maurice Renard, and J. H. Rosny the Elder.